THE SASSAFRAS SCIENCE ADVENTURES

VOLUME 1: ZOOLOGY

JOHNNY CONGO & PAIGE HUDSON

THE SASSAFRAS SCIENCE ADVENTURES
VOLUME 1: ZOOLOGY

Third Edition 2022
(First Edition 2012)
Copyright @ Elemental Science, Inc.
Email: support@elementalscience.com

ISBN: 978-1-935614-20-3
Cover Design by Paige Hudson & Eunike Nugroho
Illustrations by Eunike Nugroho (be.net/inikeke)
Phone Pictures by Paige Hudson & Erin Simons (One Line Design)

Printed In USA For World Wide Distribution

For more copies write to :
Elemental Science
PO Box 79
Niceville, FL 32588
support@elementalscience.com

DEDICATION

We dedicate this book to all children, especially our own. We hope that reading about the Sassafras twins will help you to discover the wonderful world of science.

Make the Most of Your Journey with the Sassafras Twins!

Add our activity guide, logbook, or lapbooking guide to create a full science curriculum for your students!

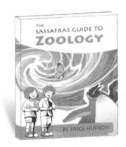

The Sassafras Guide to Zoology includes chapter summaries and an array of options that coordinate with the individual chapters of this novel. This guide provides ideas for experiments, notebooking, vocabulary, memory work, and additional activities to enhance what your students are learning about animals!

The Official Sassafras SCIDAT Logbook: Zoology Edition partners with the activity guide to help your student document their journey throughout this novel. The logbook includes their own SCIDAT log pages as well as habitat sheets and a zoology glossary.

Lapbooking through Zoology with the Sassafras Twins provides a gentle option for enhancing what your students are learning about animals through this novel. The guide contains a reading plan, templates, and pictures to create a beautiful lapbook on zoology, vocabulary, and coordinated scientific demonstrations!

Visit ElementalScience.com to learn more!

The Sassafras Science Adventures

TABLE OF CONTENTS

Authors' Note — viii

The Sassafras Guide to the Characters — ix

Chapter 1: The Adventure Begins — 1
Crazy Uncle Cecil — 1
Zip Lines and Smartphones — 6

Chapter 2: The African Grasslands — 13
Look! A Lion! — 13
Chasing Cheetahs — 20

Chapter 3: Lost in Elephant Valley — 27
Eyeing Elephants — 27
Glimpsing Giraffes — 33

Chapter 4: Off to the Desert — 41
Camel Criminals — 41
Captured With Cobras — 50

Chapter 5: Escaping the Tomb — 57
Leaping Lizards! — 57
Ferreting out Foxes — 66

Chapter 6: On to Canada — 75
Compelling Cows — 75
Buzzing Bees!! — 8 3

Chapter 7: Working on the Farm   91

Chicken Coop Cleaning   91
Swinging with Spiders   99

Chapter 8: Zipping through the Amazon Rainforest   107

Sloth Sighting   107
Tree-Hopping Toucans   117

Chapter 9: Trouble in the Jungle   125

Fearsome Frogs   125
Beguiled by Butterflies   134

Chapter 10: Diverging to Australia   143

Capturing Koalas   143
Rampant Rabbits   154

Chapter 11: Separated in China   161

Panda Park   161
Explosions and Eagles   171

Chapter 12: The Feuding Brown Mountain Hermits   177

Petrified by the Powerful Owl   177
Snared with the Sambar Deer   185

Chapter 13: Trekking in Sichuan   195

Meeting Monkeys   195
Moving in with the Mice   203

Chapter 14: Arctic Adventures   211

Arctic Reunion   211
Animals in a Flash   220

Chapter 15: Split up by the Storm   229

Summer Storms   229
Searching for a Sassafras   241

Chapter 16: A Dip in the Ocean   247

Promising Penguins   247
Comical Codfish   259

Chapter 17: Arr, Treasure Ahead!   267

Watching Whales   267
The Shivering Squid   276

Chapter 18: The Adventure Ends   285

Bonus Data   285
A Fun Surprise   293

Authors' Note

The novel you hold in your hands is both a work of fiction and a teaching tool, which creates the need for a delicate balance.

We have taken fictional liberties when it comes to the story line—to our knowledge, no one is traveling around the world on invisible zip lines. But, when it comes to the information shared by our local experts, we have done our best to accurately reflect the current scientific knowledge at the time of writing this book.

We have drawn from our personal experiences and education, as well as the following resources:

- 📖 *DK Encyclopedia of Animals*
- 📖 *DK Encyclopedia of Nature*
- 📖 *DK Encyclopedia of Science*
- 📖 *Kingfisher Science Encyclopedia*
- 📖 *Kingfisher First Encyclopedia of Animals*
- 📖 *Basher Science Biology: Life as We Know It*
- 📖 *The Usborne Children's Encyclopedia*
- 📖 *Usborne Science Encyclopedia*

In addition to these books, we have drawn on the information found on many different websites.

Please keep in mind that science is ever-changing as our technology advances and our understanding deepens. If you find an issue in this novel, please let us know and take the opportunity to discuss these new developments with your students.

The Sassafras Guide to the Characters

Throughout the Book

★ **Blaine Sassafras** – The male Sassafras twin, also known as Train.

★ **Tracey Sassafras** – The female Sassafras twin, also known as Blaisey.

★ **Uncle Cecil** – The Sassafras twins' crazy, but talented uncle.

★ **President Lincoln** – Uncle Cecil's lab assistant, who also happens to be a prairie dog.

★ **The Man With No Eyebrows** – He has no eyebrows and seems to be trying to sabotage the twins at every stop.

The African Grassland (Chapters 2-3)

★ **Nicholas Mzuri** – (muh-zur-ee) The local expert for the African Grasslands leg of the twins' adventure. He is the owner and tour guide extraordinaire for Mzuri tours.

★ **Hank** – A narcoleptic tourist who is a member of the twins' tour through the African Grasslands.

★ **Pam and Fred** – The eccentric and hilarious couple who is a member of the twins' tour through the African Grasslands.

★ **Shelley** – Nicholas Mzuri's assistant, who also happens to be a machete.

★ **Imani Mzuri** – (ee-man-ee) Nicholas Mzuri's sister, who also helps out with Mzuri tours.

The Egyptian Desert (Chapters 4-5)

★ **Princess Talibah** – (tal-ib-ah) The local expert for the Egyptian Desert leg of the twins' adventure. She is the princess of the Tuareg (twar-ehg) nomadic people.

★ **Jendayi** – (jen-day-ee) Princess Talibah's hand-maiden and friend.

★ **Hanif** – (han-if) Princess Talibah's advisor and teacher. He thinks that answers can be found in the stars, not in science.

★ **Abasi** – (ah-bah-see) Princess Talibah's sworn protector. He is also in love with the princess.

★ **Itja** – (eet-jah) The scoundrel leader of a group of bandits known as the Kekeway (kee-kee-way).

★ **Mesneh** – (mez-nuh) He helps Princess Talibah teach Itja and his men a lesson after the Kekeway ravage his village.

The Canadian Farm (Chapters 6-7)

★ **Jet (Jethro Mecklen, Jr.)** – The local expert for the Canadian Farm leg of the twins' adventure. He is also sixteen years old and friends with Edbert.

★ **Edbert Snarfuffel** – The goofy sixteen year old boy who works with the Sassafras twins on the Smitty farm in Canada.

★ **Farmer Smith** – He is the owner of Smitty Farms.

★ **Ed Lumbia** – He is the farm foreman at Smitty Farms.

★ **Tank & Billy** – They are the sons of Farmer Smith. They like to pull pranks and create problems for the twins and their companions.

The Amazon Rainforest (Chapters 8-9)

★ **Alvaro Manihuari** – (al-vah-ro mah-nee-ar-ee) the local expert for the Amazon Rainforest leg of the twins' adventure. He is also the owner of the Out on a Limb guesthouse.

★ **Arrio** – (rr-ee-o) Alvaro's assistant and helper at the Out on a Limb guesthouse.

He is a native Peruvian.

✷ **Skip, Gannon and Gretchen** – They are three trekkers that are also staying at the Out on a Limb guesthouse.

✷ **Violetta Perez** – (vee-o-leh-tah peh-rezz) One of the Perez twins who is staying at the Out on a Limb guesthouse with their father. She makes friends with the Sassafras twins.

✷ **Vancho Perez** – (vahn-ch-o) One of the Perez twins who is staying at the Out on a Limb guesthouse with their father. He makes friends with the Sassafras twins.

✷ **Ernesto Perez** – He is the father of Violetta and Vancho. He is also president of ProLog.

✷ **Ortiz** – (or-tee-zz) He is the foreman for ProLog. He works under Mr. Perez.

The Australian Deciduous Forest (Chapters 10 & 12)

✷ **Willy Day** – The local expert for the Australian leg of the twins' adventure. He is an Australian filmmaker working on a project in the Brown Mountain Forest.

✷ **Ethel** – She works at the local diner near where Blaine arrives. She makes a great plate of "hot-maybe" eggs.

✷ **Ralphy Dingo** – He is one of the infamous Feuding Brown Mountain Hermits.

✷ **Matty Mingo** – He is one of the infamous Feuding Brown Mountain Hermits.

The Chinese Bamboo Forest (Chapters 11 & 13)

✷ **Tashi Yidro** – (tah-see yee-dro) The local expert for the Chinese leg of the twin's adventure. She is a student at the local university who takes Tracey back to her home village.

✷ **Llamo** – (lahmo) She is Tashi's sister.

✷ **Norbu** – (nor-boo) He is Tashi's brother.

✷ **Amala** – (ah-mah-lah) She is Tashi, Llamo and Norbu's mother.

The Arctic (Chapters 14-15)

★ **Summer Beach** – The local expert for the Arctic leg of the twins' adventure. She was also a former classmate of Uncle Cecil's.

★ **Ulysses S. Grant** – Summer Beach's lab assistant, who also happens to be an arctic ground squirrel.

★ **Brooks Hirebro** – He is a professional snowboarder, entrepreneur and also a friend of Summer's.

★ **Yotimo** – (yo-tee-mo) He is an Inuit sled driver who finds Tracey in the arctic tundra and also a friend of Summer's.

The Atlantic Ocean (Chapters 16-17)

★ **Captain James Q. McScruffy** – The local expert for the Atlantic Ocean leg of the twins' adventure. He is a fisherman and the owner of the *Scot's Folly III*.

★ **William Atwater** – He is the first mate on the *Scot's Folly III*.

★ **Peach Beard** – The leader of the P.R.O. pirates, a band of men dedicated to bringing pirates back to the high seas.

VOLUME 1

ZOOLOGY

CHAPTER 1: THE ADVENTURE BEGINS

Crazy Uncle Cecil

Twelve-year-old twins, Blaine and Tracey Sassafras, sat in sulking silence on the very back row of the bouncy bus. It was the first day of summer break. Instead of being on their way to Camp Zip-Fire with all of their friends, they were on this bus headed to their crazy Uncle Cecil's house for the entire summer. Blaine and Tracey had done pretty well in school, especially the last semester. They had good grades in every subject, except for one. Blaine and Tracey had both failed science.

Their parents had warned them in the middle of the semester about their grades. They could still hear their father's loving but stern voice saying, "You two had better get those science grades up by semester's end or you will be sorry." As the two sat there, bouncing around on the hot and shaky bus, they were definitely sorry they hadn't worked harder in science class. All they knew was that their Uncle Cecil was some sort of scientist. Since Blaine and Tracey had failed the subject, their parents had thought it would be a good idea for them to spend the summer with him, improving their science skills instead of going to their favorite place in the entire world.

After several miserable hours on the rattling bus, Blaine and Tracey were finally at their stop. They found themselves at 1104 North Pecan Street standing on the front porch of their Uncle Cecil's house. It was an old two-story house covered in plain brown siding with a steeply pitched roof. There were a few bushes attempting to decorate the front porch, but they were mostly dead. By the looks of the cobwebs hanging in the top corners of the front porch windows, Uncle Cecil wasn't much for housekeeping.

The twins had only met Uncle Cecil one time, and that

had been at a Sassafras family reunion when they were only eight-years-old. The only thing they remembered about Cecil, other than his crazy red hair, was that he had called them "Train and Blaisey" and that he had spilled fruit salad all over himself. Now they were supposed to spend the summer with him.

Blaine, who acted very much like an older brother even though he was only older by five minutes and fourteen seconds, spotted the handwritten note attached to the front door first. It was Tracey who stepped forward to read it though.

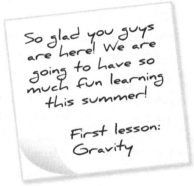

So glad you guys are here! We are going to have so much fun learning this summer!

First lesson: Gravity

The last sentence caught Blaine by surprise, who was now stepping up to look over his sister's shoulder. "First lesson is gravity? What is that supposed to mean?" Suddenly, a section of the porch dropped away and Blaine and Tracey found themselves falling through a trap door. Almost immediately, they landed on a smooth, wide metal slide, which carried them briskly down a dark tunnel. As they flew quickly through the tunnel toward a growing light, they braced themselves for impact. Slick metal gave way to soft cushions as they landed with a quiet thud on a pile of old pillows.

Blaine and Tracey, somewhat dazed, looked around at their surroundings. They were now in what looked like a basement. The room was filled with all kinds of interesting looking things. There were beakers full of different colored fluids, taxidermy animals of all sorts, bugs pinned to corkboards, a wide variety of plants sitting under lights, and a jumble of electrical wires, magnets, mirrors, and lots of other stuff that just looked like plain junk. And there, in the far corner at a cluttered desk, they saw Uncle Cecil's head of red hair. He was wearing a white lab coat and had headphones on. Whatever he was listening to, he must have the volume turned up very loud because he was unaware that they had arrived. Blaine and Tracey picked themselves up off the mound of pillows and approached their uncle. From behind, Blaine gently tapped Cecil on the shoulder. Caught off guard by the presence of someone in his basement, Uncle Cecil jumped out of his chair a few feet into the air and landed on his desk, smashing the uneaten portion of spaghetti. The surprise on his face turned to happiness as he recognized his nephew and niece. He pulled off his headphones and slid off the top of his desk. "Train! Blaisey! You guys are finally here! Welcome!" He then gave Blaine and Tracey a big bear hug, getting spaghetti all over them.

Uncle Cecil proceeded to give the twins a spirited tour of his house; their residence for the summer. Though they were still bummed about being there, it was hard not to get caught up in his excitement. He talked a mile a minute as he showed them their rooms, the kitchen, the bathroom and the living room.

"Oh, I almost forgot to ask. How did you guys like the slide down into the basement?" Uncle Cecil asked, laughing.

"Well, it certainly caught us by surprise!" Tracey answered.

"Yeah, a really nice lesson in gravity," Blaine added.

"Oh I thought you guys would like that," Cecil said, wringing his hands in delight. "That was President Lincoln's idea!"

"President Lincoln?" the twins asked in unison. "You mean the sixteenth president of the United States?"

"No, not that President Lincoln," Cecil informed as he pointed to a hole in the wall. "President Lincoln is my lab assistant. He's a very good one even though he happens to be a *Cynomys ludovicianus.*"

"What's a cyno . . . ludo . . . cianus?" asked Blaine.

"*Cynomys ludovicianus* is Latin for 'Prairie Dog,' but he never answers to that. He much prefers being called 'President Lincoln.'" A prairie dog gingerly poked his head out of the hole.

Blaine whispered under his breath to Tracey, "Uncle Cecil really is crazy!"

The twins followed Uncle Cecil back down to the basement (using the stairs this time instead of the slide) for an introduction of what they would be learning over the summer.

"Are we really going to spend our entire summer cooped up in this basement?" Tracey asked.

"Not just cooped up, but cooped up doing science. It is the most boring subject in the whole world," Blaine added.

Completely unaffected by the children's pessimism, Uncle Cecil continued. "Now, when I last talked to your father, he told me about your disposition toward science and your none-too-stellar grades in science. He also told me all the things you needed to learn about by summer's end. And golly, golly goodness, I think we can have you two loving science by the time you head back home!"

Somehow the twins didn't think so. Suddenly, the prairie dog they had seen upstairs poked his head out a hole in the wall. "Where did he . . . how did he . . ." Blaine mumbled.

"Oh, there is a network of tunnels throughout the house that President Lincoln uses to get around," Uncle Cecil responded, as if it was totally normal. Blaine, on the other hand, was still wondering why the prairie dog was called President Lincoln.

Uncle Cecil made big motions with his hands as he began to cover all that they were going to learn. "We are going to learn about the five kingdoms of living things: that is, bacteria, single-cell organisms, fungi, plants, and animals. Oh yes! We are going to cover migration, which is animals making their annual journeys over land, air, or water to find better living conditions. We are going

to study defense methods and food webs! We are goin—"

"I don't mean to interrupt you Uncle Cecil," Blaine apologized, "but why... I mean, how, are we going to do all of this?" The twins' heads were spinning at the thought of all the science they were about to get blasted with.

"Oh, I thought you would never ask!" Cecil exclaimed, as he bounded over to a table and scooped up what looked like two rock climbing harnesses. "You see these harnesses? President Lincoln and I are excited about these! Using these harnesses and special carabiners, the two of you will be able to travel all over the planet this summer and encounter science face to face."

Blaine and Tracey just looked at him dumbfounded.

"Now, I'm a scientist, but President Lincoln fancies himself as more of an inventor. We did work together on this, but it was more his idea than mine." The prairie dog clambered up on a table. "We invented invisible lines that can go anywhere on the planet. Africa, South America, Asia, you name it, and these lines can take you there! You simply get cinched up in your harness, attach it to your correctly calibrated carabiner, clip onto one of the lines, and zip bang--at the speed of light you arrive at your destination!"

Now the twins' mouths hung open in disbelief. Invisible lines? Special carabiners? A prairie dog inventor? Speed of light? Science face to face? Were Blaine and Tracey really supposed to believe this? It was Blaine who first managed to say something, but all he could sputter out was, "What?"

"Oh, yes! It works like a charm," answered Uncle Cecil, laughing giddily. "We tested it on several of President Lincoln's relatives."

The twins looked at the prairie dog, who was sitting quietly on the table, sniffing an apple core. Why hadn't they tried harder in science class?

"Now I know the two of you were originally hoping to go to camp Zip-Fire again this summer, and I know they have all kinds of fun activities there including zip lines. But you two have already gone to that camp three summers in a row. These invisible lines that President Lincoln and I have invented for you are not too different than Camp Zip-Fire. Ours, however, travel at the speed of light," Uncle Cecil said.

The first glimmers of interest flashed through the twins' eyes. Sure, all their friends were at Camp Zip-Fire, while they were stuck here with their uncle. However, if they could return to school after summer break with stories of world travel, that would still be cool, wouldn't it? But was all of this possible, or was Uncle Cecil just plain crazy?

With a sudden surge of adventure pulsing through his veins and a definite readiness to call Uncle Cecil's bluff, Blaine stepped up and grabbed one of the harnesses out of his uncle's hand. "Let's try this out, right now!" Blaine declared. Uncle Cecil leapt for joy, while President Lincoln just continued sniffing the apple core.

Zip Lines and Smartphones

A few minutes later, Blaine had his harness on, as did Tracey. She had decided she couldn't let her twin brother take off on this adventure on his own. She still seriously doubted that any of this invisible line travel stuff was even possible.

Uncle Cecil handed them the special carabiners, "Each carabiner has three rings. Always screw the locking ring shut first, you know, for safety sake. Then, turn the longitude ring and the latitude ring to the correct coordinates for your target's location."

As Blaine and Tracey attached their carabiners to their harnesses they gave each other a glance with raised eyebrows. They were definitely convinced that their uncle was crazy, but they would continue to play along, for now.

"President Lincoln and I will be able to follow your progress on the special tracking screen that we designed just for this summer!" Cecil said as he skipped over to the wall where a large flat screen TV displayed a map of the world. On the map were two small green dots in America.

"These two green dots are where you are," Cecil pointed. "When you zip from here to there, we will be able to track you on this screen."

Cecil bent over and tapped a button on his keyboard, changing the screen from a world map to an empty document page. "And this screen is where we can view all the information that you will be sending us, along with the pictures you will be sending in. Speaking of which, I almost forgot! You guys will need your smartphones!" Uncle Cecil rushed off to the cluttered desk in the corner to look for the phones.

Standing there in their harnesses, Blaine looked at Tracey and smiled, "At least we may get free smartphones this summer."

"Blaine, this is crazy!" Tracey exclaimed, not thinking about the phones. "Uncle Cecil really is insane. How are we going to make it through this summer?"

"I don't know Tracey, but we might as well try and have some fun."

Uncle Cecil returned and handed sleek looking smartphones to each child, saying, "The two of you can use these phones to communicate with President Lincoln and I no matter where you are on the planet." Uncle Cecil began talking faster and faster as he got more excited. "We have designed two applications for these phones that will be very important for your journey. First, you have an application called LINLOC, which is short for 'line locations.' It lists every topic you will be studying and the locations you need to travel to, along with the exact carabiner coordinates and names of the local experts who you should contact upon arrival. The second application on your phones here is called SCIDAT, which is short for 'scientific data.' It enables you to enter all the scientific data you will be gathering on the topics listed in the LINLOC application. You will need to take and send pictures for each topic."

Blaine and Tracey rolled their eyes at the thought of gathering scientific data. Even so, Cecil continued, "We are experiencing a little bit of a problem with this second application. If the information is not entered, or if it is entered incorrectly at one location, you won't be able to move on to the next one. If you don't progress through the locations correctly, you won't be able to make it back here to the basement. So, it is very important that all of your scientific data is entered correctly. Not ideal, I know. It is a little glitch that President Lincoln is working on." President Lincoln made a hiccup noise from his spot on the table.

"Oh! I am so excited for you two! You will be traveling all over the planet learning about all kinds of things! I know science has been like rocks in your socks thus far in your lives. But after this summer—ooh golly, golly, goodness, you are going to love it! I just know it!" More and more curious, but still not convinced, the twins smiled and nodded as if they agreed.

"So, where in the world are we going first?" Blaine asked.

"Try out that LINLOC application on your smartphone," Cecil said, gleaming. Blaine used the touch screen to open the LINLOC application. The first location listed was Kenya.

"Kenya is a country in Africa, right?" Blaine asked.

"Yes it is" answered Tracey as she maneuvered through to the LINLOC application herself on her smartphone.

"The contact person's name is Nicholas Mzuri, and the coordinates listed are latitude -2° 42' 9.08" and longitude 38° 10' 35.6". The app says it will put us in the African grasslands."

"The topics we need to cover are lions, cheetahs, elephants, and giraffes," Blaine added, as the twins continued to read through the information they were finding on their phones. Whether or not all this planet-traveling science recording stuff was possible or not, these smartphones sure were cool. Plus, the prospect of going to a place like the

African grasslands was pretty exciting.

"So are we going on a safari?" Blaine asked.

"Persactly!" Uncle Cecil shouted in joy. "Africa is just the first of many stops you will be making this summer for the sake of science. Train and Blaisey—you are going to experience and learn so much that it is going to be simply fantabulous!" Blaine and Tracey weren't fans of science, but they were fans of fun. It was only because of a failing grade in science that they were even here in their uncle's basement. They had to admit they were already having a little fun.

"Okay, are you guys ready?" Uncle Cecil asked, his face barely able to hold his smile. Blaine and Tracey looked at each other, at their harnesses and carabiners, and at their uncle's smiling and anticipatory face.

"Let's do it!" they declared in unison.

"Ok!" Uncle Cecil stated, looking over the harnesses, making sure they were snug and secure. "First things first—close that locking ring tight, and then turn your latitude ring to -2° 42' 9.08" and your longitude ring to 38° 10' 35.6." Then, zip, bang, boom, you are ready to go to the African grasslands!" The twins locked their carabiners tight and got their coordinates set correctly.

"President Lincoln wanted me to assure you that these invisible lines and coordinates are designed to get you as close to your professional contact person as possible without your arrival being detected by anyone." The twins nodded, showing they understood.

Uncle Cecil then reached under the table and grabbed two backpacks. He handed one to each twin. "Use these nifty backpacks to store your harnesses and helmets once you arrive at your locations."

The twins again nodded.

"Since you will be traveling at the speed of light, it will feel more like riding a lightning bolt than a traditional zip line. For the most part, your landings will be as smooth as butter." Uncle Cecil scooped the prairie dog up off the table, held him in his arms and continued on, "These travels will take you two a while, so it will be more than a few moons until President Lincoln and I see you again. Take care of each other. Don't let anyone else know about these invisible zip lines! Remember, you can contact us anytime and anywhere. Use those smartphones to their full capacity. LINLOC will give you your guiding information. Be absolutely sure to enter the correct data into SCIDAT so you can progress through your destinations."

Blaine and Tracey took deep breaths knowing this was the moment of truth. Either Uncle Cecil was as crazy as they suspected, or they were about to start off on the greatest adventure of their lives.

"Well, go ahead! Clip your carabiners onto the line!" Uncle Cecil cheered.

Feeling a little silly, the children opened the clips of their carabiners, pretended to hook them to a line, and then let them snap closed.

Suddenly, the twins' feet lifted a few feet up in the air. Their bodies were secure in their harnesses and attached to their carabiners, which were somehow clipped into a taut invisible line. The twins' faces were covered with an odd mixture of awe and fear.

"Isn't it amazing?" Uncle Cecil exclaimed, clapping. "As soon as you are correctly calibrated, the carabiners snap shut. They automatically connect to the correct line. And now," he said looking at his watch, "you have approximately seven seconds until you will slide off at the speed of light, zip lining to the African grasslands!"

The twins could feel their rapidly accelerating heartbeats pounding in their chests. Could this really be happening? Then, with a magnificent sonic burst of light, twelve-year-old twins Blaine and Tracey Sassafras shot off at the speed of light.

CHAPTER 2: THE AFRICAN GRASSLANDS

Look! A Lion!

It was simply exhilarating. The Sassafras twins could not believe this was actually happening. They were zipping on an invisible line at the speed of light, flying, soaring, gliding, and shooting through space like sunbeams. Uncle Cecil wasn't so crazy after all.

Then, with a sudden jerk, they came to a stop and a tingling sensation flushed through their bodies. Blinking their eyes, they couldn't see anything but white at first. Slowly, the white light began to fade, colors came, and they were able to make out shapes. They found themselves standing, but their wobbly legs could not hold them. The twins involuntarily fell to the ground, their carabiners automatically unclipped from the lines. Blaine and Tracey just looked at each other, mouths open in disbelief.

As usual, Blaine managed to say something first. "That . . . was . . . unbelievable!" he claimed enthusiastically but out of breath.

All Tracey could do was nod in agreement. Camp Zip-Fire's zip lines had nothing on Uncle Cecil's and President Lincoln's invention. So, it really was possible—they were traveling over invisible zip lines to different places on the planet. Though they had just experienced it, they still couldn't really believe it. But they were here, weren't they? But . . . where was here?

Seeing clearly now and with their legs strong again, the twins stood up, took off their harnesses, put them in their backpacks, and scoped out their new surroundings. They were in a large room that was rustically decorated. It was full of big leather couches, furry rugs, and ornate lamps. Rough wooden beams ran across the ceiling, supporting the thick thatched roof. The wooden floorboards creaked under their feet as Blaine and Tracey walked around the room, looking at all of the beautiful artwork on the walls. Most of the paintings and photographs were of animals.

A side door swung open and a lady with braided hair and beautiful brown skin walked in. "Children, children, what are you doing in here?" she asked kindly. "Everybody is supposed to be in the jeep. Come now, come now, or you two are going to miss the safari."

Assuming they should cooperate, Blaine and Tracey looked at each other, shrugged their shoulders, and followed the woman. She led them through a side door out onto a big wooden porch. The twins looked out into the sunshiny day and saw the African grasslands right there in front of them. The view from the porch was breathtaking. They really had traveled across the planet!

The woman pointed and said, "Okay, children, the jeep is right over there. Go on now, before Nicholas takes off without you." Blaine and Tracey spotted the white jeep and made their way towards it.

"You two are welcome back to Jambo Safari Lodge anytime," the nice woman assured, as she waved goodbye. The twins waved back.

"So, we landed in a safari lodge." Tracey stated.

"Yeah, pretty cool." Blaine replied.

As they approached the jeep, a big, strongly built black man wearing a wide-brimmed leather hat, a sleeveless T-shirt, cargo pants, and worn hiking boots, slid the jeep door open and greeted them with a smile.

"Welcome, children, to Mzuri tours. My name is Nicholas Mzuri and I will be your safari guide today," the man boomed, with his baritone voice.

"Nicholas Mzuri, just like the LINLOC application said," thought the twins to themselves as Nicholas helped them into the jeep. It was a big four-by-four jeep with a wide wheelbase and sliding doors on both sides. It had two bucket seats in the front and two wide bench seats for passengers in the back. Nicholas closed the door behind them and then walked around the van and climbed into the driver's seat.

There were four other people already seated in the van. On the front bench there was a man with long hair and a long beard. His eyes were shut and he was either asleep or bored—the twins couldn't tell. On the back bench, there was a rather plump couple that looked to be husband and wife. They were decked out to the max with the latest tourist apparel and accessories. Their rosy cheeks and sweaty foreheads showed that they were nervous but excited. The man sitting next to them was dressed in plain clothes and had no outstanding features other than the fact that he didn't have any eyebrows. Blaine and Tracey smiled at the four passengers sheepishly as they took their seats on the front bench.

"Children, what are your names?" Nicholas asked from the front.

"We are Blaine and Tracey," Blaine answered. "Blaine and Tracey Sassafras."

"Well, Blaine and Tracey Sassafras, we are so glad to have you with us today. Is this your first safari?"

"Yes, sir." The twins answered.

"Well then, get ready for the adventure of your lives!" Nicholas said, as he put the jeep in gear and applied his right foot to the gas pedal. Off they went, a plume of dust trailing behind them.

As they drove down the jostling dirt road, Nicholas Mzuri used his loud voice to describe their surroundings.

"There are two main types of grasslands. Temperate grasslands have cold winters and warm summers, like the grasslands found in middle and western North America. And then there are tropical grasslands, which we are driving through right now. Here, in Kenya, we have warm winters and burning hot summers. We get about ten to thirty inches of rain each year on our vast grassy fields. If you look out your windows now, you are guaranteed to see dozens of beautiful acacia and other trees dotting the rolling grassy hills."

Tracey's eyes wandered in amazement across the landscape. What a beautiful place! Blaine wanted to look but was busy trying to figure out how to separate himself from the long haired man who had laid his sleeping head on Blaine's shoulder. Nicholas looked in his rear view mirror back at Blaine and laughed.

"Oh, don't worry, my friend. Hank has narcolepsy. But he always wakes up once we get to the animals. He travels to Kenya every year for a safari. This is his eleventh trip to date." Blaine smiled and laughed a nervous laugh.

"When do we get to see the animals?" asked the plump lady from the back.

"Very soon ma'am," Nicholas said with a smile. "We should be driving up on some lions within a few minutes." The lady shrieked in delight. Nicholas continued giving information.

"Lions are a part of the cat family, found only in Africa, though they once roamed throughout Asia and Europe as well. They are the grassland's largest predator."

"P-p-p-predator?" asked the plump man. "That means hunter right?"

"That is correct," answered Nicholas. "But don't worry, sir, I will keep everyone safe. Lions are carnivores. They hunt anything that they can kill, but their favorites are zebra and wildebeest. Lions usually hunt at night and rest during the day. And as you can see, it is daytime, so don't worry my friend."

Hank jolted awake, pulling his head off of Blaine's shoulder.

"Carnivores are meat-eaters," He added, as he blinked his eyes and wiped away a small stream of slobber from the corner of his mouth.

"Hank, my friend! Welcome back to the safari," Nicholas laughed.

Nicholas began to slow the jeep down as he looked out into the grasslands intently.

"Okay my friends, I have spotted one," He declared, as he brought the jeep to a complete stop. He turned the engine off, put on the parking brake, then pushed a button on the dashboard. With a creak of fiberglass and metal, the entire roof of the jeep opened up. All six passengers gasped in awe.

"Now you can feel free to stand up and look out," Nicholas said. "The lion I have spotted is about one hundred yards out, standing at the crest of a small hill. He is a male lion—you can tell by the thick mane around his neck."

Blaine and Tracey joined the other four, as all stood up to try and spot the lion.

"C'mon, Fred, get your binoculars out," the plump lady

barked to her husband.

"Patience, Pam, patience! I can't find them in my fanny pack," Fred responded, as he rummaged through the biggest fanny pack either of the Sassafras twins had ever seen.

"Let's see—lip balm, whistles, sunscreen, fans, sunglasses . . . Oh, good heavens! There they are, at the very bottom," he said, exasperated, as he pulled out a pair of binoculars and handed them to his wife.

Pam grabbed the binoculars out of his hand and stuck them on her face. She looked out into the grasslands, albeit in the wrong direction.

Hank was the first of the six passengers to spot the lion. "Oh, there he is! I can see him now." He pointed.

Blaine and Tracey followed Hank's finger. At first all they could see was gently swaying grass, but then, just as Nicholas had said, they spotted the lion at the crest of a hill.

"Wow!" Tracey exclaimed, pausing to take a picture with her smartphone, "What a magnificent animal!"

Blaine also quickly snapped a photo, as he nodded in agreement.

"Pam, for Pete's sake, you are looking out of the wrong side of the jeep. Give me those things so I can try," Fred chided, grabbing the binoculars.

As Fred and Pam continued to fumble around with the binoculars, Nicholas began to give some more information about lions. "Lions are social animals that live in groups called prides. Prides are made up of several females and their cubs, along

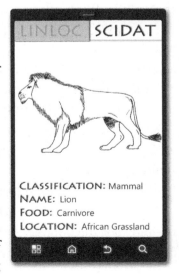

LINLOC   SCIDAT

CLASSIFICATION: Mammal
NAME: Lion
FOOD: Carnivore
LOCATION: African Grassland

with a few males—one of which is dominant."

As if on cue, the lion on the crest opened his mouth wide and let out a huge roar. The sound sent shivers down the twins' spines.

"I happen to know," Nicholas started again, "that the pride of lions this male lion belongs to has some new cubs. Does anyone want to drive in for a closer look?"

"Is it safe to get closer than this?" asked Pam, in alarm.

"No worries, ma'am," answered Nicholas with a smile. "We have never had any injuries or casualties with Mzuri tours."

Not waiting for any other responses, Nicholas started the Jeep back up and began to drive slowly toward the crest where the lion was. Blaine and Tracey were fans of fun, but this was the most intense thing they had ever done. They had definitely never been this close to a wild, uncaged lion before. Soon, they were close enough to see the other lions in the pride on the crest. They were resting in the shade of some acacia trees. There sat about a dozen more lions.

"If you look near the base of the tallest tree, you can see three cubs. They have spots when they are first born," informed Nicholas.

Blaine and Tracey immediately spotted the three cubs. They were quite adorable.

"These lions are resting right now," Nicholas continued. "When they are sitting, they usually have their paws out in front." Blaine noticed that the lion on the crest was making his way closer to the Jeep. He also noticed that the roof of the Jeep was still open. He wondered if the lion could jump up into the vehicle and the thought made him shudder.

Evidently, Pam noticed too. "Mr. Mzuri, that big male lion is coming this way," she squeaked, her eyes as big as saucers.

"P-p-predator," Fred added.

Nicholas, with no fear in his voice, responded, "Ok, friends, time to move on and see the next animal." He skillfully turned the Jeep around, and headed slowly away from the pride.

Blaine looked back to see if the big male lion was following them. He was not, and Blaine released a little sigh of relief.

"Not scared, are you?" Tracey whispered.

Blaine shook his head no, which, of course, wasn't a completely accurate response.

"Lions are mammals," continued Nicholas, as they drove away. "The four basic characteristics of mammals are that they are covered with fur, they are warm blooded, they give birth to live young, and they feed their young with milk from the mother. All the animals you see on this safari will be mammals. But I thought it would be best to start at the top of the food chain. Hank, do you remember what a food chain is?"

"Sure do," Hank responded. "It's a chain of living things that eat each other."

"That is correct," Nicholas smiled. "Next, I hope we can see a cheetah, another carnivorous cat at the top of the food chain."

Chasing Cheetahs

Nicholas left the roof of the Jeep down, as he drove out further into the grasslands. A gentle breeze blew across the passengers, which was nice on this hot, sunny day in Kenya. Blaine and Tracey just gazed out across the landscape, trying to soak up this experience. The man who had no eyebrows looked out his window as well, but Hank abruptly fell back asleep. Nicholas quietly sang a song in an African language in the front, while Fred and Pam argued about which flavor granola bar they wanted.

About half an hour passed, when Blaine and Tracey felt the

Jeep speed up. Nicholas was laughing and looking out to the right.

"Look everyone," he pointed. "We have spotted a cheetah, and it looks like he wants to race."

The twins looked out the right side of the jeep and saw a slender cat running at an amazing rate of speed. Not too far ahead of the cheetah was a herd of wildebeest. They had sensed the danger of the approaching cat and were already running away.

"Binoculars! Now, Fred!" Pam insisted, reaching toward the fanny pack.

"Now wait just a second, dear. Maybe we should try the camera this time." But Pam must not have heard her husband, because when Fred put the camera in her outstretched hand, Pam grabbed the camera like a pair of binoculars and was trying to look through it with both eyes.

"Well, mercy me, how do these silly things work? I can't see a thing!" Pam exclaimed.

The cheetah was running parallel to the jeep, and was beginning to outrun them, so Nicholas pushed down harder on the accelerator. The twins looked at the speedometer. It read forty-five miles per hour, then fifty miles per hour, but still they had not caught up with the sprinting cat.

"Man oh man, this is a fast one!" Hank exclaimed, bolting awake from his slumber. Fifty-five miles per hour, and still the cat was faster. It wasn't until the jeep reached sixty miles per hour that they caught up with the speed of the cheetah.

Suddenly, the herd of wildebeest took a hard right as a group and the cheetah darted right after them, almost close enough to pounce. One slower, weaker wildebeest was visibly lagging well behind the herd. The cheetah saw its chance and leapt into the air with claws extended and mouth open, right onto the back of the unlucky wildebeest. Both animals crashed down, disappearing behind some tall grass. The twins' mouths hung open in wonder.

"Looks like he got him," they heard Hank say.

Pam had finally figured out that she was holding a camera and not binoculars and she was snapping away. The only problem was that the lens cap was still on.

Nicholas stopped the jeep a safe distance away from where the cheetah had disappeared and began talking, "Cheetahs are also carnivores that hunt a variety of animals, but they seem to prefer zebras, gazelles, and wildebeests. And as you just witnessed, they can reach speeds of over sixty miles per hour, but only for short distances. Their slim, muscular bodies and long legs allow them to move with speed, strength, and flexibility."

Blaine and Tracey had never been interested in science. Just the thought of it had made them nauseous. But if this was science, their opinions were already starting to change. They were loving this adventure and even had questions.

"What places in the world can cheetahs be found?" asked Blaine.

"Yes, and are we going to get to see any babies?" Tracey added.

Welcoming the questions, Nicholas answered, "Today cheetahs can only be found in the plains of Africa, south of the Sahara. But they once lived in North Africa, the Middle East, and India. Sadly, cheetahs are endangered animals. But happily, we have had some baby cheetahs born in recent months. We probably won't see them on this trip, but I hear that they are all doing well. When a baby cheetah is first born, it has a coat of long gray hair and looks more like a honey badger than a cheetah. This is

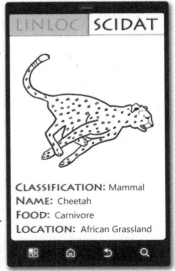

CLASSIFICATION: Mammal
NAME: Cheetah
FOOD: Carnivore
LOCATION: African Grassland

a form of camouflage. Cheetahs can give birth to up to four babies at a time. So not just twins like you, Blaine and Tracey, but triplets and quadruplets as well."

The Sassafras twins knew that they would need to remember all this information so that they could enter the correct data into the SCIDAT application on their phones. When Uncle Cecil had first told them about progressing through the different locations and collecting data, they hadn't really cared. But if all of the locations were going to be as interesting as here in the African grasslands, then they wanted to experience all of them! Plus, if all the local experts were going to be as cool as Nicholas Mzuri was, then the twins wanted to meet them as well!

The group looked out into the grassy field in the direction of where the cheetah had taken down the wildebeest. After quite a long time, the cheetah emerged, with his whiskers still red. He walked over to a nearby tree and hopped up onto a low branch, and then proceeded to climb to a higher branch, where he plopped down for a rest after a satisfying lunch. Blaine and Tracey took the opportunity to snap a quick photo with their smartphones.

"Cheetahs use their long tails help them balance and aid in climbing, running, and leaping," stated Nicholas.

"I hope he's full," stammered Fred.

"Oh, that is true," replied Pam. "I haven't seen Mr. Mzuri eat anything all day. Give me that fanny pack."

"Dear, I was talking about the cheetah," Fred said, shaking his head, but Pam didn't hear him.

"Oh Mr. Mzuri, would you like a granola bar?" Pam asked cheerfully.

Nicholas just laughed, "Yes ma'am, that sounds very nice." Pam handed him a chocolate-chip flavored granola bar. Nicholas thanked her, took the bar, and started the jeep back up.

"Okay friends, now it is off to see some elephants!" Blaine

and Tracey looked at each other, excitement in their eyes. Would there ever be a dull moment here in Kenya?

The six passengers and their driver bumped along in the jeep for another thirty-plus minutes. The twins took the time to enter the data they had learned into the SCIDAT app on their phones. They had just finished, when Nicholas brought the vehicle to a stop again.

"Well, my friends, I hope you are ready to get a little adventurous. Here at Mzuri tours, we encourage our travelers to walk on the wild side, and we are about to do just that. The plan is to go see the elephants on foot!"

"But what about the p-p-p-predators?" asked Fred. "Is it worth taking the risk?"

"No worry, guys," Nicholas responded. "We are in elephant territory now, and the only real predators that elephants have are humans. But if we get into a sticky situation, we always have Shelly to protect us."

"Who is Shelly?" asked Fred.

Nicholas reached under his seat and pulled out a huge machete. "This is Shelly," he stated proudly, "and she has never let any harm come to me."

"Oh, dear," Pam blushed, cheeks as rosy as ever.

"Don't worry, guys," reassured Hank. "This is my eleventh safari with Nicholas, and this is, hands down, my favorite part. We'll all be fine. It will be fun."

"We will only go on foot if everyone agrees." Nicholas declared.

The Sassafras twins were a little scared, but they were never ones to skirt an adventurous opportunity. Besides, Uncle Cecil wouldn't send them anywhere that they could really get hurt, would he?

"We are up for it," the twins said together. The man who had no eyebrows simply nodded in agreement. Fred, however, looked like death-warmed-over.

"Oh c'mon," pleaded Pam tugging at her husband's arm. "We didn't buy all of these fancy do-dads just to look good. Let's make this a real adventure!" Fred reached into the fanny pack, pulled out a battery-powered fan, turned it on, and aimed it right at his face.

"Okay," he finally managed weakly.

Within five minutes, the group of seven was walking out into the grasslands on foot. Even though Nicholas had assured them there was nothing to fear, they were all still a little nervous. It was now late afternoon, but the sky was still very blue and the sun was very hot. They walked down a narrow dirt path in single file. Mzuri was in front and the man with no eyebrows was bringing up the rear. Fred and Pam were lathered up with sunscreen, bug spray, and hand sanitizer. Blaine and Tracey could smell all three ointments as they walked behind the couple on the trail.

Though the grasslands looked mostly flat, they could be very deceiving. The group found this out as they very suddenly came upon a rather large valley.

"Welcome to Elephant Valley!" Nicholas announced happily, as the group began to descend down the trail. The twins could see a small lake down in the valley, but they couldn't yet see any elephants.

Nicholas stopped walking and turned around to address the group. Instead of talking, his face froze in horror, as he looked behind the group. Seeing Mzuri's face made the twins freeze too. What was Nicholas staring at behind them that was making him so scared? Was it a lion? Was it a cheetah? Blaine mustered up the courage to slowly turn his head and look behind him, but there was nothing. He couldn't see anything.

"Wait a second," Blaine thought, "Where is the man with no eyebrows? Wasn't he just walking behind me? Had a predator gotten . . ." Blaine's thoughts were interrupted by the sound of an engine starting off in the distance. Nicholas, unfreezing himself, raced past the group back up the trail. Blaine, Tracey, Hank, and Pam followed him. Fred just stood still looking like an ice sculpture. The twins were amazed at how fast Nicholas ran. There was no way they could keep up with him, but then Nicholas stopped and just stared off into the distance. Blaine and Tracey joined him, stopping by his side. Then Hank came up, and finally a wheezing Pam rejoined the group. The five could see a trail of dust starting from where the jeep had been parked.

Nicholas' face was covered in disbelief. "He stole the jeep," he exclaimed. "The man who had no eyebrows stole the jeep."

CHAPTER 3: LOST IN ELEPHANT VALLEY

Eyeing Elephants

A smartphone began to vibrate with an incoming call on one of the tables down in Uncle Cecil's basement. President Lincoln used his nose to nudge the phone across the table to Cecil's waiting hand.

"Howdy hooty!" Cecil answered the phone. Blaine's frantic voice was on the other end.

"Uncle Cecil! You have to help us! Someone stole our jeep and now we are stranded out in the grasslands!" Blaine screamed. Cecil's face wrinkled up in perplexion.

"Are the zip lines not working?" he asked calmly.

"No, the LINLOC app won't give us any new coordinates because we haven't entered all the data into the SCIDAT app yet," Blaine retorted.

Cecil could also hear Tracey yelping in the background, "The SCIDAT app says we need data on lions, cheetahs, elephants, and giraffes. We have entered the correct data for the first two, but we haven't even seen those last two animals yet. How are we going to get out of here?"

Cecil reached up and rubbed the back of his neck. He knew the twins weren't going to want to hear it, but there was one way to progress. "The only way to get to your next location is to enter all the data." Cecil stated. Blaine and Tracey responded with silence.

"Cheer up you two!" Cecil continued happily. "I am sure that you two are having an adventurous time, and besides, you are Sassafrases, and Sassafrases never give up." Cecil heard two loud sighs and then the call clicked off. He looked at President Lincoln, smiled, and declared, "Don't worry, they'll be fine."

Blaine and Tracey turned off their smartphones and began walking back to the small rock where Hank was lying. Fred and Pam were also sitting there, listening to Nicholas Mzuri. The twins had hoped that if they called Uncle Cecil, he might be able to zip them out of there without entering the data, but he had just confirmed their suspicions. The only way to leave was to learn the information, and then enter it into the SCIDAT app, but how were they going to survive this first location? They had already seen a cheetah take down a wildebeest and before that they had seen a pride of lions. Here, they were just sitting out in the open. There were no fences holding back the animals in this place, but what Uncle Cecil had said was right. They were having an adventurous time, to say the least. Plus, they were Sassafrases, and Sassafrases never give up.

The twins plopped down on the rock, near the group. The small rock they were sitting on was down in Elephant Valley, about two hundred yards from the small lake. Nicholas looked calm again now. He had been rather angry about the jeep getting

THE SASSAFRAS SCIENCE ADVENTURES

stolen; evidently, the man who had no eyebrows had somehow taken Nicholas' keys without being noticed. Nicholas had been embarrassed that he had let it happen. He had initially feared for the safety of his safari guests, but he was now already back to his old confident self. He had grown up not too far from here, and he knew how to handle the dangers of the grasslands. Besides, he had reminded everyone—he had Shelly. The combination of Shelly and Nicholas' confidence had reassured everyone except Fred, who hadn't said a word since the jeep was stolen.

Nicholas was now standing in front of the group, giving an introduction on elephants. "There are two different species of elephant—one is found here in Africa, and one is found in Asia. The African elephants, found in the grasslands, have bigger tusks and ears, while the Asian elephants are found in the forests and have a more rounded forehead. Elephants are very intelligent and really do have very good memories. They usually travel in herds of about eight to ten and are known as the heaviest animals that walk on land."

Hank, who in the middle of their perilous situation had somehow fallen asleep on the rock, bolted awake, sat up straight, and pointed across to the other side of the lake. "Look, here come some elephants now," he declared.

The group looked to see a herd of ten elephants coming out from behind a grove of trees and approaching the lake's edge. Blaine and Tracey aimed their phones and clicked a picture of the herd, while Fred shuddered at the sight of another animal. He clicked his battery-powered fan back on and aimed it toward his sweaty forehead.

Hank patted him on the back. "Don't worry, buddy. Elephants are herbivores, not carnivores. They only eat plants. Ain't that right, Nicholas?"

"Yes it is, Hank," Nicholas replied. "Carnivores eat meat. Omnivores eat meat and plants. And herbivores eat only plants.

Elephants are herbivores. So, they are not very likely to attack us, especially if they don't see us as a threat."

They watched as the elephants tromped right down into the muddy water. The biggest elephant in the herd raised his trunk and let out a loud trumpeting bellow. Nicholas started again. "The elephant that just trumpeted is the dominant male of this herd. The other elephants are probably related females, and it looks like there may be a couple of babies. Female elephants and babies never roam on their own. However, male elephants can live by themselves or travel in all male herds called bachelor herds."

Pam, who had finally figured out the difference between a camera and a pair of binoculars, now had the camera strapped over her shoulder, and she was trying to get the elephants' attention.

"Oh, herd of elephants," she called, "look over here." She began stomping around and started making elephant noises, all the while pretending that one of her arms was an elephant's trunk. The herd paid her no attention.

Nicholas looked at Pam, chuckled to himself, and then continued. "Now let me tell you, my friends, a little bit about my three favorite parts of an elephant. My favorite part of the elephant is their trunks. They use their trunks kind of like a straw for drinking, but can also use them like arms for carrying and moving heavy loads."

"What a cool animal!" Tracey was thinking to herself. Blaine was thinking about what he would look like if he had a straw for a nose.

"And as you just witnessed," Nicholas shared, "they can also use their trunks to make trumpeting calls to communicate with or warn the others in the herd. My next favorite part, is their teeth. They have large grinding cheek teeth that wear down and are replaced from the rear. Those magnificent tusks that you see are also part of their teeth. They are considered extended upper teeth that the elephant can use for digging or defense. My third favorite thing about elephants is those big ears they have."

"Which they use to fly with, right Mr. Mzuri?" Pam interjected. Nicholas looked at Pam with a smile on his face that said he didn't know if she was joking or serious.

"No, ma'am, they don't use their ears to fly, but they do use them to communicate with the herd and to keep cool in this hot climate. When they want to defend themselves, they can flare out those ears to make themselves look bigger than they actually are."

The Sassafras twins stared out across the lake at the animals in front of them. Elephants, here in their natural habitat, were quite a sight to behold. They took out their smartphones and entered the elephant information they had just learned into their SCIDAT app.

Nicholas flipped Shelly once in the air and caught it by the handle. "Well, my friends, since our jeep was stolen and we have no way to radio the lodge for help, it is time that we start thinking about building a shelter for the night. We will have to try and make our way back on foot tomorrow."

The hot African sun was beginning to get closer to the horizon and soon it would be dusk. Blaine and Tracey wondered what kind of shelter they were going to build. Would they even be able to sleep out here in the open grasslands? Didn't predators like lions and cheetahs hunt at night? And was walking back on foot really a good idea? What had the Sassafras twins gotten themselves into?

Nicholas pointed over to a bunch of acacia trees. "We will use Shelly to cut some branches off of those acacia trees." he announced, as he gripped his machete tightly. "Then, we will drag the branches over here and use them to make a circular fence around our little rock. Be very careful, my friends, because acacia trees are very thorny. Which is not a bad thing, because the thorns will help keep the predators out."

"P-p-p-predators?" Fred managed to say, finally speaking again.

"Yes sir, there will more than likely be predators out tonight looking for food. But with a nice thorny acacia fence and a big warm fire, we will be fine," Nicholas responded confidently.

Pam began rummaging through the fanny pack. "Fred, you did pack gloves in here didn't you?

"Yes, dear," Fred remarked weakly.

"Well then, help me find them and let's get to work!"

After about an hour, the group of six had an acacia barrier, with one small opening, built around their rock. There was a nice crackling fire right in the center. The sky was painted with the beautiful colors of the setting sun, and night was coming quickly to the African grasslands. Pam and Fred had graciously offered up the rest of their granola bars. The group was now finishing them off for a make-shift dinner, though everyone was finding it a little difficult to eat because they were so nervous about their current predicament. Mzuri, being the local expert he was, calmed them with stories from his simple childhood here in Kenya. The twins could just picture a young Nicholas Mzuri running barefoot through the grasslands, pretending to be a lion hunting his prey. It turned out that the nice lady with the braided hair that the Sassafras twins had briefly met at the Jambo Lodge was Nicholas' sister. Her name was Imani, and she and Nicholas had made both the Jambo Lodge and Mzuri Tours very successful by working hard to offer the absolute best service in Kenya.

After a couple of hours of stories, the sky was completely black and the night was fully upon them. The stars were shining, but it was impossible to see out past the wall of acacia branches.

The group could hear all sorts of strange noises coming from the darkness and the Sassafras twins wondered how they were going to be able to fall asleep. Hank, being narcoleptic, of course fell soundly asleep right away. Fred and Pam had blown up their inflatable pillows and were attempting to sleep right next to the small rock. Nicholas was sitting in front of the small entrance in their acacia blockade, digging his machete into the ground and humming lowly to himself. He had said that he would stay awake as guard so that the others could sleep.

Blaine and Tracey were sitting back to back attempting to lean on each other to get comfortable enough to fall asleep. Blaine thought he could hear a lion roaring from somewhere out in the darkness. Tracey watched the orange light from the fire dance around on the acacia branches as she thought about the animals they had seen that day. The two could still hear the elephants trumpeting every so often, as they both began to nod in and out of sleep.

Glimpsing Giraffes

Time passed—it could have been minutes or could have been hours, but eventually everything fell completely silent. Then barely, breaking the silence, an acacia branch cracked and then another. The sound was audible, but none of the six were awake to hear it. Nicholas was a good tour guide, but in his exhaustion, he had fallen asleep sometime during the night. Now he lay motionless, Shelly the machete by his side, right at the small entrance. Fred and Pam were snoring in rhythm and Hank remained in a deep sleep. The twins were still sitting back to back, somehow both asleep.

Crack. Snap. Acacia branches continued to break as something made its way around the fence the group had built. Then on the opposite side, closer to the entrance, more branches were snapping. Now, there were two things creeping around their acacia fort, but still the group slept.

The flames of the fire were now just smoldering embers

under a heap of ashes. The cracking and snapping turned into a rustling noise, as one of the things began to tug at the acacia fence. The other something was standing right at the small gap, blocking any exit.

Suddenly, Hank bolted awake. Immediately, he saw what the things were, but no words came to his mouth. Nicholas groaned and turned over, but didn't wake up. Shelly lay useless by his side. Fred and Pam snored on in rhythm, when a whole section of the acacia fence ripped off, leaving the group totally exposed. Hank, still unable to speak, watched as a long purple tongue made its way down toward Tracey's head.

She was having the strangest dream. In it, Blaine was being his usual self and pestering her. Only in this dream his arms were purple and he was waving them in her face. No, they weren't just purple, they were wet and purple and now he was rubbing one of his arms on her face.

"Blaine stop! Get your purple arms out of my face!" Tracey screamed.

Blaine heard his name as he winked his eyes open and stretched, waking from his sleep. Why was Tracey yelling at him? He turned around to ask Tracey what her problem was, and was stunned at what he saw. He jumped to his feet and joined Hank in speechless wonder.

There, inside of their little stronghold, was a giraffe eating acacia leaves out of Tracey's hair. Evidently some had gotten stuck in her hair when she had helped build the fence. Tracey was obviously still half asleep, as she grabbed and pushed at the giraffe's tongue and face. The giraffe didn't seem to mind her movements at all. It just wanted the acacia leaves out of her hair. Meanwhile, Blaine and Hank heard some crunching behind them and they turned to see another giraffe rummaging over the acacia fence they had made.

Nicholas sat up groggily and immediately started laughing. "Well good, morning, Mr. Giraffe. Leave that poor girl alone, will

THE SASSAFRAS SCIENCE ADVENTURES

you?" he soothed, as he gently shooed the giraffe out of the circle. The two animals trotted off together to find a more hospitable breakfast.

"She is never going to believe me when I tell her this story!" Blaine laughed with Nicholas and Hank. It was early morning, which meant they had made it safely through the night. The three looked up at the dawn sky. The colors at sunrise were just as beautiful as at sunset.

Fred and Pam began to stir, as did Tracey. "I had the strangest dream," she mumbled, sitting up, puffy-eyed.

Blaine just laughed and said, "You have no idea!"

After everyone was fully awake, the three told the others about the giraffes that had come into camp. Nicholas began to share what he knew about the animals. "Giraffes can only be found here in the African grasslands. They are the world's tallest animal and can grow to be up to twenty feet tall. It's those long necks they have that make them so towering. Their necks contain only seven vertebrae, just like other mammals. It's just that their vertebrae are greatly elongated. Their height helps them graze from the tops of trees where other animals can't reach, though many times a female giraffe will also eat from shorter trees and shrubs. A giraffe's favorite food is an acacia tree. They will eat the shoots, leaves, twigs, and as some of us just witnessed, they will even eat acacia out of people's hair." Tracey's face immediately got red at this reference to her, but she did laugh, because it was kind of funny.

Nicholas continued. "Giraffes use their long purple tongues and grooved canine teeth to strip leaves. Their thick lips protect them from the acacia thorns. Since they only eat from plants, they are classified as herbivores."

"Can you tell us about their spots?" Pam asked, with a mouthful of toothpaste, as she brushed her teeth with a battery operated circular motion toothbrush.

"Yes, ma'am," Nicholas replied. "The eight subspecies of giraffes can be differentiated by their coat colors and pattern types. But each individual giraffe has a unique pattern, kind of like a fingerprint. Their spots range in size and they help with camouflage."

"There they are again," said Hank, pointing down towards the lake. The group watched as the two giraffes re-emerged down close to the water's edge. They were so tall and their front legs so long, that they had to spread them apart wide to be able to bend down low enough to drink from the lake. Blaine and Tracey snapped a few good pictures.

UNLOC **SCIDAT**

CLASSIFICATION: Mammal
NAME: Giraffe
FOOD: Herbivore
LOCATION: African Grassland

"It looks like one of those giraffe is male and one is female." Nicholas stated. "Both genders of giraffes have short non-shedding horns up on their heads. The males use these horns when they fight, but the females are just there for looks. Can you believe that female giraffes don't give birth until after fifteen months of pregnancy? But then, it only takes the calves an hour or two to learn how to walk."

Hank clapped his hands together and laughed. "Man oh man, I never get tired of hearing these interesting facts about the animals."

Nicholas patted his most loyal visitor on the back. "Is there anything else that you remember about giraffe that I haven't mentioned yet, Hank?"

Hank stroked his long beard and thought for a second. "Only that their tails are tipped with long hairs for swatting away insects, and that they can run pretty fast on those two-toed, hoofed feet of theirs."

"Yes, yes, my friend," agreed Nicholas. "I did forget to mention those facts."

Blaine and Tracey were trying to soak in all the information they were hearing. They were enjoying their adventure, for the most part, but they were also anxious to enter all the correct data into the SCIDAT app. They wanted to progress through their locations and eventually get back to Uncle Cecil's basement. They had already entered the data on grasslands, lions, cheetahs, and elephants. Now, they just needed to add the giraffe data, and then they could open LINLOC, pinpoint their next location, and zip away.

Blaine and Tracey knew in their hearts that they couldn't leave, yet. Yes, Sassafrases never quit, but neither do Sassafrases leave friends behind in dangerous situations. So, they couldn't just leave their new friends out here in the African grasslands, not knowing if they would get back safe to the lodge or not. Blaine and Tracey would stick this adventure out. They would get back to the lodge with all their new friends and then enter the information on the giraffe. That is what they had to do.

The group of six watched as the two giraffes trotted off around the lake. Then Nicholas, turned to face the group. "It is time, my friends," he announced.

"Time for what?" Fred asked, cautiously.

"Time to try to walk back to the Jambo lodge," Mzuri answered. "I think we can make it in one day's time if we keep a good pace and don't run into any pred . . . problems."

Fred sat frozen on the rock, looking like an ice sculpture again.

"Oh, c'mon Fred," Pam chimed in, "let's do this thing, honey!" She reached in the fanny pack and pulled out a pair of insoles. She took off Fred's boots, put the insoles in, put his boots back on, and laced them up tight. All the while, Fred remained frozen stiff.

"There, Fred, now you have new, comfortable, gel-filled insoles in your boots, and those boots were made for walking, honey, so get up! Let's go!" Pam pulled her husband up off of the rock, and the two of them started marching off into the grasslands, but in the wrong direction. Nicholas chased the quirky couple down and the group headed off together through the African grasslands, back toward the Jambo Safari Lodge.

They walked well into the late morning, without much conversation and without anything too eventful happening. Nicholas kept a watchful eye out as he led the group, all the while holding Shelly tightly in his grasp. The minds of the Sassafras twins drifted back through their adventure as they walked. They still couldn't believe they had actually zipped through space on an invisible zip line. They had seen lions, cheetahs, elephants, and giraffes, up close and personal. They had met some interesting people—a narcoleptic safari enthusiast, a quirky but delightful husband and wife, an amazing grasslands expert, and a strange man who had no eyebrows. Who was that mysterious man, anyway? Why had he stolen their jeep and put them in the predicament they were in now, walking on foot through the dangerous grasslands?

Their thoughts were interrupted by Mzuri's deep voice. "We are making very good time, my friends. If we continue in this southerly direction, we can hope to reach the lodge just after dusk."

"That's funny," Pam said, looking at a thermometer. "My compass says we are going north."

Just then, Nicholas lifted his hand, as if asking for silence, while he fixed his gaze out somewhere into the grass in front of them.

"What is it?" Tracey whispered to Blaine. "Did you see anything?"

Blaine just shook his head. The twins could see the muscles in Nicholas' forearm flexing as he gripped his machete tighter. They watched their tour guide's face. It was covered with concern. What was in the grass? But as they watched, Nicholas' expression slowly changed from concern to relief.

"If my senses are correct," he declared, "we are about to encounter some zebras."

Within seconds, the group could hear the faint pounding of approaching hooves. "It sounds like an entire herd is headed this way," Mzuri stated. "The zebra is another magnificent species of mammal that the African grasslands have to offer. They are herbivores that are closely related to horses. Their black and white striped coats make it hard for other animals to spot them, and no two coats are alike."

The sound of hooves got louder and louder as the herd of zebras began to come more clearly into sight. Suddenly, Nicholas' face went from relief back to concern. The herd must have been bigger than he had first thought, and they were headed straight for the six trekkers.

"My friends, come quickly! Let us go to those trees!" Nicholas said, pointing to a dozen or so trees off about one hundred yards to their left.

Sensing the tone of urgency in Mzuri's voice, the group wasted no time, and headed immediately for the trees. Surprisingly enough, Fred was the fastest of the pack, sprinting for the trees like an Olympic runner. Hank was close behind him, followed by Blaine and Tracey. Nicholas was in the back, keeping pace with the slower Pam.

Blaine looked at the trees, and then at the approaching herd of zebras. The herd was close, but he thought they should be able to get to the trees with no problem. Just then, Blaine heard a scream of pain behind him. He looked back to see Pam tumble to the ground, holding her ankle.

He grabbed Tracey and the two rushed back to see if they could help her. Mzuri knelt down beside Pam to assess her injury.

Pam winced as Nicholas gently prodded her ankle.

"Holy moly, golly molly," she cried in pain. "I think I broke my ankle."

"No, ma'am," Nicholas responded. "I believe it is just badly sprained, but you aren't going to be able to walk on it anymore, not very fast, anyway."

Nicholas looked over toward the trees that Fred and Hank were just now reaching. The two were totally unaware about what had happened with Pam. He looked at the Sassafras twins, and stated, "Blaine and Tracey, I am going to need your help."

The twins nodded and jumped into action. Tracey grabbed the huge fanny pack that Pam had been carrying and slung it over her shoulder, grunting in surprise at how heavy it was. Nicholas and Blaine worked together to pick up Pam off the ground. They put her arms over their shoulders and helped her walk on her one good foot. Blaine looked again at the rapidly approaching herd of stampeding zebras, then at the trees, and then back at the zebras and the realization hit him like a ton of bricks. They were not going to make it to those trees before being overrun by the herd of zebras!

CHAPTER 4: OFF TO THE DESERT

Camel Criminals

The zebras' pounding hooves now sounded like rolling thunder. The herd was coming, and they were coming fast. "Zebras can outrun most of their predators," Nicholas shouted above the crescendo. "Now let's see if we can outrun them!"

He and Blaine worked together to move the injured Pam as fast as they could toward the safety of the trees. Tracey ran ahead of them in a full sprint, carrying the fanny pack. Fred and Hank had already climbed a tree and only now looked back to find that Pam had been injured. Pam grunted in pain as Nicholas and Blaine hobbled her along. The going was slow, but they were making progress.

"Too slow," thought Blaine as he glanced toward the herd, then looked ahead at the target trees. "There is absolutely no way," he thought. " Within seconds we are going to get over run by all of those zebras."

Up ahead, Tracey had reached the safety of the trees. She threw herself up on a low branch, and then immediately looked back to see if her brother, Nicholas, and Pam were going to make it. Her face wrinkled up in concern. They were still so far away, too far. They weren't going to make it. The zebras were practically upon them. But wait! What was that? Was that a jeep? Tracey climbed higher in the tree to get a better look. It was a jeep. Speeding up behind the three in a cloud of dust, wheels tearing angrily over the terrain was a Jeep!

Back on the ground, Blaine was struggling under Pam's weight, but he wouldn't quit. He had to try and help his friend, but was it a lost cause? The zebras were now only a few short yards away. He, Pam, and Nicholas were about to get pummeled. Then, seemingly out of nowhere, a jeep appeared right next to them, blocking them from the stampede. The driver of the jeep put on the brakes. Nicholas, Pam, and Blaine fell to the ground in the safety of the vehicle's shadow. Immediately, a flurry of black and white stripes shot by them. The herd of zebras passed around in a thundering stampede of snorts, hooves, and dust. The ground around them rumbled with a rhythm even faster than Blaine's beating heart.

After several minutes, the pace slowed, as the slower zebras trickled by, bringing up the rear of the amazing mass movement of animals. The three just sat on the ground until every last zebra had passed. When the dust had settled, Nicholas stood up to see who was driving the jeep.

"Imani!" Nicholas shouted with joy.

Blaine stood, helped up Pam, and looked into the jeep. There, sitting in the driver's seat with a big smile on her face, was the lady with braided hair—Imani Mzuri, Nicholas's sister.

After an hour-long ride in the jeep, the six stranded trekkers were back, safe and sound, at the Jambo Lodge. Imani had gotten worried when Nicholas hadn't returned to the lodge with his six safari guests. She had prayed for their safety throughout the night, and then, at first light, she had hopped into another one of the Jambo Lodge jeeps and begun the search. She knew the areas where Nicholas usually took his guests, but she had been very lucky to find them right before they were overrun by the herd of zebras. She had found the group, but she hadn't found the man who had no eyebrows. He had the stolen jeep and had disappeared without a trace or clue to explain his actions.

It was evening now. The Sassafras twins were alone in their room in the lodge. They had said goodbye to their new friends, and had thanked the Mzuris for all their help. They had only been in the grasslands for two days. They were really going to miss this place and the people they had met, but their scientific adventure would have to continue. They had finished entering the data entry into the SCIDAT app.

"Okay, it worked!" Blaine rejoiced. "The LINLOC app just gave us our new coordinates—latitude 20° 0' 21.5" and longitude 29° 31' 52.5." It looks like we're going to Egypt!"

"Oh, and look," Tracey added, "this time our local expert is a princess—Princess Talibah."

Blaine continued to read the information on his phone. "We will be exploring the Egyptian Desert, and looking for camels, cobras, spiny-tailed lizards, and the fennec fox. This is going to be sweet!"

It was easy to forget this was all about science, because at this point it just felt like an adventure. Could learning science be truly adventurous? The twins weren't sure, but they were giddy with excitement as they put on their harnesses, calibrated the rings of their carabiners, and let them shut on the invisible lines.

Again, in a burst of sonic energy, they found themselves zipping through open space at the speed of light. "This is never going to get old," the twins thought as they soared.

After a few moments of exhilaration, they came to a jerking stop. Wait, they hadn't stopped completely. They weren't traveling at the speed of light anymore, but they were still moving. It hadn't happened like this the first time. The twins' eyes slowly adjusted from the white light effect of the zip line travel to the color of their new location. There wasn't much color to see here, mostly just darkness. They must have landed in the Sahara desert at nighttime. They were definitely still moving, but their feet were not on the ground. They were riding something. Blaine felt around with his hands and took in a deep breath. His senses told him animal hair and animal smell. They had to be riding some sort of an animal.

The twins' eyes were now fully adjusted to their new setting, but it was so dark it was hard to see. Thankfully, Blaine and Tracey were together on the same animal. Blaine was in the front and Tracey was on the back. They were separated by a hump on the animal's back.

"Blaine," Tracey whispered. "I think we are riding a camel!"

Blaine suspected that his sister was right. Wow, Uncle Cecil's and President Lincoln's zip lines were so precise they could even land their travelers on the back of a camel! Pretty cool, but were they all alone in the desert? Where was this Princess Talibah?

The two could see the shadows of quite a few other camels moving slowly alongside their camel. Were there any people riding the other camels? Just then, Blaine and Tracey heard some faint voices to their right.

"I keep telling you, Princess," a raspy voice said. "Studying all of that biology isn't worth your time. Just try to remember what I teach you, and you will fare fine."

"Oh, leave her alone," another voice chimed in. "You talk nothing but nonsense. What our dear Princess really needs is to fall in love with me."

"You two are hopeless," a woman's voice laughed softly. "What do you think, Jendayi? Should I put them out of our hire?"

"I could hope for nothing better," another woman responded, "but I don't believe your father would allow that."

The voices the Sassafras twins were hearing were coming from other individuals that were also riding camels. By the tone of their voices and the rhythm of their conversation, it seemed as though the twins' sudden arrival had gone unnoticed. Blaine and Tracey weren't sure if they should reveal their presence just yet or not. They decided, that for right now, they should keep hidden in the darkness that the night was offering and continue listening in on the conversation.

The first woman they had heard, who the twins guessed was Princess Talibah, continued. "Yes, I know, Hanif, my father has instructed you to teach me about everything that is important to him, but my father does not know my heart. He does not know of my desire to learn about subjects not traditionally studied by women in our culture. What is there not to love about biology?"

"Take the camels we are now riding, for example. They are absolutely fascinating," the Princess spoke passionately. "Did you know, Hanif, my teacher, that these humps on their backs, made of stored fat help them survive for long periods of time without food or water? They can actually go months without drinking water because their digestive systems are extremely effective at extracting water from the plants they eat. However, when water becomes available again, they can drink up to thirty gallons in just minutes to make up for the loss. Did you know that, teacher?"

The man with the raspy voice, called Hanif, answered, "Did you read of this nonsense in one of your books? Everyone knows camels' humps are full of bad luck that causes droughts."

"Don't stop her from talking," the second male voice said, almost singing. "Her words are, to me, like sweet melodies from the morning birds."

"Abasi!" Hanif ordered. "Be quiet! You only say that because of your infatuation for her. You know she speaks nonsense."

"Yes, Hanif, my friend. Maybe it is nonsense, but it is beautiful nonsense," the other man lilted.

"Oh, these two are hopeless," the other woman teased. The Sassafrases thought they remembered her being called Jendayi. "Talibah, what else do you know about camels?"

"Just that they are the world's largest even-toed mammals, with big and wide feet that prevent them from sinking into the sand," the princess answered. "They also have two rows of eyelashes, and nostrils that can completely close, preventing the desert sands from getting into their eyes and noses. They are probably the best suited animals to live in the world's driest deserts."

"I love your biology," Jendayi encouraged, "much better than teacher Hanif's mysticism and protector Abasi's hopeless romanticism."

The two women laughed as the conversation of the four paused momentarily. It was rather cold in the Sahara desert at night, so the twins used the blankets they found draped over their camel's back to wrap up and keep warm. As the twins listened in on the conversation of the four shadows, the combination of their exhaustion, the warmth of the blankets, the slow trodding of their camel, and the darkness of night began to lull them to sleep right there on the camel's back. Before they knew it, the Sassafras twins were out cold.

Sand. Lying on his back in the sand.

Was Blaine dreaming? He gingerly moved his hands and fingers over the ground. Yes, that was sand.

But why was he lying on his back in the sand? Where was he again? Hadn't he fallen asleep next to a fence made of acacia trees?

No, wait. Something about an animal with a hump; there was a camel. Blaine had fallen asleep on a camel, but now there was sand. Sand beneath his back and sand in his hands and sand in his face. Why was there sand in his face? Blaine's eyes were met with morning sunlight as he blinked them open and reached up to wipe the sand off his face.

"Ahh ha," he heard an unfamiliar voice say. "Our last thief is finally awake."

"Thief?" Blaine thought. Then, more sand was kicked in his face.

"Stop it!" Blaine heard Tracey say. "We aren't thieves."

Blaine sat up, wiped the sand off his face, and opened his eyes wide. Tracey was sitting next to him and there were about thirty or forty very tall, very big, and evidently very angry men standing right in front of them. They were dressed from head to toe in black cloth. Most of them only had their eyes showing and most of them were also brandishing swords. The biggest one was standing in front of the rest.

Blaine looked at Tracey. "Why are they calling us thieves?" he asked.

"Because that is what you are," the front man answered for Tracey. "You are thieves—camel thieves, all six of you."

"All six of us?" Blaine thought, perplexed. Then, he looked behind him where four more people sat in the sand—two men and two women. Evidently, they were being accused as camel thieves, along with Blaine and his sister.

"And what do we do to camel thieves?" the front man asked, turning to the band of black-clothed men.

"We make them pay," one man answered.

"That is right," the front man confirmed, turning back to the accused. "We make them pay. And today we will make them pay with their lives."

Blaine and Tracey looked at each other. They both had fear and questions in their eyes.

The man continued in his deep, creepy voice. "We have something very special for the six of you today. We happen to be in the proximity of several old tombs that have long since been robbed of all their treasure by greedy caravans and foreign archaeologists. Now, they sit empty out here in our desert, miles away from anything or anyone. Today, we are going to make one of these tombs your permanent home."

Blaine and Tracey's minds were racing. Why were they being accused of being camel thieves? They had arrived in the Sahara at night and hadn't actually seen Princess Talibah or the other three people that they had heard talking. They now felt safe to assume that the people sitting behind them were the Princess Talibah, her friend Jendayi, her teacher Hanif, and her protector Abasi. They and the others were being accused of stealing these men's camels. But why would a princess and her friends steal camels?

As if reading the twins' minds, Abasi, who was very thin and very tall, spoke up. "Why would a princess steal camels?"

"A princess?" the front man questioned. "We have a princess among us, do we?"

"Abasi, you fool," said the short and round Hanif. "We must keep the princess's identity a secret!"

"No need to protect my identity," the woman stated, getting up.

"So that is Princess Talibah," thought the twins. She was not like a princess they had seen in cartoons. She was a rugged and strong desert princess. She had dark hair, dark eyes, and perfect, sun-kissed skin. She was wearing a deep blue cloak and had one diamond stud in her nose. The morning sun illuminated her striking beauty as she stood up straight and spoke with confidence.

"I am Princess Talibah of the Tuareg nomadic people. And I happen to know who you are. You are Itja, the scoundrel leader of a rag-tag group of bandits known as the Kekewey. We are not stealing your camels. You are stealing mine! When my father, the noble, wise, and powerful Abubakar, finds out about your insolence, he will have you and your men drawn and quartered."

The front man looked at his men, and then looked back at the Princess. He stood silently for a strange moment and then began laughing. "Well, Princess, everything you just said is correct, except for one thing—your father is not going to find out because none of you will be around to tell him."

That last statement made Blaine and Tracey shudder in their bones. That man did not want them to survive, let alone learn anything about the animals here. They remembered what Uncle Cecil had said about LINLOC when they were stranded in Africa. How were they going to get the information they needed for their SCIDAT app so that they could get out of there? Would they ever get home alive?

Suddenly, Abasi stood up and shouted, "I am Abasi, the sworn protector of Princess Talibah, daughter of Abubakar. I will let no harm befall her or any in her company. Her beautiful eyes shall see no misfortune, and a hand will not come against her on my watch. I will also protect her friend Jendayi, her teacher Hanif, and these two children who have found their way into her care!"

Itja swung out and knocked out Abasi in one blow. "Does anyone else want to protect the Princess?" he asked arrogantly.

No one answered as they sat in stunned silence. Two of Itja's men picked up Abasi's limp body and threw it over a camel. Next, they took lengths of rope and bound the hands of the five others behind their backs. Then, the black-robed leader of the Kekewey began leading them through the desert to the unnamed tomb.

Captured With Cobras

After a hot, sandy walk that seemed like to take hours, but really only took minutes, the group found themselves at the entrance of the tomb. It was the exact same color as the desert sand and could be easily missed if one wasn't looking for it. It was built in the shape of a pyramid, but it only stood about ten feet tall. There were steps going down to a single entrance.

"Welcome to your eternal resting place," Itja said flippantly. "I especially like this tomb, so it is fitting that a Princess will be buried in it. As an added perk, one of my men recently found a way to re-activate one of the ancient traps built into this tomb."

One of the men grunted proudly at his recognition.

"You see, this tomb has two rooms—an entry room, and a sarcophagus room. We have blocked off the sarcophagus room, so the six of you will only have access to the entry room. But that room holds for you a surprise, a deadly surprise. Archaeologists have dusted, scraped, and dug through every inch of this tomb. They have long since left it for other discoveries, but when they opened the tombs, they always left them that way. We have found that when the entrance is shut again, something very interesting happens in the entry room. I will divulge no more information. I will just let the six of you find out what happens."

The men of the Kekewey all laughed as they shoved the five, plus Abasi, who was now conscious, down the steps into the entry room of the small pyramid. They tumbled into a heap on the floor, hands still bound with rope. The Sassafras twins looked back at the entrance where Itja's huge frame was standing, blocking most of the doorway with the sun behind him and holding a lit torch in his hand. The twins had never been this scared in their lives. Hanif and Jendayi were visibly shaking with fear. Abasi sat in shame, but Princess Talibah didn't look scared at all.

She stood and faced Itja. "You are a thief and a coward," she spat out. "You and your men roam around the desert, stealing the camels of women and children, because you are too afraid to live in a community and be worthy citizens. We will escape from this tomb, and my father will find out what you have done, and then you will pay."

Itja just laughed and spat on the ground, as he stuck the torch in a holster on the wall. "Well, my dear Princess," he said. "You can share that sentiment with eternity when you get there."

With that, he turned around, walked up the stairs, and motioned to his black-robed men to close the entrance. Four of them grabbed a huge stone and began rolling it in front of the doorway. Blaine and Tracey watched as their window of sunlight got smaller and smaller. The four men grunted under the weight of the stone as they pushed it, but it was moving right down into a groove where it wouldn't be possible to move it back out. Just before it shut all the way, a gust of wind swirled around the entrance and blew the head-wrapping off of one of the men. The last thing the Sassafras twins saw before the door shut was a man who had no eyebrows.

Blaine & Tracey stared at each other with utter surprise.

"What? How had he gotten here? He was one of the Kekewey? Was it just another man who had no eyebrows? No. The twins were sure it was the same man. But how —?" Blaine and Tracey's thoughts were interrupted by a creaking sound coming from the floor.

"What was that noise?" the twins heard Jendayi ask. "Oh, Princess, I don't want to die in here."

"We are not going to die," Talibah answered her friend. "Just give me a moment. My hands are almost free of the ropes."

"How are your hands almost free?" screeched Hanif. "Bad luck. Bad luck has brought us here."

"Enough of your bad luck, dear teacher," Talibah declared. She then lifted her hands into the air, somehow free from the ropes.

"How on earth did you do that?" the teacher asked.

"I was able to hide a small, sharp stone in my cloak. Now, I can use that stone to free the rest of you," she informed. As the Princess jumped into action, it became apparent that the creaking noise was the sound of the floor opening up, as a hole in the center of it slowly began to get bigger. "So this was the 'surprise' Itja had mentioned," thought Tracey.

"The earth is opening its mouth to swallow us up!" yelped Hanif.

Everyone tried to ignore him, as Princess Talibah rushed around cutting everyone's ropes off. The room they were in wasn't very big, and the floor was receding into the walls at a rate that was making them all uncomfortable. The hole in the center just kept getting bigger and bigger. Then, to make matters worse, the Sassafras twins saw what was in the hole.

It was a pit full of snakes.

Tracey tried to scream out the word 'snake,' but when she opened her mouth, no sound came out.

THE SASSAFRAS SCIENCE ADVENTURES

Hanif had also spotted the vipers. So he screamed it for her. "Snakes! Snakes! Our bad fortune continues!"

Talibah, who was focused on her task, had freed everyone except Abasi, who was sitting on the ground in silence. "Abasi, stop sulking, and get up. How are you going to protect me if you die in this room?"

"I am so sorry, my lovely Princess. I failed you."

"Stop worrying about that. Stand up, man, and let me cut you free."

Abasi finally stood up and Princess Talibah began slicing at his ropes with the stone. The floor kept going back, back, back. The pit kept getting bigger, bigger, bigger. The snakes down in the pit seemed to be getting agitated as they slithered and hissed. Talibah successfully cut through Abasi's bonds. They were all free of the ropes, but what were they going to do now?

The floor continued to disappear. Within minutes, it would be nonexistent. The walls were perfectly flat, other than a few supporting columns. They offered no handholds or footholds for them to grab onto when the floor was gone. Just as Itja had said, the doorway to the second room was completely blocked shut. The only possible outcome seemed to be falling into the snake pit.

Jendayi was crying and Hanif was muttering something about bad luck under his breath. Abasi still looked a little dazed. Blaine's and Tracey's minds were screaming for a solution, but they were coming up blank. Princess Talibah was looking over every inch of the room for some possible clue to aid an escape. The floor continued to shrink. The snakes continued to hiss.

"Use your biology, Princess!" Hanif exclaimed. "Are the snakes in our pit here venomous?"

"Yes, they are, teacher. Those snakes appear to be cobras. Cobras are all venomous. Their venom, which is injected through their hollow teeth, stops the heart and lungs from working. That venom is produced in glands at the roof of their mouth and you must have anti-venom, or you will die from their bite."

Hanif looked sick. "You don't happen to have any anti-venom hidden away in your cloak, do you?"

"No, teacher, I don't," the Princess answered.

There continued to be less and less floor to stand on, and a bigger and bigger pit to fall into.

Talibah continued to scan the small room for a solution. She also continued speaking in an attempt to distract the others from what was occurring. "When cobras feel threatened, they can flatten their necks to make themselves look bigger, as some of them are doing now. A cobra has no eyelids or external ears, and it sheds its skin up to six times a year as it grows. The new skin grows under the old, and it splits in a process called 'sloughing,' leaving behind a transparent version of the snake."

Blaine and Tracey had been very impressed by the beautiful Princess thus far, and they were glad she knew so much about cobras because they needed it for the SCIDAT application. Even so, they really wished she would stop talking right now and figure out a way to get them out of here. There now were only a few feet of floor left to stand on. Soon they would have their backs against the wall, literally. They quickly snapped pictures with their smartphones, just in case they didn't get another chance.

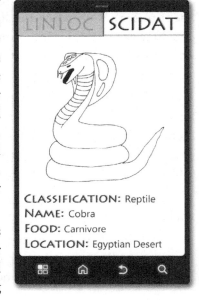

CLASSIFICATION: Reptile
NAME: Cobra
FOOD: Carnivore
LOCATION: Egyptian Desert

Nevertheless, the Princess continued. "Cobras bury their eggs in damp, warm places—kind of like this pit we have growing before us. The eggs hatch later on their own. These snakes eat small vertebrates that they kill with their venom and then swallow whole since their teeth cannot cut up flesh. Their jaws are elastic and able to stretch wide enough to swallow the meal."

The floor that was left now was only about two feet in width and still shrinking. Blaine and Tracey looked at each other. So this is how it was going to end for them. Everyone was now standing up, waiting for the inevitable. Jendayi still cried; Hanif still muttered. The Princess was still looking for a way to escape.

"Talibah, my beautiful princess," Abasi gushed. "My heart has been yours since the first time I saw you. And now, before we meet this terrible end together, I will confess my undying love for you!"

"That can wait until later, my protector," Talibah said flatly.

"What?" Abasi responded.

"I've found our way out! Everyone grab the ropes that were tied around your wrists before they fall into the pit!"

The six lengths of rope had all been carried by the moving floor toward the wall. Luckily they were all still there, though some of their ends were dangling like snakes over the pit. Everyone managed to grab their ropes.

"Now, everyone go stand beneath one of the supporting columns that line the walls, and look up," Princess Talibah commanded.

Though they were scared, and there was barely enough floor left to maneuver on, everyone managed to successfully follow Talibah's instructions.

"What are we looking for?" Blaine asked.

"There is just enough of a lip on top of each column for you to hook your ropes around," the Princess directed. "Grab each end of your rope with one hand, toss it up, and try to catch it over the top of your column. Hurry!" She had an edge of angst in her voice as she spoke. "We don't have much time left."

Holding their ropes like jump ropes, all six began tossing their ropes, trying to hook it over a column's top. The Princess hooked her rope on the first try. Blaine, Abasi, and Jendayi got theirs hooked on the second. But Tracey and Hanif were struggling. Hanif's shortness and roundness was contributing to his lack of success. Tracey was just nervous. They both kept tossing and tossing. Tracey looked down to see that the floor that was left was only about an inch longer than the length of her shoe. She also saw the eyes and forked tongues of about five hundred snakes that wanted to bite her. Tracey heard Hanif shout for joy as he was finally able to lasso the top of his column.

"C'mon, Tracey, you can do this," Tracey heard Blaine shout, trying to encourage her.

She heaved the rope up toward the lip of the column and she missed. The floor was now almost completely concealed into the wall. Tracey could only stand on her toes. Floor disappearing, palms sweating, cobras hissing, limbs shaking, Tracey Sassafras only had one more chance to hook her rope over the top of the column.

CHAPTER 5: ESCAPING THE TOMB

Leaping Lizards!

The rope seemed to float up in slow motion. Tracey had jumped as she had thrown it because there was no more floor to stand on. Her body was in mid-air. If the rope hooked over the lip at the top of the column, she would survive. If the rope missed, she would fall into the pit of cobras.

Her wide eyes watched as the rope floated up toward the lip in a reaching 'U' shape. Her hands were gripping each end of the rope as tightly as they could. Blaine and the four others watched, too, in great anticipation, hoping with all their hearts for a successful toss. Up, up the rope went toward the lip, and . . . it caught! Tracey had done it! She had hooked her rope over the top of the column.

Blaine, Abasi, Hanif, Jendayi, and the Princess all sighed in relief. Tracey smiled and sighed, glad to be alive, but they were not safe yet. All six were gripping their ropes, trying not to slip, while dangling over a snake pit. They couldn't hold on forever. The way the ropes were hooked over the column, they couldn't even let go with one hand or down they would fall. Blaine already felt his hands beginning to weaken, but for right now he was just glad his sister was alive.

"Maybe we can talk the counselors at Camp Zip-Fire into putting in a snake pit," he said, trying to be funny, but Tracey didn't laugh.

"What now, Princess?" shouted Hanif.

"Now I wanted to tell you that I forgot to mention that cobras live on every continent except Antarctica."

"Enough of your science! I am beginning to slip from my rope!"

"No need to worry, my dear teacher. When I spotted the lips at the top of each column, I also spotted what looks like a ventilation shaft. If we can all make it to the top of our columns, I believe we can all reach the ventilation shafts with relative ease."

"There is nothing easy about this!" Hanif shot back. "Just tell us the best way to climb, before we all fall into the mess below us!"

"Take the two ends of your rope and bring them together in front of you," Princess Talibah demonstrated as she spoke. Then, grab each rope with both hands and climb up the rope to the top of your column. Be sure to grip both ends of the rope or you will fall."

With grace and agility the Princess climbed her rope, reached the lip of her column, and pulled herself up into the ventilation shaft. She made it look easy enough. But would the still dangling five be able to follow her lead?

"Princess Talibah, my sweet," Abasi gushed, again full of

energy, "you move like a bumblebee dancing above a springtime flower, and I will now fly with you."

Abasi climbed up his rope to the top of the column and joined Talibah in just a few seconds, even managing to grab the torch off the wall as he went. Tracey, not wanting to be the last again, began climbing her rope and column, making sure to keep a tight grip as she went. She reached the ventilation shaft easily enough and was followed closely by Blaine and Jendayi. Though he complained the whole way, Hanif also completed the climb successfully.

Holding the torch, Abasi led the way crawling through the ventilation shaft, as there was only enough room to go one by one.

"If what Itja said is accurate about this tomb only having two rooms? "Talibah stated. "Then, this tunnel should lead straight to the sarcophagus room." The six found this to be true when they quickly came to the end of the ventilation shaft.

As Abasi held the torch out, they found themselves overlooking a room about the same size as the entry room had been. It looked identical to the first room, except that right in the center of the floor, it had a single empty sarcophagus lying on its back, open. They all carefully climbed down from the ventilation shaft to the ground and then plopped down to rest. The firelight of the torch was washing the room in a dim orange glow.

Hanif said to Talibah, "Being your teacher. I can tell you that this tomb or pyramid was built for royalty, maybe even one of your ancestors. It is designed to shoot the deceased's spirit up into the sky, but we will not be shooting anywhere, will we? We are trapped in this room with no way out. The doorway is blocked and that tunnel only leads to the poisonous cobras. Is there anything in your science books to help us now? I think not! If we could see the stars, we would see that they are not aligned for us now."

Blaine and Tracey were growing tired of Hanif's pessimism, but they both had the same passing thought, "Are our attitudes toward science like his?"

"Dear Hanif," Talibah responded to her teacher. "We will see the stars again. We will escape from this place and once again feel the desert winds on our faces. We must simply wait for a solution to present itself."

Hanif just crossed his arms and grunted.

Abasi said in his sing-songy voice again, "My heart is free, my Princess, because it is in love with you."

Jendayi laughed for the first time since they had been in the tomb. "Hopeless, absolutely hopeless, Abasi. Talibah, tell us what you have read in your biology books about our desert, now up above us."

"Oh, Jendayi, the desert is such a fascinating place," Talibah marveled. "The desert is not just sand dunes but it also has countless rocky outcroppings that are hosts to many animals and some amazing plants. The animals and plants that survive here have proven to have the adaptability needed for the hot days, cold nights, and little rainfall. Desert plants, for example, have extra-long roots to absorb any available water and cacti are especially good at storing and conserving water for long periods of time."

The Sassafras twins were amazed at Princess Talibah's vast knowledge and love of science. She did not have to study science; in fact, she wasn't supposed to, yet she loved it. Her passion for the subject was infectious.

Suddenly, Hanif let out a heart-stopping scream. "Spiders!"

Everyone looked to where he was pointing, and there, pouring out of a small crack in the wall, came a flood of something small, fast, and black. The six jumped up and moved away from the intruding mass.

"I don't think those are spiders," Princess Talibah informed. "Their bodies are segmented and they have eight legs. They are arachnids, just like spiders, but these are not spiders. These are scorpions!"

"We are waiting for that solution you spoke of to present itself, Princess!" Hanif yelled as he danced on his toes, trying to elude the small black stingers as the scorpions quickly began covering all open space.

The familiar helpless feeling overwhelmed them all. Abasi was waving the fiery torch at the arachnids, but it didn't seem to be helping. Blaine and Tracey had to shake scorpions off their shoes.

"Into the sarcophagus!" Talibah shouted. All six ran and jumped into the stone coffin. It was the only place left in the room that wasn't occupied by the stinging creatures.

Once inside, they peeked over the edge and watched the room swirl and move with prickly legs, claws, and stingers. Then a strange sound reached their ears. Was that a cracking sound? Almost like pottery breaking? The scorpions began to climb the outside walls of the sarcophagus. What would they do once the black arachnids climbed up, over, and into the sarcophagus?

The cracking noise got louder, and then all at once, the six were falling. It happened so fast no one really knew what was going on. Angry scorpions and pieces of rock were falling all around them, as the sarcophagus crashed through the floor and landed on an inclined surface. The coffin started inching down some kind of underground tunnel very slowly at first, but then it began picking up speed. The track got steeper and the rubble gave way to a smoother surface. They were now clear of the scorpions, but were they safe? Where was this ride taking them?

Abasi still held firmly to the torch. The flame now began blowing horizontally as they were zipping down the underground tunnel at an increasing rate of speed. Suddenly, the sarcophagus pitched hard to the right with a turn and almost threw them out. Musty wind whipped through their hair as they tore down deeper into the darkness. Right and left turns rolled them this way and that. Dips here, small jumps there, and even a section of track that felt like a corkscrew.

Just when they thought they couldn't go any further, the slide flattened out a bit, and with a huge splash, they hit water. The sudden stoppage of movement threw all six tumbling toward the front of the coffin. Were they stopped? Were they sinking? Surely a stone sarcophagus would sink straight to the bottom of any body of water.

But they weren't stopped. They weren't sinking. They were moving. They were . . . floating? How was that possible? There was a current to the water that was carrying them and their floating stone casket further down into the tunnel. The going was much slower and gentler now. Blaine and Tracey looked at each other with the same thought on their lips. "That was awesome," they said in unison.

"Better than any roller coaster ride I have ever ridden!" Blaine added.

"Awesome? Roller coaster? That was terrifying!" screeched Hanif. "We are now riding a boat of death straight to the center of the earth!"

"Teacher Hanif," the Princess said. "Where is your sense of adventure? Is it not amazing that some ingenious ancient Egyptian minds thought this whole experience up so many years ago? It is a wonder that the archaeologists never found this passageway."

"They must have never put the weight of six people in or on the sarcophagus," Jendayi added.

"Yes, Jendayi, you are right," continued the Princess. "There must have been a layer of clay that the sarcophagus was sitting on that was strong enough to hold the coffin itself, but not the coffin plus a lot of extra weight."

This was all very exciting to Tracey. "And the bottom of the sarcophagus must have been rounded, at least a little, allowing it to slide and now to float," she guessed.

"But to where are we floating? That is my question," interrupted the grumpy Hanif.

"We will ride the current and find out," was Princess Talibah's answer.

The underground river took the floating group calmly downstream. After about fifteen minutes, Abasi thought he saw something. "Do my eyes deceive me? Or is that sunlight I see in front of us?"

The other five craned their necks for a better view. "Yes, Abasi," Jendayi confirmed. "I think you are right! I think it is sunlight!"

As they approached the spot of interest, they found that Abasi had indeed been right. There in the middle of the stream up ahead was a beam of brilliant sunlight shooting down from somewhere up above.

"Maybe we have died!" cried Hanif. "We have found the portal for our souls to shoot to the sky."

"Or . . ." the Princess said as they floated close to the sunbeam ". . . it is a water well."

No one was surprised when the Princess was right and not Hanif. They were now out of their sarcophagus, attempting to climb up and out of the well. There was no rope or water retrieval bucket, just the stones that had been used to build the walls. They offered multiple hand holds and foot holds. The going was slow, but it was a lot easier than hanging over a pit of cobras on a precariously hooked rope. It was an extremely deep well, but the six managed to climb at a decent pace. They were anxious to get back out into the open air. As they neared the brim of the well, a noise met their ears. Was that a hissing noise?

If they had come all this way only to run into more cobras, it would be heart wrenching. The Sassafras twins didn't know if they could handle any more snakes. Abasi carefully climbed first to the top of the well and gingerly poked his head out to see what the source of the hissing noise was. He hung frozen for a moment, looking at something that the rest of them couldn't see. They all looked up at him from their places in the well, waiting for information. After a few long moments, he looked down at them and smiled. Abasi put his finger over his mouth, signaling for them to be quiet as they proceeded. He waved them up. As the five climbers reached the top of the well, the hissing sound got louder.

Peeking over the edge, they all saw what was making the hissing noise, and it wasn't what they had been expecting. There, in front of them, not ten yards from the well, was some kind of weird-looking cat trying to attack some kind of strange looking lizard. It was the lizard that was hissing, not the cat. The cat was about five times the size of the lizard, but the little reptile was warding off its attacker by hissing, baring its teeth, and swinging its spiked tail.

"A sand cat and a uromastyx," whispered the Princess excitedly.

"Uromastyx?" questioned Tracey.

"Also known as the spiny-tailed lizard," answered Talibah. "They are swift, sharp-clawed, agile reptiles that live in the hilly, rocky areas of the desert which gives them good access to shelter.

Hanif rolled his eyes as if to say, "Here we go again."

The Princess disregarded him and continued quietly, "Their scaly, watertight skin is smooth, unlike most reptiles who have rough scaly skin. This helps them burrow into their shelters better. They are cold-blooded, which means they

LINLOC   **SCIDAT**

CLASSIFICATION: Reptile
NAME: Spiny-tailed Lizard
FOOD: Omnivore
LOCATION: Egyptian Desert

don't make their own body heat. So, they have to spend time in the sun to keep warm. Their skin can even darken in the sunlight to help their bodies absorb even more heat."

The cat circled the lizard, still looking at it as a possible lunch. But the uromastyx continued to hold the bigger animal at bay with its scary looking tail and hissing.

"Some lizards will shed their tails when they are attacked, taking several months to grow them back," said the princess. "Not the spiny tailed lizard, as you can see it uses its tail very effectively for defense."

Blaine watched the duel and found himself rooting for the smaller animal. It really was a pretty cool little lizard. He and Tracey both took pictures.

"Most lizards prefer to eat meat, but not the spiny-tailed lizard," continued Talibah. "It eats mostly plants, and the occasional insect. They have adapted to the desert well and are able to get all the water they need from the vegetation they eat. One more amazing thing about them is the females can lay from five to forty eggs at one time."

"What about the sand cat?" Jendayi asked, "What do you know about it?" Talibah answered her friend, "Three things I know about it are—lizards are a main part of its diet, it is highly skilled at burrowing, and its paws are covered in fur so they don't burn on the hot sand."

Eventually, the spiny-tailed lizard's defensive strategy worked, as the sand cat gave up, and the two animals shot off in different directions. The six climbed out of the well and put their feet down on the sand. How nice it was to be out in the open again. There were sizable rocky hills surrounding the well, which was probably where the lizard and the sand cat had come from.

Ferreting out Foxes

"I think I know about where we are," Princess Talibah informed them. "If I am right, there should be a nomad camp nearby."

The group made their way on foot up the rocky hills, the sun beating down on them from the clear sky. Blaine and Tracey still had the blankets that they had gotten from the camel's back. They now wrapped themselves up as good as they could, to keep as much of the sun and heat off of them as possible. In less than an hour, they crested the hill. From this vantage point, there was already something visible out in the steaming desert in front of them. The Sassafras twins were hoping that it was the nomadic camp the Princess had spoken of and not some sort of mirage. After another hour of walking through the desert, they were grateful to find that the former was true. As they approached, Princess Talibah informed them that the camp they were about to enter was Tuareg.

"Kin to my people" she said. "We will be welcome here." The camp seemed to be abandoned. There was no one outside and the only sound they could hear was the sound of the hot wind rustling the flaps of the tents. They came around the corner of one tent and saw smoke rising from a small fire that had recently been put out. But still not a soul had been seen. No sound of animals bleating. No sound of children playing. No sound of men or women at their daily tasks, just all these tents flapping in the wind. It was rather eerie.

Suddenly, as they were passing the entrance of a tent, a long sword flashed out, glimmering in the sun, but stopping inches from Blaine's neck. He froze, as did the rest of the group. Slowly, the trembling hand holding the sword became visible, then an arm and shoulder, then the blue-robed man holding the sword stepped completely out of the tent, the tip of his blade still bobbing inches from Blaine's throat.

"Leave that boy alone!" Talibah ordered.

"I am Princess Talibah, daughter of Abubakar the Tuareg." Immediately, the man dropped the sword and fell to his knees. "Princess Talibah," he said. "It is you. Forgive me. I did not recognize you."

"Why are you so scared, my friend?" The Princess asked the man. "Why are you hiding in your tent?"

The nomad's eyes opened wide with fear as he stuttered out his answer. "Ke . . . ke . . . Kekewey."

Everyone shuttered at the word.

"Kekewey?" Talibah asked. "Itja and the Kekewey have been here?"

"Yes, Princess," the man answered, "They came not two hours ago. They kidnapped some of our children and stole all of our camels. They were very rough with us, and warned us not to follow them. They threatened to kill us. We were powerless against them. When we saw your group coming, we thought you might be members of the Kekewey returning. So, those of us that are left hid in this tent."

He stood and lifted the flap open so the six could see in. Sure enough, inside the tent there was about a dozen nomads huddled together all looking very afraid.

The Princess stepped inside the tent. She looked at her own people, who were scared, defeated, and terrorized by the Kekewey. At that moment a strong resolve filled her face. "We are going after them," she declared. Her statement was met with faces full of disbelief.

"Did you say go after them?" the man asked.

"Did you say go after them?" teacher Hanif repeated.

"Yes. We are going to go after them," the Princess confirmed with no doubt in her voice. "Itja and the senseless men of the Kekewey have been ravaging our desert long enough. They commit crimes but suffer no consequences. That will all stop today. I have had enough. My people have suffered enough. Today, we will rise and face the Kekewey. We will capture them, and they will terrorize our desert no longer!"

"But Princess," the man pleaded, trembling, "there are twice as many of them as there are of us. And they are all skilled swordsmen, as well as lifelong criminals."

"What is your name, nomad?" Talibah asked the man.

"My name is Mesneh," he responded.

"Mesneh," she said, looking straight into his eyes. "You are Tuareg. And you have inside of you what it takes to defeat these Kekewey scoundrels. You will leave your fear here in this camp, and you will march out into the desert with me and help me capture this scum called the Kekewey."

The man named Mesneh just looked at the Princess for a moment. He then looked over at the other nomads who were still bunched together. Some of them were nodding, as if to agree with Talibah's words. He looked back at the strong, determined desert Princess. He took a deep breath. "Let us march," he stated.

Tracey counted sixteen Tuareg, plus Blaine and her, making it a grand total of eighteen people who were going to go and try to capture the Kekewey. If Tracey remembered right, she had seen nearly forty bandits this morning when they'd woken up. The numbers weren't exactly encouraging. She and Blaine weren't too keen on the idea of trying to capture a band of crazy, black-robed, sword-wielding bad guys, but they wouldn't quit. They would see this adventure through.

When the Kekewey had raided them, Mesneh overheard two of the bandits talking about going that night to a place called Dark Canyon, where they would be hunting the fennec fox for its valuable fur. The eighteen now gathered in one of the tents to hatch a plan to go to Dark Canyon, retrieve their kidnapped children, capture Itja and his men, and hopefully get all their camels back.

After an hour and a half of deliberation, they had a plan that everyone could agree on, at least everyone except Hanif, who kept muttering things about fate, bad luck, and the stars. It was a risky and daring plan that borrowed many of its ideas from an ancient story Princess Talibah had read as a child. They gathered the needed supplies and headed out into the desert toward the chasm.

Mesneh, who knew exactly where Dark Canyon was, said they should arrive just after sunset, which meant it would take them several hours on foot to reach the canyon. As they walked, the Princess shared more of what she knew about the desert. Biology really was a passion of hers. Much to the Sassafrases' delight, she also spoke about the fennec fox.

"The fennec fox is the smallest of foxes. It only weighs one and a half to four pounds," she informed. " It has short legs, a bushy tail, long ears, and fur-covered paws, much like the sand cat. Its ears give it great hearing and also release heat which helps it to stay cool. Its sandy-colored fur not only helps keep it cool by reflecting sunlight, but it helps keep it warm at night, too. It is for this fur that the Kekewey are hunting in Dark Canyon now, right, Mesneh?"

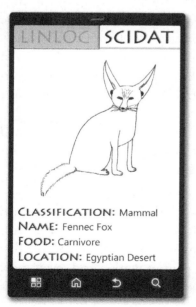

LINLOC **SCIDAT**

CLASSIFICATION: Mammal
NAME: Fennec Fox
FOOD: Carnivore
LOCATION: Egyptian Desert

"Yes, Princess," the nomad answered. "The fennec foxes can bring a good price in the markets, so many a man has been known to hunt for them. The foxes live in dens or burrows. The men will try to scare the foxes out of their burrows and then capture them in a snare. The craggy rocks of Dark Canyon have many such dens."

"Though the foxes are now being hunted, they are skilled hunters in their own right." Talibah continued. "They hunt at night and rest during the day. Their diet mainly includes rodents, insects, birds, and eggs. The fennec foxes live in pairs that each controls a certain territory. The males are called dogs, the females called vixens, and the young called cubs. The vixens give birth to live young and feed them with milk, making the fennec fox a mammal."

"Ah, the desert vixen," Abasi mused. "Someday, I hope to capture the heart of my very own desert vixen." Though everyone was nervous about the impending confrontation, this made them all laugh.

The sun began to set over the Sahara as the band approached Dark Canyon. It was not a large area, but the canyon was known for its deepness, as well as its holes full of foxes. Mesneh knew where the highest density of fox holes could be found, and he had assumed that was where Itja and his men would be hunting. His assumption turned out to be correct.

As the eighteen carefully and quietly crept up to the edge of the canyon, they could hear the shouts and evil laughter of the Kekewey. Dark Canyon was a strange place. If you stood twenty yards from its edge and looked at the horizon, you wouldn't even know the canyon was there, but as the group crawled up and looked over the edge down into the canyon, they found it to be at least one hundred feet deep and seventy-five feet wide. It was more like a big bowl than a long canyon. Down on the canyon floor, they could see the black-robed bandits of the Kekewey. The Sassafras twins wondered if the Man With No Eyebrows was still with them.

The forty or so Kekewey men were all confined to an area down in the canyon about the size of a football field. They had started some small campfires, so it looked like the bandits were planning to stay the night in the canyon, which was something that needed to happen for the nomads' plan to work. And, even more importantly, it looked like the nomads' presence at the ridge of the canyon wall had gone unnoticed.

There were dozens and dozens of holes all over the lower canyon walls and the canyon floor. By the looks of all the snares set up outside the entrances, they were the fox dens. The holes were too small for a full-grown man to climb into, but they were the perfect size for a fox.   Unfortunately, they were also the right size for a child. So, the Kekewey were using the kidnapped Tuareg children. They forced them to climb down into the foxholes to scare the fennec foxes out into the snares.

From their perches at the top lip of the canyon, the eighteen watched. Itja stood on a rock that elevated him a little above everyone else and directed the ruckus. The bandits had the children tethered to ropes. They were taunting the kids and laughing at them as they crawled in and out of the foxholes.

Mesneh stood and grabbed the sword at his side and took a step toward one of the steep trails that led down to the canyon floor.

Princess Talibah reached up and put a gentle hand on his forearm. "Not yet, Mesneh," she urged.

Mesneh looked at his Princess, then back down at the canyon. She was right. He took his hand off his sword and crouched back down, hiding himself from view.

"Our plan depends on complete darkness," Princess Talibah reminded. "We must wait for all daylight to disappear. Then, we will put our plan into action."

They were all in their places. The moonless night was completely black. The plan was about to become reality. Blaine and Tracey sat nervously on opposite sides of the canyon, gripping sticks in their hands and looking down into the darkness. All had grown still down below. Itja and the Kekewey had either fallen asleep or were sitting silently by the campfires resting from their hunting. The Sassafras twins had gotten all of their needed pictures and SCIDAT data, and they could now zip away at any time. But they would stay, as they had in Kenya, to make sure their friends were safe. This crazy zip line adventure was not only testing their knowledge of science, it was testing their courage. They were slowly realizing they could handle science and possibly even enjoy it, but could they handle the adventure?

Under the direction of Mesneh the nomad and Princess Talibah, the group of hopeful rescuers had set up flaming torches around the entire rim of the canyon. The torches were cleverly rigged with hanging clay pots that were now covering the flames, making them invisible from down below. The twins' job was to run by each torch and smash the clay pots with their sticks, exposing the flames. They would each have to run about one hundred yards. The Princess had chosen them for this job because she said they looked fast. They hoped they wouldn't let her down.

Hanif and Abasi were also in their positions. Their job was to push rolled and tied-up nomadic tents from different spots down into the canyon, causing small rock slides and hopefully a lot of noise. Princess Talibah, Jendayi, and the nomads were in various places around the canyon's rim so they could sweep down and rescue the children, and with luck, the camels, as well.

Mesneh was at the north end of Dark Canyon. He would signal the beginning of this rescue attack by smashing a clay pot-covered torch he held in his hand and shouting at the top of his lungs. They were all sitting in the cold darkness, anticipating his signal, and willing to join him in shouting. The hope was that Itja and the bandits of the Kekewey would be shocked into fear by the sudden attack, plunging their camp into chaos. It was eighteen versus forty. The percentages weren't good, but this plan was a risk worth taking.

Silence. Darkness. Eighteen speeding heartbeats.

Then, with the cry—not of a timid nomad, but of a brazen

warrior—Mesneh's voice pierced the night. The twins jumped into action. Blaine was on one side of the canyon, Tracey on the other. They shouted loudly, as they ran by each torch. They were swinging their sticks, pieces of clay flying everywhere. Tongues of fire danced and illuminated the night. Princess Talibah, Jendayi and the other nomads joined in the shouting but stayed hidden in the darkness for now. Rocks could be heard sliding down into the canyon, so evidently Hanif and Abasi had done their jobs. The arrival of sudden light and noise in a previously dark and silent place was rather shocking, even to Blaine and Tracey. They just hoped it would shock Itja and the Kekewey enough for their plan to succeed.

The Sassafras twins successfully smashed all the clay pots, and it soon became apparent that chaos was indeed breaking out down in Dark Canyon. The clanking of swords could be heard, along with shouts of fear and pain. The twins knew these sounds had to be coming from the Kekewey, because none of them had rushed down into the camp yet. Plus, the only one in their band who had a sword was Mesneh.

Mesneh and the nomads were the first to reach the rocky canyon floor, followed closely behind by Princess Talibah and Jendayi, and then the Sassafras twins, Hanif and Abasi. What they found there in the dim firelight on Dark Canyon's floor was unbelievable. Itja and the men of the Kekewey had attacked each other. The forty or so bandits all now lay injured on the ground, unable to do much more than moan in pain. All the kidnapped children were huddled together safely at one end of the camp, and the camels still stood tethered near the campfires, grunting softly as if nothing exciting had just happened.

"I can't believe it actually worked!" exclaimed Hanif in his scratchy voice.

Blaine and Tracey looked at each other, wonder all over their faces, surprised the plan had worked. Princess Talibah walked over to Mesneh and looked with pride into his eyes. She grabbed his right hand, the one in which he was holding his sword, and raised it above his head like a champion.

"Today, Mesneh, the nomad, the father, the Tuareg, has defeated his foes," the Princess declared. "He stands here now in Dark Canyon the victor. Itja, the Kekewey, now lay defeated at his feet!" The eighteen looked around and saw that Princess Talibah's words rang true. Everyone cheered.

CHAPTER 6: ON TO CANADA

Compelling Cows

Several hours later, the twins found themselves lying in a nomadic tent, happy and victorious, but also exhausted and tired. The Kekewey had been rounded up and brought back to the camp of Mesneh the nomad. Blaine and Tracey were perplexed to find that the Man With No Eyebrows was no longer among them. Had they just imagined seeing him? They just weren't sure. The next day, the bandits would be caravanned across the desert and then taken before Princess Talibah's father, Abubakar, to stand trial for the crimes they had committed. They would terrorize the Sahara no longer.

Tomorrow, Blaine and Tracey would zip off to their next destination. LINLOC had told them they would next be going to Quebec, Canada—latitude 46° 10' 18.3" and longitude -73° 6' 46.1". There they would study farmlands and gather information about cows, bees, chickens, and spiders. Their local expert's name was Jethro Mecklen. As they fell asleep, the twins thought about how excited they were about the next destination because they had never been to Canada before.

They were so tired that they slept well into the afternoon. Upon waking, they ate some of the bread Mesneh had given them and then began putting on their harnesses. "Are you ready to do this again?"

Blaine asked his sister. "Go to a whole new place and start a whole new adventure?"

"Of course I am," Tracey answered confidently. "Are you ready?" she shot back.

"Yep, I'm ready," Blaine responded. "Though I am kind of hoping this Canada leg will slow the pace down for us a bit. I've had plenty of near death experiences for one summer."

"Me, too," Tracey agreed. "Do you think we should call Uncle Cecil to see how everything is going?"

Blaine shook his head. "Naw. He has that big board he constantly tracks us with. Let's just keep going and get this crazy science experiment over with."

Blaine and Tracey hadn't talked about it specifically with each other yet, and probably wouldn't come right out and admit it, but both knew the other was enjoying this zip-line travel, all the crazy places it was taking them, and all the amazing things they were experiencing. Neither of them wanted to stop. There was too much adventure to be had.

"So, to Quebec, Canada we go?" asked Blaine.

"To Quebec, Canada we go!" exclaimed Tracey.

They calibrated their carabiners, hooked them to their cinched up harnesses, and let them snap shut. Whoosh! They were flying again—flying through places, hopping continents, while experiencing what no one had ever felt before. It was pure unadulterated exhilaration, zipping over invisible lines at the speed of light. Then, as soon as it had begun, it was over—white light slowly fading into color. They wondered where exactly they had landed this time. They stumbled on wobbly legs to the ground and waited for equilibrium to return. The first colors that came into clear view were the beautiful oranges, pinks, and purples of a morning sunrise.

"How did we arrive in the morning?" Blaine asked out

loud. "We left Egypt in the afternoon."

"Must be the time zone differences," shrugged Tracey.

They were sitting beside a lonely dirt road. The outlines of mountains could be seen in the distance, but there was nothing really around them except for barbed-wire fences, a few cows, and rolling hills covered with dew-kissed green grass. At the end of the road, they could see two figures walking slowly toward them. The twins weren't exactly sure what to do, so they took off their harnesses, put them in their backpacks, and just sat, waiting by the side of the road, to see who the two approaching individuals were. As the two figures got closer, the Sassafrases could see that they were both older teenage boys. They both had cloth bags attached to the ends of sticks, thrown over their shoulders.

"You're absolutely positive?" the first boy was saying. "You're sure they grow mostly corn and soybeans for export in this area? Because I could've sworn I heard this area had a lot of licorice farms."

The second boy just shook his head.

The first boy continued, "Yeah, for real. The farmlands' rich soil just pops that licorice right up out of the ground by the bushel." The boy stopped his sentence as he and the other boy spotted the twins on the side of the road.

"Well, hello there, you two," he said energetically. "Are you two looking for work, too? The farms out here are always looking for help in the summers. That's what me and my pal here are doing." He pointed to the other boy as he spoke. "We're both sixteen-strong-strapping-years-old. So how could any farmer not want to hire us for the summer? The two of you should come with us and see if we can't all get hired together."

Blaine and Tracey stood up and joined the two boys on the road.

"Oh, dagnabbit," the first boy declared. "Where are my manners? I didn't even introduce myself. I am Edbert Snarfuffel, and this here," he jabbed the other boy, "is Jet. What are the two of you's names?"

"We are the Sassafrases," Blaine offered. "Blaine and Tracey Sassafras. And we are twelve-strong-strapping-years-old."

Both of the teenage boys laughed a good-hearted laugh at Blaine's comment. The twins weren't sure when they were going to meet their local expert, Jethro Mecklen, but they had already met Edbert and Jet here, plus going to get hired as help on a farm with these guys wasn't a bad idea, they thought. Surely, they could gather a lot of their SCIDAT data that way. So the twins joined the older boys in walking down the dirt road.

It was a crisp, beautiful morning in Canada, which was a nice reprieve from the heat they had experienced in the grasslands and the desert. Edbert continued, "It's good to meet you two, it really is. Jet here just doesn't say much, but when he does, man does he knows his stuff," he told the Sassafrases. "Watch this, you two. Jet, tell us just one thing you know about them birds right there." Edbert pointed up in the sky toward the flock of geese flying overhead. "C'mon, man, don't be shy. Just tell us one thing you know."

"Just one thing?" Jet asked.

"One thing," Edbert responded.

"Those birds are geese," Jet informed. "They fly south each winter but return to the same area each spring."

"See, you two?" Edbert said. "Jet here is smart. He's a regular brainiac. It's just kind of hard to get the information out of him."

Jet just smiled. He obviously considered the talkative Edbert a friend, and he didn't seem to mind the pace the Snarfuffel boy kept. Jet was rather tall for being only sixteen. And strongly built, too, with dark hair and tan skin. Blaine was pretty sure Tracey already had the googly eyes over him. Edbert, however, was a short, wiry, pale-skinned boy with the lightest blonde hair the Sassafrases had ever seen. He had a perpetual smile on his face.

"I'm from down on the border," Edbert stated as they walked. "But Jet here is from all over. He's had a pretty tough life. The poor guy just can't seem to catch a break. His parents died when he was just a little kid, so he's had to fend for himself for years. He's a hard worker and you know he has the brains, but something always seems to happen that puts him back on the street. Isn't that right, Jet?"

Jet looked down as he walked. "Yep," he confirmed, "that's right. My parents were great people and I miss them. But I do fine on my own. You know they named me Jethro Mecklen ,Jr."

Blaine and Tracey shot glances each others' way. So this sixteen-year-old orphaned boy was their local expert?

"Yeah, Jethro Mecklen Jr.," Edbert said. "But he seems more like a Jet to me so I call him Jet—Jet Mecklen."

As they walked, the four approached a large gate on the right side of the dirt road. It had a big rustic archway over it that said, "Smitty Farms." Down next to the gate there was a wooden sign with a message written in spray paint that read:

"Hot diggety dog!" Edbert exclaimed. "Now we are in business."

The four walked through the open gate, across the cattle grill, and up the road toward the big farmhouse. But before they could reach the house, an old pick-up truck met them on the road. An old, gray-haired man stuck his head out of the driver's side window.

"Are you all here about the farmhand jobs?" he asked.

"Yes, sir," Edbert said enthusiastically, answering for the whole group.

"Then hop in the back of this truck, eh," the old man stated. "Farmer Smith is over in the tractor shed. This is his farm, and he does all the hiring, so I'll take you to see him."

Blaine, Tracey, Jet, and Edbert jumped in the back of the truck and then off they went. Smitty Farms was a huge plot of land that had several barns and silos of different ages and sizes spotted across it. The twins didn't know what most of the crops were, but they did recognize the fields of corn. The truck reached a large, metal-framed shed. As the old man parked, the hopeful hires jumped out of the truck's bed onto the ground. The man motioned for the four to follow him as he walked into the shed through a side door. Inside, the shed was big enough to hold three farm vehicles. There was a combine harvester, a front-end loader, and a tractor. They walked past the big impressive vehicles and into a small office at the other end of the shed. There were three people in the office— two rather hefty teenage boys sitting on an old worn couch by the window and an even heftier middle-aged man sitting in a swiveling chair at a desk covered in small tractor parts.

"'Morning, Farmer Smith," the old truck driver greeted the man in the swiveling chair. "I got a few kids with me this morning that are looking to get hired as farmhands."

"Farmhands, eh?" Farmer Smith said. "Is that old sign still out there on the gate? Well, I guess we could use some good help around here."

The big farmer looked at the twins and their new friends. "What are your names, kids?" he asked.

Edbert answered, "I'm Edbert Snarfufflel, this is Jet Mecklen, and they are Blaine and Tracey Sassafras."

"Well, Edbert, Jet, Blaine, and Tracey," Farmer Smith announced, "it's good to meet you. I see you've already met my farm foreman, Ed Lumbia." He motioned toward the old man. Then he pointed to the couch. "And these two bears over here are my sons, Tank and Billy."

The two Smith boys smiled but didn't seem too interested in the newcomers. Farmer Smith sat back in his chair and looked over the new kids standing in front of him. "So, the four of you think you have what it takes to be farmhands at Smitty Farms, eh?"

All four nodded yes, though Blaine and Tracey were both more hopeful in their nods than sure.

"We run a pretty big and versatile operation here at Smitty Farms," Farmer Smith declared. "We grow several crops and also have cows, pigs, horses, sheep, chickens, and turkeys. We already have dozens of farmhands working here, but can always use more. Do any of you even know anything about farms or farm work?" the farmer asked. "For instance, what do you know about cattle?"

Edbert looked nervously at Jet, who was looking down at the ground. The twins knew they didn't know that much about cows. They assumed Edbert didn't either. Their hopes of getting hired were hinging on Jet and his knowledge.

Jet looked up from the floor and answered Farmer Smith, "There are over two hundred and fifty breeds of cattle that are used all over the world for beef, milk, and leather. They are part of the Bovid family. They are even-toed, hoofed mammals that prefer to live in herds. Cows are herbivores and ruminants, which means they digest the grass they eat in stages within their four-chambered stomachs. They have stocky bodies, wide heads, and strong legs, and most have a sharp sense of smell and vision. When threatened, they can move with a fair amount of

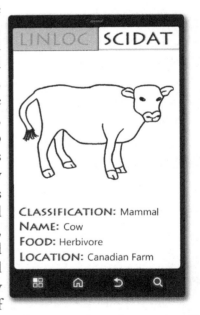

CLASSIFICATION: Mammal
NAME: Cow
FOOD: Herbivore
LOCATION: Canadian Farm

speed. In some parts of the world, cattle are used to plow and pull carts. Holstein dairy cows, the most typical breed used, can produce up to twenty-eight liters of milk per day. Only the female cows produce milk, which was originally meant to feed their babies. On most farms, dairy cows are milked twice a day by vacuum pumps that are attached to the udders. It only takes about four minutes to finish."

Farmer Smith's face gave away the fact that he was impressed. He looked at his foreman, Ed, and chuckled, then looked back at the four, now especially eying Jet. "Well, then, I will give you one day to prove yourselves," he said. "By the end of the day, we'll know if you can handle the farm life or not. We will give you several chores and see how you do. Ed here will be in charge of you, and my boys will join you, as well. Your first job will be to milk the cows that you seem to know so much about. The bad news is that our vacuum pumps are broken right now, so you'll have to milk the cows by hand."

Blaine and Tracey were speechless. Partly because they were going to be milking cows by hand, but they were mostly stunned that Jet, who was only four years older than they were, had just blasted out all that scientific information on cattle, right there on the spot. Tracey definitely had the googly eyes now.

Buzzing Bees!!

"Well, get going," Farmer Smith directed to the four. "The sun is already up, so that means we are wasting daylight.

"You, too, boys." He motioned for his sons to get off the couch and follow Ed Lumbia. The four new trial hires and the two Smith boys followed the old foreman through the shed back out to the pick-up truck. All six kids jumped in the back, and Ed Lumbia started off toward the milking barn. Edbert held his hand out to shake the Smith boys' hands as he introduced himself.

"Hello, Tank and Billy, I'm Edbert Snarfuffel, and this is—"

The one named Tank reached out and slapped Edbert's hand away, interrupting him. "You already introduced yourself in the office," the stocky boy reminded.

Billy laughed at his brother's antics. Tank continued, "We don't care who the four of you are."

"We don't care how cordial you are," he said to Edbert.

"We don't care how smart your friend here thinks he is," he said, pointing at Jet. Then, indicating the twins, he added, "And we don't care who these two toddlers you brought with you are. This is our farm and everything we say goes. Do you understand?"

Edbert still had a sort of smile on his face, but it was obvious he had been shocked by Tank's rudeness. Tank grumbled on in a haughty voice. "So, if me or Billy tells you to do something, you go and you do it. That's how it works here. Not even our dad or the old geezer driving this truck really know how it works. Me and Billy, we run this place. This is our farm. My dad introduced us as Tank and Billy, but we prefer Tank the Prank," he pointed toward himself. "And Billy the Silly," he said, as he gestured toward his brother.

Billy laughed again.

"I'm nearly eighteen years old," Tank stated, "and when I do turn eighteen, my dad is going to give me this farm. And when he does, I'll send him packing. I'll fire old Ed, and I'll make my sixteen-year-old brother, Billy the Silly, my farm foreman."

"What a bully!" Tracey thought. "You would think growing up on a farm would make a kid appreciative and a hard worker, but such wasn't the case for Tank and Billy." She hoped Blaine and she could get their SCIDAT data easily enough and zip off to the next place, but what about Edbert and Jet? She didn't know how badly Edbert needed this job, but it seemed like Jet sure did. And he seemed to know so much about farms. A place like this could be a perfect fit for him—if only it wasn't for these two rude brothers. Was this just a case of Jet Mecklen's bad luck continuing? Tracey wasn't sure, but she was rooting for the handsome sixteen-year-old Jet.

Ed finally pulled the old truck up next to an old barn. It was a big wooden structure, and the twins could already smell the cows inside. The old farm foreman got out of the cab.

Holding six metal buckets, he addressed the kids. "The cows usually get milked over in the newer barn, but as Farmer

Smith said, the pumps are broken over there. So, while the pumps are being repaired, we moved the cows to this barn, where the six of you will be milking them by hand. We need at least fifty liters of milk today, so the six of you better get to work, eh."

He handed each child a bucket and then climbed back into the front of the truck. As he began driving away, he hung his head out of the window and added, "I'll be back in a bit to pick you up, eh," as he drove off.

As soon as Ed was out of sight, Tank and Billy dropped their buckets on the ground at the feet of the four.

"Get to milking, kids," Tank ordered. Billy backed up the statement with a laugh. Then the two brothers ran off behind the barn.

Jet, Edbert, Blaine, and Tracey just looked at each other. Though they had just met Tank and Billy Smith, the two brothers had already left an impression. Getting fifty liters of milk would be much harder with four people than with six, but they were all relieved that the Smith brothers had left. Now, maybe they could focus on their task without the intimidation of the bullies.

Jet picked up all six buckets and walked into the barn with Edbert and the twins following him. Inside, there were dozens and dozens of stalls, each with a Holstein dairy cow in them. Blaine and Tracey hadn't seen this much black and white since the stampeding zebras. Jet sat down next to one of the cows and demonstrated how to best milk by hand.

"It should take about thirty minutes per cow," he guessed. Then he handed each of his three companions a bucket.

"Well, I don't see any brown cows," Edbert said, a full smile on his face again. "So I guess we won't be getting any chocolate milk today." What a delightful, yet not so bright, friend Edbert was turning out to be!

The Sassafrases picked a stall, took a picture of the cows

for SCIDAT, and then got right to work. It took a while to get the hang of it, but once they finally got the milk flowing from the cow's udder, it really wasn't too hard. At the rate the milk was filling their buckets now, the four should be able to reach fifty liters in no time. So they worked away, all determined to do a good job.

Meanwhile, Tank the Prank and Billy the Silly were also in the barn, but they were up to no good. Their presence had gone unnoticed by the four hard workers. Tank had spotted a beehive up in the rafters of the barn. His plan was to knock the beehive down with a slingshot and then run out of the barn with Billy and lock the door behind them, shutting the four newbies in with a swarm of bees and a heap of agitated cows. The two brothers thought this prank was going to be hilarious, but, as usual, they hadn't thought through all the possibilities.

Jet, Edbert, and the twins worked on, while Tank looked into the rafters. The beehive was almost directly above the stall where Edbert had chosen to milk his cow. The big stocky seventeen-year-old Smith boy crept as closely as he could without being noticed by Snarfuffel. He had already put several rocks in his pocket, and he now pulled one out, placed it in the slingshot, and aimed. Billy was stationed back near the barn door, ready to close it and snap the padlock shut when the time came.

Tank closed one eye, checked the accuracy of his aim, and then let the rock fly.

Zip! Crack, bang, thud.

He missed the hive but hit a beam, and then the barn wall, before the rock had landed harmlessly on the ground. Edbert stopped for a second, looked around to see the source of the sudden sound, but then put his head back down and continued working. The other three worked on as well.

Tank reached in his pocket and pulled out another rock. He took careful aim again, and let the rock go. This time, he made a direct hit. The rock smashed into the beehive and knocked it clean off of the wooden rafter. The hive fell from the ceiling and landed with a thud, just feet away from Edbert. Angry bees immediately started flooding out of the hive into the air. Edbert jumped up and away from the fallen hive. Tank smirked and then ran for the door. He was laughing and very proud of himself until he reached the door and saw that it was already closed. There stood Billy the Silly with a goofy grin on his face. An inside latch was keeping the door shut, complete with a locked padlock.

"Billy!" Tank yelled. "You buffoon! You were supposed to close the door from the outside—after we were out! Do you have the key to that padlock?" The look on Billy's face changed from goofy grin to fearful dumbfoundedness.

"You brain-dead pipsqueak!" Tank screamed. "Now we are locked in here with them and the bees!"

Edbert was running past the twins and Jet shouting, "BEES!" The other three jumped up from their cows full of alarm. The buzzing of the bees became louder and angrier as the insects began filling the barn. The cows began grunting and mooing in fear, kicking around, flustered, in their stalls. The four immediately began making their way toward the barn door, but they were met by Tank and Billy, running the other way. The four collided with the two big Smith boys, and all six fell to the ground.

"There are bees in the barn," Blaine shouted to Tank and Billy. "We have to get out!"

"We can't," Tank said. "My numbskull brother has locked us all in."

"Locked in?" Tracey asked. "Is there another way out?"

Tank just shook his head no. The cows were really going crazy now. They were barreling around and making a high volume uproar. The bees were filling almost all the open space in the barn as far as the six could see.

"We are all going to get stung into tomorrow," Edbert

shrieked.

Suddenly, Jet jumped up and ran over to one of the stalls and grabbed a tarp that had been hanging there. He swiftly returned and threw the tarp over the group and himself, effectively covering all six. Blaine and Tracey snapped a quick picture before pulling the tarp tight.

"Good thinking, Jet!" Edbert exclaimed.

The six hunkered there under the tarp, while crazy buzzing and mooing continued in the barn. They could hear and feel angry bees ricocheting off the tarp as they tore around in the air. They all held the edges of the tarp down as tightly as they could, so no bees could crawl in from underneath.

"Anything you know about bees that can help us out now, Jet?" Edbert asked.

Jet looked down, closed his eyes, and then began speaking. "Bees have black and yellow stripes and are related to wasps. Only worker bees have stinging tails, which they use to defend themselves but they usually die after they sting. Honeybees are ruled by a queen, who lays eggs in wax rooms called cells. The eggs grow and larvae hatch. The worker bees feed the larvae, and they grow, developing into a pupae. After time, adult bees emerge from the cells. Bees collect sweet juice from flowers called nectar and use it to make honey, which they store in cells to feed the

LINLOC **SCIDAT**

CLASSIFICATION: Insect
NAME: Bee
FOOD: Herbivore
LOCATION: Canadian Farm

young. They are highly socialized insects and have sophisticated methods of communication, using dance to point the way to nectar rich flowers. Bees and wasps are the world's pollinators, and if they were wiped out, it could devastate the world's crops."

The other five sat silent for a moment, stunned again that Jet, who was so unassuming, could just throw down information like that.

"Ok, Mr. Smartypants," Tank said. "How does any of that babble help us out now?"

"It doesn't," Jet responded. "But the axe will."

"What axe?" Tank asked.

"The axe I saw attached to the wall. If I can get to that axe, I can chop a hole in the side of the barn pretty quickly and that will be big enough for all of us to escape out of."

"But if you do that, won't you get stung?" Tracey asked, concerned.

"Probably," Jet agreed.

Then, in a flash, Jet Mecklen rolled out from under the safety of the tarp and rushed out into the angry swarm of bees.

CHAPTER 7: WORKING ON THE FARM

Chicken Coop Cleaning

Cecil sat at his desk down in the basement and perfected the finishing touches on a small rocket that he had been making. Not a real rocket, of course, but a rocket made with a one-liter plastic soda bottle, masking tape, party balloons, and drinking straws. It was one of the many science experiments he had tried as a kid and now, as a full-grown scientist, he often revisited them mainly because he thought it was fun, but also to keep himself sharp. The basic science found at children's science fairs everywhere was also the basic science found in cutting edge scientific labs everywhere. A scientist could never be too smart, too busy, or too important for the basics—or at least that is what Cecil thought. Even though he was excited about this rocket, he was on the edge of his seat about the zip-line-traveling adventure his niece and nephew were doing. After all of his careful planning, designing, making mistakes, re-planning, and re-designing the invisible lines were actually working. Blaine and Tracey were experiencing it even now. He had been watching with great joy and excitement as they had moved across the tracking screen. The green lights represented the twins as they zipped from America to Kenya to Egypt, and now to Quebec.

He had also watched on the data screen as all of the information and pictures the twins had been gathering had come in. So far, it appeared to all be completely correct. Those two really were doing a great job. He had heard the murmurings upon their arrival. They had made their dislike for science known, but since they had been on the zip lines, they had managed to enter all of the scientific data with no problems. The LINLOC and SCIDAT applications seemed to be working well and serving their purposes. The twins had only called him once, so he knew they were having fun, diving headlong into the adventure. He also knew that the science they were experiencing face-to-face wasn't going to be easily forgotten. It was going to attach itself to Blaine and Tracey's minds and hearts. Cecil was convinced that his niece and nephew were truly going to love science by the end of this summer, if not before.

Blaine and Tracey, along with Edbert, Tank, and Billy were still hunkered down under the tarp. The buzzing of the bees continued, as did the terrified grunting of the cows. So far, the kids had managed to keep the bees out of their little space there under the tarp. The five could hear the sound of an axe hitting wood, so they knew Jet had found the axe on the wall and was now chopping out an escape exit for them. The pace of the chopping was very fast and they were sure Jet was getting stung as he was trying to hurry and cut a hole big enough for all of them to get out of.

After less than a minute, the sound of the chopping stopped and Jet shouted out, "OK. It's time to go!"

The others threw off the tarp and rushed toward Jet's voice. Running through the bees was almost like running through a fog—a fog with stingers. The black and yellow insects seemed to be everywhere. The twins swung their arms in front of their faces as they ran, attempting to keep the bees away.

They could see light coming from a hole in the barn wall, and Jet was shouting, "This way, this way," over and over again.

They ran toward that light and his voice. The other three were close behind them. Suddenly, both twins were shoved to the ground by the big Smith brothers, who wanted to get out first.

"Get out of the way!" Tank shouted, as he and Billy ran past to the hole in the wall. Edbert reached Blaine and Tracey and helped them up, while the other three continued toward the exit. Tank and Billy spilled out of the hole first, then Tracey dove out into the sunlight, followed by Blaine. Edbert missed the opening and slammed right into the wall, falling to the ground. Jet, who was standing just outside the opening, reached in, grabbed Edbert and pulled him out. All six kids fell to their knees on the grass, breathing hard. Blaine lifted up his pant leg and rubbed his calf. Amazingly, he had only been stung a couple of times on his leg. He looked around and saw that his sister and Edbert didn't seem to be in too much pain, either. Tank and Billy were both plucking a couple stingers out of their hands, but they didn't seem to have been stung too many times. Then, Blaine saw Jet. His arms and neck were covered in bee stings. The expression on his face didn't show any pain, but they all knew he had to be hurting.

"Oh, man, Jet!" Edbert exclaimed. "You look like a pincushion! You are my hero, man! Thanks for getting us out of there. Thanks, man, thanks!"

"Yes, thank you, Jet," Tracey agreed.

"Thanks," Blaine also added.

Tank and Billy didn't say anything, but just sat in the grass looking at the barn. Just then, the sound of an approaching engine caught their ears. The six looked up to see that Ed Lumbia had already returned in his old pick-up. The old farm foreman parked the truck a few feet away from where the kids were sitting. He got out with a perplexed look on his face. He walked over to the six, looked at them, looked at the hole in the barn wall, and then back at the six.

"Who chopped a hole in the barn wall, eh?" he asked.

Immediately, Tank and Billy both pointed at Jet in blaming fashion.

"And where are the milk buckets, eh?" Ed asked. "Did you get fifty liters?"

"Not quite, sir," answered Jet.

The farm foreman just nodded and gingerly rubbed the white whiskers on his face. "Well, I'm not sure what happened here," he said. "But it's time to move on to your next chore: cleaning out the chicken coops."

In the back of the truck, on the way over to the chicken coops, the Sassafras twins were stewing. They were frustrated that Jet wasn't getting any of the credit he deserved. Tank and Billy sat across the truck bed from them now, arrogant smirks on their faces. Billy laughed his goofy laugh almost non-stop. It looked like they were going to get off scot-free for their beehive shenanigans. Plus, because of a prank, Jet and Edbert probably wouldn't be hired as farmhands.

"How is that right?" the Sassafrases thought to themselves. As they considered what had just occurred, they took the time to send the pictures of the bees and cows that they had taken. They also made sure to text in the SCIDAT data on both species.

Once they arrived at the chicken coops, foreman Ed gave them their instructions for their second chore of the day.

"There are about a thousand hens in these here coops," he informed. "First, let all these free range chickens out, eh. Then I need the six of you to pull out every nesting box, gather any eggs that you find, empty the soiled straw into the compost pile, and then refill each box with fresh straw. It's that simple, eh?"

It did seem simple, thought Blaine and Tracey, that was, until a gust of wind blew their way, and they breathed in the smell of the coops. It had to be one of the worst odors they had ever smelled.

"I'm going to leave you kids alone here again to do your chore. Try not to chop any holes in the wall of the coops, eh?" Ed said, as he walked over and got back in his truck. "I'll be back around lunch time," he added, as he drove off.

The twins were sad to see him go. They wished the foreman would stick around and see what good workers Jet and Edbert were, but that was not to be.

"So, what do you know about chickens, smart boy?" Tank asked, looking at Jet.

Jet remained silent.

"I said, what do you know about chickens?" Tank stepped up and stood in Jet's face. "You better answer me, Smarty," the bully pushed.

Jet just looked at the ground. With force, Tank pushed out his hands and shoved Jet to the ground.

"Leave him alone!" Tracey yelled out.

"I just want him to answer my question," Tank responded flippantly.

Blaine was pretty sure that even though Jet was a little smaller than Tank, Jet could have really walloped Tank in a fight if he wanted to, but Jet restrained himself. He remained calm and let himself be bullied. "Why," Blaine wondered.

"Just tell 'em, Jet," Edbert urged. "Just tell 'em what you know."

Jet stood up, looked at Tank and Billy, and then the scientific information started flowing. "Birds live all over the world and are the only animals that have feathers and wings, but not all can fly. All birds lay eggs, and most build nests. They have light skeletons, strong chest muscles, a tough beak, and keen vision, due to their eyes on either side of their head."

Jet paused and then continued. "Chickens are birds that can't fly. They are kept as farm animals all over the world. They are related to wild birds that were tamed by humans over four thousand years ago. Chickens can fly short distances but prefer to run or walk. In the coop, chickens develop a strict sense of seniority, commonly referred to as a 'pecking order.' In other words, the older and stronger chickens get to eat first because they will peck the younger and weaker members of the group to keep them in line. Male chickens, called roosters, have large

CLASSIFICATION: Bird
NAME: Chicken
FOOD: Omnivore
LOCATION: Canadian Farm

crests on their heads, a ruff of long feathers around their necks, and a long spike at the back of their legs called a spur. They're the ones that crow at daybreak. Female chickens, called hens, are generally smaller and less colorful than roosters. They lay eggs, which they sit on until the eggs hatch, getting up for less than an hour each day. They even turn the eggs periodically to ensure even incubation."

Jet took a deep breath and then continued, sharing even

more, "The baby chicks will hatch after twenty-one days. They have soft feathers that are different colors and patterns than their adult feathers will have. Chicks will shed their baby feathers in a process called 'molting' as they mature." Then, as soon as he had begun, Jet was finished.

"Wow, where did Jet learn all this stuff," the Sassafrases wondered to themselves.

"Well, since you know so much about chickens," Tank retorted, "me and Billy will just take a little rest while the four of you clean out the coops." With that, the hefty Smith boys walked over to a big pile of straw and sat down, with proud looks on their faces.

"Those boys are something else, aren't they?" Edbert said, probably angry yet still smiling. "No matter," he continued, "we can get more done without their help, anyways."

Jet, Blaine, and Tracey nodded in agreement, as they all got right to work. As foreman Lumbia had instructed them, they first let all of the chickens out of their coops. Blaine and Tracey got some photos as the birds walked out the door and down small ramps. Though the smell at first seemed unbearable, they slowly got used to it, as they walked down the rows of coops. They started pulling out the nesting boxes, placing eggs they found in provided crates, dumping the contents of the boxes in the compost pile, refilling the boxes with fresh straw, and then replacing them where they went. Ed was right—it was rather simple, yet it was still good solid farm work.

About an hour in, Tracey looked over and saw that Tank and Billy were passed out in the straw, both sound asleep. For justice's sake, she hoped that Lumbia would return soon to catch them napping. The four were really breezing through this chore because Jet was setting the pace. Just when they had reached the very last of the coops, Ed pulled up in the truck. Somehow, just seconds before Ed arrived, almost as if they had a sixth sense, Tank and Billy had awakened from their slumber and began acting like they had been working the whole time.

The old foreman walked over to the coops. "This chore went much better than the first one, eh?" he stated, folding his arms in front of him as he spoke. "I was expecting you to be only about half finished, but you're almost all done, eh? That's pretty impressive!"

The four were feeling pretty encouraged until Tank spoke up. "Yes sir, Ed," he agreed. "You put Tank and Billy on the job, and you get results, eh."

Ed just chuckled and turned back towards the truck. "Finish up those last few nesting boxes and then come get your lunch. It's waiting in the back of the truck for you."

Tracey stomped back over and pulled one of the last nesting boxes from the coop. She wanted to throw the smelly soiled contents from the box right into Tank's or Billy's face. How could they really take the credit for the success of this job when all they had done was sleep? They were so rude and cocky that she almost couldn't stand it. When the last boxes were done, the six walked over and looked to see what was for lunch.

"Mmm! Canned sardines!" Edbert exclaimed, enthusiastically.

Canned sardines? Neither of the Sassafrases had ever tried canned sardines, and even though they were both hungry, they really didn't want to try them now, either.

"Eat them sardines up, eh?" Ed said. "They will make you farm strong."

Blaine and Tracey watched as Jet and Edbert, as well as Tank and Billy, peeled open the tin cans, pulled out the small stinky slimy fish complete with heads, and threw them down their throats. The twins looked at each other as they both opened their cans, reached in, and pulled out the goo-covered sardines by the tail. Blaine looked at Tracey. "To adventure," he said.

"And to farm strong!" Tracey exclaimed. Then, both twins put the whole fish in their mouths, chewed a couple of times, and swallowed.

"Mmmm, canned sardines," Blaine said, not quite as enthusiastically as Edbert.

Old Ed had the kids load up in the back of the truck once again and he began driving them across the farm to what he said was going to be their last chore of the day. It would probably take them most of the afternoon, he had also said, then they would go back and meet with Farmer Smith to see if they were hired or not. After Tank and Billy had sabotaged the first chore and then taken credit for the second chore, the four weren't feeling very hopeful.

Swinging with Spiders

The mountains in the distance were a little more visible now in the full sunlight. The twins could see that the rolling hills of Smitty farms, covered with fields of different crops and animals, really were impressive. It was a beautiful day here in Quebec, if only these arrogant Smith brothers weren't here to ruin it. Ed finally stopped the pick-up in front of an old, moss-covered, rickety barn. The six kids jumped out of the truck as the foreman reached behind the bench-seat in the cab and grabbed some sledgehammers.

"Your last chore of the day here is to tear down this old barn." Ed handed a sledge to each child. "Be careful not to knock it down on top of yourselves and watch out for all of the bugs, eh. We haven't used this barn in years because it's infested with critters; mostly ants and spiders. When you're done tearing it down, be sure to put the rotten wood in one pile and any re-usable wood in another pile, eh. Any of you kids know anything about those types of critters?"

Everyone looked at Jet. All could tell he didn't enjoy divulging the information he knew, because he didn't like being the center of attention. He just wanted to put his head down and work, but by now everyone knew that he was a whiz. What the others didn't know is that he truly cherished science. His favorite was the study of animals and if he read about it, he never forgot it. He didn't like talking about it, so he spoke quickly, not to brag, but just to get the talking over with so he could get to work.

"Insects all have six legs, a pair of antennae, and a body made up of three parts. Those three parts are the head, the thorax, and the abdomen. The legs are always attached to the thorax. Many insects have two wings. They are invertebrates, which is to say, they are animals with no backbone. There are more insects on earth than any other creature. They live in every region and every habitat of the world. Ants are insects that live in colonies with a social structure. Each ant has a job to do. Some guard the nest, some gather food, and some keep the nest clean."

Jet got caught up in what he was sharing and kept going despite the fact that everyone was staring at him. "Spiders are also found all over the world, but they are part of the arachnid's class of invertebrates. They have heads and rounded abdomens with eight legs. Most have poor eyesight, but they do have four pairs of simple eyes, which work together to judge distances. Spiders mainly prey on insects, using their webs to catch the prey. The webs are made of silk, which is very strong and stretches. The prey gets stuck in one and then the spider comes along and stuns

LINLOC **SCIDAT**

CLASSIFICATION: Invertebrate
NAME: Spider
FOOD: Carnivore
LOCATION: Canadian Farm

it with venom from its fangs and then wraps it in silk to eat it later. The silk thread is made from proteins produced in the spider's abdomen, which are then drawn out of the body by spinnerets on the underside of the abdomen. Spiders spin a new web every night and eat the old web to recycle the proteins."

Ed Lumbia nodded his head, scratched his white whiskers, and then folded his arms. "Hmmm . . ." was all he managed to say.

The Sassafrases were sure the foreman was impressed with Jet's knowledge. How could he not, eh? Even so, he was a hard man to read.

"Well, I'll be back in a bit to pick you up, eh?" the old man said. He walked to his truck, got in and then was gone.

All six grabbed their sledgehammers and walked into the barn. Foreman Lumbia had definitely not been joking. There were insects crawling all over the place. There was a big red ant pile right in the center of the floor, overflowing with ants, and there were spider webs with spiders in almost every possible place. The twins snapped a couple of pictures as they looked around. They started to think about how best to start the demolition of this sad structure. They were not surprised, however, when the Smith brothers first came up with a plan how best not to work.

"OK, you four lightweights," Tank announced, "Me and Billy have a game that we want to play with you." Billy laughed in anticipation.

"It's a game we call 'Dare or Scare,'" Tank explained. "The way it works is: we tell you about a task that is either daring or scary. Then, we make you do it. Doesn't that sound fun?" snarled the oldest Smith boy.

The Sassafrases stiffened up in fear, wondering what kind of dares and scares these cruel farm boys were going to think up.

"The four feats of fear are as follows," continued Tank. "First, one of you must walk across that beam way up there, from one end to the other, without falling off." He pointed to a beam about twenty feet up in the air that ran horizontally.

Neither Blaine nor Tracey was scared of heights, but the

problem was that the beam Tank had pointed to looked completely rotten. The first dare would result in a sure fall.

Tank kept going. "The second dare is that one of you has to stand in that red ant pile right there for one minute without moving."

Tank pointed to the ant pile in the center of the floor. It looked like a small volcano and there were so many ants crawling out of it. The twins both shivered in fear.

"The third dare is that one of you has to hang onto that same high beam with your hands for one minute without falling. Only you will also have a sledgehammer tied to each of your legs."

"Where did they think up this sinister stuff?" Blaine thought.

"And the last feat of fear in our game of 'Dare or Scare' is that one of you has to eat a big ball of wadded up cobwebs." Tank and Billy both joined in laughter, evidently very proud of their backward creativity.

Blaine, Tracey, Jet, and Edbert all shook their heads and closed their eyes, not looking forward at all to playing this game.

"And just because we were raised on a farm doesn't mean we're jerks," Tank informed. "We know how to be gentlemen. Isn't that right, Billy the Silly?" Billy just nodded his head and laughed.

"So, I will be the gentleman right now and let the lady in the group go first," Tank said, pointing at Tracey.

Tracey's face went white with fear. Which dare was Tank the prank going to choose for her?

"Your name is Tracey, right?" Tank asked.

Tracey just nodded yes, still shocked.

"Tracey. I choose for you dare number . . . four. You are going to eat some cobwebs."

Tracey's face wrinkled into a disgusted frown. Blaine, Jet, and Edbert were about to protest when Tank instructed Billy to climb up into the rafters and gather up some cobwebs. Billy put the cobwebs in his left hand, the ball of silk growing bigger and bigger as Billy climbed higher, gathering more web.

"Look Billy," Tank shouted up from the ground. "Out there to your right, there's a whole mess of cobwebs there. Grab one more handful, and then we will have enough."

Billy reached out for his last handful, but as he did, he stepped on a section of rotted wood with a crack. Billy came tumbling down right toward his older brother and with a thud and a smash. The Silly crashed right on top of the Prank, followed by a heap of rotten wood and a big ball of cobwebs.

The four looked at each other for a moment, surprised at what had just happened. Then, they slowly walked over to the pile of Smith boys and rubble. Tank and Billy both moaned in pain. Tank was holding his arm, and Billy was holding his leg.

"They both have broken limbs," Jet stated, matter-of-factly. "Let's make them some splints."

"Help them?" Blaine and Tracey thought. "After all that these boys had done to them? Who was this Jet Mecklen? All life had ever done to him was mistreat him, and yet he was kind, wise, and hard-working, with no trace of bitterness."

Edbert and the twins helped Jet as he used pieces of wood and pieces of rope he found in the barn to make splints. The four carefully moved the two heavy boys outside and then, with no break at all, they jumped right into the business of tearing the old barn down. They carefully worked their way from the top down and from the outside in, methodically taking the dilapidated barn down to its core. They used their sledgehammers more like surgical tools than wild-swinging clubs. The four took aim at precise spots which were all directed by the sixteen-year-old Jet. The bugs scattered every which way, as the four quickly took down the structure. In much less time than the twins thought, they had torn down the entire barn and had sorted it into two piles of wood, a rotten pile and a good pile, just like Ed Lumbia had told them to. Now the four just sat on the good woodpile, waiting for the foreman to return, while the Smith boys were both lying on their backs in the grass, moaning.

Blaine and Tracey opened the SCIDAT apps on their phones and entered all the information they could on chickens and spiders. The first two local experts they had met had been very helpful in giving them all the information they had needed, and Jet Mecklen had been no different. He was a wellspring of information. The twins now had everything they needed to zip away to the next location, but they wanted to wait to see if Jet and Edbert got hired as farmhands.

Before long, Ed and his truck came chugging over a hill toward the six. He parked the old vehicle and stepped out. He looked at the two piles of wood and nodded his head. He glanced over at Tank and Billy lying in the grass with their splints and rubbed his whiskers. Then, he looked at the four trial hires and folded his arms.

"Your chores are done for the day now, eh?" the foreman said. "It's time to go back to the tractor shed and see if Farmer Smith wants to hire you or not. Hop in the back of the truck, and help out those two big boys, eh."

With the help of the four they had been bullying all day, the Smiths got up in the bed of the truck. Then all six, plus Old Ed in the front, made their way across Smitty Farms, back to the tractor shed where Farmer Smith was waiting on them. The Sassafras twins knew they were about to leave for their next destination, but they were still nervous for Jet and Edbert. The two teenage boys had become good friends over the course of the day, and the twins really hoped they would get hired. There was really no way to tell what Farmer Smith was going to say. After the first chore, they hadn't met their milk quota. After the second chore, Tank and Billy had taken all the credit. And after the third chore, Farmer Smith's sons both had broken limbs. Would they get blamed for that, too? They didn't know. What Blaine and Tracey did know is that Jet and Edbert deserved the jobs. Once they reached the shed, they all got out and followed Ed, the farm foreman, through the shed and into the office.

There sat big Farmer Smith in his swiveling chair. Tank and Billy immediately took seats on the couch by the window and groped at their wounds, still moaning. Ed Lumbia stood by the door. Jet, Edbert, Blaine, and Tracey stood in a line in front of Farmer Smith, waiting to see what he was going to say.

"Well, my farm foreman tells me your day was pretty eventful, eh?" the big farmer started. "I gave the four of you one day to prove yourselves. To show me that you had what it takes to be farmhands at Smitty Farms. It looks like you didn't get enough milk. You busted a hole in the side of my milking barn. You let Tank and Billy do most of the work. Then, you had a hand in breaking their limbs." Farmer Smith paused. The four gulped.

"But I know that is not exactly what happened," the farmer declared. He looked at Ed, then back at the four with a smile on his face.

"What the four of you don't know is that the six of you kids were all being watched very closely all day." Now Tank and Billy gulped. "Ed wasn't just giving you instructions today. He was watching you," the farmer said.

"But he drove off and left us at every stop," Tank yelped.

"That is what it looked like." Farmer Smith agreed. "But he didn't go very far. He always stopped a safe distance away and watched you through a pair of these," he said, as Ed stepped up and laid a pair of binoculars on the desk. Tank was stunned.

"I know about the beehive in the milking barn," Farmer

Smith informed. "And the fact that before the hive crashed down, the four of you were milking those cows by hand as fast as I've ever seen, eh. I know my boys napped at the chicken coop while you four did all the work, again, as fast as I've ever seen. I know you four tore that old barn down quickly and efficiently, even after being taunted by a game of 'Dare or Scare,' where my boys fell and broke their limbs."

Jet, Edbert, and the twins almost couldn't believe it. Their integrity was paying off. Their faces now all were smiling, as were Farmer Smith's and Ed Lumbia's. On the other hand, Tank and Billy were not smiling.

The big farmer continued, "I have never seen better workers than the four of you. The farmhand jobs are yours if you want them and not just for the summer, but full-time for as long as you want them." Farmer Smith got up out of his chair and shook their hands, as did Old Ed Lumbia.

"Proud of you," the old foreman told each of the kids.

Farmer Smith then stepped over to the couch and looked over his boys. "As for the two of you," he declared, "today confirmed my suspicions as to what you need. After your limbs heal up, I am shipping both of you off to military school, where you will hopefully learn the traits these four have shown today."

Tank and Billy both moaned even louder.

"Tell me this, though," Farmer Smith asked, looking back at Jet, Edbert, Blaine, and Tracey. "Some guy stopped by my office this morning right after you four did and told me I shouldn't hire you. He said you would sabotage my farm. That's one of the reasons we were watching you so closely, but all you did all day was prove that man wrong. Do any of you have any idea who that guy was?"

The four shook their heads no.

"Strangest thing," Farmer Smith added. "The man didn't have any eyebrows."

CHAPTER 8: ZIPPING THROUGH THE AMAZON RAINFOREST

Sloth Sighting

Light whipped across Blaine and Tracey's faces as they zipped over their invisible lines at sonic speed. They had eaten dinner at the farm with the new and proud farmhands, Jet Mecklen and Edbert Snarfuffel. They had informed their new friends that they wouldn't be staying to work at Smitty farms; rather, they would be moving on. They had said their goodbyes, Tracey doing so with the googly eyes. Then they had slipped away to open the LINLOC app. And they were now headed to explore the rainforest in Peru— longitude -4° 36' 43.26", latitude -73° 44' 34.73". They would be gathering data on three-toed sloths, toucans, poison dart frogs, and blue morpho butterflies. Their local expert's name was Alvaro Manihuari.

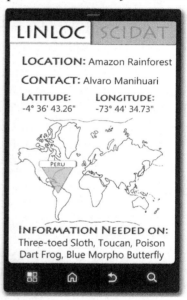

As they zipped along, though, they were thinking about the Man With No Eyebrows. They had thought that seeing him in Egypt had just been a product of their over-active imaginations, but now he had shown up in Canada as well. Who was he? Why did he seem to be following them around? And, more precisely, how was he following them around? They had sat in front of him in Nicholas Mzuri's jeep in Kenya, but they never actually talked with him. They never heard him speak a word. Even so, it was beginning to feel as if he was trying to ruin them at every turn. It seemed like he was trying to stop them from experiencing science face-to-face, but why? Why would anyone want to stop a couple of kids from zipping around the globe to learn science? The twins didn't understand, but they did know that not being able to identify who this elusive man was nagging at them.

Their travel came to a jerking stop, their carabiners automatically unclipped from the invisible lines, and they wobbled down, enveloped in slowly fading white light. In this new location they had not landed on stable ground. They felt their bodies gently rocking, even though they were off the zip lines. Had they landed on some sort of animal here in Peru, as they had done in Egypt?

Colors slowly appeared, and the Sassafras twins found themselves sitting in some kind of boat. They were rocking on the gentle waves of a rather wide river, but their boat was not just any boat. This looked to be some sort of a speedboat, with a dozen or so seats and a decent sized engine on the back.

Before the twins could figure out exactly why they were on

a boat, they saw a small crowd of people walking down the wooden dock toward them. The man in the front was addressing the group.

"To get to the guesthouse, we will be taking the highways of the Amazon Basin—the waterways. Everyone just pile in and find an empty seat. Be careful to mind the gap from the dock to the boat."

The group of people all clambered down into the boat and surrounded Blaine and Tracey, who were still wearing their harnesses. They hadn't yet managed to take them off and get them into their backpacks, but no one seemed to notice or mind.

"Hey, Alvaro, what kind of boat is this, man?" a young man with dredlocks in his hair and a big trekking backpack asked.

"It's an old but very capable speedboat," said the man who had been addressing the group. "And it is fast enough to get us to the guesthouse by nightfall. However, if something interesting catches your eye, let me know, and we will stop to take a gander."

The man named Alvaro seemed to be a tour guide. He stepped to the back of the boat and started the engine. He eased the boat out away from the dock and then propelled it up the river. Blaine and Tracey were sure this Alvaro was their local expert, Alvaro Manihuari. He was a tall and strongly built Latino man, who already given them the impression that he loved his job.

The twins looked over the others in the boat. The dredded backpacker had two friends, both with big trekking backpacks—one male and one female. The female had a couple of braids coming down amid her long brunette hair and at least ten earrings in each ear. The male also had earrings, but only one in each ear, and his hair was a sort of a short mohawk. The three backpacking friends were smiling and laughing with each other, seeming to be having a great time.

There were also three more people that looked like they were a family. A dad with his son and daughter, who looked to be about the same age as Blaine and Tracey, all three of which had dark skin and dark hair with Latino features. They also seemed to be enjoying themselves, but were definitely not backpackers or trekkers.

Then, the last and most interesting person on the boat was a man wearing only a cloth around his waist. He stood at the front of the boat and looked out into the river ahead. He must be a native of the area, the Sassafrases both thought.

Alvaro Manihuari energetically shouted above the sound of the engine as they coursed over the water. "Ah, the Amazon! There is no place like it! It is home to the lushest rainforests on the planet. There are rainforests in the tropical regions of Africa and Asia, as well, but in my humble opinion, they pale in comparison to our rainforests here in South America. The Amazon Rainforest is twice the size of the country of India, and more than half of the world's species live here. Most of the animals, flowers, and fruits are found up in the canopy, because the forest floor doesn't receive much sunlight. Rainforests are hot and humid places that get a lot of rain. However, our rainforests are shrinking fast. Much of that is out of our control, but we must do what we can to protect them. I'm excited for all of you to stay with us at Out on a Limb guesthouse so you can see firsthand the beauty of our part of the Amazon rainforests here in Peru and what we are doing to protect them."

"This is so sweet, man!" the twins heard one of the backpackers say.

It was sweet, they thought. Here they were, cruising through the Amazon on a speedboat headed to some place called the Out on a Limb guesthouse, as their adventure continued.

From the front of the boat, the native man waved his hand to get Alvaro's attention and then pointed toward the side of the river, up in the trees. All the passengers looked to where he was pointing, but neither of the Sassafras twins could see anything except trees and vegetation. Alvaro slowed the boat down and guided it closer to the bank. Then, he shut the engine off, making it quiet. The native man said something to Alvaro in a language the twins didn't understand, while pointing up into the trees. Alvaro Manihuari looked around, squinting a bit. Then his eyes lit up.

"Ah, there he is," he declared, as if he'd just discovered a treasure. "If everyone will look approximately thirty feet up in the tree that my friend, Arrio, is pointing to, you will see a three-toed sloth."

Everyone looked, casting their vision in the direction of Arrio's pointing finger. One by one, they let out "oohs" and "aahs" as they saw the strange looking animal hanging up in the tree.

"These sloths spend their lives hanging upside-down in the tree tops by their claws," Alvaro shared quietly. "They have three toes in the back and three toes in the front, and each toe ends in a long, curved claw. They hardly move at all, spending up to eighteen hours a day sleeping. They only climb down to the forest floor once every one to two weeks to go to the bathroom."

"That is crazy, dude," the packer with the mohawk said, laughing.

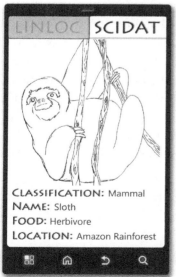

LINLOC SCIDAT

CLASSIFICATION: Mammal
NAME: Sloth
FOOD: Herbivore
LOCATION: Amazon Rainforest

Alvaro laughed, too, and then continued. "They are awake mostly at night, when they feed on leaves and fruit. This kind of diet makes them herbivores. The three-toed sloth is a mammal that gives birth to only one baby at a time. The mother will carry around the little one on her stomach for about five weeks. The baby sloth will cling to its mother's fur for the ride and, as you can see, they are about the size of small dogs and covered in hair. The sloths here in the Amazon have green algae that grows on their coats as a form of camouflage, and they also have hundreds of beetles living in their fur that feed on the algae."

Almost all of the passengers scrunched up their noses at the thought of that. "Gross," the girl about Tracey's size said.

Alvaro laughed again, and then kept going. "Unlike other mammals, sloths don't internally regulate their body temperature. Amazingly, though, they can rotate their heads through a two hundred seventy degree angle, so that they can see all around them while hanging upside down."

The twins snapped a picture with their phones, while everyone gazed up at the strange, camouflaged animal hanging up in the tree for a few more moments. Then, Alvaro started the boat back up and they continued up the river. The sun was now setting here in Peru, and the twins figured they would soon be reaching the guesthouse. They were right, and they found themselves disembarking the speedboat about half an hour later.

The group followed Alvaro Manihuari and his friend, Arrio, from the water's edge up a trail into the forest. The sun wasn't completely gone yet, but it was as dark as midnight under the thick cover of so many trees. Alvaro stopped at a certain tree, opened an electrical box that was mounted there, and flipped a switch. In an instant, the group found themselves on a beautiful, electrically illuminated path that led deeper into the rainforest. The lights were different colors in different places. There was green here, blue there, a little yellow highlighting this tree, and some red spotlighting near another area of the forest floor. It really was cool looking. The lit path led them to a hand-carved wooden sign that read—*Out on a Limb Guesthouse.*

Even so, Blaine and Tracey didn't see any kind of building anywhere, just a lot of trees and forest foliage. Was this some kind of joke?

"Dude, where's the guesthouse?" asked the trekker with the

mohawk.

Alvaro smiled and pointed up. The group looked up as Arrio, this time, flipped a hidden switch. There, way up in the canopy at the tops of the trees, was a huge tree house, beautifully illuminated with different colored lights.

"That is sick!" exclaimed the trekker girl. Only she said the word "sick" in a way that meant it was cool. The three trekkers were obviously impressed with the guesthouse, as was the father and his two children. The three of them were smiling and laughing as well. Blaine and Tracey glanced at each other, grinned, and looked back up at the tree house. This adventure continued to blow them away. Camp Zip-Fire, which used to be their favorite place in the whole world, was beginning to lose some luster compared to some of the places they were experiencing now.

Looking up, they could see that Out on a Limb guesthouse wasn't just a single tree house, but it was a network of different tree houses, connected by different kinds of bridges and walkways. It looked like a small village up in the canopy of the rainforest. Blaine and Tracey even thought they saw some . . . zip lines. Alvaro Manihuari now reached out and opened a door that was built right in the trunk of a huge round tree. The door swung open, revealing a hidden staircase inside. He smiled and requested, "Follow me!"

Everyone followed him up the long interior spiral staircase. Arrio closed the door behind them and brought up the rear. They snaked up and around before they finally came out onto a good-sized deck with a pretty wide rope bridge. One of the buildings had a sign over the doorway that said "Office." The other had a sign that said "Café."

"This is the Bienvenidos deck." Alvaro informed. "The stairwell you just climbed is the main entrance to Out on a Limb. Here on this deck, as you can see, we have the office and the café. In the office, we have maps, adventure gear, and other things that will help you better explore and enjoy the rainforest. The café is open in the morning and at night. It serves mainly coffee, juices, and baked goods, but it also has a small grocery shelf where you can buy food and drinks to pack out."

"This place is totally rad, man!" the trekker with the dreads said excitedly.

Blaine and Tracey totally agreed.

Manihuari continued, "The bridge that you see here leaving the Bienvenidos Deck leads to all our guest rooms," he shared. "However, take care, because beyond this bridge you must have on a harness and safety clip at all times, unless you are in your rooms. This bridge is the widest bridge, but past here the bridges get smaller, more precarious, and more fun."

"Sweet, dude!" Mohawk exclaimed, followed up with a, "Sick!" by trekker girl.

"There are more than bridges," Alvaro informed. "Some of the guest rooms can only be reached by swing, climbing net, or zip line." The twins felt like they had died and gone to heaven.

Alvaro opened up the office. He and Arrio began getting harnesses and safety clips for all their guests. While the father and two kids were being helped, the twins got to meet the three backpackers.

"Dude, I see you guys already have your harnesses," said the one with the mohawk to the twins, who were still wearing the harnesses Uncle Cecil had given them.

Blaine and Tracey both nodded in affirmation.

"I'm Skip," he offered. "And these are my pals, Gannon and Gretchen."

"What's up, man? Good to meet you guys," said Gannon.

"Sick place, huh?" asked Gretchen.

"Yeah, totally sick," agreed Blaine. Tracey looked at Blaine a little funny for being won over by trekker lingo so quickly.

"What are your names? You guys ever been to Peru before, man?" asked Gannon.

"We're Blaine and Tracey and, nope, it's our first time," Blaine answered. "What about you guys?"

"Our first time too," Gretchen replied. "But what a sick place."

The father and his two children walked over, all in their harnesses.

"They're ready for whomever is next," he informed.

"I guess that means us man," declared Gannon, jumping up and heading with his friends over to the office. The twins saw that the father and his son and daughter each had red straps, about a foot long with carabiners on each end, attached to their harnesses.

"Are those the safety clips?" Tracey asked. "Yes, you attach one end to your harness and the other end to the safety lines. Every bridge has a safety line," stated the boy. "So do the swings, climbing nets, and zip lines."

"This is such a fun place!" The girl smiled. "By the way, my name is Violetta Perez. This is my brother Vancho and my dad Ernesto." Her dad and brother nodded friendly hellos. "My dad is here on business, but he promised Vancho and I that he would bring us along this time."

"Nice to meet you," said Tracey. "I'm Tracey Sassafras and this is my brother Blaine."

"Yes, very nice to meet you," Violetta replied. "My dad has to go meet with some of his employees tomorrow. So maybe we can hang out a little bit."

"That would be great!" Tracey exclaimed, waving to the family as they walked out over the main bridge to go and find their guest room.

"I wonder what their dad does that he would have business

all the way out here in the rainforest?" said Blaine out loud, but Tracey just shrugged.

Skip, Gannon, and Gretchen came bounding by with their harnesses and safety clips on. "See you dudes tomorrow!" shouted Skip, as the three ran out across the bridge in search of their rooms. Alvaro walked over and handed safety clips to the twins, along with a room key.

"The two of you will be in the Hummingbird room," he stated. "Just follow the signs." The room key even had a carabiner on it, so you can clip it to your harness and not accidently drop it to the forest floor.

"Stay clipped in to the safety lines at all times beyond this bridge. You must detach and re-attach at each crossing," Alvaro reminded. "Have fun! The café opens at seven o'clock, and I will be leading a canopy tour tomorrow at eight o'clock, if you guys wanna join."

The twins thanked him and then headed out from the bienvenidos deck over the main bridge. On the other side of the bridge, there was a fork in the walkway, and a big sign with names of rooms on arrows, pointing different directions. All the rooms were named after different species of animals and plants that lived here in the Amazon rainforest. According to the number of arrows, it looked like there were around a dozen rooms in all. One arrow even pointed straight up, showing that the "Howler Monkey" guest room was a fun climb up a rope ladder in the very top of a tree. Tracey spotted the word "Hummingbird" on one of the arrows that was pointing to the right. The twins went that direction.

They walked across a bridge that was made up of separate swinging boards attached on each end by ropes to tree branches up higher. It was a fun challenge to maneuver across this crossing. Next, they tightrope-walked across a very narrow bridge only about as wide as their shoes. Both twins were careful to have their safety clips clipped into the safety lines at each obstacle. After crossing the narrow bridge, they saw another hummingbird sign pointing off to the right again. They could now see their guest room, built all by itself on an isolated tree a pretty good distance away. The only way to get to it was by rope swing.

"This is sick!" Blaine exclaimed.

"Yeah, totally sick!" Tracey said, laughing.

Blaine took a hold of the rope first, got safely clipped in, and then jumped out on the swing. He shouted with joy as he swung from the platform to his guest room, the dark rainforest floor far below him. He reached the other side with no problem. Then, Tracey used the guide-line to pull the swinging rope back to herself. With a big swing, and a shout of joy of her own, Tracey joined her brother. She took out the key and unlocked the door to their room. It was a small rustic and cozy room with a bathroom, a desk, a lamp, two chairs, and a set of bunk beds.

"We are sleeping in a tree-house tonight!" Blaine declared enthusiastically, but ten minutes later that enthusiasm had already given way to exhaustion as both the children were asleep and snoring. They had had a long, hard day of farm work and they both needed some rest.

Tree-Hopping Toucans

A buzzing noise reached Tracey's ears, but it was fine, because she was under the tarp, right? The bees couldn't get under here to sting her. It had been the handsome Jet's idea, this tarp, Tracey's eyes blinked open. Wait . . . she wasn't under a tarp. She was on the bottom bunk of a bunk bed.

"Where am I?" she thought sitting up, still hearing the buzzing noise.

Tracey now remembered. They weren't in Quebec anymore; they were in Peru in the rainforest in a tree house, but what was that buzzing noise? She climbed out of bed and walked over to the window, "Ahh haa!" Tracey said out loud. "It's not buzzing, it's humming!"

Just outside the window of the treehouse guest room was a hummingbird feeder and four hummingbirds were hovering there at the feeder. They were beating their wings so fast you could hardly see them. It was then that Tracey remembered that they were in the hummingbird room here at Out on a Limb guesthouse.

Seeing the hummingbirds made Tracey happy. What a great way to wake up in the morning. As if sensing her thoughts, one of the pretty little hummingbirds flew into the room and hovered right over Tracey's shoulder. The little pink and green feathered creature seemed to be smiling at her and singing into her ear.

She walked over to the desk and picked up a card that was lying there that had a picture of a green-crowned brilliant hummingbird on it. It said:

Green-crowned
Brilliant
Hummingbird
(Heliodoxa jacula)

There are over 300 different hummingbirds found in the Amazon rainforest. Their wings beat so fast that they hum, giving the birds their names. They use their long beaks to get nectar out of flowers. They eat nectar because it is full of sugar and gives them the energy they need to hover and hum.

"Simply magical," Tracey thought as she picked up her smartphone to look at the time. "Seven-fifteen a.m.," the clock read. "Oh no! I don't want to miss breakfast," Tracey said loudly. She picked up a shoe and tossed it at Blaine, who was still snoozing on the top bunk.

"Three-toed sloth!" Blaine shouted out as he woke up with a start. The little hummingbird zipped out of the window as Tracey said to her brother, "Get up sleepyhead, or we are going to miss breakfast."

By seven-thirty, the Sassafras twins were already sitting at the café and had ordered their breakfast. Arrio walked over, set down what they had ordered on their table, and walked away.

"Never thought I would get served cappuccino and a blueberry muffin by a man in a loin cloth," Blaine mused. Chocolate milk just about shot out of Tracey's nose as she burst out in laughter at her brother's statement.

"Wouldn't have it any other way," Blaine said, very proud of his joke. Then, he leaned forward to sip foam off the top of his cup, like he was living the high life. "What a cool guy, though, Arrio." He continued. "I wonder what his story is."

Tracey heard a familiar buzzing noise again. She turned and there was what looked like the same pink and green hummingbird hovering over her shoulder. The bird seemed like it was smiling at her. She was just about to tell Blaine when all three Perez's walked over the main bridge and approached the café. The pretty little creature fluttered away as Violetta asked, "Can we sit with you guys this morning?"

"Of course," Tracey answered. Blaine got up and added three chairs to their table. Vancho and Violetta sat down while their father went to order for the three of them.

"We are in the Crocodile room," offered Vancho. "What room are you in?"

"The Hummingbird room," replied Blaine. "It was nice and we slept well."

"I'm so excited about today," said Violetta, smiling. "Are the two of you going to join the canopy tour with Mr. Manihuari?"

"We are," the twins said together.

THE SASSAFRAS SCIENCE ADVENTURES

"It may just be the four of us and him," Vancho guessed. "We heard Skip, Gannon, and Gretchen say they were going to sleep in a little this morning and then go do a hike on their own."

"Our Dad is heading out on business right after breakfast," Violetta added.

"What does your father do?" Tracey asked.

"I am the president of ProLog," Mr. Perez answered, walking back to the table after ordering. He sat down with the children and continued, "It's a logging company based out of Iquitos, down the river. I make occasional trips out here to make sure that all the operations are running smoothly and that they are following all of the logging laws. This time, I brought Vancho and Violetta with me so that I could show them this guesthouse. It's fantastic, isn't it?"

"Yes, sir, it is," Blaine replied. "It's the coolest guesthouse we've been too!" Tracey nodded her head in agreement.

Mr. Perez continued. "This guesthouse is built on private land, and it is surrounded by protected national forest. Not too far from here, ProLog has a clear-cutting range, where we cut down all the trees in a given area and then re-plant the area to use for lumber once again. Today, I'm going to meet with Ortiz, my head manager, to make sure that we are only clear-cutting on our given land and not encroaching on the national forest. We must protect the rainforest, you know."

Arrio delivered the Perezs' breakfast and all enjoyed the delicious food while overlooking the rainforest. After they were done, Ernesto Perez said goodbye to his children and left to take care of his business. Alvaro Manihuari showed up at eight o'clock on the dot to take the kids on the canopy tour.

Blaine, Tracey, Vancho, and Violetta all followed the energetic Manihuari across all the bridges, climbing nets, swings, ladders, and walkways of Out on a Limb to the other end of the treetop guesthouse where there was a zip line platform. "Welcome to the starting line of our canopy tour," Alvaro greeted, grabbing a hold of one of the zip lines.

"I just love zip lines!" Violetta said, smiling. Turning to the twins, she asked, "Do you guys like them?"

Blaine and Tracey looked at each other with a knowing smile, and answered their friend in unison, "We love them!"

Alvaro gave the four children instructions, "Ok, kids, as usual keep your safety clips hooked securely into the safety lines at all times. This platform is the first in a series of stations that this network of zip lines will be taking us today. Some of the lines are faster and some are slower, but all will put you into good positions to see up into the rainforest canopy. I'm hoping that we will get some great wildlife sightings today, as well. There are two parallel lines that run right next to each other throughout the course, so we'll go two at a time and I will zip down last behind you. We will stop at each platform and talk about any animals you see. Are you ready?" The four nodded yes. "Who's going to go first?"

"I think that we should let the ladies go first together," Blaine suggested.

Tracey and Violetta agreed, stepped up, and hooked into the zip lines. The girls looked back and waved to their brothers. Then, with happy shouts, they jumped off the platform, letting the lines whisk them away.

As the wind whipped through Tracey's hair, she smiled. This zip line wasn't as quick and exhilarating as the invisible one, but it was still a lot of fun. The green of the canopy danced in front of her, as she zipped down side by side with Violetta, both keeping their eyes open for animals.

Back up on the platform, Blaine was waiting patiently along with Vancho and Alvaro, when he heard a buzzing noise in his ear. It startled him at first, but then he looked and saw it was a hummingbird. "Wow, this little guy is not scared at all," Blaine thought. "He's brave enough to just hover here, right over my shoulder."

"Ok, guys, it's your turn," Blaine heard Tracey shout from the other platform. The little pink and green hummingbird flew away. The boys got their safety gear hooked up correctly and then got their zip on. Zipping through the rainforest canopy over forty feet above the ground wasn't so bad after all. The boys reached the next platform and were quickly followed by Alvaro.

When Manihuari reached the four, his eyes were wide with joy. "Did any of you see the toucan?" he asked excitedly. The children shook their heads and he pointed, "Look there in the branches of that Kapok tree. Surely you at least heard them? They are some of the noisiest birds in the forest with their croaks, barks, and hoots."

Now that Alvaro mentioned it, the kids could definitely hear the birds. All their eyes followed their ears until they spotted a group of toucans high up in the trees.

"They are not excellent flyers," Manihuari continued. "So they often walk or hop along the branches, using their tails for balance. They are covered all over in black feathers, except for a few white feathers around their eyes. They also have big bright orange and yellow beaks, which are hollow inside, making their very lightweight."

CLASSIFICATION: Bird
NAME: Toucan
FOOD: Omnivore
LOCATION: Amazon Rainforest

"What do they use those big beaks for?" asked Vancho.

"Their beaks actually help them regulate their body temperature, help them to attract mates, and eat," Alvaro answered.

"Are they herbivores, omnivores, or carnivores?" asked Blaine.

Tracey gave her brother a surprised look. Was he actually paying attention and learning all of this science stuff? Maybe he was. Maybe she was, too.

"They are omnivores. They occasionally pluck small birds or reptiles from cavities within the tree with their long beaks, but they really love fruit, especially passion fruit. The toucans will toss the orange pod up with their beaks and back into their mouths, where they gobble it up."

"Such beautiful birds," Violetta sighed, and then asked, "What else do you know about them, Mr. Manihuari?"

"Their feet have two toes pointing forward and two toes pointing backward. It's a bit like the three-toed sloth we saw yesterday. The toe arrangement makes it easier for them to grip the trees," Alvaro answered, with a smile that told how much he loved the rainforest. "Also, the toucans often nest in the hollows of decaying trees, where they lay clutches of two to five eggs at a time. Both the males and females incubate the eggs until they have hatched."

The group of five stood on the high platform and watched the toucans hop along the branches as they barked out their calls. The Sassafras twins each snapped a picture with their smartphones and then got ready to move onto the next platform. Tracey and Violetta went first again, followed by their brothers, and finally Alvaro Manihuari.

Upon reaching the next platform, they all had clearly seen another animal, because sitting right there on the platform were two black-haired monkeys.

"Those are howler monkeys," Alvaro informed, as he unclipped from the zip line. "Like most monkeys, they are great climbers. They also use their tails as extra hands when swinging through the trees. Howler monkeys live in groups headed by one large male and they get their name from the calls they make to communicate with each other."

As if on cue, the howler monkeys started going crazy up in the trees. The two monkeys joined a swarm of more up in the trees. The monkeys howled as loud as fire engines and swung from branch to branch. They were creating quite a stir through the treetops.

Then, another sound reached the group's ears, a—buzzing sound. Blaine and Tracey both thought briefly that a hummingbird had returned to their shoulders, but then realized that this was not the buzzing of a hummingbird. It was a deeper and more sinister noise, like the clanking of metal teeth chewing through wood.

The children looked at Alvaro and saw that his usual smile was completely gone and had been replaced by a look of horror on his face. Then, the children saw a group of men in blue uniforms with white hard hats approaching them, with chainsaws.

Chapter 9: Trouble in the Jungle

Fearsome Frogs

There were at least a dozen of them that had just climbed out of the back of a truck. On each one, ProLog could be seen clearly written on their hard hats and blue cover-all uniforms.

"Those are men from your dad's logging company," Blaine said to the Perezes. "Why are they walking through the forest toward us, with chainsaws?"

Neither Vancho nor Violetta answered, but their faces said they were just as stunned as Blaine was.

"They are not allowed to cut in this area," Alvaro said, getting angry. "I own the plot of land that we are on, and beyond this is protected national forest. What are they doing here?"

The men kept approaching, using their chainsaws to whack away underbrush as they walked. Vancho straightened up with a start.

"I recognize the man in the front, Violetta," he said to his sister. "That is Ortiz, Father's head manager."

"But I thought that is who Father was going to meet with today," Violetta responded. "Why is Ortiz here? And where is Father?"

The rapid clanking and buzzing of the chainsaws got louder as the blue-uniformed men got closer and closer, approaching the very tree that the five were standing in. Then, as if they had rehearsed, all the men turned off their chainsaws at the exact same time, leaving an eerie silence floating through the forest air. Even the loud howler monkeys and beautiful toucans sat silently in the tops of the trees, waiting to see what would happen next. Alvaro Manihuari shouted down, knowing that now that the chainsaws were switched off, he would be clearly heard by the men.

"You cannot cut any trees down here! This is private and protected land. Take your chainsaws and leave!"

The man who Vancho and Violetta had called Ortiz slowly looked up at the zip line platform where the five were standing. A scratchy-looking beard, acne scars, and a determined frown were on his face.

"We are taking it all down," he said.

"All?" Alvaro questioned. "What do you mean, 'all'?"

"I mean all!" Ortiz shouted up. "We are taking it all down. We are taking down every tree that you see. Every tree in the national forest, every tree on private and public land, and every single solitary tree that holds up your silly Out on a Limb guesthouse and canopy tour will be gone. We are taking it all down!"

Alvaro was so angry he didn't even know what to say.

"Our father would not allow this!" Vancho shouted down. "Where is he? Weren't you supposed to be meeting with him today?"

"Your father? Oh, you mean Prez Perez?" Ortiz said sarcastically, but still with a frown on his face. "We have him tied up in the clear-cut office trailer. He wanted us to follow all the laws, but I decided, as head manager, to take the company in a different direction. I never did like your father anyway. He doesn't have thick enough skin. He doesn't have the courage it takes to break out of the binds of the law and make ProLog the dominating force that it can be. Now we are going to take it all down and we are going to start with the tree that the five of you are standing in right now!" And with that, Ortiz and the rest of the men started cutting at the base of the tree.

"Quick, children!" Alvaro quipped, urgently. "Get down the line to the next platform! Girls first!"

Wasting no time, Tracey and Violetta got hooked in and jumped out on the parallel lines and sped through the air to the next platform. They reached it quickly enough, but as the group was finding out it doesn't take chainsaws very long to cut through trees. By the time Blaine and Vancho were hooked in securely to the zip line, the men down below were already almost all the way through the trunk of the tree. As he and Vancho zipped down toward the next platform, Blaine looked back to see the blue-uniformed men step back from the trunk of the tree, as they had sliced all the way through it. Immediately, the towering tree began to fall.

"Hold on!" Blaine yelled to Vancho.

Suddenly, from behind them, the lines snapped free from the plummeting tree, and the boys felt themselves not zipping but falling. Both Blaine and Vancho grabbed ahold of the zip-line-turned-rope-swing tightly with their hands and began swinging down toward the forest floor at an alarming rate of speed. Tracey and Violetta watched with angst from the next platform as their brothers hung on for their lives. They were high enough on the lines that they did not crash into the ground, but they were not high enough to miss a big plot of ferns. Bracing for impact, both boys lost their grip as they smashed face first into the ferns. They tumbled down, head over heels onto the forest floor, leaves, dirt, and twigs exploding around them. Finally, they came to a somersaulting stop at the base of a small tree.

Alvaro Manihuari was nowhere to be seen, as the girls looked down from their perch. Their brothers had just landed hard on the forest floor, and most intimidating of all, the group of chainsaw-crazy men were now walking toward the tree that they were in. What should they do? Should they just keep zipping down the lines of the canopy tour in an attempt to escape? What about their brothers and Alvaro? They couldn't just leave them, could they? They looked down in fear as white hard hats, blue coveralls and chainsaws got closer.

But wait! What was happening? The chainsaw-carrying wayward men of ProLog were starting to fall down one by one, and the ones who weren't falling down were running away. Something was either frightening them, or attacking them, or maybe both. Ortiz looked up at the girls and shouted angrily as his men retreated towards their truck.

"You may have won this battle with your fancy little darts, but we will win the war. We will be back with more men and bigger machinery. Mark my words—we are taking it all down!"

Quickly and surely every blue-uniformed man, including Ortiz, ran or was carried back to the truck. They quickly sped away, leaving only one fallen tree behind. Tracey and Violetta just stood silent in the tree, still not exactly sure what just happened. They heard some grunting coming up from the forest floor and looked down to see Blaine and Vancho both standing up on wobbly legs.

"Are you guys okay?" Tracey shouted down.

"We'll be fine," Blaine responded. "We are both a little

scraped up, but no broken bones. We'll be fine."

Then, in the direction of the one fallen tree, the girls heard some crunching branches. They looked over and saw Alvaro hobbling toward them. He had a little bit of blood over one of his eyes and a spot on his shin, but he looked okay.

"Mr. Manihuari!" Violetta yelled, relieved. "You are all right! We didn't know where you were."

"I swung down, just like the boys, only in the opposite direction," he said.

The girls unclipped themselves from the safety lines and then used metal rungs that were secured to the tree to climb down and converge at the tree's trunk and meet with Alvaro, Blaine, and Vancho.

"What has happened to Ortiz?" Vancho said. "He has turned into a madman. He never acted like that before."

Violetta agreed and was worried. "I hope he hasn't hurt our father. Oh, poor Father!"

"He seems very determined not to let anything stand in his way," Blaine said. "He really does want to take it all down—the guesthouse, the forest, everything."

"But we can't let that happen," Alvaro Manihuari said, with resolve in his voice.

"We must find a way to stop him!" Tracey agreed, but she was still confused as to what had just happened. "What was Ortiz talking about when he said we won the battle with our fancy little darts? Why did he and his men run away?"

"I have a good idea about what happened," Alvaro said, stepping over to a nearby tree. "They ran in fear of one of the Amazon's smallest and deadliest creatures: the poison dart frogs." He reached up and used two fingers to pull a small wooden dart out of the tree's trunk, being very careful not to touch the tip. "This dart is coated with a poisonous liquid that oozes from the skin of the miniature amphibian. Did you know that the word 'amphibian' comes from the Greek words '*amphi*' and '*bios*', meaning: double life," Alvaro asked, as he showed the kids the dart.

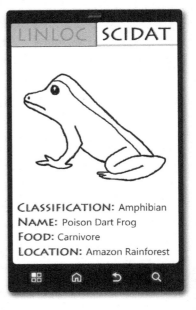

The knowledgeable local expert then knelt down and began gently rummaging through a tuft of green plants. "All amphibians, like frogs, toads, salamanders, newts, and caecilians, undergo metamorphosis, meaning they change from tadpoles or larva into adults that are able to live on land or in the water. The female poison dart frog lays her eggs either on the forest floor under leaf litter or in pools of water that collect in the bromeliad plants like these. The male frog then comes along and fertilizes the eggs, and after a week or so, the tadpoles hatch. They begin life breathing through gills and swimming in the water, but the little guys grow lungs and legs by the time they reach adulthood."

As he slowly pulled back one last leaf, the four saw just what Alvaro was talking about. There, on a thick leaf in a small pool of water, were several tadpoles and a few full-grown—though still only two inches long poison—dart frogs. They were all brightly colored, with hues of orange, yellow, red, green, and blue. The twins both carefully took a picture, grateful that Uncle Cecil just wanted pictures and not actual specimens.

Alvaro continued. "After three months, their gills shrink as their lungs develop and their tails get shorter as they gradually grow their legs. Finally, the tiny frogs leave the water for land where they grow to adulthood and the cycle begins again. These frogs eat fruit flies, ants, termites, small crickets, and tiny beetles, which they catch with their long sticky tongues and swallow whole. They have strong back legs that they use for jumping, and they are also very good swimmers. They are cold-blooded, meaning their body temperature varies with their surroundings." Alvaro paused.

"But where did the actual dart come from?" Blaine asked, pointing to the poisonous, tiny projectile that Manihuari still held in one of his hands.

Alvaro stood up and took a wide cautious gander through the forest. "Natives in this area have used the poison of this frog for generations," he said, in a sort of half whisper, still looking out into the forest as if he could see something that the tour kids couldn't.

"I believe that Ortiz and his men were warded off by natives, who were probably using handmade blowguns to shoot the darts."

Blaine and Tracey both looked out into the thick forest, wondering if the natives who shot these darts were still out there. Watching them even now.

"The poison dart frog secretes an alkaloid toxin slime that covers their bodies," said Manihuari. "The frogs' slime, which has varying toxicity, is still used by natives, who put the most poisonous varieties on the tips of their arrows. Only one animal, the Amazon snake, has developed a tolerance for the alkaloid poison, so it is able to eat the frogs."

Blaine and Tracey both gulped. They hoped the natives didn't see them as possible dart targets.

"So, Ortiz didn't just threaten us with his words and chainsaws," Vancho said. "He was also threatening the natives who live in the national forest. Right?"

"Correct," Alvaro responded. "They used their darts against Ortiz and his men because they were protecting themselves and the forest, which is their home. The natives are on our side . . . I hope." The little brightly colored poison dart frog let out a loud croak, as if saying that he hoped so, too.

"Did you know that frogs croak by moving air across a series of vocal chords in their inflatable throat pouch?" Alvaro said. "Each species has its own unique call."

The Sassafras twins hoped they could remember all the information they were getting from Alvaro about the animals. They had gotten all the pictures they needed so far, but hadn't entered any data into SCIDAT yet. Just then, Blaine heard a familiar buzzing noise in his ear. He looked and there it was again—the small pink and green hummingbird from before, hovering over his shoulder. This time Tracey saw it.

"Hey, look," she exclaimed to everyone. "My pet hummingbird has found Blaine."

"What do you mean: your pet hummingbird?" Blaine asked. "Have you seen this bird before too? He was hovering near me earlier, up on the first zip line platform."

"Yes," Tracey answered. "This same little guy found me this morning in our guest room, and again at breakfast, but I never did get a chance to show you. Isn't he cute? Does it look like he's smiling to you, too?"

Blaine looked as closely as he could at the quickly vibrating hummingbird, "Yes, I guess it does look a little like he is smiling. Is that normal?"

"No, something is not right about this," Alvaro said. "Hummingbirds don't smile, and they don't usually hover this long around people." He stepped up to take a closer look. "This is not a bird," he said, shocked, "This is a—"

But Alvaro didn't finish, because he was interrupted by a fearful yelping noise from Violetta. The hummingbird flashed away, as all turned to see why Violetta had screamed. She was covering her mouth with one hand and pointing with the other.

"What? What is it?" Alvaro asked, alarmed.

THE SASSAFRAS SCIENCE ADVENTURES

Blaine and Tracey tried to see where their friend was pointing. Had she spotted a native? Or maybe a predatory animal?

"What is it?" Alvaro asked Violetta again.

"One of the loggers has returned," she whispered.

Finally, they all saw where the frightened girl was pointing. Standing in his white hard hat and blue coveralls, trying to hide himself behind a tree not too far away, one of the loggers had indeed returned. He was holding something in his hand, but it wasn't a chainsaw. It was something smaller and black, like a walkie-talkie or a small radio. Suddenly, he turned and saw that they were all looking at him. The Sassafras twins saw his face as plain as day. It was the Man With No Eyebrows! Blaine and Tracey looked at each other with mouths open. With determination welling up in his heart, Blaine dashed out into the forest.

"Where are you going?" yelled Tracey.

"I'm going after him," Blaine shouted back. "I have to know why and how!"

As soon as the Man With No Eyebrows saw Blaine racing toward him, he bolted off quickly into the forest, but Blaine would not be denied. Blaine kept pursuing.

Alvaro, not knowing the story of the Man With No Eyebrows, and thinking Blaine was chasing the man solely for being a forest destroyer, hopped into action. "Come now, kids!" he said. "We must help Blaine catch this man. Maybe then we can have some leverage to stop Ortiz from taking it all down. I want to know why and how, too!"

Tracey, Violetta, and Vancho all followed Alvaro as he raced after Blaine. Up ahead, Blaine was hot on the trail of the Man With No Eyebrows. The blue coveralls the man was wearing were making him pretty easy to see amongst all the green of the rainforest, but he was fast and shifty. Luckily, Blaine was too. They ran on, dodging trees, smashing through brush, and stomping over the rainforest floor faster than one might think possible.

Blaine was pretty sure he was gaining on him. When he caught the man, he would finally figure out why the man was trying to thwart him and his sister, and how the man was showing up at all of their locations. Blaine was so close now he could hear the man panting as he ran, but, suddenly, the unthinkable happened. The Man With No Eyebrows disappeared, right into thin air!

Blaine tumbled down to the ground, breathing hard, and not believing what he just saw. The Man With No Eyebrows had been right in front of him, and then one millisecond later he was gone! Why? How? Blaine's mind raced. He saw that the man had dropped the small black thing that he had been holding. It wasn't a walkie-talkie or a radio. Instead, it looked to be a remote control of some kind. Just then, Alvaro, Tracey, and the Perezes came crashing through the trees and stumbled into Blaine's spot.

Beguiled by Butterflies

"Where did he go?" Manihuari asked, gasping.

"He disappeared," Blaine answered. "But he dropped this," he said, holding up the remote control.

Alvaro took the controller from the boy and looked it over. "I wonder what he was using this for," he wondered aloud. Manihuari began pulling and pushing on some of the levers and buttons. Then, suddenly, there it was again—the little hovering hummingbird.

"He's back," Tracey said. "Man, this little guy is persistent! Is he going to follow us around all day?"

But now the bird was acting strange. It wasn't stopping to hover over anyone's shoulder. It was flying around erratically, being more abrupt than graceful. The children then noticed that the bird was mimicking the movements that Manihuari was making with the controller.

"This is no bird," Alvaro said. "This is a robot."

The kids' faces all scrunched up in perplexed confusion. "What are you talking about?" asked Vancho.

Alvaro answered, "Evidently, the man Blaine was chasing, was using this remote to control this robot hummingbird." He slowly reached out and snatched the bird out of the air with one hand. The kids gasped, still not sure that this, which looked so real, could truly be a robot.

"You say this bird has been hovering around you all day?" Alvaro asked, looking at the twins.

They nodded yes.

The rainforest expert looked over the small bird he now held in his hand. He shook his head and chuckled as if impressed. "Very ingenious," he said. "Such intricate detail, It looks about as real as possible, except for the small smile painted on its face."

Alvaro held the bird where all the kids could see. Now that the hummingbird was lying still in Alvaro's hand, they could all tell it was indeed some kind of robot and not a real bird. "And if you look very carefully at the smile on the hummingbird's face," Manihuari said, pointing. "You can see a small camera lens hidden there. That logger must have been using this bird to spy on us."

Blaine and Tracey couldn't believe it. The Man With No Eyebrows was not only showing up at all their locations, he was now using spy robot hummingbirds to watch them. Who was this crazy villain? They were dying to know.

As everyone stared at the little bird in Alvaro's hand, a huge net suddenly came flying through the sky and landed over the top of the group, catching them totally off guard. The net tangled them up together in a bunch. What was this? Where had this net come from? They were all too shocked to even squirm around or try to free themselves. Then they saw his scarred, bearded, frowning face as he stepped from cover of forest out into the open.

THE SASSAFRAS SCIENCE ADVENTURES

Ortiz was then slowly joined by several of his wayward ProLog companions. "I told you we were coming back," he said gruffly.

"You didn't have to chase us." Alvaro began to push and pull at the net. "You may have chainsaws and spying cameras, as well as more men and bigger machinery on its way," the guide said angrily, "but we will find a way to stop you!"

The frown disappeared from Ortiz's face for a passing second as he scoffed at Alvaro's statement. "You will not stop us," he said confidently. "We are taking it all down."

Ortiz then instructed his men to use rope to tie the five to the net and to each other so they could not escape. The blue-uniformed men followed his instructions precisely. When they had finished, the group of five was in such a tangled mess that there was no hope of wriggling free to escape. Ortiz and his men then began walking back into the forest. As he left, he looked back at the huddled, trapped, and tangled group.

"Again, I'm telling you. We will be back. So don't worry about chasing us again. Not that you could, even if you wanted to." He paused to scoff. "When we come back with our bigger equipment, we will figure out what to do with the five of you. Right now, we must go back and take care of Prez Perez, who is still tied up in the clear-cut trailer." With that, Ortiz and his men got back in their truck and drove out of sight again.

"I am sorry that I did not succeed in protecting you children," Alvaro Manihuari said, sounding ashamed.

"No need to apologize," Blaine said. "None of this is your fault. We will figure out a way to get out of this yet."

Tracey smiled at her brother's optimism, but she doubted he was right. How were they going to be able to free themselves? How would they escape Ortiz and the other men when they returned? Vancho sat silently. Violetta began to softly cry, more out of fear for her father than for herself, Tracey guessed.

As the group sat tangled up on the ground with deflated hope, the rainforest around them began to slowly come alive again. Different varieties of birds called and whistled from the treetops. Mammals cried out, carefree, from hidden spots amongst the trees, and a smattering of beautiful blue butterflies began to rise from and float gently over the forest floor.

"Mr. Manihuari," Violetta said, still sniffling. "Can you please tell us about those butterflies?"

The Sassafras twins were both glad that Violetta had asked Alvaro about the butterflies. Because not only did they assume this was the very butterfly that they needed data on, they both would rather think about butterflies right now than think about being tied up or about meeting Ortiz again.

"I would be happy to," Alvaro answered Violetta. "That is the blue morpho butterfly." He spoke with a lingering sadness in his voice about their predicament that was somehow mixed with an excitement and passion about the subject of which he was speaking.

"Their bright blue wings are edged with black, except for the underside of their wings, which are dull brown with several eye spots as camouflage. Their entire bodies are covered by thousands of tiny scales that shimmer in the light. They have two forewings, two hind wings, six legs, and three body parts—the head, thorax, and abdomen—which makes them insects." Tracey and Violetta both made a face at the thought of insects.

Alvaro continued on. "Sometimes they head up to the canopy for mating or to sun themselves, but these butterflies spend most of their time on the forest floor, eating rotting fruits, tree sap, fungi, and the juice from decomposing plants. They feed entirely on liquids, which they suck up through a hollow tongue called proboscis. When a butterfly isn't using its tongue, it coils it up like a spring under its head. These butterflies use their antennae to detect scents of food or other members of their species."

One of the butterflies floated close to the group and landed on the net. Manihuari kept sharing. "Their life cycle begins with the female laying eggs on a branch. The eggs then hatch into caterpillars. Blue morpho caterpillars are red-brown with patches of lime green. They feed at night on plants that are part of the pea family. The neat thing is that those plants contain a toxin that the blue morpho butterflys will later secrete, making them toxic to animals. The caterpillar eats and grows quickly, and when it reaches maturity, the young insect spins itself into a pupa. Over time, it changes or metamorphoses into an adult butterfly. The blue morpho butterfly life cycle is one hundred and fifteen days from egg to death."

LINLOC **SCIDAT**

CLASSIFICATION: Insect
NAME: Blue Morpho Butterfly
FOOD: Herbivore
LOCATION: Amazon Rainforest

Though they were tied up tightly, both Blaine and Tracey managed to get their phones out and snap pictures of the pretty blue butterflies.

"Butterflies differ from moths in many ways," Alvaro continued. "Butterflies are colorful, while moths are dull in color. Butterflies fly by day, while moths fly at night. Butterflies rest with their wings up, while most moths rest with their wings flat. Butterflies also generally have long, slender antennae with clubbed ends, while moths can have feathered antennae."

The Sassafras twins suddenly had a strange sensation. Though they hadn't heard a sound, they were sure that someone was watching them. Had the loggers returned already? Was the Man With No Eyebrows spying on them again with a hidden camera? Alvaro and the Perezes must have sensed it as well, because the three of them silenced completely and stiffened up a bit. Ten helpless eyes looked out into the forest before them, wondering how many eyes were looking back at them. Who or what was it that was now silently approaching them? Then as quietly as they had approached, they appeared—eight native men carrying clubs, daggers, and blow-guns.

Blaine and Tracey watched in amazement as the men walked over the forest floor, making absolutely no noise. They were wearing only cloth around their waists. They had rings in their ears and noses that looked to be made of bone. Their bodies were partially covered in some sort of red earthy paint. And their eyes were wide and intense. The twins wondered in fear what their intention was. They hoped that Alvaro had been right when he had guessed the natives were on their side.

Suddenly, breaking the silence, one of the native men spoke. The Sassafrases couldn't understand a word of it, but it was an impressive sounding language that included sounds and tones English doesn't even have. Had the man just issued an attack call or . . .

Alvaro began laughing. Why was Alvaro laughing? "I have good news, children," Manihuari said. "These men are here to rescue us."

Blaine and Tracey let out a huge sigh of relief. Alvaro then said something back to the men in their language. At his response, the natives jumped forward, knelt down, and used their daggers to cut the five free from the net and ropes. Alvaro continued to have a conversation with the men. He then turned back and looked at the two Perez children, smiling.

"Vancho and Violetta," he said. "Let's go rescue your father! These men are going to help us!"

Both Perez children gasped and then smiled. "OK! Thank you! Let's do it!" Violetta said exuberantly.

THE SASSAFRAS SCIENCE ADVENTURES

Alvaro happily clasped his hands together, then said something to the native men, who immediately and silently turned and raced off into the trees.

"OK, you four," Manihuari said. "Let's do our best to keep up with them."

Alvaro, Vancho, Violetta, Blaine, and Tracey raced off into the rainforest, following their new native friends. "How cool was this?" the twins thought as they ran. We are racing through the Amazon rainforest, with natives carrying blow-guns with poisonous darts from frogs on a rescue mission! Awesome! Surely none of their classmates' summer breaks would include this experience.

Then, to their amazement, they were met by more natives running toward them. There was a small convergence of laughter and shouts in the native tongue. Then, who should appear other than Ernesto Perez. Arrio was standing by his side.

"Father!" Vancho and Violetta shouted out in joy. They ran and embraced their dad.

Blaine and Tracey weren't sure how Ernesto Perez had already been rescued, but they were so happy to see the Perez children reunited with their father. Alvaro Manihuari listened to the natives tell the story of what had happened and asked a few questions. Then, he came over, with a huge smile on his face, and filled the Sassafras twins in. It turned out that, at the same time the five were being cut free from their net, another group of native men were rescuing Mr. Perez from the clear-cut trailer. All the men were from Arrio's tribe, and it was Arrio himself who had planned the rescue efforts.

Ortiz and all his men had been captured. Now, they were the ones who were tied up in the clear-cut trailer, being guarded by capable, blow-gun wielding, native men. The twins hoped that the Man With No Eyebrows was among their number.

The defected ProLoggers had only managed to cut one

tree down, so they by no means reached their goal of "taking it all down." The rogue loggers would be taken to Iquitos and put to justice for breaking the law.

Suddenly, the whole group heard a crashing noise from amongst the trees. Stumbling out of the green into the open came Skip, Gannon, and Gretchen, breathing hard and looking lost. The natives looked over the three backpackers with stares as much as or more curious than the backpackers' stares over the natives.

"Dude!" exclaimed Skip. "Looks like we picked the right trail!"

"Sick," said Gretchen slowly.

The natives all laughed, as did Manihuari, the Perezes, and the Sassafrases. The three trekkers walked over to where Blaine and Tracey were.

"It looks like you guys found the right trail too, man," Gannon said. "How has your day in the Amazon rainforest been?"

"Sick!" Blaine responded enthusiastically.

Back at 1104 North Pecan Street, a man quietly walked around the two-story brown house. He was wearing a white hard hat and blue coveralls. He had nearly made it all the way around the house when he finally spotted it—a slightly cracked open basement window. He carefully knelt down and peeked through the dusty pane. No one. The basement was empty, at least for now. He knew Cecil was somewhat impulsive and unpredictable. He knew he never stayed in one place for very long. So wherever Cecil was, he could return at any moment.

The man would have to get in and get out quickly. He

quietly opened the window just enough to crawl through, and then carefully lowered himself down into the basement. He took one more look to make sure the room was empty. Then, he silently bolted over to the tracking screen. A wicked smile covered his face as he used the keyboard to bring up the document page. This would be revenge to the highest and it would be sweet.

CHAPTER 10: DIVERGING TO AUSTRALIA

Capturing Koalas

The man took off his white hard hat, and prepared to start typing on the keyboard. He knew that if he put the wrong information in, the Sassafras twins would not be able to get to their next location. But before he could start typing, information started streaming in on the screen.

Oh no! Those twins were sending in their SCIDAT information right now! Information on three-toed sloths, with a picture of the animal that the kids had taken, flashed on the screen. The information was zipping up on the screen at an incredible rate of speed. "Kids these days can text faster than most adults can type," the man thought to himself.

The wicked smile on his face had been replaced with a look of panic. He noticed a small flashing light and heard a beeping noise. The sequence of lights and sounds had started when the

SCIDAT information began coming in. This must be some kind of indicator signal to Cecil for when the twins were entering data.

Just then, the man heard something a few feet behind him. He looked back with a jerk, and saw what had made the noise. A prairie dog had just climbed up on the table and was now staring right at him, and to make matters worse, he heard footsteps coming down the stairs. What could he do? His evil plan had been thwarted. He had come at the wrong time, but he had to at least give it a try. Desperately, he swiped his hand across the keyboard, causing a jumbled mess of letters and punctuation to appear in the middle of the information the twins were texting. That might do it, he thought, as he bolted for an open window. He quickly hoisted himself up and out of the window.

Cecil Sassafras walked through the basement door just as the man's boots disappeared out of sight. "Oh, fantabulous!" Cecil said, skipping toward the tracking screen. "Blaine and Tracey are sending in their info from the Amazon Rainforest. President Lincoln, haven't those kids been ultra impressive?" Cecil smiled as he watched the data and pictures stream in.

President Lincoln just made a snorting noise.

"Why are you so grumpy?" the scientist asked the prairie dog. "This experiment is working like banana pudding and chocolate chips."

President Lincoln snorted again, jumped off the table, and rumbled over to the screen. He used his nose to tap on the incoming data.

"Link Dog, what has gotten into you, why—" Cecil stopped. He stared at the screen with his mouth open.

"Oh, no! How did that happen?" he said, referring to the jumbled patch of typing in the middle of the otherwise correct data.

It was then that he saw the white hard hat. Cecil picked it up and slowly read what was written on it.

"ProLog . . . ProLog?" Cecil looked back at the mistake on the screen and wondered out loud, "How did a ProLog hat get into the basement? And, more importantly, how will that mistake in the data affect the zip lines?"

"There. All done with the data entry," Tracey said, putting her phone away for a moment to get situated correctly in her harness.

Blaine was already cinched up and ready to go. He tapped over to the LINLOC application in his phone, excited to see where they would be headed next. Suddenly, his carabiner pulled up and he found his feet off the ground, as if he was already attached to the next invisible line. "That was weird," Blaine thought, "this isn't exactly how it had worked all the times before." Then with a silent explosion of light, he was off, only managing to see the word Australia on his phone before he zipped away.

Blaine was a little worried. "What had just happened? Was Tracey with him? They were supposed to look over all the LINLOC information and then calibrate and clip the carabiners on the lines themselves, weren't they?"

With a jerk, his zip line traveling was over. Blaine slumped to the ground, but before he could even see clearly, he began calling out for his sister. "Tracey, what just happened? Tracey! Tracey, are you there?"

No answer.

Blaine reached out his hand and felt smooth glass. Colors slowly began to come to his eyes as he continued to feel around more. There was glass on all sides of him. He was in a glass box of some kind. He stood up and tested his now strong legs and shook his head, his vision now clear. Oh, he had landed in an old phone booth.

He looked outside the booth. There was no sign of Tracey anywhere. There wasn't much of anything, actually. The landscape was pretty flat and dusty looking. The only thing he saw was a building that said "Diner." Blaine pulled out his phone and looked at LINLOC.

"Australia—latitude -37° 29' 49.37" and longitude 148° 10' 22.29", in the deciduous forest," he read aloud to himself. "Information needs to be gathered on koalas, rabbits, the powerful owl, and the sambar deer. And my local expert's name is Willy Day." Blaine exhaled. "First, I have to call my uncle to see what in the tarnation is going on."

He dialed Cecil's number. The call only got through half a ring before Uncle Cecil picked up the other end.

LINLOC SCIDAT

LOCATION: Australian Forest
CONTACT: Willy Day
LATITUDE: **LONGITUDE:**
-37° 29' 49.37"   148° 10' 22.29"

VICTORIA

INFORMATION NEEDED ON:
Koalas, Rabbits,
Powerful Owl, Sambar Deer

"Train? Blaisey? Is that you?"

"What happened?" Blaine answered with an exasperated question of his own. "The zip lines took me before I was ready, and now Tracey is not with me. What happened, Uncle Cecil?"

His uncle made a clicking noise with his mouth, like he was thinking. "By no fault of yours, some of the SCIDAT data got jumbled up. I think it is possible that . . . wait . . . Blaine . . . wait. I am looking at the tracking screen now, and the other green dot is moving."

Blaine pictured the tracking screen in his mind, and remembered that he and Tracey were represented by two green dots.

His uncle continued. "Blaine, I can see that your green dot is in Victoria, Australia, and now Tracey is zipping to . . . uh oh . . . not Australia. Blaine, your sister just landed in . . . China."

"China!" Blaine exclaimed. "Why did she land in China? Why is she not in Australia with me?"

Blaine heard some shouting on the other end of the line and heard Uncle Cecil talking to someone.

"Blaine," Cecil said, "President Lincoln said it's that glitch in the SCIDAT application."

More snorting on the line . . . then Cecil continued. "He is surprised you were even able to get to your next location, but now that you are there, you need to gather all the data and take all the needed pictures. Tracey must do the same at her location in China. Then, once you both complete all the data entry for these two locations, you should converge at the next location."

"Okay, Uncle Cecil," Blaine sighed, not completely understanding what had happened, but clearly understanding what he must do to fix the problem. "I can do that."

He ended the call and put his phone away. Though he wouldn't easily admit it, he felt alone without his twin sister. They often got on each other's nerves, but they really were best friends. Right now, he needed to focus on his task and his new location— Australia. He took off his harness, put it in his backpack and stepped out of the old phone booth just as a brown van pulled into the dusty parking lot of the diner. On the side of the van, written in yellow and red letters, was "Willy Day Productions."

"Well, that must be my local expert," Blaine thought to himself. A stocky man with curly blond hair, in his early twenties, hopped out of the driver's seat and bounded happily into the diner. Blaine had left Peru at night, but had landed in Australia in the morning. This whole different time zone thing was going to take some getting used to. The idea of a little breakfast sounded good, and it was time to meet the next local expert, so Blaine walked into the diner.

A bell over the door rang as he entered, and all five people inside gave him a long stare. There were three old men sitting at a small round table. All had steaming cups of coffee. Behind the bar was a hefty and rather gruff looking woman wearing a blue and white apron. The young man who had come from the van was already sitting at the bar on a stool, looking ready to order. Then, the woman behind the bar said, "Aye look, blokes, it's the boy who was just outside using a cell phone in the old phone booth."

"Can you imagine that?" one of the old men said. "A cell phone in a phone booth."

The small diner erupted in laughter, the kind of laughter that was not mean at all. A weak smile formed on Blaine's face.

"Well, don't just stand there, lad," the lady said. "Come over here to the bar and get some breakfast."

Blaine walked over and climbed up on the stool next to the young man.

"What do you want to eat this morning?" asked the lady, who Blaine now saw had a name tag that said Ethel.

"I don't know," he answered. "Maybe eggs."

"Maybe eggs," Ethel repeated. "Okay, and how do you take your eggs?"

Blaine didn't have any idea how he took his eggs. He wasn't even sure what taking eggs meant.

"Hot?" he said, in more of a question than an answer.

Ethel just looked at the twelve-year-old for a moment, and then shook her head. "OK, mate! One serving of hot-maybe eggs, coming right up."

The three old men at the table were still chuckling. Blaine assumed it was at him. The young man hollered at Ethel that he would have the same as Blaine. Then, he leaned over and stuck out his hand for an introductory handshake.

"Will he die!" he said happily.

Blaine took the young man's outstretched hand and shook it, but was obviously puzzled by such a strange introduction.

"Will who die?" Blaine asked.

"No, no, no," he said, smiling. "You're an American, right?"

Blaine nodded his head yes.

"Let me try again with an American accent. Willy Day," he said slowly. "That's my name, Willy Day."

Oh, now Blaine got it. This was indeed his local expert, Willy Day. Only with the Aussie accent, Willy Day sounded like "Will He Die" to Blaine's American ears. That was pretty weird and cool all at the same time.

"Nice to meet you, Willy," he said. "I'm Blaine. Blaine Sassafras."

"Well, it's good to meet you, Blaine," said Willy. "What brings you to these parts of Australia?"

"I want to learn about some of Victoria's animals," was Blaine's response.

"No kidding!" Willy said, very excited. "That's exactly what I am doing! To be more exact, I am making a documentary film about Victoria's Brown Mountain Forest. It's packed full of interesting animal and plant life."

Willy paused, looked around, lowered his voice a bit, and added, "It is also home to the infamous 'Feuding Brown Mountain Hermits.'"

"Feuding Brown Mountain Hermits?" Blaine asked.

"Ha!" one of the old men at the table laughed. "Those blokes don't exist."

"Aye," one of the other old men said. "There's no hermits in the Brown Mountains. Those are just stories made up to mask the truth."

"What's the truth?" Blaine asked, a bit alarmed.

The third old man said, "The truth is that the Brown Mountain forest . . . is haunted."

Blaine just sat, silent, somewhat daunted by the word haunted.

"Two orders of hot maybe eggs!" Ethel said, reemerging from the kitchen and breaking the silent moment. She slid Blaine's and Willy's plates down the length of the bar. Both plates came to precise stops right in front of Blaine and Willy.

"And here are a couple glasses of O.J., on the house, mates," she added, sliding them glasses of orange juice.

As they ate their eggs and drank their juice, Willy continued to tell Blaine about his film project. "The purpose of my documentary about the Brown Mountain Forest is to capture the wonder, beauty, and mystery that this deciduous forest offers. I want to figure out once and for all if the forest is haunted. If the feuding hermits really do exist. I want to highlight as much wildlife as possible. All in all, I want to make a film that the Australians of Victoria can be proud of," Willy paused. "But I've run into a bit of a snag."

"What happened?" Blaine asked, with a mouth full of eggs.

"My cameraman had an allergic reaction to something he ate yesterday, so he couldn't come with me on this trip. I mean to tell you; whatever he ate made his face swell up as big as a rugby ball. His sickness has left me in need of some help. You wouldn't happen to be available to help me, would you, mate?" Willy asked Blaine.

Blaine took a swig of orange juice, returned, "Sure Willy! I'd love to help out!"

After finishing the best eggs he had ever eaten, Blaine Sassafras was off in the old brown Willy Day Productions van, with Willy Day himself. They were headed out to the Brown Mountain Forest. The jostling ride quickly rocked Blaine into a deep sleep. He awoke with a start, after what seemed like only seconds, when Willy turned off the van's engine.

"Here we are at the trail head, mate," the young film-maker said energetically.

"Wow, that didn't take long," Blaine exclaimed, groggy-headed.

"What are you talking about, mate? We've been driving for hours. That must have been a good hard sleep you were having."

Blaine just nodded and rubbed his eyes. He loved the adventure, but he sure was missing sleeping in his own bed.

"This is as far as we can drive. We have to walk from here," Willy said. "There are two bags in the back of the van—one with camera equipment and the other with camping supplies. We can each carry one, and our hike will be just dandy. But before we start our walk-about, let's set up the cameras right here at the trail-head and do an introduction to the forest. Does that sound good, mate?"

"That sounds great," Blaine said, as he jumped into action helping Willy get bags out of the van.

In a matter of minutes, the duo had the camera set up with film rolling. Willy stepped in front of the camera with an infectious smile on his face and began a monologue with an enthusiasm that seemed to come so naturally and genuinely.

"Hello, mates! My name is Willy Day. Welcome to Victoria, Australia! Behind me stands one of the most beautiful and mysterious deciduous forests in the entire world—the Brown Mountain Forest. It is a forest teeming with amazing wildlife, some of which are unique to this part of the planet. For instance, this forest is the home of the spot-tailed quell, mainland Australia's largest marsupial carnivore, as well as the long-footed potaroo, Victoria's rarest marsupial. The Brown Mountain Forest also has some bombastic plant life! It's an old growth forest that contains over fifty types of trees, many of which are more than three hundred years old. How amazing is that!

"But, mates, this forest that stands behind me now is also steeped in deep mystery. Many locals believe it to be haunted and there have been reports of strange happenings in the forest for years. There are also the rumors about the infamous 'Feuding Brown Mountain Hermits'. So, I am here now with a camera and a desire to dive right into the heart of the beauty and mystery of Victoria's Brown Mountain Forest. Join me if you dare, mates. Let the journey begin!" Willy stepped out of the line of the camera.

"How was that, mate?" he asked Blaine.

"That was fantastic, Willy," Blaine responded. "You're a real natural. This is going to be a good documentary."

"Thanks, Blaine," Willy said, smiling. "All righty then, mate, let's get going."

A few hours into the hike, in a heavily wooded area, Willy stopped abruptly. He looked up into the trees and started whispering to himself.

"What is it, Willy?" Blaine asked in a hushed voice.

Willy turned to Blaine with an excited look in his eyes.

"I believe I've just spotted our first animal of the trip. Look there," Willy said, pointing. "About half-way up that eucalyptus tree. It's a koala!"

Blaine looked up and quickly spotted the cute animal. He immediately got out the camera, to make sure they got this koala on film. The second Blaine pushed the 'Record' button, Willy started energetically spouting off information.

"I did mention earlier that there are many types of trees out here in the Brown Mountain Forest, but the overwhelming majority of trees here are eucalyptus trees. Eucalyptuses are evergreen trees, meaning their leaves do not turn brown and fall off. Sometimes they will lose leaves in the dry season, but they lose most of their leaves to the koala, and if you'll look behind me here, mates, you will be able to spot one of these koalas part-way up that eucalyptus tree."

Willy turned and pointed. Blaine followed his finger with the camera and zoomed in to get a great close-up shot of the koala.

Willy continued on, "Koalas look like small bears, so people have called them 'koala bears' for years, but they are really part of the marsupial family, along with kangaroos. Marsupials are like mammals, except that their young are born in an immature state. Marsupial babies complete their development in the mother's pouch. When the babies are born, they are roughly the size of bees. They crawl up their mother's abdomen and into the pouch, where they will continue their development. When the little guys are ready to leave the pouch, they climb onto their mother's back until they are mature enough to go out on their own."

LINLOC **SCIDAT**

CLASSIFICATION: Mammal
NAME: Koala
FOOD: Herbivore
LOCATION: Australian Deciduous Forest

By now, Blaine had zoomed the shot back out. Much to his surprise, looking through the camera's lens, he spotted several more koalas up in the surrounding eucalyptus trees.

Willy had spied them too, and now began talking about it. "Oh, and look there, mates! Look there! Several more koalas can now be spotted!" Willy really liked to use his hands when he talked.

"All koalas live in eucalyptus forests like the Brown Mountain Forest. They spend most of their lives up in the trees eating the leaves and bark—which makes them herbivores, by the way. They only come down from the trees to cross over to another clump of trees. Koalas have strong legs and sharp claws that they use for gripping tree trunks. They climb by bringing up their hind legs in a series of jumps." Willy gave a quick demonstration before continuing on, "Although they eat up to two pounds of eucalyptus leaves each day, their diet is not particularly nutritious, so they end up sleeping for up to eighteen hours a day. Not a bad life, yeah, mates?"

Blaine kept the camera pointed at the marsupials and got some really good footage. He also snapped some pictures with his own smartphone. Then, off the two went, deeper into the forest. Blaine kept the camera out as they walked, getting some good action shots of Willy hiking up the forested trail and giving out information on the fly. At one point, the path was almost completely covered by a thick tangle of vines. The two crept and twisted through the vines, doing their best not to get bound up. They hiked on, and on as the sun got lower and lower. Blaine wondered when they were going to see the next animal. He also had the perpetual question at the back of his mind: "Is this forest really haunted?"

Rampant Rabbits

As the trail wound up and around, Blaine saw something up ahead that he thought he recognized. They were approaching a thick tangle of vines, and it looked just like the tangle they had already gone through a little bit ago.

As they carefully climbed through the vines, Willy commented, "That's strange. Didn't we already climb through these vines?"

They continued up the trail, but after they hiked a while

longer and came to the exact same tangle of vines again, they both knew something was afoul.

"Blaine, I pride myself on navigation skills and a good sense of direction. But, I'm sorry to say, I think we are walking in circles," Willy declared.

The Sassafras boy nodded, all the while thinking to himself that if he was going to be walking through a potentially haunted forest, he would rather be walking in a straight line than in circles.

"It's getting pretty dark, mate," Willy said. "Maybe we should just set up camp here—take the time to get our bearings straight and start out again in the morning."

The camping gear was all in the bag that Willy was carrying. He slid the bag off his back, opened it up, and started pulling out supplies. Suddenly, a strange moaning noise filled the breezy air. The sound made both Blaine and Willy look up into the trees with a start. The moaning slowly got louder and louder, until it changed pitches, turning into more of a howling noise. Blaine was frozen, but Willy quickly clambered over to the camera bag, carefully pulled out the camera, and started recording. He talked in a low whispery voice, as the haunting noise continued.

"Deep in the heart of the Brown Mountain Forest, we have found ourselves lost and walking in circles. Now, mates, we have been greeted by a strange howling noise. Is this forest truly haunted?" Willy asked, as he panned the camera up and around toward the treetops where the noise was coming from.

Suddenly, the howling rose up a notch and now sounded more like an eerie scream than a howl—almost like an injured animal that had crawled off somewhere to die. This new sound sent shivers crawling up Blaine's spine. Though he would have rather had them closed, Blaine's eyes wandered through the shadowy treetops, searching for the source of the scary noise, and then, just like that, he spotted it. A creature perched up on the high limb of a tree. It was hunkering up in the shadows, sitting completely still, staring right at him.

Blaine reached up a shaking hand and pointed. He tried to get Willy's attention by saying "Look," but the only thing that came out of his mouth was "Loo—" Willy followed Blaine's pointing finger with his eyes and his camera, and within a few seconds, he spotted the strange creature, too. The sight of an unknown screaming and howling creature, sitting up in a tree and looking down at him, was scaring Blaine to the core. Yet, he couldn't take his eyes off of it. How was it managing to make such a loud noise without moving? And were those spikes coming out of its back?

"Look, mate," Willy said, pointing slowly here and there.

Blaine looked and saw that Willy had spotted several other creatures in different high and shadowy treetop spots. The eerie sound continued seeming to randomly jump between screams, howls, and moans. It was so loud that it seemed to envelop the two movie-makers. Then, a sound somewhat like short horn blasts chimed in and added to the noise. Much to Blaine's and Willy's surprise, every time a horn blast sounded off, they were being hit with some kind of liquid. Splat! A big glob of something hit Blaine right in the face. He reached up to wipe it off and found that the projectile liquid was slimy, like mucus. Gross! Were the spiky-backed treetop shadow creatures spitting at them?

Blaine was scared. He felt like screaming and running off into the forest, but he knew that wasn't wise. He kept his composure as best he could. Willy was still holding the camera, getting this whole creepy experience on film. Blaine started to walk over closer to where Willy was, but just as he began to move, he felt something fast and hairy brush against his leg, and he froze again.

"What was that?" he whispered, barely out loud.

Then something brushed against his other leg. Zip! Whoosh! Zip! Several small hairy things brushed by him. Blaine squinted in the darkness and saw that floods of small things, hairy and alive things, were pouring out of holes in the bottoms of the trees and the tree roots. They were charging right at him and Willy!

"Willy!" Blaine yelled. "We are being attacked by hairy . . . haunts!"

Willy Day just laughed. "No, Blaine," he responded, not a hint of fear in his voice. "We are being attacked by rabbits, mate. Well, not really attacked as much as greeted, I would say."

Blaine looked down around his ankles at the swarm of fur and spotted several pointy rabbit ears hopping by, but he was still trembling.

"No worries, mate," Willy reassured, trying to encourage his twelve-year-old camera man. "These mammals are herbivores that feed mainly on grass and plants. They aren't going to nibble on you."

Willy handed Blaine the camera. As he did, he said, "I think I've figured it out."

"Figured what out?" Blaine mumbled to himself as he hit the "Record" button.

Willy talked into the camera which was now set on night vision. "One of our big questions was: 'Is the Brown Mountain Forest haunted?' We have been confronted this evening by circular trails, eerie howls, spitting horn blasts, and creepy tree-top silhouettes." Willy paused and let Blaine swoop around with the camera to capture the sounds and pictures that Willy had just mentioned.

Willy continued. "The easy answer would seem to be that 'yes,' the Brown Mountain Forest is haunted, but when the rabbits were released upon us, I believe the truth was also set free. My theory has always been that the supposed 'hauntings' in Brown Mountain Forest were all the handiwork of one of the infamous hermits. Now that we have spotted so many rabbits, I think I know which hermit it is. In just a moment, mates, I will call out his name and see if he will reveal himself, but first I want to tell you about

THE SASSAFRAS SCIENCE ADVENTURES

these wonderful creatures that are hopping all around our feet."

Blaine held the camera close to the ground to get some great night vision footage of rabbits bounding toward them as Willy continued to talk. He also pulled out his smartphone and captured the moment.

"Rabbits are an invasive species, meaning they are not natural to Australia. They were introduced in 1788 by the Europeans, and they are responsible for the loss of many plant species. Rabbits were originally only found in the Mediterranean, but nowadays humans have introduced them all over the world. Rabbits can have from one to nine babies in a litter and can have up to seven litters per year, which makes for a lot of rabbits mighty fast! The babies are born hairless and blind, so the mother keeps them in the burrows, where they are born, for about three

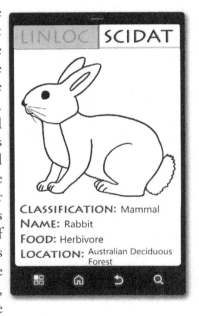

LINLOC   SCIDAT

CLASSIFICATION: Mammal
NAME: Rabbit
FOOD: Herbivore
LOCATION: Australian Deciduous Forest

weeks, until they are strong enough to survive. Rabbits dig their burrows, not only to give birth, but also to provide protection from predators and shelter from the weather. These cute little mammals are actually pretty good at eluding predators out in the open, too. They use their large hind legs for bounding away with speed."

Willy stopped, smiled, took a deep breath, and then started talking again, but more slowly now. "Back to those Europeans in 1788, called the First Fleet. There were one thousand and thirty souls in the First Fleet, made up of 753 prisoners and 277 military personnel. They arrived in eleven ships, on January 19th, 1788. It was the idea of one of the Naval Officers, a man by the name of Hezekiah Dingo, to bring rabbits along on the First Fleet's journey to Australia. Many of his counterparts did not agree with him, but Hezekiah persisted and brought the rabbits anyway. Hezekiah's rabbits and their quickly multiplying descendants ended up ravaging everything green in sight, almost leading to the starvation of the entire First Fleet. This is why Hezekiah and his family were banished from the group. They were forced to live in solitude, and the Dingo name became forever associated with the Rabbit Incident of 1788."

Willy dramatically paused and then continued again with a wry smile, "In the research I've done, I have come to learn that one of Hezekiah Dingo's descendants now lives alone out here in the Brown Mountain Forest. I believe that this descendant I speak of is one of the Feuding Brown Mountain Hermits. The releasing of the rabbits only confirmed my suspicions."

Blaine listened to Willy now with special interest, but he was still pretty convinced the forest was haunted. In all their conversations thus far, Willy hadn't given any detailed information about either of the two hermits.

The eerie noises still broadcasted all around them as Willy continued. "I am going to now call out into the dark forest, mates, and see if I can get this hermit, this descendant of Hezekiah Dingo himself, to respond. If he doesn't answer, we will never know the truth about Brown Mountain Forest, but if he does answer, we can find out the real story behind this mysterious forest."

Blaine was still mostly frozen but, now, more out of anticipation than fear. Was there really a hermit out there somewhere in the darkness? Or was this place just haunted? Blaine hoped they were about to find out.

Willy Day cupped his hands around his mouth and then shouted at the top of his lungs, "Ralphy! Ralphy Dingo!"

CHAPTER 11: SEPARATED IN CHINA

Panda Park

What had just happened? Had Blaine just taken off without her? Tracey had seen Blaine get pulled up into the air by the next invisible zip line, and then he had disappeared! That wasn't how it was supposed to work!

Tracey quickly opened up the LINLOC app on her phone. The next destination listed was Sichuan, China—Latitude 30° 38' 16.53", Longitude 104° 2' 48.01". They were to gather information about giant pandas, golden eagles, golden-haired monkeys, and mice. The local expert's name was Tashi Yidro. Tracey quickly put her phone away and calibrated her carabiner to the correct coordinates. Within seconds, her carabiner and the next zip line connected, and off she went, hoping she was right on Blaine's trail.

Light streamed and swirled around as she zipped through places, but she was not thinking about that. She was wondering about what had gone wrong with the lines. She was sure that she and Blaine had entered the right information from their Peru leg into the SCIDAT application. So why hadn't she and Blaine zipped off together? Was her twin brother just horsing around? Was he playing another one of his practical jokes on her? Well, it wasn't funny, and she would tell Blaine exactly that when she saw him in just a few seconds.

Her traveling came to the usual abrupt stop, and her eyes were greeted by the customary white light. Her eyes were briefly blinded and she had to wait for her sight to return. She started calling out for her brother, "Blaine! What just happened? Blaine! Blaine, are you there?"

No answer. But she could hear the voices of many others. And all these voices sounded like they were speaking . . . Chinese.

As her vision cleared, she realized she had landed in a public place. Though it had been night in Peru, it was morning here in China. As the morning sun shone gently into Tracey's eyes, she saw that she was sitting on a wooden bench on a school campus of some kind, maybe a college campus? There were scores and scores of people walking over a wide sidewalk, right there in front of her. So many people, in fact, that none of them seemed to notice her sudden appearance.

Tracey sat there feeling a little awkward in her harness and helmet and a lot alone without her twin brother. She reached in her bag, pulled out her phone, and dialed up Uncle Cecil.

"Blaisey! Are you okay?" She heard her uncle's voice as he answered and the tone of Cecil's voice let Tracey know he was genuinely concerned.

"Yeah, I'm okay," she answered. "But what happened? Where is Blaine? Why am I alone in China?"

"President Lincoln and I think the SCIDAT information from your last location was sabotaged."

"Sabotaged?" repeated Tracey.

"Yes," her uncle replied. "You and Train entered the most recent data correctly, and you got all of your pictures in. What has happened is in no way your fault."

"Sabotaged?" Tracey parroted again. "Did someone else mess up our data? I thought that if the incorrect data were entered, we couldn't even get to the next location! So, how did I get to

China? And where is Blaine?" Tracey asked, exasperated, as she was trying to figure it all out.

"That glitch with the SCIDAT application that I mentioned before you two first took off has proven to be very unpredictable," said Cecil. "So our best guess is that the sabotage led to you two being sent to different locations. As you already know, you are in China, but your brother is in Australia."

"Australia?" Tracey inquired with alarm. "He's in Australia? When is he going to get to China?"

"He's not," was Cecil's answer. "He needs to collect all the correct data at his location in Victoria, Australia. You need to collect all the correct data at your location in Sichuan, China. When the two of you do that and get it all into SCIDAT, you should converge together at the next location."

That was not the solution Tracey wanted to hear, but she understood what needed to be done.

"Okay, Uncle Cecil. Bye," she cracked out weakly as she tapped her phone to end the call.

Tracey took a deep breath and watched all the people pass in front of her. She missed her brother. He could be a pest sometimes, but he really was a good brother and sincerely was her best friend. Tracey determined right then and there that she would toughen up and brave this one on her own. Yes, she was more comfortable when Blaine was around, but she would prove now that she could fly solo and handle her business just fine.

She took off her harness and helmet and stuffed them in her backpack. She was just about to leave the bench, when a young girl carrying a backpack of her own approached with a shy smile.

"Hello," said the skinny girl. She was not much taller than Tracey, she had rosy cheeks, straight black hair, and wore a long dark skirt.

"Hello," Tracey responded.

THE SASSAFRAS SCIENCE ADVENTURES

"Welcome to our university," said the girl. "My name is Tashi Yidro. What is your name?"

Tracey smiled. She had found her local expert. "My name is Tracey Sassafras. Very nice to meet you," she responded.

Tashi invited Tracey to walk around campus with her. As they walked, Tashi showed Tracey everything of interest on the university campus. But what was most interesting to Tracey is that Tashi was studying zoology, which, as Tracey found out, was the science of animals. When Tracey mentioned that she would love to see some of China's animals, Tashi got very excited.

"I am about to take a trip back to my hometown. You should come with me," Tashi said. "The Panda Reserve is on the way, and if we are lucky, we will spot many other animals as well. There are also some interesting animals in and around my hometown."

"Where is your hometown?" Tracey asked.

"I am from a small Tibetan village out in the mountains of Sichuan. The best way to get there is by bus."

"That sounds great!" Tracey responded happily. "I would love to visit your village!" The two girls began making their way off campus toward the bus station.

What the two girls didn't know is that they were being followed. He hadn't seen Tracey arrive on the bench, but he had been watching Tracey and Tashi the whole time they had been talking and walking around the university campus. He had just overheard their conversation about riding a bus back to Tashi's hometown. As the two girls now walked down the busy sidewalk toward the bus station, he followed them at a safe distance. He knew he would be on that bus, too.

A couple of hours later, Tracey Sassafras found herself sitting next to her new friend, Tashi Yidro, on a bus stuffed full of people, headed out into the mountains of Sichuan, China. Their first stop was the Panda Reserve, and then they would get on another bus that would take them to Tashi Yidro's hometown. Neither one of the girls noticed that the one who was secretively following them was on the bus too, sitting three rows behind.

The densely populated city they started from was very flat, but before Tracey knew it, they were in the mountains. The highlands were lush and green, with a misty fog hanging in the air. Tashi Yidro cheerfully shared information as they bounced along on the bus.

"The forest out there is a bamboo forest, which is mostly found in China, Japan, and other East Asian countries. Bamboo is an evergreen plant that is the largest member of the grass family. It is one of the fastest growing plants in the world. The stem is hollow and we use it for food, building, and a variety of other things."

Tracey gazed out of the bus window as Tashi spoke, drinking in the beauty they were passing by. Every place she had been on the zip lines had a unique beauty all of its own. The bamboo forest of China was no exception to the list. All the local experts Tracey had met had been so passionate and excited about the science in their parts of the world. They had inspired her to see that science was worth knowing and here was Tashi Yidro, an absolute delight, and worthy local expert.

When the bus got to the reserve, everyone piled off the big vehicle and started making their ways excitedly out onto a broad network of footpaths. Almost all had their cameras out and were happily chattering about the prospect of spotting a panda. Tashi led Tracey to a trail that no one else was on. The two girls hiked down through the bamboo and as they walked, Tashi excitedly whispered to Tracey, "I have a surprise for you, Tracey. I have been here many times, and I know where they have some red pandas."

"Red pandas? I thought that all pandas were black and white?" Tracey questioned.

"Well, red pandas are not really pandas. Both giant pandas and red pandas eat bamboo and have some other similar characteristics. So, when these animals were first classified, the two animals were put in the same family. It turns out that the red panda is the only living member of its family and it's more closely related to the raccoon than the giant panda," Tashi explained.

As the girls approached a small fenced in enclosure, Tashi continued, "Though this is a reserve, where most of the animals roam free, there are a few enclosures around the premises to help zoologists and veterinarians observe the animals to make sure they are healthy. If we are lucky, there will be some red pandas we can see."

The girls walked along the fence, and sure enough, after a couple of minutes, they saw two red pandas.

"Wow!" exclaimed Tracey.

Tashi laughed and then started to share a couple more facts about the animals. "They can easily climb trees with their sharp claws. Red pandas hunt at night for small animals, but they will also eat eggs and bamboo shoots."

The girls watched as the two cute little red pandas crawled and rolled around in the enclosure for several minutes. Then, Tashi led Tracey further down the trail, and she now began talking about the giant pandas she hoped they would see soon.

"The giant panda is an endangered animal. There are fewer than three thousand still found in the wild because they were once hunted for their fur, which is of a beautiful black and white. The fur is waterproof and thick enough to keep out the cold. Another reason the giant panda is endangered is because their forests are being cut down, which is why I love this Panda Reserve so much."

The mist that had been on the road also floated there above the trail, mysterious and beautiful, all at the same time. He saw Tracey pull out her phone as she listened to Tashi. She was ready to capture a picture of the pandas once they saw one, but what she didn't notice was that he was still following them. They were the only ones on this certain trail and the two of them were walking almost fifty feet in front of him. He was silently stepping behind them, ducking behind trees and clumps of bamboo when he needed to. His backpack was full, and he was anxious to open it up, take out some of the contents, and give the girls their "surprise." For now, he kept his distance and listened, as Tashi was now talking about newborn giant pandas.

"At birth they weigh less than five ounces and have to be carried everywhere," Tashi shared. "They are teeny, tiny, blind, and pink. They aren't able to walk until they are a year old, but after about ten weeks, they do start to crawl. Giant pandas have one to two cubs at a time, and the cubs stay with their mothers for eighteen months before they are ready to be out on their own."

Then, off the left side of the trail, out near a thick bunch of bamboo stalks, the girls spotted a giant panda. The big bear was just sitting there, crunching on bamboo.

"Wow! He's just right there. What a cute fuzzy looking guy!" Tracey exclaimed, as she snapped a picture.

Tashi continued on with the information as the girls stood and watched the animal. "The giant panda loves to eat bamboo. It has an extra pad on its front paw that works a little like a thumb and helps it to grasp the stems of the bamboo. One panda can eat up to six hundred bamboo stems a day."

"Six hundred stems a day?" Tracey repeated as a question.

LINLOC SCIDAT

CLASSIFICATION: Mammal
NAME: Panda
FOOD: Herbivore
LOCATION: Chinese Bamboo Forest

"Six hundred," Tashi affirmed. "They spend twelve to fifteen hours a day eating. They have large, powerful jaws for crushing the tough bamboo stems. The shoots are crushed between their flat teeth, and the nutrients are released. Their throats have a tough lining to protect them from splinters. Even so, most of the tough bamboo fibers pass straight through their digestive systems."

Suddenly, the forest air was filled with the sound of an explosion. Not just one explosion but a series of explosions. Tashi Yidro ducked, and Tracey nearly jumped out of her shoes. The giant panda grunted and quickly rumbled off into the forest, out of sight. The explosions continued with loud popping and cracking noises and even some screaming-type sounds.

"What is happening?" Tracey shouted to Tashi, her heart racing. "What is that?"

Tashi looked up, scanning the forest behind them. "Fireworks," she responded. "Somebody is setting off fireworks."

Both girls reached up and covered their ears until the fireworks stopped.

Tracey looked at her friend with wide eyes, "Tashi, those fireworks were so loud and so close! Why would someone set of fireworks in a Panda Reserve?"

Tashi Yidro frowned. "They should not have done that. It is against the rules to have fireworks here."

The girls stood up and walked back up the trail, looking for the source of the explosions. They only had to take a few dozen steps until they found a pile of used and burned up firecrackers. The girls just stared at the pile of red paper and black ash. Whoever had set off these fireworks had been practically right behind the girls, but there was no one around. He or she had seemingly disappeared right into thin air. Tracey wondered if the Man With No Eyebrows was back, yet again, to wreak havoc with her travels.

The girls saw a whole company of people now approaching

them on the trail with the sound of agitated voices and running feet. They were pointing and shouting at the girls in Chinese. Both girls stood there by the pile of used up fireworks, frozen. They were a little scared, as they realized they were about to be accused of the crime. The group of people, led by a short man that looked like some kind of security guard, ran up and surrounded the girls. They continued in raised voices and accusatory points and gestures. It was all in Chinese, but Tashi didn't need to translate for Tracey. Tracey knew exactly what was happening. They were being accused of setting off the fireworks, and they were going to be escorted out of the Panda Reserve.

Tashi tried to explain to the guard and the others that it wasn't she and Tracey who had set off the fireworks, but it was of no use. The short little guard grabbed Tracey and Tashi by the arms and walked them back up the trail to the front gate of the reserve. He pushed them outside the gate and then locked the gate behind them. Tashi Yidro hung her head as she apologized to Tracey. She was obviously very embarrassed.

"Don't worry, Tashi," Tracey encouraged her new friend. "It's not your fault we had to leave the reserve. I had a wonderful time in the reserve, and we got to see a giant panda, so no worries, friend."

Tashi managed a small smile as the two girls headed over to the parking lot with the buses and found the one that was going to Tashi Yidro's hometown. They bought a couple of tickets and plopped down in their seats.

What the girls didn't know was that he was already on the bus. He still had his backpack, and it still had plenty more fireworks in it. His plan in the Panda Reserve had gone off without a hitch. He had scared the girls half to death, and then they, rather than he, had been blamed for the small explosion. Now, here he was, still trailing them, and they were totally unaware of it. He laughed to himself in anticipation. The next little explosive stunt he was planning would be even better than the first.

Explosions and Eagles

Their second bus ride of the day took the girls further out into the mountains and to higher elevation.

Tracey quickly fell asleep, but awoke suddenly to the sound of a loud honking horn. The first thing she saw was a huge orange truck barreling right toward them. She gasped, thinking a collision was coming, but the bus driver calmly maneuvered the bus around the oncoming truck. Tracey reached over and grabbed Tashi's arm.

"We were almost in a head on collision," the Sassafras girl stated, more than a little alarmed.

Tashi, who had been sleeping herself, blinked her eyes open. "What? Oh, yes. Don't worry, Tracey, they drive a little differently here than what you are used to. We will be fine." With that, Tashi closed her eyes again and fell right back to sleep.

Tracey, however, was frazzled. She was extremely tired, but there was no way she could go back to sleep now. Tracey stared out the window at the road ahead, with tense muscles and straining eyes. They were on a very narrow road that didn't have any kind of road stripes or guardrails. It looked like it should be a one-way road, but it was functioning as a two-way road for big buses and huge trucks. There was a towering mountain on one side of the road and a steep drop-off to a snaking river far down below on the other side. Even so, the bus driver was not treating this like a precarious road at all. Oh, no, he was driving as fast as one might think a big bus could go, and he was swooshing up the narrow road, zipping around blind mountain curves like he had no care in the world.

Tracey let go of Tashi's arm and grabbed the armrest instead. She held on so tightly that she was sure she would leave permanent indentions. Eventually, the road straightened and leveled out a bit, and Tracey was able to breathe a little more easily. She laughed to herself. Who would have known a bus ride could be more intense than traveling at light speed on an invisible zip line? Tracey looked again out the window. They were still in the mountains, but much higher than they had been before. Tracey could still see towering peaks everywhere, but now many of them were sparkling with white snow on the tips.

Boom! Pop! Pop! Snap! Pow!

An explosion sound suddenly ripped through the bus. Shocked, the bus driver jerked awkwardly at the wheel, which sent the bus careening toward the side of the road. Tashi Yidro shot up, wide awake, just as Tracey was ducking her head down for cover. The huge vehicle spilled over and off the edge of the pavement. Luckily, there was no steep cliff here, but they were now speeding and bouncing down a substantially large, rocky hill. The bus driver pushed his foot down on the brake pedal, but nothing happened. He gripped the steering wheel in terror and vigorously pumped down over and over again on the brakes, but something was wrong. The brakes weren't working.

The excruciatingly loud sound of fireworks gave way to the screams of the passengers and the sound of rocks hitting and scraping the bottom side of the bus. The bus rolled, bounced, and shook down the wide gravelly knoll, until it finally came to a slamming stop against a large boulder. Tracey and Tashi flew up and hit the backs of the seats in front of them, but they were not hurt and were just glad the bus had stopped. For a moment, everyone just sat still in stunned silence, not believing what had just happened. Then, the bus driver stood and turned toward the passengers. He slowly eyed every one of them, and everyone could see his blood starting to boil as he started shouting in Chinese.

Tashi looked at Tracey and whispered, "He wants to know who set off the fireworks. I hope we don't get blamed again." Tracey hoped not, too.

The bus driver made everyone get off the broken bus, and he checked the contents of everyone's bags as they did. After all the bags were searched, no fireworks were found. Everyone stood in a sort of half-circle and looked at the battered bus. It had scrapes and dents on every side and was leaking all kinds of fluid. It was clear that no one would be riding out of there on that bus.

The bus driver was still angry, but he did care about his passengers. He gave everyone two options. They could either stay by the bus to wait for another one to come pick them up or they could walk back up to the road and try to hitch a ride or walk to wherever they were going. Tashi and Tracey chose the second option.

"It may be a whole day before another bus gets here," Tashi said, as the girls walked the hill. "Besides, my hometown is not too much farther up the road, and we can make it before it gets too dark. More than likely, we can find someone with a small truck or a tractor that will give us a ride."

Except for one other boy, Tashi and Tracey were the only two passengers who decided to walk instead of wait. Once they reached the road, Tracey took in a big deep breath, partly because the high altitude made it a little harder to breathe than normal, but mainly because the scenery was so . . . well . . . breathtaking. It had been beautiful from behind the bus window, but now, walking out in the open and breathing in the fresh air made the mountains and the sky seem that much prettier. Tracey was taking in all the beauty, but deep down inside she was also a little worried. She was assuming it was the Man With No Eyebrows who had somehow set off the fireworks at the reserve and on the bus, but she also wondered if he was also the one who had sabotaged her and Blaine's SCIDAT data. Why was he so bent on their failure? How could they stop him when he was so good at being elusive? Tracey didn't know, but she wanted answers and the sooner would be better than later.

The two girls continued up the beautiful lonely road. All was silent except for the sound of their shoes hitting the pavement as they walked. As far as they knew, they were all alone except for the young boy who was walking by himself way behind them. They walked on like this until Tashi broke the silence with a happy and surprised laugh.

"Look, Tracey," she squealed, pointing up into the clear blue sky. "It's a golden eagle!"

Tracey looked up and saw the big bird floating way up high, with wings fully expanded.

"The golden eagle is one of the most widespread eagle species and it can be found all over Asia and Europe," Tashi said excitedly. "It got its name from the golden collar of feathers around its neck. It can have a wingspan of over seven feet."

LINLOC **SCIDAT**

CLASSIFICATION: Bird
NAME: Golden Eagle
FOOD: Carnivore
LOCATION: China

Tracey watched the eagle swoop and soar, treating the open sky like its own personal playground. She reached for her smartphone and snapped an image of the moment.

"Their outer feathers are very strong and powerful, while

their inner feathers help to reduce air resistance and give them their ability to soar." Tashi Yidro continued. "Their soft down feathers trap air that helps to keep the eagles warm."

The golden eagle arched way up in the sky and then shot down like a bullet toward the earth, as Tashi went on, "The eagle's eyes face forward so that they can judge distances accurately. Their eyes are larger and keener than a human's eye, which gives them the ability to spot their prey from long distances."

Tracey held her breath because it looked like the bird was going to sail right into the ground, but just before the eagle crashed, it changed trajectories and started flying right above the ground.

Tashi smiled as she spoke, enjoying watching Tracey watch the eagle. "Golden eagles have strong wings and large hooked bills, both of which make them very good hunters, but they don't use their bills for killing prey. Instead, they use their powerful talons. A fully grown golden eagle can pick up prey that weighs up to ten pounds. It can also fly fast and chase its prey until the catch is exhausted and unable to escape."

The girls watched as the eagle reached out with those strong talons that Tashi had just spoken about, and plucked up what looked like a rabbit. It then flew back up into the sky, where it was soon joined by another eagle.

"Oh!" Tashi exclaimed. "That must be this eagle's mate. Did you know that golden eagles mate for life and return to the same nest each year? Their courtship consists of an intricate flying dance they perform in pairs."

That last bit of information made Tracey laugh out loud. It was a funny thought to think of these eagles performing dance routines in pairs.

Tashi continued, "They nest in cliffs or trees and they lay one to three eggs per year, which hatch after forty-five days."

Both girls watched the two eagles dance in the sky until they were out of sight and then they continued their walk up the road. The boy that had been walking behind them was gone now. He must have taken another route to wherever it was that he was going. So now it was just Tashi and Tracey alone on the road. Tracey was a little surprised they hadn't seen any cars pass by, when suddenly, another explosion sound rang out from the silence.

"Not again," Tracey thought, as she shouted to Tashi, "Is that more fireworks?"

Tashi's face was filled with a fear that Tracey had not yet seen and her eyes wide with horror. "Not fireworks," she shouted to Tracey, above the loud cracking noise.

Tracey followed her friend's gaze up the mountain and her face filled with the same horror as the two of them screamed, "Landslide!"

CHAPTER 12: THE FEUDING BROWN MOUNTAIN HERMITS

Petrified by the Powerful Owl

No one answered. The weird sounds continued. The rabbits kept trickling by and those strange creatures still sat motionless in the tops of the trees. Even so, Willy Day, the passionate and fearless Australian documentary filmmaker, would not be deterred. Again, he shouted out into the darkness of the Brown Mountain Forest.

"Ralphy Dingo!" Only this time he didn't stop with the name. "I know who you are, Ralphy!"

Willy shouted loud enough to be heard over all of the haunting noises.

"I know you are a descendant of Hezekiah Dingo! I know your family was banished to solitude by the First Fleet because of the rabbits. I know you probably think your family name is forever stained, mate, but I know something else about your family that most people either don't know or have forgotten."

Blaine held on to the camera and successfully captured Willy's call out-to Ralphy Dingo on film. The twelve-year-old was still scared, but he was also skeptical. Did Willy Day really think there was a hermit out there right now, within earshot, listening to what he was saying? The idea that the Brown Mountain Forest was either haunted or feuded over by a couple of hermits had both seemed far-fetched back at the diner. However, right now, standing in the dark, with all the strange things going on around them, Blaine thought the haunting theory felt a little more feasible.

On the other hand, Willy Day was convinced there was a hermit listening to him right now, so he continued to yell out. "I know something your family did that is honorable and legendary.

The famous Captain Cook was one of the first to discover Australia, and he named the first city 'New South Wales,' which no one much liked. It was Hezekiah Dingo that suggested they change the name of the city to Sydney. Everyone loved it, and the name stuck. To this day it is called Sydney, and it is adored worldwide as the pride of Australia. It is the Dingos we have to thank for that, Ralphy! And I will do all in my power, through this film I am making and otherwise, to make sure everyone knows."

As soon as Willy finished his last sentence, all of the scary sounds stopped. The dark forest was quiet except for the slight sound of rabbits still scurrying around. What had happened?

Then, softly, the silence was filled with the sound of crying. Somebody was sniffling and sobbing only a few feet away from where Blaine and Willy were standing. Slowly, a short old man stepped out from behind a tree. He approached the two of them, and without stopping, he walked right up and hugged Willy. The filmmaker had truly believed that the Feuding Brown Mountain hermits existed, but to be hugging one of them right now was a little more than shocking. The look on his face showed how much he couldn't believe what was happening.

"It's been a long time," the old hermit croaked, "since anyone has said anything nice about the Dingo name. Thank you," he said, still crying a bit.

He then came over and hugged Blaine. The old bearded hermit was dirty, and Blaine felt awkward hugging him. In the end, he was just glad that the hermit had decided to be nice. Old Ralphy Dingo then invited the two into his dwelling and even carried both their bags for them. His shack, as Blaine would have called it, wasn't too far from where they had been standing in the tangle of vines. It was just four boards, serving as walls, and a tin roof. Inside there was one flickering candle near a heap of animal skin blankets. Ralphy invited the two filmmakers to sit down.

Suddenly, without even asking, the old man grabbed the camera and turned it on. He started talking and Blaine could tell by the smile on Willy's face that this was a good thing. Blaine had assumed that all hermits would be shy and quiet, but that wasn't the case with Ralphy Dingo. Maybe it was because he hadn't seen people in so long, or maybe Willy's kind words about his family had softened him up. Whatever the reason, Ralphy was happy and gushing.

"I'm so glad all of my frighteners, as I call them, didn't scare you two away. I designed that circular trail to get people all bumpuzzled. It had you two pretty confused, am I right?" Ralphy paused to laugh, obviously very proud of himself. "Then, when night began to fall, and you two stopped, I got you shivering with the wind hollows, the horns, the shoots, and the rabbits!"

"Did you design all these frighteners yourself?" Willy asked Dingo.

"Oh, yes!" Ralphy said, smiling. "I have hoses hooked up and strung every which way. The hoses attach to hollow pieces of wood that I carved into different shapes. When I blow into the hoses, the flowing air makes all them strange sounds that had you two pale as ghosts. For fun, I added some water hoses to the mix that use water siphoned from the stream. So now, when I blow into those hoses, it makes a trumpet-type sound, and then shoots slimy creek water out at you!"

Now Willy was laughing along with Ralphy, but Blaine still wasn't so sure why all of this was so funny. "What about the rabbits?" Willy asked. "How did you manage to release them like that?"

"Well, you know a Dingo is gonna have him some rabbits, mate," Ralphy said. "I have enough rabbits to drive a man insane. I keep them in cozy little cages in the bases of several hollow trees. They get a little stir crazy in those cages, so when I pull the lever, simultaneously opening their hatches, they shoot out like a cheetah after a wildebeest."

Most of Ralphy's explanations made sense to Blaine, but he was still wondering about those scary creatures up in the trees, so he asked Ralphy Dingo about it. "What about those big spiky-backed, monster-looking things that sit motionless up in the tree branches? What are those?"

Ralphy laughed louder than he had yet. "Oh! You saw those? Wonderful! Those are my treetop scarecrows! I was wondering if those silly things were worth putting up there or not, mate. So those creeped you, did they?"

"Yes, they definitely creeped me," Blaine responded, a smile finally coming to the twelve-year-old's face.

The unlikely trio of friends talked on. They conversed more about Ralphy's strange family history, and about Willy's short filmmaking career. But the demeanor of the conversation changed when Willy asked Ralphy about the other Brown Mountain Hermit. Ralphy stopped laughing, and his face immediately became sullen.

THE SASSAFRAS SCIENCE ADVENTURES

"I'm sorry," Willy apologized. "I didn't mean to offend you."

"Oh, it ain't you, mate," Ralphy responded with a frown on his face. "It's just that I hate that bloke."

"So it's true? There is another hermit living in the Brown Mountains?" Willy asked.

"Yeah, there's another hermit, and he lives way too close, if you ask me," Ralphy said in disgust. "Can't much call myself a hermit with that no good scoundrel hanging around, now, can I?"

"Why don't you like him?" Blaine asked.

"Why don't I like him?" Ralphy repeated the question like the answer should be obvious. "I don't like him because these are my mountains. Then, he came along saying they were his mountains and we've been feuding ever since. Make no mistake about it, I am much more of a gentleman than he is, mates. I set up frighteners around me to keep people out, but he has set up actual traps, designed to hurt people. He's dangerous, mean, dirty, and downright impolite. You two should not go anywhere near him."

"I researched his family history, just like I investigated yours," Willy said. "And while he and his family have some stains, he also has some heritage to be proud of. His name is Matty? Right? Matty Mingo?"

Ralphy made a face, like the actual name Matty Mingo smelled bad. "Yeah, that's his name, mate. Matty stinking Mingo."

Willy shrugged off Ralphy's disdain for his fellow hermit and began telling the Mingo story. "Much like your family introduced rabbits to Australia, the Mingo family introduced the sambar deer into Australia. In 1860, Matty's great, great grandfather, Mephibosheth Mingo, brought a small boatload of sambar deer and released them into the Australian wild, and like the Dingo rabbits, the Mingo deer overpopulated and ravaged local plant species, but that is not what drove the Mingo family into solitude. Their humiliating family incident happened nine years later when gold was found here in Victoria. The Mingo family jumped into gold mining with both feet. In the summer of 1869, Mephibosheth Mingo found the largest gold nugget in recorded history, weighing in at seventy-seven kilograms. He invited the local newspaper to do a story on him and his nugget, but to his humiliation and dismay, the very next day, John Deason and Richard Oates found a gold nugget one kilogram bigger, and the newspaper did the story on those two mates instead. To add insult to injury, when the inspector came to look at the Mingo nugget, it was found to be not gold at all, but fool's gold. Mephibosheth Mingo became the laughingstock of the gold mining community and he and his family retreated to the solitude of the Brown Mountains."

Willy paused to catch his breath. "Now, Matty Mingo , his great, great grandson, lives out here somewhere alone, living the life of a hermit. But what most people don't know is that the Mingo family later did something wonderful, for Victoria, in particular."

"Hmpf!" Ralphy snorted. "I don't much care what Mingo's family did that was wonderful. The bloke is a mean and nasty human being, and I don't like him. Nothing is going to change that."

"Even so," the resilient Willy said. "I would like to try and make contact with him."

"That's impossible!" Ralphy grabbed a couple of the animal skin blankets and tossed them at Willy and Blaine. "Your kind words about my family have made us friends," said the old man. "But I am a hermit. I like my solitude. You're welcome to rest here tonight. But tomorrow, I'll show you back to the trail, and off you two go. Just forget all about Matty Mingo."

There was a sense of finality to what Ralphy Dingo said, so Willy didn't push him. The three lay down in the small shack like sardines in a can. After a few minutes, Blaine's eyes were feeling heavy, but just as they slid shut, a loud hooting noise sounded out in the darkness just outside Ralphy's dwelling.

Blaine sat up, wide awake again. "What was that?" the Sassafras boy asked. "Was it another one of your frighteners?"

Ralphy just chuckled. "No, it's not a frightener, but rest easy, mate, it's just a book bok."

"A what?" Blaine asked.

"A powerful owl," Willy said, chiming in. "The largest owl in Australia, sometimes referred to as a book bok."

Willy got up, grabbed the camera, and stepped outside. Blaine followed him, knowing they were going to try and catch a glimpse of this owl. The dark forest in front of him didn't seem so scary, now that Blaine knew it wasn't haunted. He felt a little silly for ever thinking that it was. He and Willy strained their eyes out in the darkness looking for the bird. They heard another hoot. Willy was the first to spot it. Ironically enough, the bird was perched up on one of Ralphy's treetop scarecrows. Willy handed the camera to Blaine, and jumped right into a monologue about the bird.

CLASSIFICATION: Bird
NAME: Powerful Owl
FOOD: Carnivore
LOCATION: Australian Deciduous Forest

"The powerful book bok, or what most people call the powerful owl, is a part of the hawk or owl group of birds. It is covered with feathers that are especially soft, which allows it to fly silently. Its quiet flight not only prevents prey from knowing that the owl is coming, but it also makes it easier for the owl's ears to detect even the slightest noise while in flight."

Blaine was amazed that here, even in what felt like the middle of the night, Willy was just as energetic and excited about science as he was in the daytime. Willy continued on. "The powerful

THE SASSAFRAS SCIENCE ADVENTURES

owl's hearing is so sensitive that not only can it hunt at night, it can hunt on a completely dark and moonless night. The shape of its head is such that it hears sound on one side a fraction of a second sooner than on the other side, which allows it to pinpoint the location of the sound. It has large eyes, which gives it good vision; however, it cannot move its eyes in their sockets. Instead it moves its head, which can turn three quarters of the way around. So, the owl can see in front and behind of where it sits."

As Blaine was filming, he was thinking about how cool this documentary was going to be. There was science and mystery in the Brown Mountain Forest. It really was worth checking out. He was glad that he could be a part of sharing it with others.

"Look there, mates!" Willy said excited. "The owl is taking off after something!"

Blaine watched through the lens of the camera as the powerful owl swept silently down to the forest floor, reached out with its large powerful claws, and caught what looked like a mouse.

"Whoa! That was pretty amazing, wasn't it!" Willy said caught up in the moment.

"The powerful owl is a bird of prey that hunts mostly at night, catching mainly mice, as you just saw. The owl swoops down with its feet out and talons, spread to kill the prey by piercing it with its talons. The carnivorous bird also eats rabbits, which are not in short supply in this forest!"

With its vermin meal firmly in its grasp, the owl flew off into the dark forest beyond the view of the camera. Blaine had barely managed to snap a picture of the owl before it vanished.

"Probably off to feed its chicks," Willy was saying. "Powerful owls generally lay between one and two eggs a season. Unlike most birds, the owl doesn't wait for all the eggs to be laid before incubating them. Owls begin incubating immediately, which means their chicks will hatch several days apart. The baby chicks are covered with soft down feathers that keep them very warm after they hatch."

Willy and Blaine concluded their filming for the day, put the camera away, and bunked down for the night in Ralphy Dingo's small shack. What Willy hadn't told Blaine was that he had no intention of heading back out of the forest the next day. He wanted to wake up before dawn, slip quietly away from Ralphy's place, and go look for Matty Mingo.

Snared with the Sambar Deer

The next morning, Blaine awoke to being gently dragged out of the shack by his feet. He almost shouted out, but then he saw that it was Willy Day that was doing the dragging, with a big goofy smile on his face. Willy motioned for Blaine to be quiet, helped him up off the ground, and handed him a backpack. It was still very dark outside, though hints of dawn could be seen in the east.

All was quiet, except for the sound of Ralphy Dingo snoring, when Willy whispered to Blaine, "Sorry to wake you up like that mate. Are you ready for some more film-making?"

Blaine nodded that he was. Then off they went, quietly tromping away from the Dingo dwelling. Blaine was thinking about all that Ralphy had said about the other hermit, Matty Mingo, especially about all of the kinds of dangerous traps he was supposed to have. Blaine wondered if that was true, or if old Ralphy had just been blowing smoke.

The hike that morning wasn't as easy as it had been the previous morning, but Blaine was glad that they weren't walking in circles anymore. About an hour into the hike, the sun finally peeked out, attempting to pierce through the tree cover. Blaine was about to say something cheerful about the sunshine when he snagged something with his foot. He looked down to see that he had walked into a small vine strung across the trail, but before he could put all his thoughts together, a huge tree branch came swinging down onto the trail right toward him and Willy. Somehow, Willy managed to duck under the assaulting branch, but Blaine wasn't as lucky.

The branch hit the boy in the sternum with a force that knocked him off his feet and sent him tumbling backward down the trail. Blaine rolled to a painful stop, with the air completely knocked out of his lungs. Willy stood back up from his ducking position and began making his way toward Blaine to see if he was alright. As he did, his foot caught another carefully strung trip-wire vine, summoning another big swinging branch down toward the trail. Blaine tried to call out a warning, but he was still too breathless. The swinging branch smacked Willy hard in the back, catching him just below his backpack, and sending him sprawling directly toward Blaine. The young filmmaker, with camera in hand, smashed right into the twelve-year-old, knocking the breath out of Blaine a second time.

The two laid on the trail in a heap for a few moments until both were able to fully catch their breath again. "Well, mate." It was Willy who managed to speak first. "I guess Ralphy was right about Matty Mingo having some dangerous traps."

Blaine nodded in silent agreement, gingerly rubbing at his sore chest. The two picked themselves up and slowly continued up the trail, while being very careful to search with keen eyes for trip-wires. They spotted several, managing to step over them and avoiding any more powerfully swinging branches.

The forested trail turned to the right and then led down into a sort of ravine, with high walls of dirt, rock, and roots on either side. The two hikers followed the trail downward, still being careful to watch each footstep. Suddenly, a strange scraping sound reached their ears. They looked behind them, toward the mouth of the ravine. Blaine had never seen anything like it. In the trunks of about thirty or forty large trees, sliding doors were scraping open.

Blaine wondered if something was about to come out of the tree trunk doors, like maybe more rabbits, when his question was answered. Almost immediately, huge rocks started clunking down through the hollow trees and shooting out of the openings. Rock after large rock spilled out of the trees and started rolling down into the ravine right toward Willy and Blaine, like a stone tidal wave. The moving pile of tumbling rocks blocked the ravine's mouth, and the walls on either side of them were too steep to climb. So that only left one option—RUN!

Willy and Blaine turned and bolted down the steep trail, deeper into the ravine. Gravity and inertia propelled the rocks forward; they were gaining on the two. Even at the age of twelve, Blaine had already been chased by a lot of things, but never by a pile of rocks. His chest still hurt from getting bushwhacked and the backpack he was carrying was heavy, but he pushed forward, running as fast as he could. Willy ran, too, still holding the camera and getting this whole crazy experience on film. The rolling stones were continuing to gain on them, and in a matter of seconds, they would be crushed under an avalanche of rock.

Just then, Blaine felt his foot trip on another wire. "Fantastic," Blaine thought. "Just what you need when being chased by a pile of rocks—a giant tree branch to swing down and knock you into oblivion,"

Blaine braced himself for impact. He didn't know if he was going to get hit first from behind or from in front. He tried to shout out a warning to Willy, but he couldn't because he was . . . flying? And there was Willy right next to him, also floating up into the air. What was happening? Blaine managed to look down and see that both he and Willy were being pushed up into the air, out of the ravine, by a huge catapult-looking contraption. So they weren't flying; they were being catapulted up and out of the ravine! Evidently, the vine trip-wire Blaine had just run over was for this catapult, not another bushwhacker branch.

Just as the wall of rolling rocks crashed into the base of the catapult, the contraption thrust both of its riders out free into the air. Both soared through the air, ungracefully, with flailing arms and legs. The relief of not being crushed by the stones had been extremely short-lived. Now the emotion was dread from knowing that they would soon be landing from their flight. They soared up out of the ravine, over the ravine wall, and down into a pit on the other side. They both landed hard, so hard that all Blaine could see were stars.

"That was absolutely crazy, mate," Blaine heard Willy say.

Blaine thought that was quite an understatement. Slowly, Blaine's sight returned, but all he could see was brown. The pit they had landed in was a big and deep pit with high, unclimbable walls of dirt. Blaine felt around his body. Amazingly, he didn't seem to have any broken bones. He started to stand up to try and shake some of the dirt off himself, when he heard a rustling noise coming from a far dark corner of the pit. Blaine looked at Willy, who was sitting right next to him and had heard the sound too.

"What was that?" Blaine whispered.

"I don't know, mate," Willy answered, also whispering. "But whatever it is, it's alive."

Willy handed Blaine the camera, which was somehow not even scratched after all the rough and tumble they had taken it through.

"I'm going to go take a peek, mate," the curly blond-headed filmmaker stated.

He stood and slowly tiptoed into the shadows of the pit, toward the rustling noise. Blaine held the camera steady, unsure of where to point because all he could see was brown dirt and shadows. Blaine could hear Willy's footsteps, but then they fell silent. He could hear the rustling noises, but then it all fell silent. Blaine sat alone, in the dark pit, in complete silence for what seemed like forever. What had happened to Willy? What had been making the rustling noises? Why had it all fallen silent? Then, with an explosion of snorts and hooves, an animal with large antlers burst out of the shadows, heading right toward Blaine and the camera. The boy ducked down as the animal jumped over him. It reached the pit wall, kicked off of it with a couple hooves, and then bolted back off into the shadows

Willy Day then ran back into view with a look of joy on his face, shouting, "Did you see that, mate?"

"Yeah, what was that?" Blaine responded.

"That was a sambar deer, one of the largest deer in Asia. It belongs to the family of even-toed mammals that includes cows, pigs, and camels, among others."

Blaine picked himself up and followed Willy into the pit's shadows to try to get another glimpse of the deer. Willy continued giving information as they slowly walked, giving Blaine a chance to film the whole thing.

CLASSIFICATION: Mammal
NAME: Sambar Deer
FOOD: Herbivore
LOCATION: Australian Deciduous Forest

"The sambar deer is frequently hunted. It lives in woodland habitats and uses the trees and undergrowth for shelter, food, and protection. Its brown color helps it to blend into its surroundings, making it very hard to spot. Especially in, say, a brown pit. The young are typically covered with spots for camouflage as they hide in the brush for the first several weeks of their lives. The fawns come out only to feed."

The duo stopped as they saw the deer again, who was now just standing still, looking at the two. it knew there was no way out of the pit.

"How do you think he got in here?" Blaine asked as he took out his smartphone and snapped a quick picture.

"I guess he was trapped by a hunter or maybe he got catapulted in here just like we did, mate."

"Look at those antlers," uttered Blaine in awe. "Aren't those amazing?"

Willy nodded, smiling, and then continued to feed information into the camera for his documentary; "Each year, male deer grow new sets of antlers, adding one point for each year of growth. During breeding season, they use the antlers to fight with each other to determine who the herd's leader will be. As you can see, mate, they have slender muscular bodies with long thin legs, making them graceful and swift runners, which helps them to escape predators. They are very alert animals, with ears that can move to pinpoint a noise. They are plant eaters exclusively, preferring to graze on grass or eat the occasional leaves, twigs, shoots, flowers, or fruit."

Hearing about grazing made Blaine hungry. He didn't want to graze on grass or twigs, but some "hot maybe eggs" from Ethel's diner sounded pretty good right now. He wondered how they were going to get out of this pit. He wondered what Matty Mingo, the hermit, would do to them if he found them here. The chance of escape from this place seemed slim, but surely between him and Willy, they could figure something out. Just then, something slapped with a thud against the pit wall. It was a gnarly, braided rope, and it looked to be made out of vines. The two looked up to the brim of the pit and saw the bearded, smiling face of Ralphy Dingo.

"I knew you two blokes weren't listening to a word I said about the dangers of Mingo. I knew you were going to go and look for him," he said, chucking. "Now look what you've gotten yourselves into. Go on. Grab the rope. Pull yourselves out of there, mates. Let's haul that poor deer outta there, too, while we're at it."

Ralphy Dingo wasn't a very big man, but he was a very strong man. He managed to pull the deer and both young men out of the deep pit in a matter of minutes. The sambar deer bolted off into the forest, disappearing amongst the brown and green. He was glad to be free.

Blaine and Willy were also glad to be free from the pit, but that gladness faded when they heard an unfamiliar deep, gravelly voice say, "Back in the hole. All three of you!"

Blaine, Willy, and Ralphy all turned to see an old man with longer hair and dirtier clothes than even Ralphy. He was standing right behind them, holding some sort of string in his hands.

"Matty stinking Mingo!" Ralphy seethed in disgust, as he spat on the ground.

"Good to see you again, Ralphy," Matty responded sarcastically. "I see you haven't left my forest yet."

"It's not your forest," Ralphy retorted immediately. "It's mine. I was here first!"

"So you say, Old Man," Matty came back. "But the Mingos were here long before the Dingos!"

"Oh, rusty bucket!" Ralphy shouted. "The Dingos laid claim to these mountains at least a century before the Mingos came along."

Blaine and Willy just looked at each other with perplexed, squinted eyes, as the two old hermits argued on and on like small children. However, the argument came to a halting stop when Matty Mingo angrily said, "Oh, yeah, but I got something you don't have. I got dynamite!"

Mingo pulled out an old box of matches and Blaine suddenly realized the string Matty was holding wasn't a string at all; rather, it was a fuse.

"Dynamite?" asked Ralphy, stunned. "You wouldn't!"

"Oh, yes I would," said Matty Mingo, in his deep voice. "I know you have all your fancy frighteners strung up everywhere, making weird noises at night. But that is child's play, Dingo. My traps are better than your frighteners, and besides, my ancestors were gold miners. They left me an endless supply of the red boom sticks—enough to blow up this entire mountain range. This fuse I am holding now leads to just an introduction of the explosive power that I possess."

"You wouldn't," repeated Ralphy Dingo. "You wouldn't blow up our mountains, would you?"

"Well, now, that is the question of the moment, isn't it, mate?" Matty sneered, as he still held the fuse and the matches.

Breaking up the conversation with a dash of boldness, Blaine Sassafras stepped right in between the two Feuding Brown Mountain Hermits.

"Enough, you two!" shouted the boy. "No one is going to blow anything up. It's time to make peace. Willy, you have to tell Matty here what you know."

The two hermits were stunned into silence by Blaine's boldness, and Willy Day took the invitation to interject. "Matty Mingo, I know what happened to your great-great-grandfather, Mephibosheth Mingo in the 1860's," the young Australian filmmaker said to the fuse-wielding hermit. "I know about the sambar deer, and I know about the seventy-seven kilogram nugget of fool's gold. I know those incidents drove the Mingo family into solitude, and it seems that is all people want to remember your family by. But what almost everyone forgot is that great and praiseworthy cause that the Mingo family started and championed for Victoria. It was the Mingos who laid the first good roads in the province of Victoria, resulting in an influx of industry and trade that made Victoria one of the wealthiest and proudest provinces in all of Australia. If it wasn't for the Mingo family, many in Victoria would still be living in squalor."

THE SASSAFRAS SCIENCE ADVENTURES

Everyone now stared at Matty in anticipation, wondering if this revelation of truth about his family would defuse this explosive situation. The old hermit's wrinkled and dirty face looked emotionless, but then one tear formed in the corner of his eye, trickled over his eyelid, and cut a small stream there in the dirt on his cheek.

"I didn't think anybody would ever remember the roads," he whispered softly.

Matty dropped the fuse and threw the matches into the pit. He held out his hand in front of Ralphy. "Truce?" he questioned.

Ralphy Dingo just looked at Matty's hand, waiting there in mid-air for a handshake. Blaine and Willy both stepped back, hoping that Ralphy would accept the truce. The air was thick with anticipation.

After a few moments, Dingo relented. "Truce, and not only a truce," he added, shaking his ex-enemy's hand, "but also a friendship."

The two hermits smiled. They not only shook hands, but even hugged each other. Blaine was amazed how truth and forgiveness could wash away years of bitterness and quarrelling. Matty Mingo invited everyone to his dwelling, which was built just inside the entrance of a mineshaft.

That day, Ralphy Dingo and Matty Mingo became the Friendly Brown Mountain Hermits. Willy Day had gotten all the footage that he needed to complete a stellar documentary. And Blaine got all of his SCIDAT data entered into his smartphone. Now, it was time to see if the SCIDAT glitch had been fixed. It was time for the Sassafras twin to see if he could successfully reconnect with his sister. It was time to zip.

CHAPTER 13: TREKKING IN SICHUAN

Meeting Monkeys

The cracking and tearing sound changed to a rumbling and grumbling, as about fifty feet of the left side of the rock wall started crumbling down from the top. The rocks were coming down fast from the tall mountain and gaining more rocks and power as they came. The landslide would smash the girls with full force in seconds if they didn't move fast. Tashi pulled Tracey's arm, breaking her out of her staring daze, and the two girls sprinted up the road. If she was going to survive, this would have to be the fastest forty-yard-dash of Tracey's life. The Sassafras girl ran fast, almost as fast as Tashi, who managed to outrun Tracey, even in her long Tibetan skirt.

The avalanche of landsliding rocks was now almost upon them, as rocks free of the big mass began to rain down on the road all around them. They ran on in full sprint, knowing they couldn't stop, even if they thought they were far enough out of the way. With a deafening smash, the river of rocks washed across the small mountain road, crushing the pavement and flowing well onto the other side.

Tashi had made it out unscathed, but Tracey was hit by a rock about as big as a rugby ball. It just clipped her leg, sending her into a helicopter-type spin up into the air and then down onto the road. She landed in an awkward, twirling thud.

Rocks continued to rumble down, making the pile that lay across the road continually higher, deeper, and wider. Tracey had missed the full brunt of the landslide, but she was still in danger of the rolling stones. She had managed to remain cut- and scrape-free after her spinning collision, but as she went to stand up to continue her run to safety, she realized she couldn't. She had the biggest Charlie horse known to man.

Tashi Yidro saw her friend struggling and raced back to help her. The Tibetan girl threw one of Tracey's arms over her shoulders, and helped Tracey hobble quickly, out of harm's way.

The girls plopped down to their seats on the road only after they were well out of the way of the landslide. At this point, the big rocks finished falling, but small rocks continued to skip and slide down, adding to the top of the massive pile that now lay across the road like a mountain.

"Are you okay?" Tashi asked. "Did you get injured badly?"

Tracey was massaging her thigh where she had been hit by the rock. "No, not badly. It's just a Charlie horse."

"A Charlie horse?" Tashi questioned, not knowing that English phrase.

"Yes, a Charlie horse," Tracey responded. "Kind of like a big knot in your muscle. I'll be fine. I just need to walk it out. It will be sore, but I will be okay. Thank you so much for helping me."

"You are welcome, but I am so sorry this has been such a perilous journey," Tashi apologized.

"No problem, friend," Tracey said cheerfully. "Peril means adventure and adventure means fun, right?"

Both girls managed a laugh, as Tashi helped Tracey up so they could continue on up the road. Tracey limped pretty badly at first, but the longer she walked, the better her leg felt. The limp slowly started going away, and to make things even better, after less than an hour, they spotted a tractor pulling onto the road. It was full of smiling people in Tibetan clothing. As soon as the tractor load of people saw Tracey and Tashi, they waved for them to come and get in.

"We can ride with them!" Tashi said, happily. "Some of them are my neighbors. They will take us in the right direction."

The two girls walked over to the tractor and were helped up into the tractor bed by the happily chatting Tibetans. It wasn't a big vehicle. It had a small coughing engine in the front, one seat for the driver, and a small tractor bed for hauling. Today that bed was hauling a small crowd of people, a group of which Tracey was now glad to be a part.

The driver shouted something to Tashi over the noise of the engine, and Tashi responded in a language Tracey didn't understand. The driver then cranked the old machine into gear, and with a belch of black smoke, they began chugging up the mountain road.

"These neighbors of mine are field workers," Tashi told Tracey. "They will take us to the field they are going to harvest. The good news is that field is just one mountain over from my village. My sister and brother are both living on that mountain. My sister lives at the bottom and my brother lives at the top. I hope I get a chance to introduce you to both of them today."

Tracey smiled there on the back of the tractor as she sat, squashed among the friendly Tibetan field workers. Sure, Blaine wasn't here to experience all of this with her, but she was still having a blast.

He reached up and wiped away a bead of sweat from just above his eyebrow. He hadn't meant to start the landslide. Yes, he was trying to scare them half to death with the fireworks, but he wasn't trying to literally kill them. He had followed the girls when they were the only two who had decided to walk out instead of wait for a replacement bus. That had singled him out a bit too much, he thought, but he just hung back far enough on the road so they wouldn't recognize him or pay much attention to him. He knew where Tashi and her American friend were headed. So when he got the chance, he had taken a foot trail up the mountain to the left of the road—a shortcut to Tashi's village. He had been walking along the high ridge, watching them walk on the road far below, when he had accidentally stumbled over the rock that had started the landslide.

The landslide had nearly crushed the girls, and he felt sincerely sorry about that. But that still wasn't going to stop him from going through with his master plan. The fireworks in the Panda Reserve had been great, the fireworks on the bus had been even better, but the fireworks prank he had planned for tonight would be the greatest, by far. After Tashi and her friend made it home to her village and fell asleep along with all the other villagers, he was going to string, drape, and fill the entire village with fireworks. It would definitely scare them half to death and, in his opinion, it would be the greatest fireworks display of all time.

Right now, he just had to beat the girls to the village. He wanted to do so without him or his backpack full of explosives being seen. He had narrowly escaped being found out when the bus driver had started checking everyone's bags, as he made them get off the bus after the wreck. He had managed to carefully open the bus window, drop his bag outside, and then retrieve it after he got off the bus. That had been too close for comfort. Tonight, he could not have any close calls like that.

Now, he would hike to Tashi's village quickly, hide himself, and then wait for cover of darkness to execute his prank. He knew people would probably wonder why he was stalking Tashi Yidro with pranks like this. And he kind of wondered himself. But he liked her and thought she was the nicest and prettiest girl at his university, so this is how he was showing his affection, as strange as that may be.

The jostling, yet fun, tractor ride lasted for about half an hour, and then they arrived at the harvest field. Tracey jumped off the tractor, feeling great now that her Charlie horse was mostly gone. A Tibetan girl, who was already out in the field when they arrived, raised her hands and shouted for joy, as she ran toward the tractor.

"That is my sister," Tashi said, happily.

Tashi's sister came up and joyfully greeted Tashi, welcoming her back to the mountains. Tashi then introduced Tracey to her sister, using both English and Tibetan, so that everyone understood. Tashi's sister's name was Llamo and she warmly greeted Tracey. After a fun conversation with some translation, Tracey found out that Llamo and her fellow workers were harvesting wheat and barley, which they would then sell to vendors who would take it to the city. But Llamo was now free to hike up and over the mountain to the village with Tashi and Tracey. They also planned to stop and see their brother, who lived in the monastery at the top of the mountain, on the way to the village.

It was now mid-afternoon, and Tracey was wondering how long it would take for them to hike to the village. It was a sunny day, but the top of the rather large mountain they were about to trek over was hidden by low-lying clouds. The two Tibetan sisters assured Tracey that they would make it to the village in time for dinner. So off the three girls went, up a trail that started right there in the golden field of grain.

There wasn't an abundance of flat land out here in the mountains of Sichuan, so it was interesting to see how resourceful the Tibetan farmers were with their fields. The fields were carved by hand into the bottoms of the mountains, almost like giant stairs. It is absolutely beautiful, thought Tracey, as she hiked up through the many different levels of the network of cascading fields.

The girls hiked up along the series of switchbacks, gaining altitude as they went. Eventually they were up in the clouds. Tracey was breathing hard because of the strenuous hike and the high altitude, but Tashi and Llamo looked as though they were just taking a nice Sunday stroll through the park. They weren't taking any deep breaths, and there was not a bead of sweat anywhere on them. Tracey guessed that, since they grew up in this mountainous area, their bodies were used to the elevation.

As they hiked on, Tracey was also wondering how it was possible to build any kind of building up so high. The sisters had said they were going to visit their brother in a monastery. How did the people get all the building materials up the mountain to build the monastery? It was pretty amazing to think about.

Rather abruptly, the narrow dirt trail they were hiking turned into stone steps. Tashi, who was leading, turned and said, "These steps lead up to our brother's monastery. We are almost there, Tracey."

But Tashi's "almost" must not have meant what Tracey's 'almost' meant because, as Tracey looked up, she couldn't see an end to the stone staircase that kept going up, up, up. She certainly didn't see a monastery. All she saw were stairs disappearing into the clouds. She also saw an interesting-looking animal bounding around on some of the steps just ahead of them.

"Look!" Tracey said, pointing. "A monkey!"

Tashi and Llamo both gasped in delight.

"You are right, Tracey," Tashi said. "That is a golden-haired monkey, Sichuan's most prevalent primate, other than humans, of course. We get to see them up here by the monastery all the time because the monks like to feed them."

The monkey bounced around on the steps and then hopped off the stairway. He climbed a tree to the top and jumped from that tree over the stairs to another tree on the other side of the stairway. Then, he climbed down that tree and started bobbing around on the steps again. Tracey laughed as she thought, "What a peculiar and funny show of skill and energy."

The three girls kept walking up the stone steps closer to where the primate was. As they did, Tashi Yidro, who was proving to be a very capable zoology major and local expert, shared more information on the golden-haired monkey, "They get their names from the golden hair they have all around their heads. The reason we can see them up here in the mountains where the weather is often cold is because their fur is a bit thicker than many other primates. They are mammals, and very intelligent ones. The monkeys can hold things in their hands and even solve simple problems. As we just saw, those hands are strong and flexible, perfect for grasping tree branches, which makes them very good at climbing trees. Their long tails also help them with balance."

When the girls got too close for comfort, the monkey jumped off the steps and bounded back into the tree branches. That is when Tracey spotted a few more golden-haired monkeys, including some babies.

"Oh, look," she said, snapping a picture with her phone. "How cute!"

Tashi and Llamo agreed and showed so with "oohs" and "aahs" of their own. "They live in troops of up to two hundred animals in the summer," Tashi said. "But only twenty to thirty in the winter. The males can weigh up to twenty pounds, while females are closer to thirteen pounds. Their babies are usually born from March to June, after a gestation of about six months."

CLASSIFICATION: Mammal
NAME: Golden-Haired Monkey
FOOD: Herbivore
LOCATION: China

Llamo opened the bag that she had been carrying and pulled out some small oranges. She set them down on the stone steps, as she motioned for the monkeys to come down out of the trees and get the fruit. The monkeys jumped around and made some hoots and howls like they were debating the decision, but none of them came down.

"Golden-haired monkeys are herbivores, and their primary source of food is lichens," Tashi explained. "But they will also eat tree bark, leaves, flowers, and fruit when they have the chance."

Llamo continued to call, but the monkeys didn't come down to the stairway to grab the oranges. At least not until the girls continued on up the steps away from the small stack of fruit. After that, a whole group of the monkeys scrambled down from their places in the trees. They fought over and gobbled up the oranges. Tracey giggled at the funny primates as they continued their journey higher into the clouds.

Her giggling soon turned to labored breathing because of the ever present high altitude. But altitude or no altitude, Tracey

Sassafras would trek on, following her Tibetan friends.

Moving in with the Mice

Then, there it was, at the top of the forever staircase: the monastery. It stood on the very tip top of the cloud-shrouded mountain. It was a rather big structure, made with stones and held together with dirt mortar. It was painted in a blood red color and had a dirty, ornate, golden roof. There was a big stone wall surrounding the monastery, and the staircase they were now almost finished climbing led to the one gate that led through that wall. Without even stopping for breath, Tashi and Llamo walked right through the gate and into the courtyard, happily chattering in their native tongue.

Tracey followed them in, and what Tracey saw in the courtyard was not at all what she expected to see in the courtyard of a mountain top monastery. There were monks in their traditional robes playing a game of basketball! They had two baskets and a full court. They were playing what looked like a real game, complete with one monk serving as a referee. There was also a full crowd of cheering fans, all of whom were monks themselves. Tracey couldn't believe it. First of all, how did they have the lung capacity at this altitude to run full speed on a basketball court, and secondly, weren't monasteries supposed to be quiet and serene? This place looked more like a bustling schoolyard than the grounds of a monastery.

Tracey smiled as she watched a tall bald-headed monk hit a long arching fade-away jumper from behind the three-point-line, his robes flapping in the wind. The crowd cheered. There were even monks watching from the second floor windows of the monastery, and evidently one of those monks was Tashi and Llamo's brother. When he spotted the girls, he excitedly waved and motioned that he was coming down to meet them.

"That was our brother," Tashi told Tracey happily. "He is going to hike down to the village with us. His name is Norbu."

Tracey was happy to meet the girls' brother, Norbu, but she was even happier that Tashi had just said the word "down." She didn't know if she could have walked any more in the up direction. Norbu emerged from the doorway of the monastery and hurried up to the girls with a smile on his face. He had a plastic sack full of soda cans and was holding a smartphone of his own. He held out his other hand to greet Tracey.

"Hello," he said in English. "Nice to meet you!"

"Nice to meet you, too," Tracey responded. "Your sisters told me you are going to hike down to the village with us."

Norbu just looked at Tracey with an awkward smile on his face, and then began laughing, his sisters joining him. Tracey just stood there perplexed, wondering why the three were laughing.

"Tracey," Tashi said through giggles. "I am so sorry. The only thing my brother can say in English is, 'Hello, nice to meet you.'"

"That explains the awkward smile on Norbu's face," Tracey thought as she joined her friends in laughter. Norbu said something to Tashi in Tibetan and then pulled a can of soda out of the sack and handed it to Tracey. He also held up his smartphone, but then put it in his pocket.

As the Sassafras took the can, she thanked him, while Tashi translated, "He said you look thirsty, so you should drink something. He also said he would let you surf the internet if you wanted to use his phone, but the monastery's Wi-Fi isn't working right now."

"Basketball, soda, and Wi-Fi," Tracey thought as she opened the can. "Not what I expected at all, to see on top of this mountain."

Tashi, Llamo, and Norbu all had sodas as well, before the four left the monastery courtyard and started down a trail on the opposite side of the mountain from where they had hiked up. It was already starting to get dark, so Tracey was relieved when Tashi pointed out that you could already see their village in the valley down below. They still had a way to go, but they were now going down, which was much faster than going up.

So down, down, down they went on the dirt trail. Within an hour, they had already reached the outskirts of the village, but it was almost dark outside. Tracey could see spots of dim light coming from the windows of the two- or three-dozen houses nestled together in a clump in one of the few flat spots in the valley.

The houses were small, but each of them was three stories tall. They were made out of stone held together with dirt mortar, just like the monastery had been, but they weren't painted. On the other hand, the trim was painted in a beautiful mixture of black, white and red. The windows were especially interesting, because even though they were built in the standard rectangle shape, the black paint around them made the windows look like trapezoids.

Tracey followed the three siblings down a tight little lane through the cozy village. On either side of the lane, firewood was stacked up as high as a tall basketball-playing monk, serving as a kind of fence for each house. They cut to the left, walked a few yards, and then cut back to the right. Then Llamo, who was leading, reached out and pushed open a gate as Tashi turned to Tracey. "We are home," she announced, smiling from ear to ear.

They walked up a stone path and then stepped through a doorway; the huge wooden door was already standing open. On the first floor, the room they stepped into was completely dark and smelled somewhat suspect. Tracey thought this seemed very strange, and then to add to the strangeness, she heard some snorting coming from somewhere in the dark room.

Tashi, who must have been sensing Tracey's confusion, said to Tracey, "The first floor is where the animals live. We have two pigs down here now that you can probably hear and smell. But don't worry, friend. Carefully follow me to the stairs."

Tracey put her hand on Tashi's shoulder and followed her

to a steep staircase that Llamo and Norbu were already walking up. As they began to carefully climb the narrow steps, Tashi continued. "On the second floor, we have a kitchen and a living area where we eat dinner. Then on the third floor, we have several bedrooms where you can sleep tonight."

When they made it to the second floor, the four stepped into a large room that was being illuminated by one single bare light bulb. A very old looking lady, with a smile on her face that looked like it was held there permanently by all the wrinkles, stood up from the small stool she had been sitting on near the stove. She shouted joyful salutations in Tibetan.

"This is our mother," Tashi said. "We call her Amala."

Amala greeted her three children by pinching their cheeks and poking at their stomachs as if she thought they looked too skinny and might be on the brink of starvation. Though she hadn't been formally introduced to Tracey, she did the same to the twelve-year-old girl. Tracey smiled an awkward smile as the beautiful old wrinkled lady grabbed at her face and poked her stomach. Amala beckoned for all her children and Tracey to sit down next to the stove. Then, she immediately started rummaging around the room, grabbing different items Tracey assumed would be mixed together and cooked for supper.

Tracey looked around the simple yet ornate room. There weren't many items in the room other than the black iron, wood-burning stove, the stools, and a hodgepodge mix of antique cooking pots and utensils. Yet, contrasting that simplicity, every wall was covered with brightly colored Tibetan-style paintings. Tracey was glad the house had a stove and that they were sitting around it, because even though it was summer, it got pretty cold up here in the mountains at night.

Amala continued to scurry around, and started throwing ingredients into a huge wok that was sitting on the stove right in front of them. "I can't wait for you to try Amala's cooking," Tashi exclaimed. "I hope you like it!"

It looked like Amala was making a sort of soup. Whatever it was, it smelled very strange and looked even stranger. Tracey hadn't been able to recognize anything that had gone into that wok yet, but Tracey's Tibetan hosts were being so kind and hospitable that there was no way she was going to offend them by not eating whatever they put in front of her.

Suddenly, Tracey felt something run across her foot. She squeaked and picked her feet up off the ground quickly. She looked down just in time to see a long tail slip into a small hole in the wall. Tashi laughed at Tracey's reaction.

"It was a mouse," she said. "We have a lot of them in the house because we don't believe in harming them. Do they bother you?"

Tracey thought that should have been an obvious answer. But she kept a straight face as she squeaked out, "Maybe a little bit."

"Mice can have ten litters per year, with up to twelve babies per litter. They are all over the place in our village. We mostly see them at night, though."

Now Tracey couldn't stop looking at that small hole in the wall, as Tashi continued, wondering if that mouse or one of its babies was going to dart out and run over her foot again.

"Did you know that baby mice are born hairless, blind, and without ears, so they are completely helpless for the first few days? After two weeks they can leave the nest and I'm sure there are many nest hidden in the walls of our house."

That was not what Tracey wanted to hear.

"Mice are found all over the world and are the most numerous and diverse group of mammals on the planet," Tashi continued. "They are rodents with long tails and sharp front teeth. They eat seeds, grain, fruit, insects, and sometimes human food, so they are considered omnivores."

THE SASSAFRAS SCIENCE ADVENTURES

There it was again! The mouse darted out of the hole, ran over Tracey's foot again and then down into a crack in the floorboards. Tracey gasped and all her muscles tensed up. She had been somewhat expecting the mouse to pop out again this time, and she knew she needed a photo for her SCIDAT app, so she managed to snap a quick picture.

Tashi acted as if it was nothing out of the ordinary as she continued giving information on the little furry scurries. "Mice have a good sense of sight, hearing, and smell, as well as highly sensitive whiskers for finding their way in the dark. Oh! And I almost forgot to tell you that their teeth grow constantly, so they must continually gnaw at things to keep them from getting too long."

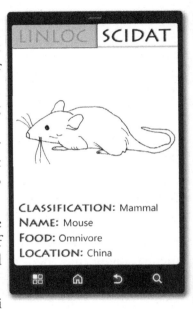

CLASSIFICATION: Mammal
NAME: Mouse
FOOD: Omnivore
LOCATION: China

Just then, Amala came over and dished out a bowl full of whatever was in the wok and handed it to Tracey.

"Are you hungry?" Tashi asked.

Tracey looked at the strange smelling bowl of floating things as she thought about hairless baby mice and gnawing teeth. She then replied in the most gracious voice possible, "Yes, I am. Thank you so much."

Then, with all four of her Tibetan friends watching her in anticipation, she put a big bite in her mouth.

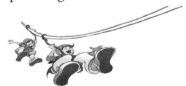

THE SASSAFRAS SCIENCE ADVENTURES

It was time. It was dark enough now that everyone in the village was inside. Not a soul was outside. The work was finished for the day, and they were all now gathered around stoves eating dinner or watching TV, if they had one. It was time. Time to set this splendid plan into motion. If he had calculated correctly, he had saved enough fireworks to string them on or around every house in the village. He, of course, had saved the biggest and brightest for Tashi's house. If he timed it correctly, the explosions would start about the time everyone was going to bed. It was going to be amazing and they were all completely unaware of what was coming. He quietly stepped out of the outhouse he had been hiding in and began his task.

Tracey somehow made it through the entire meal without gagging. These were some of the loveliest people she had ever met, but the food was not her favorite. Though she was now done with her bowl of soup, she was still not sure exactly what it was that she had eaten. She was now sipping a cup of what Tashi had called "yak butter tea," but it didn't taste like tea at all to her. More like liquid buttered popcorn, if that were possible. She was finding out that there was no hope of actually finishing the cup of tea, because every time she took even the smallest sip, Amala would fill her cup back up to the brim.

Though the cuisine was difficult, the relationships were not. Tracey was having so much fun listening to Tashi, Llamo, Norbu, and Amala laugh and talk. Tashi kindly translated almost everything for Tracey so that she felt included. It was a nice visit.

After a couple of hours of fun, it was time to go to bed. Tashi walked with Tracey up to the third floor, using a flashlight to light their way. She showed her the room that she would be sleeping in. It was a small room with dirt walls, a bare timber ceiling, and a pile of animal fur blankets. Tracey's first thought after Tashi said good night, gave her the flashlight, and headed back downstairs, was to wonder how many mice nests there were in the room. The Sassafras was so tired, though, that she snuggled down into the blankets and tried to go to sleep.

It had been another long day and she now had all the data she needed to enter into SCIDAT app from this leg. Hopefully, once she did, she would be reunited with Blaine. First, she needed to get a good night of sleep. She was so tired that even the thought of mice gnawing on things and scurrying over her wouldn't prevent sleep from coming. Eventually exhaustion prevailed, and her eyes began to shut.

"Wait! What was that?" Tracey shot back awake. A loud strange sound filled the entire village. Tracey's mind raced, "Was that the sound of fireworks or landslide? Or was it something else even worse?"

CHAPTER 14: ARCTIC ADVENTURES

Arctic Reunion

As Blaine let his calibrated carabiner snap shut and felt the next invisible zip line go taught, the thing that was on his mind was reuniting with his twin sister. Sure, he'd had an exciting time in the Brown Mountain Forest making a film with Willy Day, but science face-to-face just wasn't fun without Tracey. So now he hoped they could get past whatever glitch had thrown them off onto different courses and reunite.

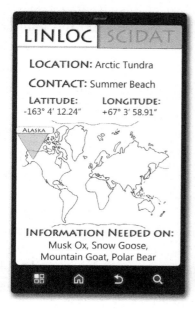

He had been careful to enter all the correct data and pictures into SCIDAT. LINLOC had told him that his next destination was the arctic tundra of Alaska—Longitude +67° 3' 58.91", Latitude -163° 4' 12.24". Next thing he knew, he was zipping there now at the speed of light towards his destination. The local expert that he was supposed to find was named Summer Beach and the next round of animals were the musk ox, snow goose, mountain goat, and polar bear. However, more than finding the expert or the animals, Blaine wanted to find Tracey.

The Sassafras boy came to a jerking stop as the zip-lining concluded. He slumped to the ground to wait for strength and sight. He sure hoped Uncle Cecil and President Lincoln were right about this glitch being overcome-able.

It was a loud sound and a familiar sound that now filled the small Tibetan village. Tracey jumped up from the pile of animal fur blankets, clicked on her borrowed flashlight, and made her way down the dark stairs. Tashi was there to meet her on the second floor.

"Is that sound what I think it is?" Tracey asked her friend.

"That depends on what you think it is," Tashi replied, sounding a little worried. "I have lived in this village since I was a little girl. I have heard this sound before, but never this loud or intense. What does it sound like to you?"

"It sounds like dogs barking," supposed Tracey. "But not just a few dogs. Lots and lots of dogs, and they sound extra mad. What do you think is going on?"

"I don't know," answered Tashi. "We should go and find out."

The two girls, along with Llamo, Norbu, and Amala, made their way out of the house and toward the sound of the barking dogs. Their flashlights shone circles of light on the wood-lined footpath, but they also illuminated something else. There were strings and strings of fireworks draped all over everything. The fireworks were on the stacks of wood lining the path, every gate they passed, and even on all of the houses. Tracey now had two questions racing through her mind.

"Why were all the dogs barking? Why were all the fireworks there? Had the Man With No Eyebrows followed her all the way out here to Tashi's village?"

Within a few minutes, the five of them reached the center

of the village where the loud sound of barking was coming from; seemingly all dogs in the village were barking angrily at the top of their lungs. Every person from the village seemed to be here now, and they were all pointing their flashlights at the object causing all of the barking. There, in the middle of the village, a boy was clinging to the top of a statue that stood there. The statue wasn't very tall, but it was just tall enough to keep the trembling boy out of the reach of all the angry dogs. A couple of the men from the village were shouting things over the noise of the dogs to the boy. Tracey couldn't tell if they were accusing him or trying to help him. She looked over at Tashi just as the girl gasped.

"I know that boy," she said. "He is one of my classmates at the university."

The men continued to yell as the boy began to answer. Thankfully, Tashi translated for Tracey.

"They are asking him why he climbed on top of the statue . . . He is saying it's because the dogs were chasing him . . . 'Why were the dogs chasing you?' the men are asking . . . 'Because of the fireworks,' he says. 'I am the one who put up all the fireworks.'"

"Wait a second," Tracey thought. "It was this boy, Tashi's college classmate, who had strung up all the fireworks here, not the Man With No Eyebrows?"

Tracey wondered if he had also set off the fireworks on the bus and at the Panda Reserve. The men, who now seemed as angry as the dogs, continued to question the young man.

"They asked him why he put fireworks up all over the village . . . He answered that it was because he likes . . . ," Tashi didn't finish her sentence.

"Likes what?" Tracey asked.

"He said it is because he likes Tashi Yidro."

Tracey's mouth dropped open. Why would Tashi's classmate string fireworks all over her village if he liked her? Boys were so weird. One of the men who had been questioning the boy walked over to Tashi. He asked her several questions and Tashi nodded. The man then pointed at the dogs, then at the boy, then back at the dogs. Tashi reached up, grabbed the man's arm and shook her head, answering whatever his question had been with a bold "No!"

The man immediately turned, shouting some instructions to his fellow villagers, who proceeded to wrangle up all the barking dogs. The noise died down, as every villager slowly left and every dog was taken away, leaving the boy alone with an audience of only Tashi, her friend, and her family. Even though all the dogs were now gone, he was still clinging to the top of the statue in fear.

Tashi walked over to the statue with her brother Norbu. She spoke some kind sounding words to the boy. Then, she and Norbu helped him down. Tracey walked with the Tibetan family as they led the boy back to their house. She watched as they gave him a warm dinner and a place to sleep for the night.

Tracey slept okay that night, considering her disdain for mice and her nagging curiosity as to what exactly Tashi had said that saved the boy from the villagers and their dogs.

In the morning, over another steaming cup of yak butter tea, Tracey found out that the answer was quite simple. The man had come over and asked Tashi if she knew the boy. When she had confirmed that she knew him, the man asked her if they should let the dogs teach the boy a lesson as punishment for his devious behavior. Tashi had said "no," and then added that they should forgive him. The village had agreed, and away they all left with their barking dogs, leaving the forgiven boy alone with Tashi and her family.

Tashi's classmate sat with them here now, huddled around the stove as he sipped butter tea. He had confessed to all the firework incidents from the previous day and asked for forgiveness. Tashi and her family had pardoned him for all of it.

With the closure of her adventure here in Sichuan, Tracey

had reconnecting with Blaine at the forefront of her mind. She had entered all the SCIDAT data and pictures, and now it was time to see if the glitch that had sent her and her brother to different locations was fixed.

She walked upstairs to the third floor and opened the LINLOC app. The arctic tundra of Alaska was the next location listed. The Sassafras girl put on her harness and calibrated her carabiner.

"Alaska, here I come," she said aloud. "I hope that's where you are, too, Blaine." Then away Tracey zipped at the speed of light.

As the white light slowly faded into color, Blaine saw that his view didn't actually change that much because he had just landed in a big field that was covered with a fresh dusting of snow. Not only did he not see Tracey, he didn't see much of anything.

So far, they had landed on, in, or near something, but what was this place? What was this field? It had to be at least a mile wide in every direction. He did see quite a few trees and mountains in the distance, but they weren't close. How was he supposed to run into a local expert out in the middle of this field in the middle of nowhere?

Suddenly, the ground opened up and swallowed Blaine. He felt himself falling into darkness, but then landed with a thud on something metallic or maybe hard plastic. Something about this felt oddly familiar to Blaine as he began sliding downward on some sort of underground slide. It was a spiral slide, and he found himself cork-screwing down deeper into the earth. Then, up ahead, he saw light, and he was sliding right toward it. He reached the end of the slide and flew right off, careening into a nicely cushioned landing area.

Blaine rolled to a soft stop, then picked himself up and looked around. If he wasn't mistaken, he was in some kind of underground science lab, reminiscent of Uncle Cecil's basement—except this was no old basement. This was a pristine, cutting-edge, state of the art science lab. It seemed to have much of the same kinds of things that Cecil had in his basement, except this place was clean, neat, and organized. Everything was encased with a slick black or white finish. There were specimens displayed in beautifully lit tubes in the center of the room. There were liquids of different colors, flowing in perfectly equidistant tubes running the length of the ceiling and then down pillars to somewhere under the floor. There were egg-shaped doors, built right into the walls, seemingly with no hinges or knobs. There were several translucent floor to ceiling touch-screens with data and pictures. What was this place? How did it get built underneath the middle of a field in Alaska? And who lived here or who operated this place?

These were all questions buzzing through Blaine's mind as one of the egg-shaped doors made an electronic sound and began to slowly open. Before the door even opened all the way, a slender,

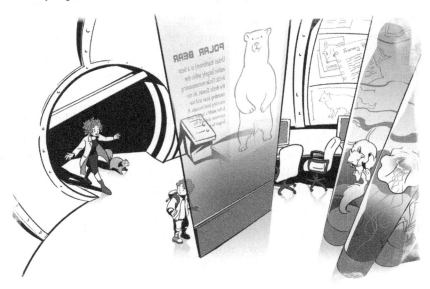

frizzy, blond-headed woman in a paint-spattered lab coat ducked through the opening and ran toward Blaine with her arms outstretched.

"Blaine Sassafras!" she shouted in joy. "You are finally here!"

Blaine was dumbfounded, as the woman ran over and nearly tackled him in a hug. How did she know who he was? Was this . . .

"I'm Summer Beach!" the woman said, interrupting Blaine's thoughts. "And I get to be your local expert at this location! Sweet mustard and ham on rye! Isn't that exciting?"

"Where is Tracey?" he managed to get out among Summer's joyous hello celebration.

"She is on her way!" Summer giggled. "As a matter of fact, she should be arriving in a few short seconds!"

Tracey was pretty sure she had just landed in snow. Not deep snow, but snow nonetheless. As her vision came, her suspicions were confirmed. She had landed in a huge empty field powdered in snow. She stood up as her strength returned, and her first thought was a discouraged one: "Well, I guess we didn't beat the glitch. I've landed in the middle of nowhere and Blaine isn't anywhere to be seen."

She might have continued in that line of thought if the ground hadn't suddenly opened and swallowed her up. She was falling through the darkness and then she was sliding through the darkness on a spiral slide. Hadn't something like this already happened once this summer? She slid down through the darkness toward a growing light, left the slide, and flew through the opening in a somersaulting tumble, landing in a well-padded landing area.

She hopped up and was greeted by a happy, familiar face and an even happier unfamiliar face.

"Tracey Sassafras!" said the pretty, but frazzled-looking, woman that Tracey didn't know. The woman then proceeded to run over and wrap up Tracey in a huge, happy, dancing hug. As Tracey awkwardly hugged the woman, she saw Blaine's smiling face over the woman's shoulder. She couldn't tell if he was laughing because he was happy to see her again, or if he was laughing because he knew something about this woman that she didn't, or maybe it was both. Regardless, they had overcome the glitch and were now reunited.

The woman eventually let go, and Tracey ran over to her brother to give him a hug. Blaine thought she was coming to give him a high-five, so Tracey was met with an accidental slap in the face, which didn't really hurt. They laughed, and the twins were back together.

"This is our local expert, Summer Beach," Blaine said, introducing his sister to the hyperactive woman.

"Sweet tuna salad on wheat!" Summer exclaimed. "I am so glad you are here and that the two of you are together again, and that now all four of us are together!"

"All four of us?" thought the twins. They had only counted three. Just then, Tracey saw something small and brown skitter across the floor and her muscles tensed up. Was it another mouse, like in Tashi's house? Blaine saw it, too, and was equally shocked. Then, there it was again, scurrying across another section of the floor. It climbed up a table leg and just sat on the tabletop and looked at them.

"What is that?" Blaine asked, alarmed.

"Not what is that," replied Summer, smiling. "But who is that? That is Ulysses S. Grant, my capable lab assistant and resident inventor. Not Ulysses S. Grant the eighteenth President of the United States, but Ulysses S. Grant, the *Spermophilus parryii*, or, as we would say in non-scientific language, Ulysses S. Grant, the arctic ground squirrel."

"Ulysses S. Grant, the arctic ground squirrel?" Tracey asked.

"Who serves as your lab assistant and resident inventor?" Blaine asked, adding to Tracey's question.

"One and the same," Summer pronounced, beaming.

The twins didn't even need to have a conversation to know that they were both thinking the same thing—their local expert here in Alaska was like a girl version of Uncle Cecil. Plus, she already knew them. How did she know them? Also, she had been expecting them. Did she know about the invisible zip lines?

Summer walked over to the table, picked up Ulysses S. Grant, and put him on her shoulder. She looked at the twins with a very kind look on her face, like she knew what the twins were thinking.

"Cecil forgot to tell you, didn't he?"

Blaine and Tracey just shrugged, sincerely not sure if their uncle had forgotten anything or not.

"Cecil and I are friends," Summer explained. "We used to go to school together. We were classmates all the way through junior high and high school. We both loved science, so we were in a lot of classes together. I was pretty good at science, but Cecil was always the smartest in the class—and the most handsome, I might add." She paused before she added, unabashedly, "Cecil Sassafras, what a dream boat!"

The twins had to laugh a little about this last statement. Their Uncle Cecil may be a lot of things, but dreamboat wasn't one of them. Apparently, though, Summer Beach would disagree with them on that.

THE SASSAFRAS SCIENCE ADVENTURES

Animals in a Flash

"Your Uncle Cecil and I have kept in touch with each other over the years," the quirky scientist said, continuing. "Even when I moved here, to the arctic tundra, to take this science station job. Cecil knows about all the projects that Ulysses S. Grant and I are working on out here, and we also keep up with all that he and President Lincoln are working on in the basement. I was especially excited when they started the invisible zip line project."

At this, Summer actually jumped up and down. "Sweet corned beef and hash on pumpernickel!" she shared, enthusiastically. "Just the thought of traveling around the globe at the speed of light and experiencing science face-to-face! Wow! So cool!"

The twins knew that if this was the first time that they heard this line, they would have thought this happy lady in front of them was a lunatic, but since they had already experienced the zip lines for themselves, they had to agree—it was so cool. Summer moved so quickly around as she continued talking that the twins were surprised that Ulysses, the arctic ground squirrel, was able to hang on to her shoulder.

"Then, when Cecil told me that his niece and nephew were going to come visit him this summer and that he was going to put them on the lines and send them around the world to see science face to face, I was so excited! Then, when he asked me to be one of the experts, I almost lost my head! And now you two are finally here! I almost can't stand it, I'm so happy." Summer took a break from talking and hugged the twins.

Then she continued. "Cecil has been keeping me updated on your status. I even have a tracking board of my own, here in the lab."

Summer walked the twins over and showed them one of the translucent floor-to-ceiling data screens. Sure enough, there was a world map with illuminated lines to and from all the location they had already been.

"The two of you have been doing such a good job entering your SCIDAT data," Summer said. "You have been listening to your local experts and getting all of the information texted into your phones by memory. I have been so impressed! And man, the adventures you guys have been having! Sweet banana, honey, and peanut butter on white, they have been amazing!"

Though she was a little hyperactive, Blaine and Tracey really liked Summer Beach. They agreed with what she had just said—their adventures, thus far, had been amazing.

"We are going to do something a little different, though, here in the arctic tundra," Summer said, walking over to another one of the see-through screens. "Here, in my lab, we have the ability to upload the SCIDAT data on the animals directly from my computer system, straight to your phones! Isn't that exciting?!? Now, I don't want to rob you of any adventure, so we will still go out and take the actual pictures of the animals in their natural habitat, but all of the other data you will get right here on this screen."

Summer moved her fingers quickly across the almost invisible touch screen and brought up information on the musk ox. She read aloud what was written there on the screen.

"Musk oxen can be found in Alaska, Canada, and Greenland. Due to over-hunting, they were once wiped out of Alaska and Northwestern Canada, but they were re-introduced into parts of Alaska in 1935 and have since thrived. The musk ox is a herbivore related to sheep and goats. In the summer, it feeds on grass, lichens, and moss, but in the winter, it feeds on arctic willows. It has a thick shaggy coat to protect it from the cold. Its long outer layers of coarse hair protect them from snow and rain, while its thick, dense under fur keeps it very warm. Alaska now has several musk ox farms, where their wool is collected and used to make winter clothing.

"The males emit a heavy odor, called musk, to attract females for mating and to mark their territory. They will also charge into each other until one of the males gives up for the right to breed with a certain female. Females give birth to one calf after an eight to nine months gestation period. Amazingly, the calves can keep up with the herd after only a few hours of life, and will begin eating grass after two months.

"Adult oxen will gather together in a defensive huddle when threatened. Every adult will stand with its back to the center of the huddle and its horns facing toward the attacker, which makes for a formidable sight."

When Summer finished reading, she tapped around some more on the screen until she reached a tab giving her the option to send. She looked at the twins and smiled.

"Here it comes!" she said, as giddy as a school-girl.

She tapped "Send" and immediately Blaine and Tracey both felt their smart phones vibrate as the musk ox information uploaded directly into their SCIDAT apps.

"Well, that was much easier than hanging over a pit of cobras," Tracey said.

"Or cleaning out chicken coops," Blaine added.

"Don't worry, you two," Summer said, as she lifted her eyebrows up and down quickly. "I have a surprise for you that is sure to fill your adventure sails with wind, but first let's go ahead and find and upload the data on snow geese."

She whipped her fingers around the screen some more and quickly brought up a file.

"Snow geese belong to the family of water birds known as waterfowl." Summer read aloud. "They spend more time on land than ducks and swans do. The geese do have two webbed feet and a boat-shaped body that enables them to swim well when they need to. Snow geese travel in large family groups called flocks. They travel together to look for food and warn each other of weather and predators with a loud honking call. They migrate from the Gulf of Mexico to the arctic every summer."

Summer continued. "Geese are generally larger than ducks and have much longer necks. They are herbivores that eat grass, marsh plants, and grains. A goose uses its broad bill to grip and rip grasses and plants. It also has a sharp 'tooth' on the side of its beak that it uses for tearing the toughest stalks. A mother snow goose will build her nest on an area of high ground, using plant matter and feathers. She will lay three to five eggs and then incubate them for twenty-two to twenty-five days before they hatch. Baby geese are called 'goslings'. Within a few hours of birth they can swim, walk, and find food." As Summer finished reading, she again started spontaneously jumping around again.

"I just love it!" she said. "I love science! I love the animals of the Arctic! And I love you guys! This is so fun!"

She again found the "Send" tab on her screen and pushed it, sending all the information on snow geese directly to Blaine's and Tracey's SCIDAT apps. Their phones both vibrated in confirmation.

"OK! Now I am so tempted to get out and see the animals immediately!" Summer exclaimed, as Ulysses S. Grant jumped off her shoulder to a nearby desk. "Especially since we have more hours of sunlight here in Alaska than all the other places you have been so far, but it is late. The two of you probably need to get some rest. How have you guys been dealing with the sonic lag?"

The twins just looked at each other and shrugged. Neither of them had any idea what sonic lag was.

"Oh, I guess that's another thing Cecil forgot to tell you about. Oh, he is debonair, but he is also absent-minded. Sonic lag is a more extreme version of jet lag. For instance, when you fly on an airplane to a different time zone, the time difference throws your body's inner clock off a bit. However, the two of you have not been using airplanes to travel. You've been going at the speed of light. So, for you, it's almost more like time travel than airline travel. For example, when you two go to sleep here in a few minutes, it will be your second time to sleep tonight."

Blaine and Tracey were baffled at the news of this. Summer could see that, and she continued her explanation.

"Tracey, you were just in China, and China is sixteen hours ahead of Alaska's time. Blaine, you were just in Australia, and Australia's time is nineteen hours ahead of here. So it's already tomorrow in China and Australia, but it's still yesterday here."

The twins still didn't really get it. Maybe it was because they were so tired, or maybe it was the sonic lag messing with their bodies' inner clocks. Regardless, they were both happy about the prospect of a little sleep. Summer could tell the twins weren't going to grasp this concept right now, so she changed the subject.

"I think you guys are going to love the sleeping pods that Ulysses S. Grant designed. They are so cozy and comfortable. I know you will be so rested when you wake up tomorrow."

Ulysses S. Grant nudged a small button on the wall, and a small compartment opened up that was filled with nuts.

"Ulysses!" Summer said in a not very believable scolding tone. "How rude! The least you could do is show Cecil's niece and nephew their sleeping pods before you think about your stomach! Sorry guys," she said, apologizing to Blaine and Tracey.

"He is indeed a squirrel, so he loves nuts as well as berries, moss, and lichens. He keeps his food hidden in compartments around the lab. I'm not sure why. I guess it just reminds him of how he lines his burrow with food for the winter. He has a funny work schedule. He hibernates in his burrow all winter, snuggled up in his musk ox fur blanket. So we don't see him for several months but, man, he really goes at it in the summertime! Anyway, let me show you the sleeping pods." Summer led the twins across the lab, as Ulysses continued to feed his face.

The scientist pushed two sleek buttons on the wall, and immediately two of the egg-shaped doors began to open up. The two entrances each revealed a very small room, just big enough to fit one bed, but the one bed that was in each was the most comfortable-looking mattress that either twin had seen in quite a while. Summer could see that both children were happy, so without saying anything else, she just left them to it.

Blaine and Tracey weren't sure how long they slept, but one thing they did know is that when they woke up, it was the most rested they had been since they had gotten on that bus to go to Uncle Cecil's house. At about the same time, they came stumbling out of their egg-shaped pods. Ulysses S. Grant was right there on the floor to greet them. He bumped another place on the smooth wall, popping open another hidden compartment. This one was filled with what looked like trail mix. Blaine was hungry and took the squirrel's gesture as an invitation to breakfast. He reached in the compartment, grabbed a handful, and stuffed it in his mouth.

"Is it good?" Tracey asked.

Blaine nodded, not even attempting to say anything with his mouth so full. Tracey grabbed a handful as well and munched away.

Summer appeared with bounces and smiles, just a few minutes later, entering from one of the doors. "Well? How did you guys sleep?"

"Fantastic," the twins said in unison.

"Those sleeping pods are pretty magnificent, are they not? And I see that Ulysses shared his breakfast with you," Summer said, as she spotted crumbs everywhere.

She pushed a button and several holes along the baseboards opened up, and a hidden vacuum sucked all the crumbs into the holes. Summer smiled as she could tell the Sassafrases were impressed.

"That's one of the ways we keep the lab so clean. The vacuum system is yet another one of Ulysses S. Grant's inventions, but if you think that's great, you should see something else that he invented! Sweet black olives and meatballs on a hoagie! Follow me and I'll show you!"

Summer exited the lab through the same egg-shaped door she'd entered from. This doorway led to a long hallway, also shaped like an egg. Neat lights ran horizontally the distance of the hallway. Every so often, there would be a door or a button, but this hallway was leading straight to somewhere, and the twins soon found out where that was. They came out of the hallway into a very big dome-shaped room, and there in the middle of the room on a big red-and-white-checkered circle, was a helicopter.

"Ulysses S. Grant invented the helicopter?" Blaine blurted out, totally shocked.

"No, of course not," Summer responded.

Tracey closed her eyes and shook her head, embarrassed for her brother. Summer laughed.

"This isn't a helicopter. It does look like a helicopter and it operates like a helicopter, but it is twice as fast as a helicopter. It's a heli-quick-ter."

"A heliquickter?" the twins asked.

"Yep, a heliquickter," Summer confirmed. She then clasped her hands and began jumping in place. "So, are you two ready to go see some arctic animals?"

The twins answered by climbing on board. A few moments later, the heliquickter's blades were spinning, the domed roof was opening up to a clear blue sky, and Blaine and Tracey were suited up in heliquickter gear, complete with helmets that had built-in headsets. They were listening to Summer speak to them over the headsets as she carefully handled the heliquickter's cyclic control stick, lifting it slowly off of the red and white landing pad, out through the roof, and up into the Alaskan sky.

"I know this heliquickter is no light-speed zip line, but it does enable us to fly all around Alaska really quickly. The plan today is to fly first over a musk ox farm, then down to a place called Cook Inlet to see some snow geese. After that, we will head up north to see if we can find some polar bears and mountain goats. Have your smart phones ready, you two, and let's get some great pictures!!"

CLASSIFICATION: Mammal
NAME: Musk Ox
FOOD: Herbivore
LOCATION: Arctic Tundra

Then, off they went, chopping over Alaska at a very high rate of speed. Within minutes, the twins spotted a whole herd of musk oxen. Summer slowed the heliquickter down and sort of hovered over the herd. This was a fun vantage point to view the animals. The twins hadn't experienced this yet and both got good pictures. They gave Summer the thumbs up, and then off they went again, in search of some snow geese.

"Alaska is so green. What a beautiful place!" Tracey thought as they flew just over the treetops. In contrast, she knew there would be snow when they headed north.

In no time, they reached Cook Inlet, and sure enough, there were flocks and flocks of snow geese. Summer lowered the heliquickter down near the banks of the water, where she had seen several nests, but as she did, a whole bunch of geese took off as a group, flying into the air. Summer followed behind them, and soon they were flying at the same speed and height as the birds, almost like their heliquickter was part of the flock.

Blaine and Tracey were able to get some great mid-air, in-flight pictures of the snow goose. The twins were loving this. The animals here in the arctic were totally cool, Summer was crazy but cool, and this heliquickter that Ulysses S. Grant had invented was awesome. They liked how it could hover in one spot or fly as fast as a bullet. With the data for both the musk ox and the snow goose now successfully entered into SCIDAT, the trio flew north in search of the next two animals. The twins knew this leg of their travels was going great. What they didn't know is that they were headed directly into a storm.

LINLOC **SCIDAT**

CLASSIFICATION: Bird
NAME: Snow Goose
FOOD: Herbivore
LOCATION: Arctic Tundra

CHAPTER 15: SPLIT UP BY THE STORM

Summer Storms

"While rare, they do happen!" Summer Beach shouted through the headsets. "Especially the further north you get, but a summer arctic storm this big has totally caught me off guard!"

The twins hung on as Summer jostled around with the heliquickter's controls. The big flying machine rose and fell in an alarming fashion as blasts of wind and snow whipped it around in the sky.

"Much of Alaska is considered to be taiga, which is a moist sub-arctic forest dominated by coniferous trees. Also plentiful are lichens, mosses, and some grasses. It has super cold winters, with lots of snowfall. Half of the year, the taiga has temperatures below freezing. The summers are usually rainy and humid, but evidently, we are far enough north into the tundra to get blasted by an arctic storm," Summer explained.

Just then, the biggest windblast yet smacked into the heliquickter and sent it into a flailing spiral. The entire control panel went haywire, with gauge lights flashing on and off, and needles dancing around like windblown reeds. The doors on both sides of where the twins were sitting suddenly ripped open, inviting in gusts and swirls of cold white wind. Summer was doing an admirable job of attempting control over the aircraft; she was remaining fairly calm, especially for her impulsive self, but nothing seemed to be helping.

She was still shouting to the twins through the headsets, but her voice was breaking up. "Blaine and Tra . . . parachutes . . . und . . . seats . . . jump out and . . . the . . . or . . . blades will cut right through . . . OK?"

The heliquickter continued to roll and pitch. A crash at

this point seemed inevitable. Tracey, who deciphered the broken message more quickly than her brother, rapidly undid her seat belt, got down, and ripped up her seat. She found a parachute stored there and she slipped it on, securing the pack around her torso. Blaine, who had the words, "blades will cut right through" echoing through his mind, shook himself from frozen disbelief and quickly followed in the steps of his sister.

Suddenly, the heliquickter began a plummet straight toward the white earth below, just as Blaine lifted his seat. He saw his parachute, but just as he reached for it, the heliquickter jolted to the right and flung the Sassafras boy right out of the open door. Blaine's body disappeared, falling into a fog of snowy white.

Tracey couldn't believe what she had just seen. She screamed at Summer through the shaking haze, but the scientist couldn't hear her and the headsets were evidently totally inoperable at this point.

Summer pulled back on the stick, and suddenly the heliquickter had its first real burst of power since they had been hit by the storm. They shot back up higher into the sky, pounding through the storm nose first. Frantically, Tracey tried to get Summer's attention to let her know about Blaine, but she could barely hold on, much less move up to the front where Summer was.

She shouted into her headset, "Blaine fell out! Blaine fell out!" But Summer couldn't hear her.

Higher and higher they went up into the sky. So high that Tracey thought at any moment they might burst out of the clouds and into the sunshine on top of the storm. Then, with a disheartening beep, the entire control panel went dark and dead. The heliquickter stalled at its apex, and its blades completely stopped spinning. It began a free fall plummet through the storm straight toward the earth. Summer looked back at Tracey with fear in her eyes.

Tracey still couldn't hear Summer, but she could read her screaming lips. "Jump! Tracey, jump!"

Tracey did not want to jump; this was sheer peril. Yes, she had ridden invisible zip lines at the speed of light, but this was not the same carefully calculated travel. This was parachuting out of a free-falling aircraft, but the Sassafras girl knew she had to do it. She looked at Summer Beach, who was frantically punching around at the control panel, trying to restore life.

Tracey supposed this was the last time she would ever see the energetic and friendly scientist. Then, without any more hesitation, the twelve-year-old dove right out of the open door into the arctic storm. She managed to avoid getting hit by any part of the falling heliquickter as she soared out into the sky. As soon as she could, she pulled the cord and out came the chute. It immediately filled with air and jerked Tracey up, stopping her inertia.

She was now at the mercy of the storm, as wind and snow tore across her face and body. It whipped her parachute around like an autumn leaf. Thinking about poor Summer and the heliquickter, Tracey listened for an explosion, but never heard one. Maybe because all she could hear was blustery gusts of wind. She had no idea how close she was to landing as she floated down because the ground, at present, was just as white as the sky. Down, down, down she went until finally she landed with a cold, hard thud in a huge bed of snow. Her chute fluttered down and draped over the top of her.

Tracey just sat there in disbelief. She was sad, exhilarated, and mad all at the same time. She was sad because she had just lost Summer. She was exhilarated because she had just lived through the escape of a plummeting aircraft. She was mad because she had lost her brother again, and now she was all alone.

Summer had been so nice and was already beginning to feel familiar because of her connection to Uncle Cecil, and now she was gone. Plus, Tracey had just been reunited with Blaine. They hadn't even had a real chance to tell each other about their respective experiences in China and Australia, and now they were already separated again. By the way Blaine fell out of the heliquickter, she assumed she would never see him again, either. Tracey began to cry. Was she the only one still alive?

Snow kept falling and began to cover her parachute, which was covering her, as the Sassafras family motto kicked that negative thoughts out of her brain. "I am a Sassafras," Tracey declared out loud. "And a Sassafras never quits."

Tracey picked herself up out of her would-be ice tomb and gathered up her parachute. She pulled out her smartphone and opened the compass application. Then, with the determination that only a Sassafras knows, she headed north in search of the next animal.

Eventually, the storm let up and the snow stopped falling. Tracey found herself walking across the flat white barren arctic tundra. The vast nothingness made the battle against loneliness that much harder. She trekked on, taking one difficult step after the next, in shin-deep snow. Tracey scanned the horizon for any movement or any sign of life, though it was hard to tell exactly where the horizon was because the sky and the ground looked so much alike.

The storm had stopped, but the wind was still blowing. It swept across the tundra with an eerie, almost silent whistle, relentlessly pounding at Tracey's frame. This was the first time this summer that Tracey had been truly alone. She had been separated from Blaine but had been with Tashi, her local expert. But now there was no Blaine, no expert, no color, no landscape. Just Tracey and the windblown white.

Wait, what was that? Tracey still only saw white, but now part of the white in front of her was moving. She stopped and squinted, trying to see better. Yes, that was definitely movement. She glanced down right in front of her in the snow and saw a huge paw print. She looked back toward the white movement and now recognized animal fur. She then saw a black nose, two eyes and a mouth. Tracey's heart soared. She had found a polar bear!

But then Tracey's heart sank. She had found a polar bear. She was alone in the arctic tundra, face to face with a polar bear. If the bear decided to attack, there was nowhere to run; there was no safe place to hide. Panic attempted to rise up and choke her, but she squelched it. She had to be brave.

She didn't know how she was going to get all of the needed SCIDAT data without a local expert helping her, but she could at least try to get a photograph. She held up her phone and snapped a picture. Tracey looked at the snapshot to make sure you could make out the bear amongst all the white. To her relief, you could.

Tracey began to back away from the huge mammal, when suddenly, the polar bear rose up on its two hind legs and made a loud roaring noise. Tracey shuddered and fell backwards into the snow. The polar bear came down to all fours and began a charge straight toward her.

"Really!" Tracey thought. "Could today get any worse?"

THE SASSAFRAS SCIENCE ADVENTURES

She had lost her brother again. She had lost her local expert. Now she was being charged by one of the largest carnivores on earth, with no place to hide. She knew she was about to die. She just hoped it would happen as quickly and as painlessly as possible. The wind blew. The polar bear charged. And Tracey just closed her eyes.

Within seconds, she was hit full force. Her body flew up in the air and then landed with a thud on a pile of fur. Now she was moving. Moving at a very fast pace. She was riding something. She was riding the pile of fur. Tracey slowly opened her eyes expecting to see white fur and probably some teeth or claws, but that is not what she saw. The fur was brown. And it was attached to some kind of wooden frame. It was a fur blanket, attached to a . . . sled?

She heard what sounded like a thousand footsteps, coupled with determined panting. She looked up and over the frame and saw that she was being pulled on a dogsled by a pack of sprinting huskies.

She looked behind her and saw that a tall stone-faced man was driving the sled. He looked down at her, acknowledged that she was there, and then looked straight ahead again. He was covered from head to toe in some kind of very warm-looking animal skin clothing. The only thing not covered was his face, which was wrinkled and leathery. A huge dagger hung from a belt around the man's waist, but, other than that, he seemed to not have any more supplies or equipment. There was just one man, his knife, his sled, his dogs, and now a rescued twelve-year-old girl.

Tracey looked out into the tundra and spotted the polar bear again. It was now far away, and this dogsled was going fast. She was safe, but where was she going now?

THE SASSAFRAS SCIENCE ADVENTURES

The landing was so much softer than he had expected it to be. Falling from a heliquickter, one would expect to land hard and dead. But as Blaine hit the ground, it felt more like he was landing on a mound of snowy pillows than on hard earth. But when he hit, he didn't stop. He was now sliding at a fast, crazy pace down the side of a mountain.

Blaine tried to gain some kind of control over his careening body. It proved to be difficult, but eventually he did. That is, right before he fell into a huge crevasse. He landed hard but kept sliding, because again he had landed on a slant. He was now on ice, not snow, sliding down a curvy natural ice slide, zipping through the under regions of a glacier.

Blaine had no idea where this slide was going, but wherever that was, it was going there fast. The walls of the slide turned from white to dark as he slid down deeper into the glacier away from the surface. He reached out with his hands and pushed out with his feet, trying to stop himself, but it was of no use. He was going too fast and the ice slide was just too steep. He was now sliding through complete frozen darkness. Blaine braced himself, not knowing when the underground slide was going to come to a crashing stop.

When he saw it—light was up ahead. He was going to make it out after all. He shot out of the icy tunnel slide, like a cannonball, and landed in a huge snowdrift. Blaine lay there for a moment, glad that he had finally come to a stop. Then, he slowly crawled out of the hole he had just created. At this point, the storm seemed to be letting up a bit, and Blaine could see that he was still on the side of a big mountain.

His thoughts turned elsewhere. What happened to Tracey and Summer? Had the heliquickter gone down? Had the girls survived? Abruptly, Blaine's thoughts were broken off by another voice.

"That was totally sick, dude!" Blaine looked around but didn't see anyone. "Up here, man. Above the ice cave you just blasted out of!"

Blaine looked up on top of the tunnel exit. And there, standing on a little snowy ledge, with a snowboard attached to his feet, was a young man. He was decked out in snowboarding gear—hat, goggles, coat, gloves, pants, and boots. And on all of his gear was the word "Hirebro."

"What up, man?" he said. "I am Brooks Hirebro, professional snowboarder and entrepreneur, and I have seen a lot of wicked cool stuff in my day, but you sliding down through that glacier was the coolest thing I've ever seen. Totally sick, bro! What's your name, man?"

"Um, Blaine. Blaine Sassafras."

"Dude, Blaine, you must be an adventureholic! Is that what brings you up here into the mountains? Adventure?"

"Well, kind of," Blaine answered. "But actually, I'm looking for polar bears and mountain goats."

"Polar bears and mountain goats? No kidding? I can't help you with any polar bears, but I just saw a whole herd of mountain goats on a rocky outcropping about four hundred yards that way," said Brooks, pointing off toward the west. He slung off his backpack and unzipped it.

"Here you go, dude," he said, throwing Blaine a pair of Hirebro snowshoes. "If we hoof it, I bet you they will still be there."

Within minutes, Blaine was walking behind Brooks, who was carrying his snowboard and now also had on a pair of snowshoes. They walked toward the out-cropping where the snowboarder had seen the mountain goats. It amazed Blaine how much easier it was to walk on snow wearing snowshoes instead of regular shoes. As they trudged, Brooks offered the Sassafras more information about himself.

"Yeah, dude, I'm only twenty-two years old, but I've already started my own company to feed my own adventure addiction. My company's name is Hirebro, just like my last name. Our slogan is 'Adventure Fuel.' We make anything and everything that fuels adventure. Pretty sick, huh, bro?"

"Pretty sick," Blaine answered.

"There, dude, look!" Brooks said, stopping and pointing.

Blaine looked and, sure enough, several yards in front of them, huddled on and around a rocky place on the mountainside, was a herd of a couple dozen goats or so. Blaine reached in his backpack for his smartphone so he could take a picture, but he couldn't find it.

"What? Where did it go?" Blaine said aloud.

He checked all of his pockets and then re-checked his backpack, but his phone was nowhere to be found.

"What's wrong, man?" Brooks asked.

"I can't find my phone," Blaine said, disgusted. "Now I can't take a picture of the goats."

Here Blaine was, on the side of a snowy mountain. Separated from his sister again. With no phone and no local expert. How was he supposed to get the SCIDAT data?

"What am I supposed to do now?" Blaine asked

"No worries, dude," Brooks said. He reached into his own pockets and pulled out his own smartphone. "I'll just take a picture for you, then you can send me your phone number, and I'll send the picture to you."

"Sick. Thanks, man!" was Blaine's relieved response.

Brooks Hirebro snapped a nice close-up picture of one of the mountain goats and showed it to Blaine. He nodded his approval.

"All right, dude. Now you gotta check this out!" Brooks said, getting very excited.

THE SASSAFRAS SCIENCE ADVENTURES

He opened up his backpack again. This time, he pulled out what looked like a snowboard that was cut in half.

"What's that?" Blaine asked.

"It's the first folding snowboard, dude!" Brooks happily showed it off.

He folded it out, revealing that it was indeed a full snowboard. It had nice small hinges and locked open tightly, leaving a perfectly waxed, smooth bottom.

"It's perfect for packing, and it rides just as nice as a regular snowboard. Hirebro is going to reveal this bad boy to the world this coming ski season. It will be in stores everywhere! But I will let you take it for a spin right now! What do you say, man?"

Blaine stood there for a second thinking. His main desire and priority now was to find his sister, Summer, and the heliquickter. He didn't know if he could afford to take the time to go snowboarding with Brooks. But then again, he wasn't even sure which direction to go, so down this mountain was as good a place as any to start.

"Sure, Brooks," Blaine responded, taking the folding snowboard from the professional. "I'll try this bad boy out."

Very excited that he had someone to try out his new product, Brooks handed Blaine a pair of boots that clicked securely into the folding snowboard. Then, he got back on his own board. Blaine got his boots clicked in, took a deep breath, and pointed the nose of the board downhill.

"You do know how to snowboard, right dude?" Brooks asked.

Blaine nodded yes. The twelve-year-old had never actually snowboarded, but he had been sledding with his family, but only down a short hill. This was pretty much the same thing, right?

"All right then, dude!" Brooks said with a big smile on his

face. "Let's do this!"

The pro-boarder jumped up into a one hundred eighty degree spin, landed back on the snow, and started his downhill run. Blaine thought that looked cool, so he tried it too. But he only managed about a ninety degree jump, and then he landed sideways on his board. He tumbled head over heels a couple of times, before he somehow managed to land back on his board in the correct fashion. He found himself going downhill . . . fast.

He looked down the mountain in front of him to see Brooks doing all kinds of jumps, spins, and tricks, but it was all Blaine could do to simply stand up on the board without falling down. He was now going so fast that he knew any kind of crash would hurt, so he began to maneuver his back foot toe-side to heel-side, heel-side to toe-side, causing the back of the snowboard to act like a kind of rudder.

"Wow, that was nice!" Blaine thought. "You can actually steer this thing." He coasted on down the mountain now at a little more of a manageable speed.

Brooks Hirebro continued to amaze Blaine up in front. He treated the slope more like a playground than a snowy mountain. Blaine saw that Brooks was speeding right toward a huge drop-off. Instead of stopping or swerving around, the boarder just soared right off of the edge and did a series of spins and jumps, before landing safely back in fresh powdery snow.

The Sassafras didn't even entertain the idea of trying the same stunt, so he steered around the rocky drop-off and continued boarding down at a decent pace. Eventually, the slope started to flatten out, and Blaine saw something up ahead that made his heart soar. It was the heliquickter! So Summer had somehow managed to save the craft from crashing!

Now he was going to be back with Tracey. Summer could help them with the rest of the SCIDAT data, and all would be well. Blaine finished his mountain run, stopping right near the heliquickter. Brooks had already taken off his board and was climbing into the heliquickter's open door. Blaine followed close behind him and was glad to see the smiling Summer again, but where was Tracey?

Blaine put one of the radio equipped helmets on and heard that Summer was already talking to him.

"Blaine! Oh, Blaine! I am so glad you're okay! When you fell out in the storm, I thought we may never see you again."

"I'm glad to see you too, Summer, but where is Tracey?"

Summer's face lost its smile for a second. "She parachuted out somewhere on the other side of this mountain range. I hope we can find her."

Blaine's heart tried to sink, but he decided not to let it. Yes, he and Tracey were separated again, but this time it was only by a mountain range. They would find his sister; he was sure of it.

"Blaine," Summer said, interrupting his thoughts. "I'm glad you met my friend, Brooks Hirebro. We often see him up here in the arctic circle in the summer time when most of the snow in other places has melted."

Brooks just nodded and gave Summer a fist bump.

"Now, let's go find Tracey!" the scientist said, using the control stick to lift the heliquickter off the ground.

Blaine glanced up at the aircraft's control panel. Everything seemed to be working properly. He hoped so. He really didn't feel like riding in a heliquickter-gone-haywire again. Blaine just happened to put his hand down between the crack in the seats, and what did he feel but his smartphone! It had somehow fallen out of his pocket and managed to make it through the whole plummeting aircraft thing without falling out. He held it up and showed it to Brooks, who gave him a thumbs-up, confirming that he remembered about sending Blaine the picture of the mountain goat. Summer took the hovering machine up over the mountains. Though the heliquickter had the ability to go very fast, she flew it rather slowly this time. All three riders kept their eyes peeled for the female Sassafras.

Searching for a Sassafras

Tracey clutched the warm animal skin blankets tightly as the sled cruised on. They had been on flat tundra for a while, but they were now well up into the snowy mountains on a narrow trail. Tracey glanced up at the driver's face again. He still hadn't said a single word. He just kept his gaze straight ahead, focused on their course.

Tracey wondered if he was an Inuit. The dogs mushed on, pulling and running without any hint of stopping. The trail wound up the mountain, leading through the white woods and around big jagged rocks. At one point, because of the density of the trees, the path spit them out of the forest and onto a rocky ledge. Now there was snow covered foliage on one side and a huge icy drop-off on the other side. Tracey still had her parachute, but it wouldn't matter if the sled went over the cliff.

Though Tracey hadn't heard the driver speak, she somehow already trusted him. There was something very calming about his demeanor. The huskies pulled the sled along the high precarious trail, like they'd done it a thousand times before. Tracey was actually really enjoying her current mode of transportation. It was almost like she was getting her own personal sleigh ride, but then, up ahead, she saw something that made all of the pleasant feelings go away.

An old, large, rotten tree had evidently had enough. Maybe

it was the years of hanging onto the mountainside or maybe it was the current weight of the snow it was holding. It had decided now was the time to topple over, and it was falling down right in front of them. Tracey screeched, certain that the dogs were going to get smashed by the huge falling tree.

Instead, what happened was the huskies dodged the falling timber by turning suddenly to the right straight toward the drop-off. The tree crashed on the path. The dogs pulled the sled to the edge as the driver cranked on the reins. Tracey closed her eyes and waited. Were they falling?

She opened her eyes again, and all she saw was open space under the sled. The dogs had somehow slipped around the fallen tree and were still on the snowy trail, their collective legs churning for all they were worth. The dogs huffed, puffed, hauled, and pulled, using all the strength they had. To Tracey's relief, they somehow managed to pull the dangling sled back up onto the path. Tracey gasped and then exhaled in relief. She looked back at the driver, whose face remained completely unchanged. On up the trail they went, as if nothing out of the ordinary had happened. The trail led them back into the woods and then into a mountaintop clearing.

What Tracey saw there took her breath away. There, sitting on a flat spot in the middle of the clearing, was Summer Beach's heliquickter. And who was standing beside it but Summer Beach herself, as well as Blaine, along with a guy she didn't recognize. How was this possible? How did Blaine survive his fall? How did Summer keep the heliquickter from crashing? The need for her questions to be answered paled in comparison to her desire for a reunion.

The quiet driver took the sled right up to the heliquickter and then stopped. Tracey stumbled off the sled and went straight up and hugged her brother.

"I'm so glad you're alive! I thought you were dead."

Blaine didn't say anything. He just hugged her back.

THE SASSAFRAS SCIENCE ADVENTURES

Not even an hour later, Summer Beach was safely landing the heliquickter back on the red and white landing pad down in the underground dome-shaped room. During their ride, Tracey had been amazed to hear how Summer had managed to resuscitate the heliquickter's power and pull it up out of its nose dive. She was also wowed by Blaine's story of falling out, landing on the mountain, sliding through the glacier, encountering the mountain goats, and then snowboarding down to safety. Tracey had recounted her story of parachuting blindly into the blizzard, her tough hike across the tundra, her run-in with the polar bear, and her whole dog-sledding experience. Blaine had spotted Tracey on the dogsled from the air, and that is how Summer knew to land the heliquickter and wait in the clearing, where she knew the trail would lead.

It turned out that Summer also knew the dogsled driver. He was an Inuit named Yotimo. Summer had thanked him for saving her friend. Yotimo had simply nodded and then rode off into the snow. They had dropped the professional snowboarder, Brooks Hirebro, back off on the top of a mountain so he could get another run in, and now here they were back in Summer's lab.

The Sassafras twins still hadn't heard each other's stories about Australia and China, but they planned to recap those stories after they got all of their SCIDAT data entered for this leg. The twins followed the rejuvenated and bouncy Summer down the long egg-shaped hallway back toward the lab.

"Sweet tuna fish and ranch on crackers!" Summer said. "I'm so glad you guys are both okay! Now we can keep this adventure going and keep the science coming. You two are unstoppable!"

They reached the lab and Summer walked right over to one of the translucent floor-to-ceiling data screens. She slid her fingers around a bit and brought up information on polar bears. Blaine and Tracey both pulled out their smartphones. Blaine was still relieved that he hadn't lost his phone; that would have been a tragedy. Brooks had already sent him the picture of the mountain goat, so that gave the twins all four pictures they needed for this leg. They had the SCIDAT info on the musk ox and the snow goose, which Summer had given them before the heliquickter ride. Now, Summer was about to give them their remaining information.

This was easy, getting the SCIDAT data sent straight to their phones. But both twins had decided they preferred having the local experts with them, talking through the animals as they saw them.

"Polar bears are the world's largest meat-eating animal," Summer relayed by reading the information on the screen. "They are found only in arctic regions of Alaska, Canada, Russia, Norway, and Greenland. They typically live alone, except during breeding season, when they travel south to feed on salmon. They are excellent hunters, eating mainly seals, but also fish, geese, and ducks."

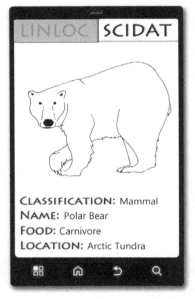

CLASSIFICATION: Mammal
NAME: Polar Bear
FOOD: Carnivore
LOCATION: Arctic Tundra

"And almost Sassafras," Tracey thought, shuddering as she remembered her scary encounter with the large carnivore.

"Polar bears are excellent swimmers," continued Summer, "because their large furry feet make good paddles. They live mainly on ice flows, so they occasionally need to swim from one ice patch to another. They can swim for up to twenty-five miles. Polar bears are the only northern bears that don't hibernate in the winter."

Summer paused and looked over at the twins, asking "Did you guys know that hibernation is a state of rest or deep sleep that some animals do to avoid the cold winter?"

Blaine and Tracey smiled as they responded in unison, "No,

but we do now!"

Summer laughed and then read on, "However, polar bear females do hibernate in dens when they are pregnant to give birth. Polar babies are about the size of a rat when born. They weigh less than two pounds at birth but grow quickly. After several months in the den, they venture out for the first time with their mother, but they stay with her for up to two years. Polar bears have a thick oily coat of white fur and a layer of fat, or blubber, that protects them from temperatures that are below freezing. Their hair is hollow, so it can trap heat like a greenhouse. Also, an oily substance on their fur makes it waterproof." She stopped and did one of her now-familiar happy dances in place.

The twins really liked her, but they wondered what Uncle Cecil thought about her. The exuberant scientist sent the polar bear information to the twins' phones and then flipped around on the screen until she found information on mountain goats.

She started reading, "The mountain goats of Alaska are one of two all-white, hoofed species in Alaska. They are often confused with the Dall sheep, but mountain goats' horns are short and black. Goats belong to the cattle family. Males are called 'billies,' females are called 'nannies,' and their young are called 'kids.' Mountain goats are hardy climbers that can survive some of the highest mountains. They are found all across the northern hemisphere in cold mountainous places. They have split hooves with hard edges and soft centers that act like suction cups and gives them stability on slippery rocks."

LINLOC **SCIDAT**

CLASSIFICATION: Mammal
NAME: Mountain Goat
FOOD: Herbivore
LOCATION: Arctic Tundra

Blaine thought about the

group of goats he'd seen way up on the snowy mountain, standing comfortably on that rocky out-cropping like they were standing on flat ground. He chuckled to himself, thinking about how cool it would be to have suction cup feet.

"The Mountain goat has a long, shaggy winter coat that blocks out the cold." Summer continued reading. "Around June, it sheds its winter coat and is left with a soft summer coat that grows into a full winter coat by the time the season comes around again. Mountain goats are herbivores that feed on grasses and plants, but they will eat almost any plant matter to survive, including trees and shrubs. Some goats have been domesticated and are used for their wool, milk, and meat."

Summer finished reading the information and then quickly found the "Send" tab to upload it wirelessly to the Sassafrases' phones.

"OK, Blaine and Tracey, now your SCIDAT data is complete for the arctic leg!" the scientist declared, excitedly.

The twins poked around on their phones and got all of the data and pictures sent in to Cecil's basement. They then opened up their LINLOC apps.

"What's the next location?" Summer asked, with wide eyes and a huge smile.

CHAPTER 16: A DIP IN THE OCEAN

Promising Penguins

Light rushed across their faces and through their hair. They were still so amazed that this was actually happening. That their crazy yet amicable Uncle Cecil, with the help of a prairie dog, had really invented these invisible zip lines. At this point, Camp Zipfire was but a dot in their memories and science was becoming a friend. They were learning, and it was fun. They were going to cool places all over the world, and they were making great friends along the way. Their most recent local expert had been fantastic. They had really liked Summer Beach and her arctic ground squirrel, Ulysses S. Grant. Plus, it had been nice to meet someone who already sort of knew them.

They had just left her cool underground lab after completing their SCIDAT data for the arctic leg and catching each other up on their separate adventures in Australia and China. Now, they were soaring through places at the speed of light, excited about going to their next location, which LINLOC said was South Georgia Island—Latitude -37° 2' 45.23", Longitude -54° 37' 17.00". Their local expert's name was James Q. McScruffy, and they would be seeking information on king penguins, codfish, blue whales, and squid.

They braced for the anticipated landing, but this time,

instead of landing with a jerk, they landed with a splash. The shock of going from being enveloped in light to being enveloped in freezing cold water was almost overwhelming. What had happened? Had the LINLOC longitude and latitude numbers been off a bit? They had never landed in water before.

Both twins held their breath and struggled to get to the surface, which proved to be next to impossible because they were still blind and weak from the zip line travel. Blaine tried to pull with his arms and kick with his feet, but he just didn't have enough strength yet. He felt his body sinking deeper into the icy cold water. Tracey was also trying for all that she was worth to swing to the surface, but she just couldn't. The freezing, numbing water didn't help. The twins both felt like their lungs were about to explode. Their strength slowly began to return, but would it come to them quickly enough?

Blaine let the last bit of remaining air out of his lungs, causing a few bubbles to come out of his mouth. Then he gave a big kick with his legs. It worked! His legs moved, his strength had returned! He frantically clawed his hands and arms at the water and kept kicking his legs, swimming upward. How far beneath the water was he? He opened his eyes. The zip line light was gone, but he could still see nothing but murky water. He couldn't tell how far he had to go to reach the surface.

Tracey also found that her strength and sight had returned. She was also ripping through the water, trying to reach the surface. At practically the same time, both twins' heads came exploding out of the water. They opened their mouths wide, gasping for much-needed breath.

"Men overboard!" they heard someone call loudly. And then again, "Men overboard!"

Almost immediately, two life rings slapped down in the water close to where the Sassafrases were. They both managed to swim over and grab a ring. Blaine and Tracey both just hung on as they were pulled up into a big steel boat, but what was happening? Blaine was feeling very light-headed as several strong arms pulled him safely from the ring to the boat. The last thing that Blaine remembered before slipping into unconsciousness was seeing the name, *Scot's Folly III*, written on the boat.

"Hypothermia," was the first thing Blaine heard as he began slowly regaining consciousness.

"Hypothermia," Blaine thought. "Doesn't that mean something about your body being too cold? But I feel so warm."

He opened his eyes and saw that he was wrapped in blankets and was sitting by a small space heater in some kind of cabin.

"Ahhh, that-a boy," he heard a kind voice say.

He looked toward the door and saw a big strong man, dressed in a navy-blue uniform of some kind topped off with a stocking cap, smiling at him.

"Blaine! You're awake!" he heard a more familiar voice say

from right beside him. He looked up and saw that Tracey, too, was wrapped up in blankets and sitting by the space heater.

"Nice to meet you, Blaine," the uniformed man said. "My name is William Atwater. I'm the First Mate on this vessel, and I was just telling your sister here that, amazingly enough after your spill in the water, neither of you seems to have suffered hypothermia. A minor miracle, considering how frigid the water is down here in the South Atlantic."

"Why did I black out?" Blaine asked.

William stepped forward and took his own seat on the opposite side of the glowing orange space heater. "Well, though it doesn't look like you have hypothermia, your body still suffered a traumatic experience. So, both you and Tracey blacked out. Luckily, we managed to get you aboard before you lost your grip on the life rings. Which I thank you for, because I really didn't want to have to jump in after you." The First Mate chuckled, smiled a kind grin, and changed the subject. "So, are the two of you excited about seeing the penguins tomorrow?"

Blaine and Tracey both nodded that they were. "We are not only excited about seeing them, but also about learning about them." Tracey added, "I guess James Q. McScruffy is kind of an expert on the penguins and other animals in the area?"

William Atwater frowned and laughed at the same time. "You mean Captain McScruffy? Yes, I suppose he is an expert about anything that floats on, lives near, or swims under the water, but good luck getting any of that knowledge out of him. He is my Captain. He is a good man, and I respect him; but he is a gruff old sailor, and he's not one for much conversation."

The twins looked at each other with worried glances. This didn't sound very promising. Atwater took his stocking cap off, scratched the top of his head, and then put his hat back on.

"I have learned a couple of secrets in my years of working

with the old man," the First Mate offered. "He doesn't offer up information on any of the animals he knows about, but he is also a mumbler. If you can get close enough to him when he spots an animal, he will talk all about it under his breath, spouting off information like water from a whale's blow hole. He just can't help it, but it will be a real challenge getting close enough to the Captain to hear him. He has this thing about personal space."

Blaine and Tracey looked at each other again, huddled there in their blankets. This one was going to be challenging.

"The second trick I have learned is grape soda," Atwater continued.

"Grape soda?" the twins asked, confused.

"Yes. Grape soda. That old sailor likes grape soda like a mermaid loves the sea. If you can get him to drink enough grape soda, he will yap your ear off. It'll be all you can do to get him to stop talking at that point. I hide a whole bunch of soda in the—"

Just then, the cabin door swung open and smashed against the wall. First Mate Atwater jumped up from his seat and saluted the burly man now standing in the doorway.

"Are these the two deckhands that fell overboard today?" the old man asked in a mean, not-to-be-messed-with voice.

"Yes, sir, they are, Captain," Atwater replied. He wasn't scared, but he was respectful.

"Arrrr . . . Have them to report to me quarters in fifteen minutes sharp for disciplinary action!"

"Aye, aye, Captain," Atwater retorted, saluting once again.

The old captain glared at the twins for a second, then left, slamming the door closed behind him. The twins sat in their seats, frozen from fear and not from the water.

William Atwater relaxed and smiled. "Well, that was Captain James Q. McScruffy. Such a lovely fellow, isn't he?"

THE SASSAFRAS SCIENCE ADVENTURES

Fifteen minutes later, Blaine and Tracey Sassafras found themselves looking at a door, trembling, while waiting on the first mate to knock. "Don't worry, you two. You'll be fine. He really is a good man."

Somehow, after their one brief encounter with the captain, the twins didn't think so.

Atwater knocked, and the three stood at the door waiting on an answer. They waited . . . and waited . . . but no one answered. Atwater knocked again, but still no one answered. William reached up and slowly pushed open the door.

What the twins saw next was not at all what they expected. Though the entire boat was made of steel and had a modern design, looking into the captain's quarters was like looking back centuries in time. The way it was furnished made the twins think that the captain must have taken all the decorations and furniture from a dead pirate when he wasn't looking. It was completely trimmed in dark stained, old-smelling wood—the floor, walls, ceiling, everything. It was full of antique furniture, and there were telescopes, globes, hourglasses, swords, coins, interestingly shaped bottles, maps, paintings, wooden barrels, old hats, miniature ships, and more.

Right there, in the center of the room, behind a thick ornate wooden desk, sat the captain in a high-backed chair. He was turned toward the window and was gazing silently out into the growing darkness of night. He seemed completely unaware that they were there. The twins, with trepidation, wondered if he would, at any moment, turn toward them and explode in grumbles. But then they saw something in his hand that gave them hope. It was a bottle of grape soda.

If First Mate Atwater had been right, as crazy as it sounded, the grape soda might just help lighten the angry captain's mood a bit. With William Atwater leading the way, the trio took a few steps closer, across the creaking wood floor toward the desk.

Suddenly, the old captain jerked toward them in surprise. "Arrr, what do you scallywags mean by sneaking up on me in me quarters?"

Atwater jumped to attention, and Blaine and Tracey nearly jumped out of their skin.

"Reporting with the two deckhands that fell overboard earlier today, Sir," William responded.

"Ah, yes," Captain McScruffy snapped, easing back just a little bit, but still keeping the wrinkled frown on his face. "The two clumsy deckhands. What were you two land-lubbers trying to do, check the bottom of the sea for leaks?"

The twins just stared at the captain blankly, assuming the question he'd just asked was rhetorical.

"The rules of this ship state that if a member of the crew falls overboard and survives, they must then face disciplinary action for their foolish movements."

The twins had never been so tempted to tell a local expert about the zip lines. They didn't want to find out what kind of disciplinary action awaited them for presumably falling overboard. Even so, they knew that Captain McScruffy wouldn't believe them if they told him, so they stayed standing silently before him.

He rubbed his sandpaper-like white whiskers and then looked over at William. "Arr, you may go, First Mate. Leave these two numbskulls here, and I'll decide what to do with them."

William nodded his head, saluted, and then left, sneaking in a reassuring wink toward the twins before he exited. The Sassafrases didn't feel very reassured. They were both wondering what discipline awaited them.

James Q. McScruffy slammed both of his hands down on the top of his desk and stood up from his chair. He was a man of average height, not nearly as tall as William Atwater, but right now he was towering over the twins and staring at them with unblinking eyes The captain broke off the stare after what seemed like an eternity and picked back up his bottle of grape soda. He walked over to the window, tilted back his head, and drank almost all of the contents of the soda bottle in one drink. Then, he stared out into the dark moving ocean.

"Do you two want to hear a story?" the old captain asked, in his deep gravelly voice.

The twins looked at each other in surprise. A story sure sounded better than disciplinary action.

"Yes sir, Captain, sir?" Blaine answered, not so confidently.

"Me father was a ship captain, as was his father, and his father before him. It was me great grandfather, James R. McScruffy, that started our family out on the water, and on the water we have stayed. Arr, the sailor's life was made for McScruffy, and McScruffy was made for the sailor's life."

The old captain grabbed another bottle of grape soda and started on it as he continued. "Me father was a fisherman, me grandfather was a navy man, but me great-grandfather, now he was a treasure hunter. Me myself, I have tried the fishing and I've tried the navy, but like me great-grandfather before me, I am a treasure hunter at heart."

More grape soda went down the gullet before he continued. "One blustery evening, somewhere out in the South Atlantic, so the story goes, me great-grandfather James R. McScruffy alighted from his ship, The *Scotsman*, and took to sea in a rowboat. He was going to check on a floating wooden chest that was spotted by several of the crew. There were whispers among the men that the floating chest carried a curse, because every sailor knows that if a chest has treasure doesn't float. But me great-grandfather, brave soul that he was, was the only one courageous enough to row out to the floating chest and find out what was inside. That is, he and his tried and true pet, Folly the Ferret."

THE SASSAFRAS SCIENCE ADVENTURES

"You mean, Polly the Parrot?" Blaine interrupted, totally enthralled in the story.

"No, you scallywag!" McScruffy admonished. "I mean Folly the Ferret, the best pet a sailor's ever had. Arrr, Folly had a jovial spirit, a disarming demeanor, and she loved me great-grandfather. She stuck with him like stink on a pirate. 'Twas her that rowed out with James R. McScruffy that night, just the two of 'em, to see what was inside the mysterious floating chest. The winds were fierce and the waves were a rollin', but the brave duo reached the chest with no real problems. Me great-grandfather reached out his hand to pull the floating chest from the water, but just as soon as he did . . ."

The captain paused in his story, took another swig of grape soda as he eyed the twins who were literally on the edge of their seats. Blaine and Tracey had both forgotten all about any disciplinary action and were now totally into this old ship captain's story. "What? What happened?" Tracey asked urgently.

McScruffy looked back out the window and continued his story. "But just as soon as he did, the biggest squid a man has ever seen torpedoed up out of the icy water, swallowed up the chest and slammed into the rowboat. Arrr, the force of the monster's fury broke the little wooden boat right in half. Me great-grandfather, who was quick with the blade, managed to pull his dagger from its scabbard and cut the giant beast just under its eye, but not before the monstrous squid took poor Folly down into the icy deep with him."

"Great-grandfather McScruffy dove in after his beloved ferret, but it was of no use. The squid was just too fast and powerful a swimmer. Arr, that monster took the floating chest and Folly down to depths where no man can go."

Blaine and Tracey just sat with their mouths open in wonder at McScruffy's story. The old captain walked back over to his desk and pulled open a drawer. He reached in and carefully pulled out what looked like an old leather map.

"Me great-grandfather escaped with his life that day but left his heart down at the bottom of the briny blue with his poor Folly. He never did return to the waters of the floating chest and the giant squid, but he did sketch up a map and a poem of clues on how to get back there, if ever a soul would be brave enough to return. He also changed the name of his ship that day from The *Scotsman* to *Scot's Folly,* in memory of his beloved pet." Captain McScruffy put the leather map down on the desktop where the twins could read it.

Tracey read aloud the words written on the worn and tattered cut of leather.

"Start ye lubbers
At ole Georgia South
The king here is penguin
With codfish in mouth
From their icy beach
Head south if ye dare
Don't ne'er be fooled
By the sparkles 'neath there
Next through the wide calm
Whether weepin' or smilin'
Keep ye eyes peeled
For yon movin' island
The last spot of land
'Fore the end of the world
The timbers be shiverin'
The rocks shake and whirl
That's where ye'll find him
The biggest of all
Faint not ye heart
When he comes to call
Snatch up the chest
Don't gag or lolly
Hold fast to your dagger
And care for your Folly"

THE SASSAFRAS SCIENCE ADVENTURES

The twins now had forgotten all about the captain seeming mean, just as the captain had evidently forgotten that he was supposed to act mean. Maybe it was the grape soda. Maybe it was the children's interest in his story, but he was definitely smiling now.

"And that's where we are going right now," James Q. McScruffy said. "We will take this fantastic ship, *Scot's Folly III*, and we will follow me great-grandfather's map. We will find that giant squid and have our vengeance for Folly. Arrr, and if we are real lucky, we'll find that mysterious floating chest."

Blaine and Tracey had loved the captain's story, and now appreciated his enthusiasm, but his end goal wasn't possible, was it? There was no way that floating chest or that giant squid could still be there, could there?

"I have dedicated these latter years of me life to this cause," Mc Scruffy said. "To completing me great-grandfather's story. To avenging poor Folly the Ferret."

The captain took one last swig of grape soda and then set the empty bottle down on the desk. He looked at the Sassafrases as he ordered, "Go back to your quarters, you two, and get some shut-eye. For tomorrow morning we start at ol' Georgia South."

Sun shone through the circular window waking both Sassafrases up after a good night of sleep that included dreams of treasure and tentacles. They rushed to the deck and the first thing they saw made them smile. Penguins! Hundreds and hundreds of them were waddling around on the shore of an icy island that you could easily see from the ship. The twins got a good picture of the birds. Deckhands and crew members scurried around doing their chores in the morning sunlight, and there, leaning on the rail of the starboard side of the ship, was Captain James Q. McScruffy. He was looking out at the penguins.

The twins rushed over, greeting him with a, "Good

morning!"

The captain looked at them with a wrinkled scowl on his face. "Arr, good is the mornin' that you two deckhands be doing your chores. So, this must not be a good morning."

The twins were taken aback a bit by the captain's gruffness, but then remembered the captain's mean demeanor they had experienced the first time they met him.

"Why are you standing so close to me?" McScruffy barked. "Have you heard nothing of personal space?"

The Sassafrases backed up a bit, wondering exactly what they were supposed to do now. Blaine spotted a bucket that had a mop and some rags in it. He skipped over, pulled out the mop, and tossed the rags to his sister. Tracey, catching her brother's plan, immediately jumped into action and started using the rags to clean off the railing close to where McScruffy was standing. Blaine went to work, mopping the deck in the captain's general area as well. The twins remembered what First Mate William Atwater had said about Captain McScruffy mumbling information. They hoped they were now close enough to hear him, if indeed he did offer up any animal information.

McScruffy calmed down and seemed satisfied that the twins were working. He gazed back out at the penguins, and, sure enough, Captain McScruffy started mumbling about the birds.

"King penguins, the second largest species of penguins, are found on South Georgia Island and along the coast of Antarctica. They have golden-orange patches on their ears, bills, and upper chests. They are birds that can't fly. However, they are excellent swimmers and seem to fly through the ocean, using their stiff wings as flippers and their tails and feet for steering."

Both Blaine and Tracey were straining their ears to hear the captain, barely getting everything he said.

"Penguins have water-proof feathers," McScruffy mumbled

LINLOC SCIDAT

CLASSIFICATION: Bird
NAME: Penguin
FOOD: Carnivore
LOCATION: South Georgia Island

on. "A thick layer of fat to help them stay dry and warm in the icy waters. They can jump above the surface of the water, like a dolphin, so that they can breathe when swimming quickly or to get back up on land after being in the water. Penguins hunt and eat fish or krill, which makes them carnivores. They have spiky tongues which help them to grip slippery fish."

The twins worked and listened as Captain McScruffy continued talking, under his breath. "Penguins are black and white as a means of camouflage. When they are swimming, they appear dark from the top, and pale from below, making it harder for predators to spot them from either vantage point. Penguins come out of the water to lay eggs and raise their chicks. They usually lay one to two eggs at a time, which both the mother and father will take turns incubating. Once they hatch, the chicks will huddle together while their parents go to the sea for food. The chicks cannot go into the ocean until they have grown their waterproof adult feathers."

The First Mate had been right. The captain really did just spout off information on animals when he thought nobody was really paying attention. Luckily for the Sassafrases, they had been paying attention.

Comical Codfish

Suddenly, the captain stood up straight and pulled a telescope out of an inner coat pocket, "Well shiver me timbers; looks like we have got company!"

Up to this point, Blaine and Tracey hadn't seen any other boats than the ones they were on. They now saw a single boat in the distance, but they wondered why that was a problem. Why would one boat shiver the captain's timbers?

"Weigh anchor!" McScruffy growled loudly. "Onward now with *Scot's Folly III*!"

A uniformed crew member ran over to a control box and flipped the switch to the winch that pulled up the anchor, but he was met with a small explosion of sparks.

"Captain!" the man screamed more than a little alarmed. "The winch! It's broken! I can't weigh anchor!"

Captain McScruffy rumbled over to the man like he was going to wring his neck, but luckily for the crew member, First Mate William Atwater showed up out of nowhere and intercepted the mad James Q. McScruffy.

"Captain, the winch has had this problem before," Atwater stated. "It's an electrical problem. The wires are fried. Let me fix it."

"All right, First Mate," Captain McScruffy barked. "But no lollygagging. Arrr, because that's a pirate ship me sees on the horizon."

"A pirate ship?" thought the twins. Those didn't exist anymore. Did they?

The strong first mate Atwater ripped the top of the control box off with one yank, revealing a tangled mess of smoking wires. With no hesitation, he plunged his hands in to try to find and fix the problem. Meanwhile, the rest of the crew scurried around the deck like flustered ants. Captain James Q. McScruffy paced back and forth along the starboard rail, fighting with his telescope. The "pirate ship" got closer and closer as *Scot's Folly III* remained stationary. William Atwater worked frantically to repair the winch.

"Arrr, what have they got on that ship?" the twins heard McScruffy mumble. "A jet-propelled engine? I've never seen a ship cut so fast through the water."

Atwater seemed to be making headway. He had some wires reconnected, but the approaching ship was cruising full speed ahead right at them.

"What if it really is a pirate ship?" Blaine whispered to Tracey. "What do you think they will do to us?"

Tracey shrugged. "I don't know, Blaine. I've never run into a pirate ship before, but I have read the stories. The pirates aren't usually the good guys."

Atwater worked on, McScruffy paced on, and the pirate ship continued to approach. Finally, William Atwater exhaled.

"Got it," he declared, stuffing the wires back down and reattaching the control box's top. He flipped the switch and immediately they all heard a cranking noise and the sound of chain rubbing against metal. Whatever William had done had worked! The anchor was coming up! Everyone on deck cheered. That was until they all realized it was too late.

The pirate ship was now too close for them to get away if they needed to escape. The entire crew grew quiet, as did the captain and the first mate. The pirate ship came within firing distance. Blaine and Tracey were amazed at the sight. This was no normal boat that had accompanied them here off the shores of South Georgia Island. It was a real pirate ship, straight out of the pages of a storybook. It was completely made out of wood. It had three masts, complete with sails and crow's nests. The business end of cannons could be seen protruding from the side of the boat and atop the proud vessel flew a large black flag with white skull and crossbones. The flag wasn't like other pirate flags that the twins had seen, because just after the skull and crossbones was a big white question mark.

As the boat got even closer, the twins could see that everyone on board the wooden boat were even dressed like pirates of old. What a strange sight. What was this pirate ship and its crew about to do to *Scot's Folly III* and its crew? Why had they approached so quickly?

There were some pretty big and nasty looking characters staring them down right now from the deck of this imposing pirate ship. An eerie silence cloaked both boats and their crews, as the stare down continued. The pirate ship was now close enough to reach out and touch. Suddenly, the littlest one of the pirate's crew jumped up on the railing and threw a plank down that spanned the distance of the two boats.

"Well, hidee-ho there, dear buddy friends!" the little man said in a squeaky voice. "My name is Peach Beard. Not sure if they call me that because my beard is more like peach fuzz or because the few wisps that I do have are a peachy-type color. But, regardless, that's what they call me, and I represent these fine men you see here of P.R.O. Pirates."

The entire crew of *Scot's Folly III* remained silent, but now more out of being dumbfounded than any kind of fear. Even Captain McScruffy, who had probably seen it all, stood there with his mouth open in disbelief, with nothing to say.

The skinny little pirate continued. "The P-R-O stands for Piracy Resurgence Organization. We know that in recent years, decades, and centuries, the number of true pirates and pirate ships has dropped dramatically, almost to the point of nonexistence. Piracy just isn't as prevalent as it used to be and, really, who wants to imagine a world without pirates? P.R.O. Pirates wants to change the tides. We want there to be a great and glorious resurgence of piracy! And we need your help, crew members of the . . . " Peach Beard paused until he spotted the name of their boat painted on the bow. " . . . *Scot's Folly III*. With one time individual donations of $29.99, each of you can help fill the high seas with pirates once again! What do you say, dear buddy-friends?"

The biggest scowl the twins had seen yet crossed Captain McScruffy's face. He grabbed the plank that Peach Beard had laid down and shoved it back onto the pirate ship.

"Arrr. We don't take kindly to solicitors here on *Scot's Folly*," the captain growled.

Peach Beard, not at all dampened by McScruffy's gruffness, kept trying to sell his organization's idea. "The donations don't have to be $29.99. They can be smaller. $19.99? $12.99? Does anyone want to donate?"

"Fire up the engines!" McScruffy called out loudly.

"OK, that's fine." Peach Beard continued. "No donations today, but would you at least like to fill out a survey? If you do, you will receive a free P.R.O. Pirate's lapel pin."

"Take your lapel pin and be gone!" McScruffy yelled, as the *Scot's Folly III* crew broke from their stances and hustled back to work, some of them chuckling, some of them shaking their heads at the silly pirate solicitors. The anchor had already been pulled up all the way, thanks to First Mate Atwater, and *Scot's Folly III* was now moving in the water away from the P.R.O. Pirates' ship.

However, skinny little Peach Beard would not be deterred from a possible sale, "OK. Nice meeting you fine folks. If you change your minds, we are having a boat washing tomorrow on the other side of the island, and a bake sale next week. Feel free to stop by and donate then if you change your minds."

At this point, instead of shouting back, Captain McScruffy was just trying to tune Peach Beard out. The two boats got further apart and the P.R.O. Pirates didn't pursue. They just waved goodbye and smiled.

"Look us up online—www.propirates.net!" Peach Beard merrily shouted across the distance. "We take donations there, too, and accept all major credit cards!"

Captain McScruffy just shook his head and growled in disgust, "Arrr, solicitors."

THE SASSAFRAS SCIENCE ADVENTURES

He turned his gaze away from the retreating pirate ship toward the icy shores of South Georgia Island, where a group of king penguins had found a large school of fish and were banking on a feeding frenzy. Probably to get his mind off the solicitors he evidently disliked, he started mumbling about the fish the penguins were catching. Blaine and Tracey got back to their chores and tried to stay close enough to the captain to hear what he was saying.

"Codfish are like most other bony fish, in that they have a backbone and a basic skeleton. But they differ from them because they don't have a swim bladder to control their buoyancy. Instead, they have a reduced amount of minerals in their bones and increased fatty tissue that gives them a near neutral density."

The twins strained to hear as they snapped a quick picture with their phones. They were amazed that such a grumpy old man knew such detailed specifics about the science around him. What a strange but cool old sea captain.

They listened on as the mumbling continued, "Codfish are covered with scales, which help reduce drag as they swim. They have strong fins which they use to move through the water. The codfish, like all other fish, needs oxygen to breathe, but instead of breathing in air, they absorb oxygen from the water as it passes over their gills. They're cold-blooded, which means they cannot regulate their own body temperature. So, to survive these temperatures, they have a chemical in their blood that acts like anti-freeze and their spleen is able to filter any ice crystals that might form in their blood."

CLASSIFICATION: Fish
NAME: Codfish
FOOD: Carnivore
LOCATION: Atlantic Ocean

"Codfish eat smaller fish and

crustaceans, such as krill, which makes them carnivores. They often swim in groups called schools, mainly for safety because so many fish together can confuse a predator, making it hard for them to single out and catch one fish. Arrr, but the king penguins aren't being fooled right now, are they? Almost all of them waddle around proudly with codfish in mouth."

The Captain stood up straight and shouted to whoever was that was supposed to hear his command. "Due South, me lad! Take us due South!"

What the captain had just said suddenly struck a chord of memory in both twins. As James Q. McScruffy lumbered off toward the wheelhouse, Tracey skipped over to her brother.

"Due South, Blaine," she said, excited. "Does that remind you of anything?"

"The poem on the map the captain showed us last night, right?" Blaine responded.

"Right," Tracey said. Then, she quoted the first two stanzas from memory,

> *"Start ye lubbers*
> *From ol' Georgia South*
> *The King here is penguin*
> *With codfish in mouth*
> *From their icy beach*
> *Head south if ye dare*
> *Don't ne'er be fooled*
> *By the sparkles 'neath there."*

"Don't be fooled by the sparkles 'neath there," Blaine said, repeating the last two lines of the poem. "I wonder what that means?"

CHAPTER 17: ARR, TREASURE AHEAD!

Watching Whales

The Sassafras twins had already entered their data about king penguins and codfish into their phones. They also had good pictures of both. They now stood on the cold deck of *Scot's Folly III* as the ship headed south, talking about some additional information that they heard the Captain James Q. McScruffy mumbling about.

"Over two-thirds of the earth is covered with salt water oceans," Tracey said. "Isn't that amazing?"

"Yeah, it's amazing, but it's not the SCIDAT data that we need," Blaine was saying.

"C'mon, Blaine, be honest," Tracey said. "You can't tell me you aren't enjoying learning science face-to-face. Who cares what we need for SCIDAT? It's fun to know. Yes, Uncle Cecil is crazy, but learning science by traveling on his invisible zip lines has been a blast. It's not anything like sitting in a boring classroom, looking at a black and white textbook, listening to our monotone teacher saying, 'blah, blah, blah,' about science. You have to admit that."

"Yeah, I'll admit it," shrugged Blaine. "My attitude toward science is changing. Everything we've lived through the last few days has been pretty cool. So, go ahead, what else did you hear Captain McScruffy say?"

Tracey smiled at her brother and then continued on with what she heard. "Did you hear what he said about invertebrates? More than ninety-eight percent of the world's animals are invertebrates. They're animals without a backbone or hard internal skeleton. Some have a hard exoskeleton or a fluid filled skeleton, but not a hard internal skeleton like you first think of. I heard the Captain mumble that shrimp, jellyfish, worms, clams, starfish, crabs, and insects were all invertebrates."

"Yes, Tracey, this is all very interesting," Blaine interrupted. "But I'm getting tired of sneaking around close to the captain, straining to hear him. We need to find that secret stash of grape soda First Mate Atwater was talking about. I like listening to the loud, talkative, grape soda filled Captain more than the quietly mumbling version."

Tracey nodded in agreement.

"Speaking of . . ." Blaine said, snapping to attention. "Here he comes now."

"Arrr. What are you two deckhands standing around chatting for? There is work to be done. There is always work to be done!" growled Captain McScruffy.

"Captain!" a tall skinny deckhand shouted, pointing out into the water. "Look! Something shimmers under the water!"

Practically all of the crew rushed over to where the tall, skinny deckhand was standing and looked over the railing into the water. The twins joined the crew, along with the brusque old sea captain. They immediately spotted what the crew member had been pointing at and opened their eyes wide in wonder. There wasn't just one shimmering something; there were thousands of shimmering somethings. Different members of the crew started spewing off the same questions and statements that were in the twins' minds.

"What could it be that shimmers like that?" one asked.

"Is it a lost treasure?" another questioned.

"It has to be treasure," another speculated.

"Gold! Silver! Precious jewels!" yet another crew member exclaimed. "This is why we sail the high seas! For treasure such as this!"

The lights in the twins' eyes sparkled in rhythm with the shimmering mystery under the sea. There was something alluring about these lights. Something almost hypnotizing. Blaine had a sudden urge to jump in and swim under the water to touch, see, and feel whatever it was that shimmered. Many of the crew had the same hypnotized look in their eyes that the twins did. A sparkling treasure such as this was something to be embraced, something to be explored, something to be found.

Suddenly, with a shout of joy, one of the crew members dove over the side and swam down toward the shimmering lights. He was quickly followed by a dozen or so treasure-blinded crew members. Blaine felt an ecstatic urge well up inside of him. He grabbed the ship's railing and hoisted himself up to jump overboard. Just as he was about to dive in, a big leathery hand grabbed his arm.

"Don't ne'er be fooled by the sparkles 'neath there," stated Captain McScruffy, looking right in Blaine's eyes.

The sandpapery voice and grip of the captain's hand broke Blaine free from his joyful trance. One by one, the men who had chosen to jump overboard began to resurface, yelping and gurgling in pain.

"It's not treasure that shimmers down beneath her," one

managed to say. "It's jellyfish—glowing, stinging jellyfish."

The crew members that hadn't jumped grabbed life rings and threw them to their peers, but the glowing jellyfish were agitated. They floated closer to the surface, repeatedly stinging the men in the water until the deckhands were pulled up onto the boat. The men yelped and screeched in pain. Blaine was now very thankful that Captain McScruffy had stopped him from jumping in.

"Silly sailors," said the captain, laughing at the foolishness of his crew. "They'll be pretty sore for a while, but they'll be fine."

As the Captain walked away, Tracey nudged her brother in the ribs. "You weren't really going to jump in, were you? Did you forget what the map said?"

"Yeah, I know," Blaine retorted. "The Captain just reminded me. 'Don't ne'er be fooled by the sparkles 'neath there,' but it was like I was hypnotized of something. What did it say next? Wasn't it 'Next through the wide calm, whether weepin' or smilin'; keep ye eyes peeled, for yon movin' island?'"

"Yep, that was it," Tracey confirmed. "I wonder what it means."

The twins looked out over the waters they were sailing. They didn't see a single wave. The waters were completely still, except for the ripples caused by *Scot's Folly III*. They then looked across the deck where the men who had been stung by the jellyfish were moaning in pain. Their friends who had stayed in the boat were poking fun and laughing at them.

"It's not funny," the twins heard a stung one say.

"Yes, it is, mate!" his buddy laughed. "I can't believe you were fooled by the jellyfish."

The stung-one kept moaning as he smiled and admitted that he had indeed been bamboozled into thinking there was treasure.

"Well, I think we're in the wide calm, and I see weepin' and smilin'," Blaine pronounced. "So, we better keep our eyes peeled."

"For yon' movin' island," Tracey finished her brother's sentence.

Just then, First Mate Atwater walked up.

"Hello, Sassafras twins," he declared with a smile. "How is the learning going? Have you gotten any information out of the old geezer?"

"We have, but barely," Blaine answered. "It is so hard to hear him when he is mumbling. Do you have any grape soda we can give him? He drank a bunch last night. Instead of disciplining us, he told us all about his great-grandfather, Folly the Ferret, and a giant squid."

Atwater laughed. "Ah, yes, the old leather map that leads to the whereabouts of the infamous giant squid. Indeed, we are following the directions on that map right now. The Captain must have his vengeance, and the crew thinks that treasure awaits, but, to answer your question, yes I can get you some grape soda."

The twins looked out into the perfectly calm water with William.

"Do you know what yon' movin' island means?" Tracey asked the First Mate.

"I'm sorry to say that I don't, Tracey," William replied. "This is my first time to sail this far into the South Atlantic. In all my years working with McScruffy, we did some treasure hunting, but we mainly just fished up farther north and tried to make ends meet. The Captain only told me the story of his great-grandfather recently. Captain James Q. McScruffy is getting up in years and maybe he figures this will be his last great adventure. The treasure he's hunting for now could be his legacy."

The Sassafrases continued their gaze out over the water.

"Is it normal for the sea to be this calm?" Blaine asked the

First Mate.

"No, this is very strange. I've never seen anything like it."

Suddenly, Blaine spotted something out in the distance. A huge, dark mass began to surface. Then, as soon as it had appeared, it disappeared.

"Did you guys see that?" Blaine shouted out, but neither Atwater nor Tracey had seen it. There! Blaine spotted it again. The dark mass appeared in a different spot this time, but again it disappeared as quickly it had appeared.

"There it goes again!" Blaine screamed, desperate for his companions to see what he'd seen, but, again, neither Atwater nor his sister had seen the moving mass.

"It was right out there!" Blaine declared, pointing. "It was a big mound of gray, almost like a small island. It came up, then went right back under."

Blaine had the passing thought that maybe he was delusional again, like just before when he had wanted to jump in after the shimmering jellyfish. He widened his gaze, hoping to spot the moving mound again.

"It's a blue whale," said a familiar gravelly voice from behind the three.

They all jumped around to see Captain McScruffy standing there, scowling. Without saying a word, William Atwater slinked off to tend to whatever duty was his at the moment, leaving the Sassafras twins alone, helpless in front of the gruff captain. They had seen his nicer side the night before, but this wasn't it. How they wished they had some grape soda now. Were they about to receive disciplinary action for standing around?

Suddenly, a spray of water exploded up some thirty feet into the air. The twins turned around just in time to see the fountain of water. It was a whale! The same moving gray mound Blaine had seen. Then the one whale was joined by two more whales. The

Sassafrases pulled their smartphones out and took a picture.

"Arrr. Put your fancy doodads away and find some work to do," snarled the Captain.

Blaine and Tracey immediately obeyed by putting their phones away, but they weren't quite sure what work they should find to do. They began wondering around the deck aimlessly. The Captain stared them down the whole time Just when it looked like James Q. McScruffy was about to boil over on them in anger for their lollygagging, First Mate Atwater reappeared with an armful of grape soda bottles.

"Simmer down there, Capt'n," he said, tossing a bottle to McScruffy. "Have a cold soda."

The Captain growled but obliged. He popped off the lid and took a big chug of the purple liquid. And then, as if the soda shot straight into his bloodstream, the Captain started talking about whales. The twins listened in amazement.

"Blue whales are not fish. They are mammals because they feed their young with milk. They are also warm-blooded and breathe through lungs, not gills. Their bluish-grey skin is almost hairless, but they do have a thick layer of blubber to keep them warm. Arrr, and get this, you scallywags. Blue whales are the largest animals in the world. They can be over one hundred feet long, and weigh up to one hundred tons. For your information, that's the size of fifteen elephants. Their massive weight is supported by the water they live in. If they were to ever be stranded on land, their own weight would crush

CLASSIFICATION: Mammal
NAME: Blue Whale
FOOD: Carnivore
LOCATION: Atlantic Ocean

their internal organs."

Captain McScruffy poured out the entire contents of the first bottle into his mouth, and then reached for a second one, which William Atwater was already handing him.

"Blue whales belong to a group of whales known as baleen whales." McScruffy continued. "This means they catch their food by filtering the water around them through a comb-like plate in their mouth, equipped with bristles that capture the food. These guys feed on the tiniest creature in the ocean, krill, which makes them carnivores. Blue whales can eat up to two and a half tons of krill each day. They move through the water using their tail fins.

"And, as you saw, young lad, every hour or so they must surface to get new air," The Captain stated, pointing at Blaine. "They are so huge that they look like moving islands when they surface. When they do, the whales blow stale air and water out of their two blowholes on the top of their heads. They also take in fresh air. As winter approaches, the blue whales will migrate toward the equator. They will do this every year during their lifetime, which averages eighty to ninety years."

The Captain finished his information on blue whales, and then finished his second bottle of grape soda. He reached into his pocket and pulled out the old leather map he had shown the twins the night before. He began reading the poem that was written on the map from the beginning.

"Start ye lubbers
At ole Georgia South
The king here is penguin
With codfish in mouth
From their icy beach
Head south if ye dare
Don't ne'er be fooled
By the sparkles 'neath there
Next through the wide calm

Whether weepin' or smilin'
Keep ye eyes peeled
For yon movin' island,"

The twins now understood the poem up to this point. But they were still bumpuzzled by the next stanza, as the Captain read it.

"The last spot of land
'Fore the end of the world
The timbers be shiverin'
The rocks shake and whirl,"

James Q. stopped there for a second, paused, and then said, "Arrr, me great-grandfather has been spot on thus far with his clues. We are heading straight for our encounter with that beguiled giant squid. Something I have longed for me entire life, but first we must pass by the most terrifying island in the southern seas. A place they like to call, Shivering Timbers Island."

"What's so terrifying about it?" Tracey asked.

"What's so terrifying, you ask?" the Captain shot back as if that was a silly question. "Why, no other than the fact that it has no living inhabitants. And the fact that it is the last small patch of land before thousands and thousands of miles of nothing. The island . . . is . . . how do I put this tenderly for your wee young ears? Arrrr . . . the island is . . . alive."

"Alive?" both twins questioned, not at all believing the Captain.

"That's not possible," Tracey retorted.

"Oh, is it not, my dear? Well, we shall soon find out, shall we not? For I can now see the spoken-of island appearing as a spot on the horizon.

The twins looked, and surely as the Captain had spoken, there was one tiny island way out in the distance. The Captain again held up the map and finished the poem.

"That's where ye'll find him
The biggest of all
Faint not ye heart
When he comes to call
Snatch up the chest
Don't gag or lolly
Hold fast to your dagger
And care for your Folly"

The Shivering Squid

Captain McScruffy grabbed yet another grape soda bottle from First Mate Atwater and took a swig with a contemplative look on his face.

"So, do you think we'll really find him, Captain?" asked Atwater. "After all these years, do you think the squid is actually still there?"

"I hope so, First Mate. With all that is within me, I hope so," the Captain answered in a low growl. "I plan to finish the story me great-grandfather started. I will exact revenge for Folly the Ferret, and I will see what's inside that floating chest."

The twins didn't really know what to believe at this point: maybe this whole thing was just a tall tale, or maybe it was a blossoming legend planted in a small pot of truth. Whether it was true or even possible, they had to admire the Captain's determination and resolve.

"Can you tell us anything about just squid in general?" William asked, helping the twins out a little.

He gave a knowing wink to the Sassafrases, as McScruffy started talking off in that direction.

"Well, of course I can!" the Captain growled. "Squids are related to octopuses, except they have ten arms instead of eight, two of which are a bit longer and have suckers all along them. They are scary underwater carnivores, I tell you. They use the suction

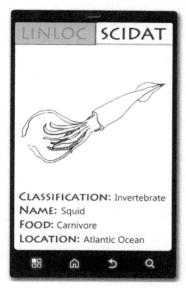

CLASSIFICATION: Invertebrate
NAME: Squid
FOOD: Carnivore
LOCATION: Atlantic Ocean

cup covered arms to capture their prey, which mainly consists of crabs, shellfish, and other fish. Arrr, though it wouldn't surprise me if some of the larger squids have the tenacity to go for prey much bigger. There are all different types of squids that range in length from less than an inch to up to sixty-five long feet. The one that smashed me great-grandfather's rowboat had to be at least sixty-five feet long, if not even a little longer.

"The squids get around using jet propulsion. It squirts water through a siphon, which is a muscular tube behind the head that can swivel to help it go in the direction it so desires. It can also change color to match its surroundings to attract a mate or to show emotion, such as anger," the Captain paused here and looked to be changing in color a little, himself, to red, as he thought about the giant squid that he so disliked. He took a calming swig of grape soda and continued.

"Squids have ink glands. When they are threatened, they squirt out a cloud of ink into the water, which confuses their attackers. These foul beasts are found at every level of the ocean. They have keen eyesight, large brains, and fast reaction times. Arrr, they are some of the fastest swimmers in the water."

"A formidable foe, Captain," Atwater said.

"A formidable foe, indeed, First Mate," the Captain growled. "But soon, this devious foe will be outdone by McScruffy."

Shivering Timbers Island was now much closer, and the

twins also noticed that the wide calm stretch of water they had been sailing through was now beginning to become choppier. Waves were starting to rock the boat a bit. Even though it wasn't yet evening, the sky began to grow dark, as if a storm was approaching. The crew of *Scot's Folly III* continued about the boat doing their duties. They grew a little quieter, though, and all were sure to kept one eye on the approaching island. They had heard the terrifying stories.

A light mist began to fall, causing everyone to don their rain gear. Everyone, that is, except Captain James Q. McScruffy. He just let the rain fall and drench him. It dripped from the brim of his sailor's hat and ran over the wrinkles of his determined, unchanging face as he stared out toward the island.

First Mate Atwater handed Blaine and Tracey some rain coats and rain pants as he shared, "Better put these on, you two. The rain will only get harder, and the storm is bound to get worse."

After the twins got all the rain gear successfully on, they looked up to see through the mist that Shivering Timbers Island was now close and clearly visible. It was thickly covered with different kinds of trees, some tall, some short. The ground that you could see was not dirt or sand, but rock. This wooded island was quite an anomaly this far south in the Atlantic because all the other land the twins had seen thus far had been mostly ice. But they didn't see what all the fuss was about. This island wasn't all that strange, and it definitely wasn't scary. Why was this place steeped in legend?

Mist kept falling, darkness continued to set in, and *Scot's Folly III* came within a few dozen feet of the island's shore. Suddenly, the air was pierced with the sound of something like a high-pitched scream. The shrill sound sent chills down the Sassafrases' spines. They looked around on the deck, thinking maybe it was one of the crew members that had made the sound.

"It's not a person that is making that sound," Captain McScruffy said from his statue-like stance. "It is the trees."

"The trees?" Blaine and Tracey both thought. "How is that possible?"

Then, very steadily, the high-pitched shrill was joined by more shrieks and some deep moans. All the different sounds mixed together like voices from an otherworldly choir. Then, all at once, the trees of Shivering Timbers Island started shaking. Not softly or slowly, but wildly and disorderly. Branches clapped together, leaves flew off and freely fluttered in the wind. Even the trunks of the trees shook and swayed. Then the rocks joined in the revelry as they started shaking and bouncing up off the ground like popcorn kernels on a hot skillet. The frightening sight made both Blaine and Tracey weak in the knees.

"Captain!" the same tall skinny crew member who'd spotted the sparkling jellyfish shouted. "The island! It's pulling us in!"

"It is true," thought Tracey. "The island does seem to have a pull all its own that is now pulling *Scot's Folly III* closer to its shaking shores." The twelve-year-old girl looked over at the Captain, who remained completely still in his stance, seemingly not at all concerned about the wildly dancing island. He just stared out past the island, thinking about what was out beyond under the water.

The boat pulled closer and closer into the island's embrace. What would happen of the boat and the crew upon contact? The howling of the trees was now so loud that some of the crew were actually covering their ears with their hands. The shaking of the island was getting progressively faster, turning almost into a vibration or a shiver.

Just as *Scot's Folly III* was about to ground into the island's rocky shore, the boat was spit out by a current into deeper water. Then, just as soon as it had started, it stopped. The sounds of the island went silent, and the shaking stilled.

As the boat floated out, Blaine looked over at Tracey. "Weird," was all he managed to say.

THE SASSAFRAS SCIENCE ADVENTURES

Tracey thought what they had just experienced was a little more than weird, but that word would have to sum it up for now.

Now, on the other side of Shivering Timbers Island, the twins noticed that the waves were a little bigger, and the mist had turned into a cold rain. Most intimidating of all, they now faced nothing except open water and an ominous black and stormy sky.

"That's where you'll find him, the biggest of all," the Sassafrases heard Captain McScruffy say to himself.

Still standing like a statue, the old man was locked in an unbreakable gaze out over the sea. The roll and pitch on the deck of *Scot's Folly III* now became a little harder to handle as the vessel went up and down, down and up, riding the growing waves. Every member of the crew had looks of anticipation on their faces. Some were anticipating great treasure; others were anticipating grave disaster.

"Arrr, there she rolls 'cross the tops of the waves like a dream made of driftwood!" the Captain shouted into the storm. "I've spotted it. The floating chest!"

The entire crew ran over to the starboard side, where their Captain was standing, and craned to see what James Q. had spied.

"The Captain is right!" one shouted out. "I see it, too! There's the floating chest!"

"So it is real," thought the twins, as they joined the crew in their gander out into the waves. Sure enough, bobbing in the water a couple hundred feet out, was what looked like an antique wooden treasure chest.

"Let out the motor boat!" the Captain shouted, breaking from his stoic stance. "I'm going out yonder to see if it's treasure or curse that floats there. Arrr, maybe we might just lure in a sea monster while we're at it," James Q. quipped, with a wry determined grin on his face. The twins now noticed that the Captain was toting a huge dagger shaped somewhat like an anchor.

"First Mate Atwater," he growled. "You're coming with me!"

Evidently, this sudden duty came as a surprise to the First Mate, and the angst on his usually kind and confident face gave him away. He followed the Captain down to the lower deck, where they could board the motorboat. The entire crew had forgotten any and all chores that they had. They were all now glued to the adventure story that was unfolding before them. The Captain and his First Mate climbed into the motorboat, which was actually a tough, inflatable raft with a motor. They trolled out in the direction of the floating chest. The First Mate sat at the engine. The Captain leaned out over the small bow.

"Faint not ye heart, when he comes to call," whispered Tracey slowly, scared for the two.

The rain fell and the waves rolled. The sky was dark and the water even darker, making it impossible to see if there was anything lurking under the waves. Closer and closer they got to the floating chest. The entire crew was watching with bated breath.

The pair had been moving slowly and carefully in the motorboat, but they slowed down even more now that the chest was almost close enough to reach out and touch.

"Snatch up the chest, don't gag or lolly," Blaine quoted. "Hold fast to your dagger . . ."

". . . and care for your folly," Tracey finished for her brother.

Captain James Q. McScruffy was now exactly where his great-grandfather had been years before. How was that possible? No one really knew, but here he was, about to reach out and see what was in the mysterious floating treasure chest. However, at least he had the benefit of knowing about the giant squid. He also had a faster boat, a bigger dagger, and a burly First Mate instead of a ferret.

Blaine and Tracey held their breath as the Captain reached out a steady hand to snatch up the chest. Just then a huge wave surged up and slapped the chest away from the Captain's reach. The twins let out a breath, but then held it in again as McScruffy and Atwater quickly tracked the chest down and the Captain again reached for it. His strong, weathered hand reached out.

The Sassafrases looked for quick, darting shadows, and then . . . James Q. McScruffy snatched up the chest. He pulled it up into the small boat, and the twins saw a rare smile on his face, but that smile soon faded when the Captain realized the chest had a huge lock on it. He made a gesture to Atwater, signifying to turn the motorboat around and take it back to *Scot's Folly III*. Then he pulled out his dagger and immediately started working at the lock. Some members of the crew were still watching anxiously, but many were now laughing with relief.

"He got it!" the Sassafras twins heard one man say. "Now Captain can get that crazy chest open, and we can all see what's inside!"

William Atwater zipped the motorboat around and started heading toward the ship. Suddenly, a huge head torpedoed up out of the water and smashed into the motorboat, which sent it into a spin. The treasure chest flew up into the air, out of McScruffy's grasp.

Everyone watching from the ship gasped. It was the giant squid. It was real, not just legend. The motorboat slapped back in the water, its motor completely shattered. Captain McScruffy had managed to hang on, but First Mate Atwater was now missing. The giant squid dove back under the water, but then quickly returned for another attack on the small boat. This time it used its sucker-covered arms and wrapped the little boat up like it was trying to crush it and pull it down into the deep. Its head came up out of the water, and there the twins saw it. The squid had a big scar underneath its eye. Was this really the same giant squid that had attacked James R. McScruffy and taken down Folly the Ferret?

James Q. McScruffy now pulled out his anchor-shaped

dagger, let out a loud growl, and sliced the giant squid underneath its other eye. The squid made a strange noise, squirted out a cloud of ink, and then let go of the boat, but Captain McScruffy wasn't done with his nemesis. He grabbed a length of rope from the floor of the motorboat and threw out a lasso toward the squid.

The would-be noose fell short. The giant squid swam free, darting away from the Captain. McScruffy snarled in disgust as he pulled the lasso back in for another attempt, but it was too late. The squid came up out of the water again, off in the distance, near where the mysterious chest had landed. The twins got a picture before it tangled up the free-floating chest in its arms and then slowly submerged. It gave McScruffy a good, long staredown before it and the chest finally disappeared beneath the water. Just then, everyone heard a splashing sound out in the waves.

Blaine and Tracey looked down, and there was William Atwater, treading in the icy water, gasping for breath.

"Man overboard!" Blaine shouted.

Later that night, Blaine and Tracey Sassafras found themselves sitting in the familiar warm orange glow of a space heater. Except this time, it wasn't them wrapped up in the blankets—it was First Mate Atwater.

The *Scot's Folly III* crew had gone back to their duties. Captain James Q. McScruffy had withdrawn quietly to his quarters, and the twins had come down here to attend to the tired and shivering William, who was sleeping now. The legend of the giant squid and his floating chest would surely continue on. No resolution had been reached today. Instead, only more mystery had been added to the tale.

The Sassafrases had just finished entering their SCIDAT data. Blaine flipped over to LINLOC to see what their next location was, "Uncle Cecil's basement!" he exclaimed in surprise.

Tracey looked at the LINLOC on her phone, and it

confirmed what her brother just said. There were no animals listed, nor a local expert, only coordinates. It just simply said, "Uncle Cecil's basement." Suddenly, a wave of conflicting emotions flooded through both twins' hearts. They didn't know whether to be happy they were finished, or sad that the adventure was over.

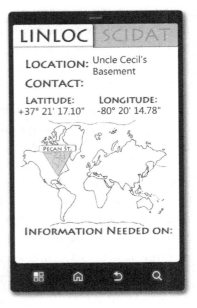

"So that's it?" Blaine sighed. "We're done?"

CHAPTER 18: THE ADVENTURE ENDS . . . OR DOES IT?

Bonus Data

How was he supposed to stop these kids? He had left them marooned in Kenya, shut them in a tomb in Egypt, tried to stop them from working on the farm in Canada, spied on them with a robot hummingbird in Peru, and he had even tried to sabotage their SCIDAT data. Nothing had worked.

These Sassafras kids just wouldn't give up. He hadn't tried to scheme against them in Australia or China. He thought that maybe them being separated would make them quit, but it hadn't. He knew he couldn't follow them at Summer's without being detected, so he hadn't bothered. He had missed their leg in the Atlantic Ocean because he was tied up trying to come up with a creative plan. If he wanted to stop them, he was going to have to up his game.

It really wasn't the kids that he wanted to stop. He had nothing personal against them. His real beef was with that no-good uncle of theirs. The person he despised like no one else on earth, that silly Cecil Sassafras, who had been his nemesis for years. He had secretly been following all of Cecil's inventions and science experiments. He had been monitoring where he was in the process of every project he was working on down in that messy basement of his. He had been especially interested in Cecil's invisible zip lines. At first, it was something that seemed so far-fetched, but now it was a reality. He knew, too, that this was Cecil's prize project for the sake of science and his favorite ever invention. That knowledge had made him want to sabotage this project even more, so he could destroy Cecil's dreams.

He had his reasons for this hatred, buried deep down in his

hard heart. Cecil Sassafras had wronged him a long, long time ago, and he had never forgiven him. His bitterness toward Cecil was his driving force. Cecil probably wasn't even aware that he had ever wronged him. It was more important, for now, that Cecil wasn't aware that everything he was doing was being monitored, and that some of those things were even being copied. The man preferred to think of it as borrowing, not stealing. Cecil wasn't aware, yet, that he wasn't the only one with invisible zip lines.

One thing was for sure—he wouldn't quit scheming until he stopped those kids. He would work relentlessly until he came up with and executed a plan that worked.

He grabbed his wireless mouse and brought his monitor back to life. His lab was much more organized than Cecil's but not even close to as state of the art as Summer's. He used to have so many more scientific materials down here. He had fancied himself as a scientist, too, and used to apply his hands to projects and inventions, but now his basement lab was dominated by computers. Now, his hands were busy with the work of revenge. He had monitor after monitor, keypad after keypad, along with tangled cords running to and fro, and wireless lights blinking. All there for the same purpose—to watch what Cecil Sassafras was doing, "borrow" his ideas, and then use those ideas to crush Cecil's dreams.

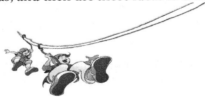

As Blaine and Tracey Sassafras zipped over the invisible lines one last time, they really tried to soak up the experience. When would they ever get to do anything like this again? "Never" was probably the answer to that question. They had been more than a little upset when their parents had put them on the bus to go to Uncle Cecil's house for the summer. They had moaned at any mention of science. They had thought their crazy uncle was truly insane when he first told them about invisible zip lines that would enable them to travel all over the globe.

But here they were now, shooting over those very lines like rays of light. What about all the science they had experienced? None of it had been boring. They had just had a plethora of adventures, living through some fun and some perilous situations, but it hadn't just been the settings or the situations that had been enjoyable. The actual learning part had been a blast, too.

Though Blaine and Tracey hadn't talked to each other about it specifically, they both knew what the other was thinking. They were twins, after all. Blaine knew Tracey's disdain for science was gone, and Tracey knew Blaine's was gone as well. Not only was any disdain for science gone, but science just might now be their new favorite subject.

The lines came to a jerking stop, but before they could even stand or see, they could hear their uncle's voice shouting in elation and his hands clapping in joy.

THE SASSAFRAS SCIENCE ADVENTURES

"Train! Blaisey! You did it! You made it back to the basement! Well done, you two!"

As the twins' senses started normalizing, they both felt their smartphones vibrate like they had just received a text message. "That's strange," they thought. They didn't even know their phones had been enabled to receive texts.

When their vision finally became clear, the first thing they saw was Cecil's huge smiling face and President Lincoln up on his table.

"Welcome back!" Cecil said, with arms upraised and spread out wide.

Upon seeing their uncle, the Sassafrases both realized that they had missed this eccentric man. He was quirky and disorganized. He almost always said their names wrong, but he was their uncle. He was family, and they loved him.

They both stood up, went over, and gave Cecil a big hug. Tracey reached into her backpack and pulled out her phone to see if she had really received a text. Indeed, she had. There, in a rectangular box on the screen of her phone, the heading of a new message read, "Bonus Data."

"Bonus data?" Tracey said. "What does that mean?" She showed her uncle the text. Blaine got his phone out and saw he had the same message.

"Oh, prickly pears!" Cecil exclaimed. "I forgot to tell you about the bonus data, but do not be alarmed. Bonus data is a good thing. Bonus data is a list of extra-fun scientific facts that you are receiving because you successfully made it through all your locations and back to the basement. It's fabtastic stuff! Some of this info you may have already learned on your travels, but much of it you probably haven't," Cecil said, like an excited parent waiting for their kids to open their Christmas presents.

Tracey began reading the bonus data listed in the text:

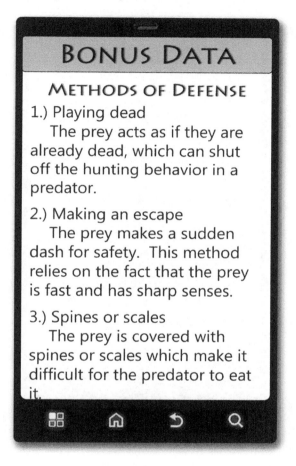

"Man, that's a long text," Blaine thought to himself as he listened to his sister read, but that was okay because as Tracey read, Blaine was thinking specifically about some of the animals they had seen that had displayed these exact traits listed here in the bonus data. It was much cooler, thinking about what he had experienced, than just reading the facts.

Tracey read on:

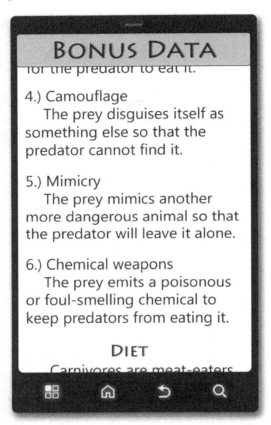

BONUS DATA

for the predator to eat it.

4.) Camouflage
   The prey disguises itself as something else so that the predator cannot find it.

5.) Mimicry
   The prey mimics another more dangerous animal so that the predator will leave it alone.

6.) Chemical weapons
   The prey emits a poisonous or foul-smelling chemical to keep predators from eating it.

DIET

Carnivores are meat-eaters

Tracey was loving reading through all the bonus data because it was helping her reminisce through the amazing journey they had just taken, but she needed a break. She paused and then said, "Okay, Blaine, your turn to read."

Blaine smiled as he declared, "Awesome! Bring on the bonus data."

Cecil smiled too. His niece and nephew were already like different kids than the two science-haters that had arrived at his house just a few days earlier.

Blaine picked up where Tracey had stopped:

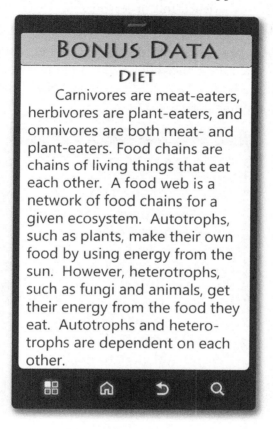

BONUS DATA

DIET

Carnivores are meat-eaters, herbivores are plant-eaters, and omnivores are both meat- and plant-eaters. Food chains are chains of living things that eat each other. A food web is a network of food chains for a given ecosystem. Autotrophs, such as plants, make their own food by using energy from the sun. However, heterotrophs, such as fungi and animals, get their energy from the food they eat. Autotrophs and hetero-trophs are dependent on each other.

When Blaine paused to take a breath, Cecil started clapping again as he exclaimed, "Oh, golly, golly goodness. I'm happier than a *Cynomys ludovicianus* with a big juicy coleoptera! You're back! You did it! How did you two like it? What did you learn? Tell me about everything."

"It was sick!" Blaine exclaimed, enthusiastically.

Cecil looked confused. "Sick?" he questioned.

"No, I mean 'sick' like 'cool' or 'awesome,'" Blaine explained. "We loved it. There were a few times when we thought we might not survive to tell anyone about it, but man! What an adventure! What a great experience full of learning new stuff and non-stop excitement!"

Tracey was just about to share her thoughts about their zip line travels when she glanced down at her phone and noticed there was a bit more bonus data, "Hey, guys, we missed the last part of bonus data on migration."

BONUS DATA

MIGRATION

Animals migrate over land, water, and air, making annual journeys to find better living conditions. Some travel short distances; others travel from one end of the globe to the other. Birds migrate using an internal compass that relies on the sun and stars to help with position. Other animals find their way by following their parents or the rest of the herd.

Tracey looked up as she finished reading with a satisfied smile on her face. However, the smile abruptly turned into shock as she saw something that made her shudder. There, on Uncle Cecil's computer desk, next to the keyboard, sat a white hard hat with "Pro-Log" written on it.

A Fun Surprise

"Uncle Cecil," Tracey said cautiously, "why is there a Pro-Log hard hat in your basement?"

Cecil looked over at the hard hat, and the expression on his face changed from exuberant to worried. "That hat appeared on my desk in the middle of your journey about the time your SCIDAT data got jumbled up. I have a theory as to where it came from."

All the twins' elation over completing their zip line task was slowly draining out of them at the sight of the ProLog hard hat.

Cecil continued. "My theory is that we have a saboteur. I believe that someone actually snuck down here into the basement and purposely messed up your SCIDAT data. Then, they must have forgotten their hard hat when they left."

Blaine and Tracey looked at each other, knowing that Cecil's theory was right. The ProLog hat being here in their uncle's basement could mean only one thing. A series of memories cruised through both twins' heads like a multi-car pile up. They could picture his face as clear as day right now in their minds—The Man With No Eyebrows.

There he was, staring blankly out the window in the back seat of Nicholas Mzuri's jeep. There he was, dressed in a black robe, shoving a rock down to block them in the tomb with Princess Talibah. There he was, wearing this very hard hat standing out in the woods, spying on them with a robot hummingbird at the Out on a Limb guesthouse. After Peru, they hadn't seen him, but the thought of him was always in the back of their minds. Was he lurking somewhere just out of sight? Watching their every move? Devising new plans to thwart them?

"We know who the saboteur is, Uncle Cecil," Blaine said.

"It's the Man With No Eyebrows."

Cecil's eyebrows raised up to the top of his forehead.

"The Man With No Eyebrows?" he asked, surprised.

"Yes, the Man With No Eyebrows," Tracey confirmed.

"What does he look like?" Cecil asked.

"He doesn't have any eyebrows," Blaine responded.

"No eyebrows?" the eccentric scientist inquired.

"No eyebrows," the twins said together. "He's the Man With No Eyebrows. We saw him at more than one of our locations."

President Lincoln made a loud chattering noise as if he was adding his own exclamation point to the conversation. Cecil put his hands in the pockets of his lab coat and started walking around the messy basement, muttering to himself. The twins could practically see the wheels in his mind turning. He came back over to the twins with his head down and his hands in his hair. All at once, he pulled his fingers out of his hair and looked up with wide eyes, his red hair now sticking up high in the sky.

"The hard hat here. Plus, being spotted at multiple locations around the globe. Train, Blaisey, do you know what this means?" Cecil gasped. "The only reasonable conclusion is that we are not the only one with . . ." Cecil stopped, not able to finish the sentence.

The twins finished it for him, ". . . invisible zip lines."

Their uncle nodded and then plopped down in the squeaky chair behind his computer desk and closed his eyes. Blaine and Tracey hated seeing their uncle like this. They didn't even know that he was capable of being discouraged until now, but, really, why did this revelation even matter? Sure, the Man With No Eyebrows had tried to stop them. He had sabotaged their SCIDAT data as well as used his own invisible zip lines to travel around trying to stop them from learning their science and progressing through their locations, but he had failed. He hadn't been able to stop the twins. They had made it back to the basement with all their scientific data. So what was the big deal? Why was Uncle Cecil so discouraged?

"Oh, Uncle Cecil," Tracey comforted in an encouraging voice. "Don't be so blue. Who cares if the Man With No Eyebrows has his own invisible zip lines? We should be celebrating, right? He wasn't able to stop us. Blaine and I were able to complete our science adventure, regardless of that no good, eyebrowless man. We made it. We finished."

Cecil sat up straight and opened his eyes. "Finished?" he said as if that word was preposterous. "Who said anything about being finished?"

"We're not finished?" Blaine asked. "We went to all the LINLOC locations. We entered in all the SCIDAT data. We sent in all the animal pictures, and we made it back to the basement. Science learned. Adventure had. That's a wrap, right?"

The discouragement on Uncle Cecil's face slowly began to disappear and was replaced by his customary smile. "Oh, slippity slappity!" their uncle said, happy again. "Sometimes being forgetful leads to great surprises for others."

Blaine and Tracey looked at each other, confused, and then back at their uncle. "What did you forget to tell us?" they asked in unison.

"You're not finished with your summer science adventure, you two. You've only just begun!"

Cecil jumped out of his chair and bounded over to a table that was covered by a sheet. He charismatically tugged the sheet off the table, revealing a whole heap of science experiment materials.

"After you complete each subject, LINLOC will direct you to come back to the basement," Cecil explained. "The subject that the two of you just successfully completed is zoology, but this is just the first of eight subjects that we are going to be covering this summer."

THE SASSAFRAS SCIENCE ADVENTURES

Cecil reached into the pile of materials and pulled out several objects, lining them up at the edge of the table.

Giddy as a schoolboy again, Cecil shared, "You will be studying the subject of botany."

He pointed to a flowerpot with a small green sprout, one of the items he had lined up. Then, pointing to a tiny globe, he said, "You will also be getting data on earth science. Next is geology and then astronomy."

Cecil pointed at a box of rocks and a tangled up solar system mobile hanging just above the table. Then, he pointed at the rocket that he had recently made out of a two-liter soda bottle, tape and string.

"This nifty little rocket here represents physics, the last subject you'll cover, but you'll be studying chemistry before that." Cecil pointed to a strangely shaped beaker with some liquid in it.

"However, your next subject, the one you will zip out for tomorrow after a good night of sleep in a comfortable bed here at the house is . . ." He paused as he pointed to the last item lined up there on the edge of the table. "Anatomy!"

The item on the table was a plastic human skull. "Tomorrow, your summer science adventure continues with the study of the human body!" Uncle Cecil exclaimed.

Blaine and Tracey just stared at the skull. Only a few minutes ago they had thought their zip line travels were over, a thought that had made them partly happy and partly sad. Happy because they thought they had completed the task, but sad because they hadn't really wanted their adventure to come to an end. Now it was clear that their mission wasn't over and, again, they were partly happy and partly sad. Sad because right now they were tired and didn't feel like their brains could handle any more scientific data. On the other hand, they were happy because they had truly grown to love science, and they didn't want this adventure to end.

Blaine and Tracey Sassafras slept soundly that night, dreaming of fennec foxes, blue whales, toucans, and cheetahs, along with old ship captains, desert princesses, and quirky scientists. Their zoology adventures had been incredible!

What adventures could the next subject possibly hold?

The Sassafras twins would soon find out . . . starting tomorrow . . .

FOLLOW THE SASSAFRAS TWINS ON THEIR ANATOMY LEG!

The adventure doesn't have to end just because you've finished this book! The summer-long, science-filled, adventure-packed journey continues for Blaine and Tracey with a look at the human body. In *The Sassafras Science Adventures Volume Two: Anatomy*, you will visit locations like:

✯ An ancient tomb in Ethiopia to learn about the skeletal system;

✯ A garbage landfill in Texas to study the digestive system;

✯ And a bistro in Italy to experience the five senses!

The twins will meet a variety of local experts who help them along the way to learn about the different systems of the human body. Don't miss a single tooth key, garbage digestion system, or delicious meal. Start reading today to learn about the human body in a way you'll never forget!

VISIT ELEMENTALSCIENCE.COM/SASSAFRAS START YOUR NEXT ADVENTURE!

11461944R00174